W9-DJC-278

Praise for *The Glasswrights' Apprentice*

"This is a splendid tale, one which captured me from start to finish. Bravo—nicely done."
—Dennis L. McKiernan

"Rani Trader is a real, complex, bewildered person trying to make sense out of a real, complex, bewildering world. From its rich imagery to its all-too-believable class system, this first novel will absorb and intrigue you, right up to the unexpected ending." —Nancy Kress, author of *Maximum Light*

"Ms. Klasky creates remarkable characters. . . . The result is an absorbing reading." —*Romantic Times*

"[A] fun and colorful adventure, and a solid first novel." —*Locus*

"A fine fantasy novel . . . a fast-paced action thriller that has wide appeal. . . . Rani is a wonderful heroine overcoming many obstacles just to remain alive, but clearly this book is a winner because of the depth of the culture described by Ms. Klasky, which makes for a real world setting."
—BookBrowser

"Klasky's future novels . . . will be worth waiting for."
—The SF Site

SEASON OF
SACRIFICE

Mindy L. Klasky

A ROC BOOK

ROC
Published by New American Library, a division of
Penguin Putnam Inc., 375 Hudson Street,
New York, New York 10014, U.S.A.
Penguin Books Ltd, 80 Strand,
London WC2R 0RL, England
Penguin Books Australia Ltd, Ringwood,
Victoria, Australia
Penguin Books Canada Ltd, 10 Alcorn Avenue,
Toronto, Ontario, Canada M4V 3B2
Penguin Books (N.Z.) Ltd, 182–190 Wairau Road,
Auckland 10, New Zealand

Penguin Books Ltd, Registered Offices:
Harmondsworth, Middlesex, England

First published by Roc, an imprint of New American Library,
a division of Penguin Putnam Inc.

First Printing, January 2002
10 9 8 7 6 5 4 3 2 1

Copyright © Mindy L. Klasky, 2002
All rights reserved

Cover art by Jerry Vanderstelt
Cover design by Ray Lundgren

 REGISTERED TRADEMARK—MARCA REGISTRADA

Printed in the United States of America

Without limiting the rights under copyright reserved above, no part of
this publication may be reproduced, stored in or introduced into a
retrieval system, or transmitted, in any form, or by any means (electronic,
mechanical, photocopying, recording, or otherwise), without the prior written
permission of both the copyright owner and the above publisher of this
book.

PUBLISHER'S NOTE
This is a work of fiction. Names, characters, places, and incidents either
are the product of the author's imagination or are used fictitiously,
and any resemblance to actual persons, living or dead, business
establishments, events, or locales is entirely coincidental.

BOOKS ARE AVAILABLE AT QUANTITY DISCOUNTS WHEN USED TO PROMOTE
PRODUCTS OR SERVICES. FOR INFORMATION PLEASE WRITE TO PREMIUM
MARKETING DIVISION, PENGUIN PUTNAM INC., 375 HUDSON STREET, NEW
YORK, NEW YORK 10014.

If you purchased this book without a cover you should be aware that this
book is stolen property. It was reported as "unsold and destroyed"
to the publisher and neither the author nor the publisher has received
any payment for this "stripped book."

To Ben,
the only brother I'll ever have

ACKNOWLEDGMENTS

Season of Sacrifice would not have been possible without the help of many people: Richard Curtis (who patiently listened to plan after plan for the release of this novel); Bob Dickey and the rest of the Library staff (who provided constant support and understanding for my "other" life); Laura Anne Gilman (who made this book much better by asking hard questions and not settling for halfhearted answers); Jane Johnson (who listened to a hundred and one plots that didn't grow up to be *Season of Sacrifice*); Bruce Sundrud (who read each chapter first); the Washington Area Writers' Group (who first started asking the hard questions); and of course, my family (who listened to me babble and told me it would all work out).

Finally, I want to give special thanks to Frank Patry and Sharon Keir, who created my Web site and helped me discover the perfect look when I had no idea what I wanted. Their handiwork is on the Web at:

www.sff.net/people/mindy-klasky

1

Alana Woodsinger watched from the sloping beach as Reade raced along the cliff top, waving a branch high above his head. The five-year-old boy's clear soprano rang out over the crashing surf as he cried, *"Hevva! Hevva!"*

The meaning of the word was lost in time. Some of the People said that it came from the ancient word for spring; others said that it came from "herring." Still others said it was the last remaining sound of the Unspeakable Names of all the Guardians.

Whatever the mystery, whatever the magic, Reade had strong lungs, and his natural energy was boosted by his pride that the fishermen had chosen him to be the huer at this first fish harvest of the season. That pride was even greater because Reade was performing the annual ritual in front of visitors, in front of Duke Coren and his men.

The duke . . . Alana tore her gaze away from the boy, seeking out the visiting nobleman. She swallowed hard against the by-now familiar pounding of her heart. The duke had lifted one wry eyebrow when Alana told him of the traditions surrounding the first harvest, managing to convey tolerance and amusement without speaking a word.

Before Alana could find Duke Coren on the crowded beach, though, she was caught again by

Reade's shouting. His voice arced like a gull's cry as he waved his branch and guided his fishermen toward their first spring catch.

Nothing could be more mystical. Nothing could be more simple.

Exotic inland visitors or no, every year the first harvest began the same way, with the excitement of a young huer calling out to the boats that tossed on the icy water. Those same boats rose and fell, driving schools of silvery pilchards into newly repaired nets. Reade, like all the lucky, sharp-eyed children chosen before him, directed the frenzy from his vantage point on the cliff, signaling with his branch so that the last of the boats could close in around the fishes' dark shadows.

The men hauled in their nets, and Reade's voice was drowned out by the People's excited chatter as the first boats returned to shore. The little boy dropped his furze branch, his job complete. He scrambled down from the promontory and was quickly lost among the other children who whooped at the water's edge, helping the fishermen drag their laden nets to shore.

Alana resisted the urge to order the riotous youngsters back to the safety of higher ground. She made herself trust Teresa, Reade's mother, and the other young mothers who guarded their children with the caution of a seagoing people.

Of course, little Maida led the mayhem, jealous of her twin brother's prize place on the cliff. She was always determined to stir up mischief among the children, even those who were older and larger than she. Her shrieks of revenge as she chased Reade into the crashing surf were enough to make Alana's breath come short, but Reade fought back valiantly, grasping his twin by her ankle and pulling them both under a breaking wave's icy shower.

As Teresa strove to bring order to her wrestling

children, Alana could not help but remember how she herself had frolicked on the same tongue of rocky sand not very long before. Now, though, she was required to wear the woodsinger's multi-colored cloak, a riotous patchwork of the Guardians' colors—brown and red, blue and white.

The Guardians had chosen Alana. The Tree had called her.

Even as that thought raised the hairs at the nape of Alana's neck, she reached out reflexively for the Tree's consciousness. The giant oak had stood on the cliff above the beach since the Great Mother had created this Age, ever since she had called the Guardians into being, and they had shaped the world with earth and air, fire and water. Even when Alana had been a child, even before she'd been called to serve as woodsinger, she had known that the Tree watched over the People, a tangible symbol of the Guardians' spirit forces. The Tree watched over the People, and the People cared for the Tree.

Now, though, as woodsinger, Alana knew so much more. She knew that the Tree remembered the life of every single one of the People. It absorbed their stories with the words the woodsingers chanted, soaking up their lives like sunlight and water and earth. Year by year, the Tree added to its enormous girth, girdling itself in another circle of bark. The oak combined all the Guardians' forces—earth, fire, water, and air—to become the physical embodiment of those spirit forces that had shaped the world. The Tree was like a living emblem of the Great Mother herself.

And year by year, the Tree added to its memories, drinking in more tales of the folk who lived on the Headland of Slaughter. It recorded how the Great Mother was worshiped, how the Guardians were honored. It recorded how the People lived. The holy and the ordinary—no detail was too small for the Tree to remember.

Even now, Alana could feel the giant oak's awareness tug at the back of her mind. It whispered to her about another huer, generations past, one almost as young as Reade. It reminded her of another spring day, when the pilchard run had been so great that three boats were swamped, pulled over by the weight of the fish in their nets. The Tree reminded Alana that the People had lived this ritual for centuries, and it pulled at the woodsinger, luring her up the steep path to the top of the cliff. The Tree wanted her to share the story of today's huer, of today's catch. It wanted to add to its store of knowledge.

Alana drew her patched cloak closer about her. Surely the Tree could be patient. It must be able to wait until she had tasted the first of the ocean's offering in this new season. She wasn't going anywhere, after all.

But the Tree was insistent, stirring deep inside her thoughts like the memory of a sweet dream after sleep has crept away. Alana sighed and shifted her cloak over her shoulders, pulling her red-gold hair out of the way. There would be time enough to feast after she had told the Tree of the spring harvest. She climbed the steep path up the cliff face.

Reaching the oak, Alana shivered against the stiff breeze that skipped through the Tree's branches. Freshly unfurled leaves trembled in eager anticipation of news from the fishing expedition. Now that the pilchard season had started, Alana would spend many long days by the oak. She had already begun to prepare the Tree for the fishermen's labors, breaking the earth above its massive roots, roughing up the ground to receive the new-caught fish that she would offer up in gratitude for past guidance, in hope of future support.

Breathing deeply from her steep climb, Alana lay one long-fingered hand on the trunk's rough bark, as if she were calming her own pounding heart. Even as she felt the whorls beneath her palm, she remembered the first time she had caressed the bark, the time that she had come to the oak at the behest of all the People, petitioning to become the Tree's woodsinger.

That visit had culminated in her drinking from the Tree's deepest sap, swallowing the bitter dregs from a cup that had been carved from an ancient oaken branch. Even as she swallowed, she felt the doors opening in her mind, and she wondered at the stinging sap, wondered at the power of the tannin that coated her tongue. And she heard the woodsingers who had tended the Tree before her. She listened to those women, awakening deep in her mind. That was when she became the woodsinger. That was when her roots were planted, her path was set.

"Ah, the fair Alana seeks refuge by her tree."

She started at the unexpected voice, but managed to paste a smile across her lips before turning to the intruder. "Duke Coren."

No wonder she had not been able to find the nobleman on the beach! He must have been here on the cliff all along, watching Reade hue in the boats. Alana shrugged off a strange feeling of uneasiness at the break with tradition, at the interference the man might have created by being so near the huer. Nevertheless, she remonstrated with herself, the harvest had been accomplished without any problem. All was well on the headland.

The woodsinger remembered to drop a curtsey, as a woman of culture might, a woman from distant Smithcourt. As she bobbed her head, she admonished herself not to notice the sun glinting on the embroidery that spanned the duke's broad chest. His coat of arms was picked out in splendid thread—a black background with a golden sun, all emblazoned with a bloody knife.

Alana's formal gesture made the duke laugh, and he threw back his mane of chestnut curls. His teeth were bright against his narrow lips, almost lost in his beard. His eyes half closed with amusement as if she had told a brilliant tale, and she reminded herself that he only meant to compliment her with his excess. His courtly manner made her nervous, though, and her fingers flew to her hair, anxious to do something, anything. She settled for twisting the silky strands into a loose knot against her neck.

The duke studied her for a long minute, as if he were measuring out grains of gold. His silent scrutiny made her even more uncomfortable than his laughter had, but now she was blessed with the familiar flush of angry irritation. None of the People would ever be so bold, so insulting as to gape at the woodsinger. Even a child as young as Reade knew that the wood-singer was special. Different. Apart.

"My lord." She captured a hint of the chill breeze in her words. "The wind is strong here on the headland. I'm sure you would be more comfortable on the beach. The feast should begin momentarily."

"Perhaps the feast is not what I had in mind." She barely made out his words, tangled in his beard and his inland accent. "Tell me, woodsinger, why do your people call this the Headland of Slaughter?"

"That has been its name forever, since the beginning of this Age."

"But the name is so . . . harsh."

"Our lives are harsh, Your Grace. There have been terrible shipwrecks on the rocks below. Men have lost their lives when they sailed too close to shore." Even as Alana spoke the words, she felt the stories stir inside her mind. Yes, the Tree knew about those lost lives. It knew the People who had been forfeited to the sea, lost to the Guardians of Water. The Tree remembered.

The duke responded, obviously unaware of the swirl of stories that surged beneath Alana's thoughts. "And yet your people continue to live in the shadow of such tragedy."

"The People could live no other way, Your Grace. The Headland of Slaughter *is* our life." When he quirked an eyebrow skeptically, she fought an indignant blush at what must seem the simple way of fisherfolk. She continued with vehemence, though, as if she needed to convince him, as if she needed to justify her people's ways.

Even as she wove her arguments, a gnawing voice nibbled at her thoughts. *Could* she justify the People? Could she justify her own father's death? She shuddered and pushed away *that* story, the first one that she had ever sung to the Tree. When she spoke again, her voice quavered. "The sea makes us different from you inland people." She swallowed and set aside the tales that were closest to her heart. "For instance, you surely noticed that there are no dogs among us?"

She made the statement a question, and he nodded tersely before she continued. "And we made your men tie up their own dogs, far from our village. That is because of the Headland, because of a great storm that blew, decades before my own birth. Three ships foundered on the rocks, and bodies washed ashore for a fortnight. There were more corpses than the People could bury promptly—men and women and little children, too. The dogs got to the bodies before the People did."

Alana's jaw hardened with revulsion, and she swallowed against the sick taste that rose in the back of her throat. Her disgust was triggered by the Tree's recollection, by its instant retelling of the horrors, deep in her mind. She could smell the rotten meat on the beach, see the bloated corpses that trailed fine hair and tangled clothing. She could hear the snarling curs fighting for morsels, snapping at each other for a reeking human hand.

The woodsinger raised her chin defiantly, as if the duke had challenged her. "We drove out every last dog from the village, Your Grace. They could not be tolerated with a life like ours."

"But dogs are useful, woodsinger! They hunt; they herd. I should think you would keep them to ease your lives."

"Ease is not a luxury for fishermen. We'll never again see a dog gnaw a child's corpse. Our children fear dogs more than you fear the sea."

"I do not fear the sea, woodsinger." The duke's denial was automatic, but Alana noted the wary eye he cast toward the rocky beach.

"You should."

The nobleman ignored the warning. "But you, woodsinger. You are more than a superstitious fisherwoman." Duke Coren's eyes glinted again with unruly energy, and Alana pretended that she chose to take a step backward. Letting her fingers trail against the Tree, she met the duke's penetrating gaze. He smiled as if he knew the trembling in her belly, and when he spoke, his voice was so soft that she had to lean close to hear him. "Tell me, woodsinger. What exactly *is* your role among your people?"

"I serve the Tree, so that the Tree may serve the People."

"Serve the People?"

His laugh was a mongrel's harsh bark, and Alana swallowed the unfamiliar taste of scorn. Last autumn, when she had first donned her woodsinger's mantle, she would have felt the need to turn to the great oak immediately, to console it by singing of the People's faith. Now, she was wiser, and she knew that the duke's ignorance could not harm the massive oak.

"The Tree is not like those that grow in your inland forests." She sighed as she struggled for words to explain. "Oh, I don't know how to make you understand! The Tree was the first creation of the Great

Mother. It is the embodiment of the Guardians, of the spirits that shaped the world, shaped the People. The Tree *is* earth and air, fire and water. It is all the world around us. It lives for the People, and we live for it."

"Fair words, my lady. But what can a tree do for you, beyond offering shade in the summer and acorns in the fall?"

"The Tree holds all the history of the People!" Alana clenched her teeth in exasperation, knowing that she must sound like a superstitious child. She cast a quick thought into the deep pool of the woodsingers who had lived before her, plumbing the memories that the Tree held in trust. No ready words, though, shimmered to the surface of that murky darkness. No other woodsinger had fed the Tree stories about the frustration of describing the giant oak to an inland duke.

Maybe Alana could find a real answer in the unread tomes that filled her little cabin, in the leather-bound journals that earlier woodsingers had kept. Perhaps her sister woodsingers had chosen not to sing directly to the Tree about inlanders' ignorance; they might have chosen to protect the giant oak from such shameful stories. Alana would read the records her sisters had left, by firelight, after the harvest festival was complete. On her own for now, though, Alana tightened her voice and tried again.

"When a child is born, Your Grace, I bring it to the Tree. I sing to the Tree of the newest member of our village, and the oak learns. It remembers. When I rest my hand against the Tree's bark, it . . . it speaks to me. I hear voices inside my head, voices of all the woodsingers before me. They tell me things, tell me stories of the People who have lived before."

The duke stared at her as if she were speaking gibberish, as if she were a child telling hobgoblin tales by the fireside. She raised her chin defiantly. "When I am with the Tree, I can see the storms that have beaten the Headland. I can see the years of good harvests and bad." She gestured toward the roots, toward the neat troughs that she had dug as the ground began to thaw. "I bring the Tree some of our first harvest. I lay the fish on the earth, and I cover it. The fish seeps into the roots, binding the Tree to us. The Tree remembers, and it reaches into our lives, into my mind."

She could read the skepticism on his inland face, his patent disbelief. She knew that he was going to say something, was going to try to humor her as if she were telling stories about talking coneys or flying horses. She cut him off before she could see scorn twist his lips. "The Tree is the core of our lives, Your Grace! Every fisherman takes a piece of it onto his boat, so that the Tree will know him and remember him if he does not come home."

Her throat closed around those last words. She had not yet found the strength to reach into all the Tree's memories of her father, into the stories her predecessors had sung about her da. Her father's story ended with Alana becoming woodsinger herself, for old Sarira Woodsinger had perished trying to sing Alana's father home, trying to guide four fishermen through a brutal autumn storm. His story, their story, ended with Alana donning the Guardians' patchwork cloak, taking up the title and responsibility of woodsinger.

Duke Coren's skepticism creased his forehead into a frown. "A tree remember? What sort of witchery is that?"

Alana forced herself to step away from the oak's quiet comfort, to stride to the outer reach of its branches. Her voice was cold as she answered, "Perhaps, Your Grace, you will understand better if I show you."

Forcing down the chill behind her words, she began to chant deep in her throat, a soft sound like a mother's lullaby. Another breeze skirled through the new-green leaves, but she ignored it, opening her mouth to voice the hymn that rose within her. The tune was wordless, a whisper about the People's lives, about the festival that spread across the beach.

Alana sang of the long line of huers who had cried out from the Headland, of the fish that had just been caught. She sang of the strange men who had come with Coren, of the anger barely hidden behind their inland beards. She sang of the dogs that were chained well away from the People, and the power of the man who stood before her, and his skepticism about the woodsinger.

As she sang, a stillness fell over the hill. The breeze calmed in a pocket around the two humans and the Tree. The children's laughing cries on the beach below melted away, swirled into the sudden silence. Alana felt the Tree listen to her, felt it add her words to its great store of knowledge. Inside her mind and her heart, she sensed the massive oak measuring the request that she had not quite dared to make.

A single branch began to lower.

Her song turned into a laugh when she glimpsed Duke Coren's amazed face. She reached up toward the branch, and the Tree moved like a supple cat, curving to greet her and caress her cheek with a whisper of fragile leaves. She strode closer to the living wood, tracing the branch back toward its heart in the tree's trunk. She followed a path that was as thick as her wrist, her neck, then her waist.

When she reached the limits of the great Tree's flexibility, she settled her hands on the rough wood. Her sung notes wrapped around the Tree's essence, melding with the living bark. For just a moment, her heart beat with the fresh sweetness of oaken sap, and her soul settled into an otherworldly calm, layer on circular layer of peace. She was no longer Alana Woodsinger, hoping to impress a worldly duke. For a single, timeless instant, she *was* the Tree; she was the oaken daughter of the Great Mother, the living essence of the Guardians in all the world.

And then her heart beat again, and she was a woman once more, an ordinary woman standing beside a branch that quivered in a sudden gust of wind. She lifted her hand from the oak, not surprised to see its valleys and peaks etched into her skin, carved over the lines of her own palm. She sighed and shook her head, not noticing when her hair fell free of its improvised knot. Coren appeared not to notice either, for he gazed intently at what the Tree had revealed.

"What in the name of the Seven Gods is that?" His gruff surprise grounded Alana rapidly, and she bit back a smile at the skeptical finger he pointed toward the bark.

She barely had to touch the patch of wood to lift it from its nest. Perfectly symmetrical, the wooden globe was carved into an intricate star, tiny points striking out against the air like a night-black snowflake. As Alana turned the star before the duke's eyes, she saw his interest sharpen until it was as penetrating as one of the carved points.

She smiled. "The children call it a woodstar, but the real name is a bavin."

"A 'bavin'?" He stumbled over the unfamiliar term.

"It's an old word. The first woodsingers learned to ask the Tree for them. When a bavin is lit, it burns without consuming the wood. Each boat we make receives a bavin. The woodstars are set in the prow, so that the Tree can track us out at sea. As woodsinger, I always know where my people are, by watching through the bavins."

"How many does the tree hold?"

"Hold?" The question puzzled her, startled her almost as much as the avaricious gleam in his eyes. She felt the Tree's sudden concern, its disquiet at the inlander's question. Unconsciously, she settled her hand against the fresh bavin scar, as if she were gentling a newborn colt. "We've never tried to find out."

"If you cut down this branch, do they just come rolling out?"

"Oh, no." Alana laughed uneasily. "The Tree does not contain bavins until we ask it to. Even then, it does not always give us woodstars. It must believe that we *need* a bavin before it makes the sacrifice." She realized that he could not understand until he had examined the Tree's gift, and she tossed the carved sphere to the man. She saw his surprise as his fist closed around it, as he registered how light it was. "The Tree has chosen to give this one to you. Take it as a keepsake of your time with the People."

He stared at the bavin for a long minute before secreting it in a leather pouch that hung at his waist. When he bowed, she felt as if she were a noblewoman in Smithcourt's royal castle. She shoved away the uneasiness that the Tree swirled into her thoughts. After all, what could an oak tree know of nobility? What could it know of the king's distant court? How could any woodsinger have told the Tree about the strange ways of Smithcourt?

Duke Coren bowed fluidly. "And may I see you to the beach, my lady?"

She paused only long enough to caress the Tree, to thank it once again for its gift and to feel the balm of its comforting acknowledgment at the back of her mind. "I would be honored, Your Grace."

Such courtly words were foreign to the People, but Alana had practiced for nearly a fortnight, since Duke Coren had arrived, leading a train of packhorses laden with trade goods. After the visitors' troublesome dogs had been banished to the village's perimeter, the People had been pleased with the duke's riches. They longed for the smooth linen that Coren brought to trade; it was crisper and softer than their own rough wool. There were other items as well—trinkets of colored glass that pleased parents and children alike, hardened leather for shoe soles, and iron knives worked by near-magical smiths.

The people had no iron anywhere near the Headland. They needed to trade for all the metal they required, for cookpots and hardware for their boats and for precious knives. The People's need was one of the many incongruities of life on the Headland. Devoted as the People were to the Tree, to the living essence that combined all the Guardians' forces, they still needed to bargain for iron, for the other major gift that the Guardians had crafted when they created this Age. The People remembered the Guardians' ancient power over earth and air, fire and water; they knew the forged power of the dark metal that was not theirs. They consoled themselves with the force of the Tree, and they traded when they could.

During Duke Coren's visit, the People marveled that the nobleman wanted so little in exchange for the precious goods he brought. All he asked for were barrels of salt fish and oil, left over after the easy winter. Those, and a handful of purple and white clamshell beads. The entire visit had carried the excitement of Midsummer Day, although it was barely spring.

That excitement was heightened by Duke Coren's proclamation that he traded in the name of the king. Of course, the westlands were ruled by the distant king in Smithcourt, but no lord from so far inland had ever deigned to travel all the way to the Headland. The People had lived for generations as complacent subjects, raising their cups to their absent, distant liege. They enjoyed the fact that they were not ground under some noble heel on a regular basis, even if that meant that the price of iron remained high, that trade in linen and beads remained rare.

Nevertheless, the presence of a nobleman spurred a giddy excitement among all the People. There were even rumors that Duke Coren hoped to ascend to the

Iron Throne when he returned to Smithcourt after this journey. After all, even the People had heard of the king's untimely death the previous year, of his passing without an heir. *That* gossip was strong enough to make the journey to the edge of the kingdom. Duke Coren supposedly claimed the crown because of the wealth that he had poured into the dead king's treasury, wealth from trading in lands so distant that the People could not imagine their names.

On the duke's first night in the village, when all the People were gathered about a warm hearth sipping ale, the nobleman had handed out presents. Excitement had fluttered beneath Alana's breastbone. She had told herself that she had no use for a silver brooch, and it was completely inappropriate for a strange man to proffer the sturdy linen sash that gathered the colors of the rainbow and nestled them about her narrow hips. Nevertheless, it would have been rude to decline his gifts. Besides, there was the village to think of—if she, the woodsinger, refused her presents, then the People could not accept theirs.

Therefore, she kept Coren's offerings, and she found herself drawn into conversation with the generous lord. He went out of his way to make her feel at ease. He was an ambassador of good will, and it was her duty to pave his way among the fishermen. It was not *his* fault that she was drawn to him in ways that were not entirely proper for the People's woodsinger, especially not a woodsinger who had been called to her post before settling on a husband.

Alas, that was one seaside tradition that Alana was *not* going to divulge to Duke Coren. There was no reason for him to learn that she was sworn to a life dedicated to the Tree, that she would never be permitted to settle in a cottage with a man, to raise children, to divide her attention between a family and the Tree. Of course, if she had found her mate before being called to serve the oak, things would have been different. . . . The Tree would have made its choice knowing her commitment to her family. But Alana had had no family when the Tree chose. She had had no distractions. The Tree would not tolerate her divided loyalty now. She would remain alone.

Through no fault of her own, she would remain alone.

Repeating that rule to herself even now, Alana stumbled as her hard-soled winter shoe turned on a stone. Before she could catch herself, Coren's hand was under her elbow, steadying her with a quiet strength. "Careful, my lady," he murmured, and she was startled by the sudden breathlessness that closed her throat. She forced herself to look down at the stony path, to focus on the earth underfoot. She thought she heard the duke chuckle beside her, but she refused to meet his piercing eyes.

His hand was still on her arm when they emerged from the scrubby ocean grass onto the beach. The People looked up in expectation, and a sudden hush fell over the crowd. Laughter and a reed flute's dancing notes slipped away in the crash of breakers. Alana saw the gossiping glint in Goodwife Glenna's eyes, and she jerked her arm away from the duke as if she'd been burned.

Goody Glenna was the oldest of the People. The crone's hearing might be going, but her eyes were sharp, and Alana knew that the old gossip was recording this latest tidbit to share by the communal ovens on the next baking day. Alana sighed. She was already tired of the Women's Council watching her every move. She knew that she was not permitted a husband. She had accepted that she was sworn to the Tree.

"Alana!" The woodsinger whirled to face Sartain, the current leader of all the People. The fisherman was short and muscular; like most of his folk, his body had been shaped by hauling nets heavy with fish. His back was stooped from years of repetitive labor, and his hands were horny pads, callused by decades of service on the People's coracles. Sartain's eyes were carved deep in his face, protected by a web of lines etched by sun and wind.

"Yes, Sartain?"

"While you've kept our guest up on the bluff, the feast has been laid. We can't have the duke saying that the People lack hospitality, can we?" Alana heard a good-natured smile behind the fisherman's sea-salt words. "Come, woodsinger, let us begin the feast."

Sartain turned and led the way to the strip of firm sand, still dark from the ocean's tidal soaking. When a restless silence had once more fallen over the beach, he spoke. "My People," he began, and then, with only a gull's cry for competition, he stumbled through a few formulaic greetings, awkwardly daring to clap his hand on Duke Coren's shoulder. "Your Grace," Sartain continued with gruff modesty as he realized the presumption he had taken, "I would not bore you with an old fisherman's words." He looked about in embarrassment and gestured toward one of the People. "Maddock, stand forward and speak to the duke."

Alana watched Maddock flow beside the Fisherman with a stoat's grace, his teeth white against his dark skin and darker hair. Maddock was one of the few men among the People who had ever ventured beyond the Headland of Slaughter. Last year, he had journeyed inland to trade salt fish for precious iron and tin and to meet with the royal census takers, declaring how many men, women, and children lived beside the sea. Now, Maddock spoke for all those People, using flowery language to admit pride and gratitude.

Alana's breath caught in her throat as she watched the young man proclaim the People's hospitality. As if unconsciously, Maddock let the wind tug the edge of his cloak, flaring the fabric to accentuate his broad shoulders. The casual fist that he set against his hip was a subtle reminder of his strength, and Alana caught herself wondering for the hundredth time how his strong hands would feel against her flesh, against the naked skin of her back. . . .

She shook her head in annoyance. Of course she thought of the young fisherman that way—he did everything he could to make every girl in the village pine for him. It was certainly no coincidence last summer that he had not finished his bath when the girls came to draw cooking water for the Midsummer Feast. He purposely used the village common to practice his fighting forms, wearing nothing more than his breeches as he swung about his smith-precious iron sword. He had his own reasons for tending the spitted lambs at the summer festivals, sweltering by the heat of the fire so that the flames drew out a glow on his bared chest.

Old Goody Glenna reveled in the attention all the girls paid to Maddock. Each day she found a new tale to tell, a story of the woe that had befallen some smitten slip of a girl when she accepted the sort of invitation that Maddock kept open. Alana, searching her knowledge from the Tree, knew that only a fraction of Goody Glenna's stories were true. Nevertheless, the young woodsinger also knew that it was her duty to help keep the village girls in line.

She had intended to do just that, late last fall, when she had confronted Maddock for the first time since donning her woodsinger's cloak. With a grin, the man had admitted every one of his faults, casting his dark blue eyes toward his feet with a child's heart-stealing shame. Alana had caught herself wishing he would brush against her as he left the clearing or, better yet, that he would not leave at all. . . .

Foolishness.

When Maddock finished his speech, Sartain invoked the traditional blessings of earth, fire, water, and air. With the Guardians' names still hovering over the People and their guests, laughter broke out. The young twins, Maida and Reade, recommenced their game of tag, and a drum joined the flute's rollicking voice, dancing amid the crash of waves.

After filing by the great iron cooking pots, Alana settled on a convenient outcrop of rock, a little removed from the crowds of boisterous people. She pulled her iron dagger from her waist, smiling at the rich present that her father had given her long before he met the Guardians of Water.

Now, Alana used the treasured blade to salute her father with the sea's first harvest, carefully picking the flesh from a steaming pilchard. She was grateful that Sartain had led his early morning fishermen to such bounty—all of the People were tired of the salt fish that had sustained them for the winter.

Sartain was clearly in a celebratory mood as well, for he ordered the young men to break out a barrel of apple wine. As Alana looked over the rim of her earthenware cup, she noted that Coren and his followers did not partake of the sweet, cool stuff. Perhaps their inland palate was accustomed to finer drink. It was a failing in the man, she mused, but not a deadly one.

"Hmphhh! He does not deign to drink our apple wine! Perhaps m'lord would prefer mead from the king's court!"

Alana did not need to turn about to chastise the complainer; she did not even need to listen to the woodsingers' quiet murmurs at the back of her mind to identify the speaker. "Hush, Landon. I think, instead, that he is loathe to take something that we clearly hold so dear." She set down her dagger and forced herself to face the lanky young man. While she knew that Landon's long face *could* be pleasant, an ugly frown distorted his features now. A sea breeze chose that unfortunate moment to skip across his brow, stressing the fact that he had already lost the better part of his hair.

She frequently had to remind herself that Landon was only four years her senior. His cautious ways and his receding hairline lent him an aura of conservative seniority almost as great as Goody Glenna's. There was a time when Alana had found his maturity compelling. Things had not gone well, though, since the winter solstice, and the woodsinger delicately forced her thoughts away from a memory as prickly as the bavin she had just sung for Duke Coren.

Landon made that retreat easier as he grumbled, "I'm certain *you* would know about his thoughts, Alana. What secrets did he whisper to you by the Tree? Did you actually give him that woodstar you sang?"

"Were you *spying* on me, Landon? What I do with the Tree is no interest of yours!"

"The Tree belongs to all the People, Alana. Not to you, and certainly not to some cursed inlander. Look at him, the way the women wait on him! It's not like he's even eating the tidbits they offer."

"You sound like a child! What has Coren ever done to you?"

"Ah, so now he is 'Coren.' Not 'my lord' and not 'the duke,' but simply Coren."

"You know the People have never put much stock in titles! If I didn't know better, I'd think that you were jealous."

"Jealous? Not I, woodsinger. I am nothing but a humble tracker, interested only in the welfare of our People. I live only to serve, following game to feed our folk when the Guardians of Water are not kind." His words were stewed in bitterness.

"You know that's not what I meant, Landon." If only she could take back the words she had spoken on the longest night of the year. . . . As she'd stared at his offering of mistletoe berries, she had been so certain that he would understand her. He *knew* that she was pledged to the Tree now, that as woodsinger she could have no husband.

Of course, Landon also knew the exceptions to the ancient rules. He knew that a married woman could keep her husband, keep her children, and still serve the Tree. He had argued that Alana should fight to change the old rules, should broaden them to include a maiden who had found her true love, but had not quite married before she was called to the Tree.

Alana had swallowed hard at the thoughts his arguments implied. She had averted her eyes from his mistletoe berries, from the confession that she had managed to ignore for months. Instead, she had chosen her words carefully, telling Landon that serving as woodsinger was a sacrifice. She must give up her freedom for the good of all the People. She must forfeit her decisions, so that she could offer up gratitude to the Tree that had watched over her since birth. She tried to explain that the Tree that had chosen her had plucked her from the black-rimmed pit of despair after her father was lost to the Guardians of Water.

When Landon had refused to accept Alana's explanation of her duty to the Tree, she had been forced to point out that he was a hunter, a tracker, a man who lived his life looking *inland*, away from the Tree. Even if she had been inclined to overthrow generations of tradition, Alana had tried to say gently, she could not break the rules for him. She only just managed to avoid the true admission, the one that would have stung him beyond reason: Alana was not a smitten maid. She did not love Landon.

Now, the woodsinger took a deep breath to explain again. Before she could find the hackneyed words, though, she was interrupted by a flurry of activity at the far end of the beach.

For an instant she could not discern individual shapes in the confusion. Then she saw that the People were running, screaming, flinging about trenchers of food. As Alana glanced reflexively at the cliff, at the Tree, she saw clouds of dust billowing from the steep path to the beach. Swirled into the dust, screaming as if in battle, were the inlanders' great horses. The massive beasts were ridden by Coren's men, by dark-liveried soldiers who bellowed at their mounts, even as they hurtled toward the beach.

The shouting would have been disturbing. The sight of war-horses caparisoned for battle would have been frightening. The thick-throated cries of Coren's men would have been terrifying. But there was a greater horror coursing down the path to the beach.

There were dogs.

Dogs charged among the People, forcing grown men to step back in ingrained fear and revulsion. One mastiff ripped at Sartain's sleeve, and Alana saw the fisherman pull back from the slavering jaws with his own snarl of disgust. The dogs were the People's greatest nightmare, sprung to full life on the sandy beach.

Before the woodsinger could move, a high-pitched scream ripped through the melee. "The inlanders are taking my babies! They're stealing the children!"

The anguish in the voice froze the People, and even as Alana recognized that Teresa was the source of the heartrending cries, she began to search the crowd for the twins. She found them before the others could react, but what she saw chilled her blood.

Maida was in the arms of Coren's lieutenant, struggling like a fish caught in a net. Her little body twisted and pulled, and she thrashed her head about as if she were determined to break her own neck if she could not be free. One well-placed kick landed against the inlander's armored solar plexus, but the man's strong right arm merely tightened across the girl's vulnerable throat. He transferred his fury to the soft flesh and tiny bones. Maida kicked one last time and then slumped in the soldier's grasp.

Reade was tangled in Duke Coren's own arms, struggling with the terror of a trapped coney. Coren's beard jutted out like a broken tree limb, and his thin lips twisted in a snarl.

Before Alana could cry out, the duke raised a silver-chased dagger. The pommel was set with a heavy ruby that glinted across the beach, mirroring the bloody knife embroidered on Coren's chest. With the smooth gesture of a man dispatching a stubborn fish, the duke brought the hilt down, smashing into the tender flesh behind the boy's ear. Reade continued to struggle feebly, but the inlander had no trouble hoisting the child onto his huge destrier.

And then, as suddenly as it had begun, the terror was over. The People stared in ragged ranks as the soldiers swung up on their horses, leading their slavering dogs up the steep cliffside path. Teresa's harsh sobs meshed with the waves, and a lone gull cried out as the inlanders rode off with the twins.

2

Alana gaped at the chaos around her.

Some of the People had run up the steep cliff path, following Coren's soldiers, bellowing threats and shaking their fists. Their only weapons, though, were brands that they had grabbed from the cookfires and an occasional iron knife. The leader of the Men's Council showed enough foresight to seize one of the gaffs from the fishing boats, but even he was defeated by the inlanders' dogs, driven back down the cliff face to the frantic turmoil on the beach.

The vast majority of the People had been too afraid, too startled, too overwhelmed to even think about pursuing their attackers. They had scattered across the narrow beach like flotsam after a storm. Children screamed in terror; mothers sobbed. Men lunged savagely toward the cliff path, only to spin back toward the sea in impotent fear.

Dogs. Armor. Swords. Deceit. The inlanders could defeat the People without even trying.

"The Guardians have abandoned us!" Alana heard one young mother cry, and the words were taken up by others.

"Cursed us!"

"Destroyed us!"

The Spirit Council, at least, managed to respond to *that* threat. The quartet of soothsayers flowed together, rising up from the People's ragged ranks as the cries of despair broke against the cliffside. As if they had planned a worship ceremony on this day of first harvest, the four councilors joined hands and began chanting the Creation Hymn.

The prayer told of the People's place in the world, the People's creation on the fifth day, after the Guardians of Earth and Air, after the Guardians of Fire and Water. The words were traditional, as comforting as a mother's arms. As the councilors chanted, the People grew calm, bespelled by the fragile blanket of familiarity.

The Spirit Council chanted louder then, raising their joined hands above their heads and marching out into the breaking ocean, as if this were midsummer's eve and the Festival of Cleansing. "And the Guardians of Water brought grief into the world, washing the world in salt, salt tears," they chanted, their words sharpening as they walked into the swirling seawater.

The hymn served its purpose.

The children stopped their wailing, shocked into silence by the sight of four adults, chest deep in the ocean, by the tumble of familiar religious words. Grown women swallowed their keening, turning their attention to the councilors. Even the men looked to the Spirit Council, and a few raised ragged voices in the hymn. "And the People were created, molded from the earth, cast in the fire, washed in the water, and cooled in the air."

"Molded from the earth," repeated the Spirit Councilor who had devoted her life to the Guardians of Earth. Many of the People took up the chant: "Molded from the earth! Molded from the earth!" as if the words would protect them from soldiers brutal enough to use dogs against innocent folk.

"Cast in the fire," cried the man who had pledged his life to the Fire Guardians. "Cast in the fire!" One woman's voice rang out louder than the others, and

Alana saw Teresa, the twins' mother, stagger from the foot of the cliff toward the Spirit Council. "Cast in the fire," the People echoed, desperate for restored order.

"Washed in the water." The People gathered around Teresa, as if she were a bride being presented at her wedding ceremony, rather than a widow, bereft of her husband, newly stripped of her children. "Washed in the water! Washed in the water!"

"Cooled in the air!"

As if to mock the praying councilors, a huge wave rose up, breaking above the heads of all four soothsayers. Alana caught her breath as the wave crashed onto the beach, but when it sucked out to the open ocean, she saw that all four of the councilors had kept their feet. Kept their feet, yes, but not their grip on each other's hands. The councilors stumbled into a rough square, fighting to stand on the shifting sand, to remain steady against the freezing, seething ocean.

Alana watched the Spirit Council, but she heard other voices in her head. She heard the woodsingers before her, telling the Tree of tragedies, of desperate, unexpected losses among the People. She heard about offerings made when ships were lost, when fishermen failed to return from the open sea. She heard about the gifts that were given to the Guardians to placate their primal forces, to encourage the Guardians to accept the People who stumbled in among them, all unready and unwilling.

So, with the Tree as her private teacher, Alana was hardly surprised when the Spirit Council shifted its chant from the Creation Hymn to the Song of Sacrifice. Two doves, they cried. Two newborn lambs! Sacrifices on the altar in the Sacred Grove would pave the Guardians' path for the children. Blood would buy a safe road for the twins, smooth their passage to the Guardians' world.

Alana watched in horror as the People spiraled into the Spirit Councilors' chant, joining the councilors' acceptance that the children were already lost to the People, were already sacrificed to the inlanders. "Two pure doves!" the foursome cried. "Two white doves! Offer them up for the children!"

"Two white doves!" rose a jagged cry from the beach, and Alana watched Teresa stumble away from the People clustered on the sand, staggering into the shallows and the center of the square formed by the four councilors. "Two white doves!"

"Two white lambs!" the councilors changed their chant. "Two white lambs!"

"Two white lambs!" Teresa cried, and her voice broke like a gull's, shattered by despair and loss. A wave broke against her, stealing her breath with its icy spray, but she stiffened her spine against the deadly chill. She raised her arms above her head, letting the ocean snag the clammy white of her widow's weeds like clotted foam. "My two white lambs!"

Alana shuddered against the hypnotic power that rolled in from the ocean, the force gathered by the Spirit Council as they knit together the People. She heard the voices in her own head, the other woodsingers who had watched other Spirit Councils join together in other times of crisis. She knew, the Tree knew, the other woodsingers knew that the Council could save the People. They would gather the People together, would turn them from one terrifying disaster back to the harsh reality of daily life on the Headland of Slaughter.

Alana took a step closer to the ocean, closer to the five people who braced their shuddering bodies against yet another frozen wave. She opened her mouth and filled her lungs, ready to cry out to the Guardians, ready to pray for the twins to be delivered safely to the Other World. Ready to admit that the twins were lost.

Before she could speak, though, Goody Glenna hobbled to her side, hissing just loud enough for the woodsinger to hear: "There'll be time enough to flatter the Guardians after the children are recovered." When Alana turned to her in shock, Glenna continued saltily, "Earth and air, fire and water—we can worry about placating the Guardians *after* we have our children back."

Alana closed her mouth and opened it again, fumbling for words. For just a moment, she continued to cling to the web that the Spirit Councilors had spun, to the order and stability that they offered the People. Then, she realized the horror that had opened before her, the defeat that the People had been willing to accept.

Before Alana could form words, before she could still the Spirit Council, Goody Glenna stumbled down to the very edge of the water. The old woman planted her gnarled walking stick in sand that had grown stiff after the last wave, as if she were claiming the beach in the name of the treacherous crown.

Her action shocked the People into silence, and she called out in a natural break of the Spirit Council's chant: "Three *people*, fisherman!"

It took a moment for Sartain Fisherman to step forward. "Goody?" he asked, and Alana could tell that he thought the old woman had gone mad.

"Order three people to follow the duke and win back the children."

"But the Spirit Council—"

"The Spirit Council is rushing things, don't you think? The children have not yet been sacrificed. They have not yet been called by the Guardians, by the Great Mother."

"But Goody Glenna, you saw the soldiers! The duke . . . he had dogs!"

"And we have men! Men and women, strong fisherfolk." Glenna glared at the Spirit Councilors, at the drenched Teresa. "We can get our children back."

"Get them back? But how?"

"Three people," the old woman repeated.

"Three!" Sartain blustered, looking out at the five adults who stood in the ocean, as if he were weighing relative power. "Goody Glenna, you can't be serious! The inlanders used *dogs.*"

"I was here, fisherman." Glenna ignored the people shivering in the swirling water, pointedly not acknowledging the callused hand that Sartain thrust toward them. "I saw what the inlanders did. They're ruthless. They're trained. We won't defeat them by weapons. We must sneak after them and steal back our children."

Glenna timed her pronouncement to end with the crash of another wave. Alana could not help but realize that the Spirit Councilors looked silly standing in the shallows, shivering, stumbling as the ocean sucked away from the beach. Teresa lowered her hands to her sides, gathering her arms about her belly and hugging her streaming widow's weeds closer to her frail form.

Goody Glenna ladled out a healthy dose of her aged cynicism as she called out: "What are you doing there in the ocean? You're going to catch your death of cold, all of you! Then we *will* need to sing the Song of Sacrifice."

Teresa's lips were the color of slate. The councilors were chilled as well; all five people had begun to shiver uncontrollably, with tremors that might have been mistaken for religious fervor, if another wave had not chosen that moment to break above their heads.

"Get out of there, fools!" Glenna snapped. The five soaked people stumbled meekly toward the shore. "Help them!" Glenna ordered the people nearest the water, and it took only a moment for warm cloaks to find their way around the councilors' shoulders, around Teresa's shivering form. "More cloaks! Build up the cooking fires! And bring them cups of apple wine! Now!"

The People rushed to comply.

Alana saw relief in the villagers' faces as they followed orders, as they accomplished small tasks. Order was returning to their world. They knew how to warm sea-drenched folk. They knew how to save people from the ocean's chill. They knew how to fight to survive.

Glenna waited until each of the five waterlogged people held a mug of apple wine, and then she turned back to Sartain. "You're wasting time, fisherman. Time that could mean those children's lives."

Sartain spluttered, "Who would you send to rescue them, Goody Glenna?"

"A soldier, a tracker, and a healer, our best." The old woman's eyes flickered over the crowd. "Maddock, Landon, and Jobina."

Alana bit back an exclamation of surprise. Certainly, Maddock was a logical choice—he was most familiar with the inland territories after his eastern journey the previous year. Landon, too, made sense; he could track a newborn lamb through spring storms. But Jobina?

Goody Glenna answered the woodsinger's question before Alana could speak. "The men have the skills we need, and I would think of sending them alone. But Jobina is a healer, strong in her craft. And she knows the Songs of the Dead."

That last admission chilled Alana, even as she recognized the logic of sending someone who could fight for the children's souls, someone who could guide them to the Guardians' world if the battle were lost.

All eyes turned to Jobina, who stood on the edge of the ocean, her loose skirts flirting dangerously with the waves that crashed on the pebbly sand. She had seen to it that the councilors' cloaks were gathered close under their chattering chins; she was topping off the apple wine in the leather mug that Teresa barely managed to grasp in her shivering hands.

When the healer felt the People's scrutiny, she inclined her head gracefully, her auburn hair shimmering like a curtain across her narrow features. "I am honored by your words, Goody Glenna, and by the Council's faith in my abilities." Her husky voice, however, did not quite capture the humility of her speech. The wind tugged at her blouse, slipping it free from one shoulder. The healer seemed oblivious to her exposed flesh, although Alana noticed that a number of the men paid closer attention to the woman.

"Such modesty," Goody Glenna answered, and Jobina at least had the good grace to look abashed as she plucked at her blouse. "So." Glenna turned to the fisherman. "We should send three to follow our children. And the woodsinger should sing a bavin, so that we may track their progress."

"A bavin!" Alana exclaimed.

Goody Glenna snorted in annoyance. "Of course! We have to know how our people fare on the road."

"But the bavins are for our *boats*!"

"They're for our *need*. And we've never had a greater need than this."

"But—" Alana began, thinking that she had only followed bavins out to sea, had only stretched the Tree's awareness toward fishermen, toward the ocean and the Guardians of Water. Would the bavin even work if she cast her attention over land? Would the Guardians of Air and Earth support her questing eye?

Alana reflexively cast her question into the pool of the Tree's knowledge, into the shimmering circles of thought that lay just beneath her own consciousness. She could feel the earlier woodsingers, awakened by the tumult of all that had happened on the beach. Alana plunged her question into their midst and almost reeled with the force of the replies.

"Stolen children?" whispered one ancient voice. "Like the stolen bull of Cumru?"

"Children!" remonstrated a younger voice. "Not animals, children!"

"Ah, like the time that madwoman Shinda took her daughter away from the People."

"She took her daughter from her husband, Shinda did."

"It wasn't her husband, it was her father. . . ."

The voices chased each other, circling around their ancient stories like rings on a tree stump. Alana felt the confusion of their histories break over her like a clammy ocean wave, and she staggered toward one of the rough boulders strewn upon the beach. There might be an answer in the People's past, but she did not have the strength to find it. Not now. Not with the voices spinning out of control in her mind.

And yet Goody Glenna was waiting for some sort of reply, for some confirmation that Alana would sing another bavin. The old woman scowled as Alana blinked up at her. "Th— the voices . . ." she trailed off, confused by the tumult inside her head. If only she could gather her *own* thoughts, form her question clearly in her *own* mind. "I don't know how to track a bavin over land."

Glenna grimaced. "We don't have time to hear what you know and don't know, girl. If you can't get the voices to tell you how, you can check the wisdom in the woodsingers' journals. You should find *something* useful there." The old gossip sounded as if she were scolding a wayward child, and Alana's flush of embarrassment was scorching. She should have thought of the journals. She should have thought of all the woodsingers' tools at her disposal. Before she could make an excuse, though, Glenna snagged her with stone-sharp eyes. "Will you sing us a bavin so that we have a chance to track the twins?"

Alana stammered, "I can't! I've already sung one woodstar today, the one I gave to Coren."

There was a gasp among the People, for they did not know that Alana had given away one of their treasures. "All the more reason," Goody Glenna countered. "You'll be reaching out to track the first woodstar. Ask the Tree to let you follow two bavins. Ask the Tree to help us save our children."

Alana wanted to argue. She could not do what Glenna demanded. After all, it was the Guardians of Water who had brought Alana to her station. Water had taken Alana's da, had cost old Sarira Woodsinger her life as she tried to sing home the bavins of those hapless sailors. Water had left the Tree without a singer, opening the path for Alana's true calling. She might convince herself that she had grown to understand the ways of Water in her two seasons as Woodsinger. But Earth? Air? What did she know of those elements? What had she learned in the short time since she had embraced the oak?

Nevertheless, she heard the command in Glenna's voice, the iron strength that she had known and followed since she was a child, younger even than the stolen twins. Alana must try to help her People, even if she was not certain that she had the strength to do as Glenna ordered. Even if she did not yet have the knowledge to plumb the Guardians of Earth, of Air, to follow a bavin across the land. . . . She must find a way.

Alana turned on her heel and made the long climb up the cliff to the Tree. Along the way, she consciously squelched the rising clamor of the voices inside her mind, the memories of woodsingers who had stretched their powers, who had tried to push the Tree to new tasks, to new directions. She did not want to hear if she was making a mistake. She did not want to know if it would be impossible to track a new-sung bavin over land.

Instead, Alana forced herself to stare at the hoof-marks on the path up the cliff, to make out the claw scrapes from Duke Coren's dogs.

She had brought this disaster upon the People. She had welcomed Duke Coren and his gifts. If she had refused his fine linen sash weeks before, the duke would have ridden away. If she had ordered him to take his trinkets and leave the People, he would not have stolen the children.

She was the *woodsinger*! She should have sensed that something was wrong. She should have realized that no inlanders could be so interested in the People, willing to trade so much for so little. She should have listened to her sisters' voices in her mind, reached out for their wisdom before the duke could steal away the twins.

When Alana gained the top of the bluff, the Tree accused her with its lowered branch, with the clean white scar where she had sung Coren's bavin. She brushed her hand across the smooth wood, raising her fingers to her lips and touching her tongue to the sharp sap that had bled into the Tree's offering. The taste reminded her of the potion she had drunk, moons before, the full cup of the Tree's blood that had transformed her into a woodsinger. Shaking her head, she tried to clear her mind, to empty her thoughts of everything except her need, her love of the Tree, and her faith that the giant oak could help to save the children.

The harder she tried to concentrate, though, the more she heard the People shuffling behind her, their breath harsh as they recovered from the steep climb. Out of the corner of Alana's eye, she spied Jobina, glimpsed one seductive arm as the woman raised healer's hands to tame her wayward blouse. The wood-singer caught Maddock staring at the healer as well, frank speculation on his face. It only took Alana a moment to locate Landon then, to catch the tracker sneering at the two who would be his companions. Would be his companions, that was, if Alana were successful.

She reminded herself to pay attention, to focus on the Tree. She was the one attuned to the oak; she was the one who could sing the bavin. She *must* sing the bavin. She must not betray her people again, as she already had by letting Coren stay among them.

Try as she might, though, Alana could not still her thoughts. No words rose to her lips, no chant to please the Tree and draw out its spirit. Embarrassed and angry, Alana finally ducked beneath the recriminating branch that had lowered for Duke Coren's woodstar. When she was on the Tree's landward side, she forced herself to take four deep breaths, to calm her heart with the cool spring air.

Then, without conviction, she began to sing. She told the Tree of her shame, of her fear for the children, of the terror on the beach. She told the oak how she remembered holding Maida and Reade as infants. She sang of how she needed to help the children; she needed to bring them back. And by the time the Tree lowered a branch, Alana no longer thought of the People standing on the cliff behind her, waiting, hoping, praying.

The second bavin was as perfect as the first, prickly and black, like the opposite of a star. Alana's fingers closed tightly around the darkened wood as she fought against a wave of fatigue. When she unclenched her fist, bright beads of blood stood out on her pale, pale flesh.

The People crowed over the treasured woodstar, then wasted no time returning to the village. They laid out provisions for the three travelers, rounding up their fastest horses and gathering together charms to summon the Guardians' protection. Sartain placed the new-sung bavin on a leather thong and settled the woodstar around Maddock's neck. The sun was already dipping toward the horizon as Maddock, Landon, and Jobina headed east.

Alana watched with the rest of the People until the trio of riders was out of sight. Then, parents gathered children against their breasts and headed to their homes, building up fires against the nighttime chill. Husbands and wives stepped a little closer to each other, silently grateful that their own children had been spared.

As Alana turned toward her cottage on the edge of the village, Goody Glenna came out of the darkness. The old woman blinked in the glow of her lantern. "You'd better light a rush lamp tonight. Read those journals from the old woodsingers and learn how to do your job."

"I'm tired, Goody. I need to sleep." Alana could not keep her hopelessness from weighting down her words. Two bavins in one day . . . What difference could it possibly make? She knew something of Coren's determination and charisma. She knew the power of iron, of swords and armor. She knew the People were outmatched.

"We're all tired, woodsinger, and we'll be more tired before this is over. I never thought that *you* would be the one to give up so easily."

"Give up!" Alana choked on her angry protest. "Goody Glenna, I'm not giving up! I sang two bavins today!"

"And now you say you're too tired to learn how to use them. Was your father too tired to watch over you when you were a child? Was he too tired, after he'd spent a long day on his boat, hauling in fish for all the People?"

"My father is gone, Goody Glenna," Alana said bitterly.

"Aye, and a good thing that he is. That man would die of shame if he saw how quickly you've lost faith."

"I haven't—" Alana started to protest again, but Goody Glenna had already turned away, shuffling off into the night. "I haven't lost faith," Alana whispered to herself in the darkness.

She walked to her home and huddled disconsolately on her doorstep. She *should* go inside. She should light a rush lamp and pull down the dusty tomes, bury herself in the words of the wise women who had sung to the Tree through the ages.

She was so tired, though. Tired and alone. She missed her father more now than she had since the horror of identifying his bloated and stinking corpse on the beach, since the nightmare of Sarira Woodsinger's death. Her father would have made this all right; he would have saved the children for her, somehow.

Her father was gone, though. And now, Maddock had left as well—Maddock whom she had watched all through the winter. And Landon, who had watched her. And Jobina, too—all gone to save the children, children who even now might be dead or dying.

Sighing, Alana gathered her patched woodsinger's cloak close about her shoulders and made her way out of the village. She might be too tired to read, too tired to study ancient journals. But she could still reach to the Tree for comfort, ask it to teach her what she needed to learn. After all, the Tree had balanced earth and air for all its life. It knew the ways of those Guardians. It knew the feeling of those elements. It could touch its own bavin, if only she asked it properly.

When she got to the giant oak, she leaned against its trunk. Breathing deeply of the fragrant loam, of the earth that she had turned to receive the forgotten offering of first harvest fish, she tangled her thoughts in the Tree's essence. She urged the oak to reach out to its own wood across the leagues, across the expanse of Air and Earth.

The stretch felt different, darker and harder than the reach for a bavin across Water. Alana shifted her mental grasp, struggling for a new, awkward balance.

With each beat of her heart, though, she moved through the Tree's rings, closer to the core of the oak that she had sworn to attend. Stories clutched at her, snagging her consciousness like branches. She caught her breath, and she could make out her own voice, echoing through the wooden heart, telling the Tree about the People's lives for two long seasons. Then, she heard Sarira's voice, chanting older stories to the Tree. Sarira Woodsinger told about the birth of twins, the rare double blessing of Reade and Maida. Alana melted her consciousness over the Tree's, following round and round the ring that had recorded the children's arrival.

And when at last Alana exhaled, she was no longer the exhausted daughter of a drowned fisherman. She was no longer the People's woodsinger. Instead, she was the living essence of the Tree, stretching across earth and air, from ringed wood to a distant bavin. She was a frightened five-year-old boy who was farther from his village than he had ever been in his life.

3

◄═━◄∞►═►

Mum would be angry.

Reade knew that he shouldn't have been playing by the water's edge. Mum had told him a thousand times that if he wasn't careful, the Guardians would take him away.

But it wasn't his fault this time! It really wasn't.

Maida had found a stinging eel in the water, and Reade was only trying to help her catch it. Her hands were too small to close behind its neck frill. Hadn't Mum told him that he needed to watch out for Maida now, that he had to be like Da?

One moment, Reade had been trying to help Maida, reaching toward the eel's bulging throat. Then, there had been screaming, and snarling dogs. Duke Coren had come to him in the tidepool, wrapping a mailed arm around his belly. "Hold still," the duke had hissed through set teeth. "Hold still, and you won't be hurt."

Reade had struggled, though, and there had been a flash of sun, and a wave of pain that made everything around him go dark as night.

And the first thing Reade thought upon awakening was that Mum would be angry. Over and over, the words pounded through his head, until he forced himself to open his eyes. A forest circled around him, looping about in a swooping, sickening dance. Giant oaks turned upside down and planted themselves up-side down in the grey, cloudy sky.

Reade's belly twisted inside him, and he barely managed to pull free from Duke Coren's commanding grip, to hold his head over the duke's armored leg. A thin stream of vomit trickled from his lips.

The duke stopped his horse immediately, leaping off the animal to help Reade down. The nobleman gave him a clean white cloth to wipe his face, and Reade spat out the worst of the taste from his mouth. Then, the duke passed him a canteen of water. Reade looked at the man suspiciously, trying to think past the ache in his head.

"Wh— where's Mum?"

Duke Coren's jaw tightened, as if he were angry with Reade, but the man's voice was calm. "She's back with the People, Sun-lord. Back at the Headland of Slaughter."

"And Maida?"

"She's up ahead. She's riding with my man, Donal."

"I want to see her!" Reade's fear surged upward with the flipping of his belly. He wanted his sister. He wanted his mum.

"You'll see her soon enough, Sun-lord. We have to get you cleaned up first."

"I want to see Maida!" Reade made the mistake of whirling around in the direction Duke Coren had pointed, and his head suddenly bubbled up above his shoulders, as if it would float away in the forest. He stumbled forward and found himself retching again, his belly clenching around emptiness as his mouth filled with a sour taste.

"Ach, Sun-lord," Duke Coren said gravely. "I was afraid you might be ill." Something about the man's voice reached through Reade's tears, made the boy remember when Da had come to sit with him last spring, when Reade had the fever that refused to yield to Healer Jobina's strongest tisane. "Take a deep breath now, Sun-lord."

"Maida," Reade whimpered. "I need to see Maida."

"Aye, Sun-lord. You shall see her soon enough."

Reade did not see her then, though. His mind kept doing funny things, like when his fever ran so high that he could see the Guardians of Air flitting above his bed. He knew that only moments before he had been riding in front of the duke, fighting his quavery belly. Now, he was shivering in a wicked breeze, standing before the soldiers in nothing more than his small-clothes. His teeth began to chatter uncontrollably, and he crossed his bare arms over his chest.

Duke Coren stood before him with a bulky, cloth-wrapped bundle. Reade tried to look away from the man, angry with himself for being sick in front of the duke. "Where's Mum? I want my mum!"

The duke only laughed kindly and knelt before him. "Ah, Sun-lord. Your spirit is unbroken even if your head hurts." Reade surprised himself by bursting into tears. "Come here, little man. I've new robes for you, clothes befitting your status. After you've put on your robes, you can see Maida."

Maida! Of course! Reade was supposed to watch out for her, to protect her. He might as well put on the golden robes. He'd look silly if his lips turned blue, like when he'd eaten the entire basket of berries last summer. Reluctantly, he moved to the duke's side.

Duke Coren began to shake out the fabric bundle, revealing yards of cloth-of-gold. Reade stared in awe. Not so long ago, he had worn nothing but a baby's shapeless dress. He could still remember the day when Da helped him into his first pair of breeches.

The cloth that the duke offered now was finer than anything Reade had ever seen among the People. He would be dressed better than Alana Woodsinger! Reade let Duke Coren help him with the heavy fabric.

And help he needed. The duke knelt beside him, taking up yard after yard of the shimmering cloth and draping it around Reade's narrow shoulders, wrapping it around his slight waist. When the boy was covered from head to toe in the rich fabric, Duke Coren nodded with satisfaction. Almost as an afterthought, he reached beneath the cloth and pulled out a woodstar. Reade had not even realized he wore the bavin.

"Here, Sun-lord. I gave this to you while you slept. It was created by your woodsinger and you should wear it, as the leader of your people in exile." Reade flushed with pride as Duke Coren centered the woodstar on his chest. If the duke were giving such great gifts, this frightening journey could not be all bad.

The bavin gave him courage to demand again, "Where's Mum?"

"She's back at the Headland, Sun-lord. Don't you remember? You don't need her anymore."

"Where's Maida?" Reade asked, feeling funny that he'd forgotten Mum was gone, that he'd forgotten she was back among the People, far away.

"She's sleeping. Over there." The duke nodded toward the far side of the clearing, and Reade could make out a pile of saddlebags. Maida was leaning against one, her eyes closed. Her face was dirty, as if she'd been playing in the People's fields, and her hair had come loose from her tight braids. She was wrapped in cloth-of-gold, though, bound up as thoroughly as Reade was himself.

"Maida!" Reade called.

"Hush, Sun-lord. Let her sleep. She's tired from our journey, and we've a long way to go yet."

"Where are you taking us?"

"To Smithcourt, Sun-lord."

"But why? Why can't we go back to Mum? Why can't we go back to the People?"

"Your time with the People is over, Sun-lord. It is your destiny to ride to Smithcourt."

Destiny. That was a word out of a grown-up's story, a word bigger than Reade could imagine. He stayed silent for a moment, overwhelmed by the thought of riding away from all the People. He closed his hands about the bavin hanging on his chest, and he felt a little braver. After a moment, he tugged at the stiff golden cloth. "Why do I have to wear this? Why can't I wear my breeches?"

"We want to honor you, Sun-lord. Among my people, you are destined for the greatest glory we can bestow. You and your sister." Before Reade could ask another question, Duke Coren gestured toward his horse. "Come now, Sun-lord. We must ride. We can't linger if we are going to get to Smithcourt in time."

"But—"

"Sun-lord. Now!" Reade gasped at the stern note in Duke Coren's voice, and he was amazed to see the nobleman's hand clench into a fist.

Reade *always* asked questions. Reade always asked and Mum always answered, question after question after question, until she finally sent him outside to play with the other boys. Mum never got angry at questions. She never yelled just because Reade was talking. And she never, never hit him. She never even curled her fingers into a fist.

Reade swallowed all the things he wanted to know—how far was Smithcourt? In time for what? Why was Duke Coren honoring Reade and Maida? Why was Maida sleeping? The duke lifted him onto the horse's broad back. By the time Duke Coren swung up behind him, Maida was settled in front of Donal. They left the clearing before Reade could learn anything more.

As the day wore on, Reade tried to sit straight on the horse. He clutched at the animal's ample mane when the beast resumed its gallop. Every step of the great roan jolted him a little more in the saddle. Before long, he was crying again, great gasping sobs that caught in his throat, while his nose ran and his eyes streamed.

How was he to know that the inlanders' huge horse would hurt so much? Da would never have let Reade ride the stallion. Da had punished Reade when he even petted the border pony, last autumn.

Da. Reade fought against a choking sob. He mustn't think of Da now. Mum said that Da had gone to fish with the Guardians, along with those four other men. Mum said Reade must be brave, like Alana Woodsinger. The woodsinger's da had gone fishing, too, and had left to be with the Guardians of Water.

It wasn't fair, though. Da had forgotten his promises. He'd said that he and Reade would go out on their own boat that spring. He had promised that Reade could help bring in the nets. But Da had gone on ahead, gone off to fish by himself.

When Reade thought of fresh, sweet fish, his belly gurgled. He was doubly empty from being sick and the long hours they had traveled. He turned in the saddle to look up at Duke Coren's bearded face. The man's eyes glinted beneath his heavy brows, and Reade wondered if he'd be allowed to ask a question now. His spirits lifted when Duke Coren growled, "Aye, Sun-lord? What do you need?"

The duke's words were strange. Reade knew that the nobleman could not really mean to call him a lord. Lords did not come from the People. Lords lived in faraway places, in giant villages called towns. They lived in amazing cottages called castles. People bowed down before lords and did their bidding. Lords dressed in fancy robes and ate meat whenever they wanted.

"Supper please, Y-your Grace. I'm very hungry."

"Then supper you shall have." Reade was cheered by the duke's smiling voice, and only a few minutes later, he was lifted down from the high horse. His legs shivered as he stood beside the road, shaking as if he'd just been caught in a winter storm. They felt all funny and bendy, the way they did when Reade chased after the bigger boys for an entire afternoon. Before Reade could test a few steps, Donal came over to place Maida beside him. Both men moved away then, walking off among the other soldiers as they shouted orders.

"Maida?"

It took a long time for his sister to turn toward him, a long time for her to blink and make her eyes focus. She looked like she'd been asleep, dreaming so deeply that she didn't recognize him. "Reade?" she asked at last, as if she weren't certain of his name.

He was frightened by her voice, by how the one word shook, but he smiled like a big boy. "It's all right, Maida," Reade made himself say, pretending that he was Da, pretending that he could protect his sister.

"I'm scared, Reade. I want Mum."

"It's going to be fine. We're going to be all right. You don't need to cry." He didn't know if he was making up a story as he spoke the words. He didn't know if they were going to be fine. But his belly felt a little better when he spoke out loud, and he didn't feel quite so much like crying himself when he told Maida not to.

Before Maida could say anything else, Donal walked back to the two of them. His eyes were hard, like old Sarira Woodsinger's when she'd caught Reade spying on the Spirit Council meeting. The soldier started to say something, as if he were going to order the children not to speak to each other, but then he shook his head, pursed his lips and whistled. Reade only had an instant to wonder at the shrill sound, and then one of the inlander's dogs bounded to Donal's side. "Aye, Crusher," the soldier growled. "Keep an eye on these two. Make sure they don't move."

Reade caught his breath at the dog's size. Dogs ate boys. Dogs ate boys and girls and men and women. They tore them apart with their sharp teeth, and they swallowed the little pieces down their dark, smelly throats. They scratched at little boy bodies with their blood-black claws, and they crunched on whatever bones were left over.

Reade shook like the leaves on the trees above him, trembling as if he had been dunked in the ocean in the middle of winter. He heard Maida moan beside him, and he wanted to tell her that he would protect her, that he would keep her safe, but he could not think of the words. He could not think of anything except that dogs ate boys.

Donal barked some other command to the massive beast and then strode away. Crusher sat on his haunches, his head almost level with Reade's own. The boy did not let himself meet the dog's dark brown eyes, did not let himself see how hungry the dog was. Crusher opened his mouth and began to pant, his breath stinking like rotten meat.

Reade forced himself to stand as still as he could, trying to forget the trembling ache in his saddle-sore legs. He made himself not see the men setting up camp. He made himself not hear the little sobs that caught in Maida's throat. He made himself not feel the hot trail down his leg as he wet himself, and he did not move his toes in the muddy puddle that formed beneath his golden robe.

Dogs ate boys.

Reade could not keep from starting, though, when Duke Coren strode back across the site. "Crusher!" the duke exclaimed, and the dog tilted his ears toward the man, all the while keeping his eyes on the children. Duke Coren followed the animal's gaze, and Reade quailed beneath the double stare.

He and Maida had been bad. They had been afraid. They had asked to go back to the People. They had

asked, repeatedly, for Mum. They had disappointed
Duke Coren. And now, Duke Coren could feed them
to the dog.

"All right, Crusher." The duke snapped his fingers
and made a gesture with his hand, as if he were tossing
a hunk of meat to the far end of the camp. The dog
rose to all four feet and edged his nose beneath the
duke's hand for just an instant before trotting away
from the children.

Reade's relief washed over him like a wave on the
People's beach. He dared to fill his lungs with air.
Duke Coren had saved him, saved him and Maida,
even though Reade had been bad! He stepped for-
ward, away from the clinging mud beneath his feet.
For just an instant, his heart clenched as he saw Duke
Coren register that mud, and a hot flush of shame
painted the boy's cheeks.

The duke nodded slowly, and said, "Come along,
Sun-lord. Sun-lady. Your supper is ready." Reade was
so relieved at the kindness in the duke's voice that he
almost ran to the man, almost threw himself against
the duke's armored chest. That was how Reade used
to launch himself at Da. When Da came back from
fishing. Before Da had gone off to fish with the
Guardians.

Maida hung back, though, and Donal finally had to
drag her over to the cookfire. Even when the soldiers
gave her food, she only sat and cried. She wanted
Mum, and she hated the hard bread that the soldiers
told her she must eat. Reade showed her how she
could hold it in her mouth and work her tongue
around it. She could make it soft enough to chew.
That made her stop sniffling for a little while. Reade's
chest swelled like a bantam rooster. Mum would be
proud of him.

Before Reade could ask for a second helping of
bread, the duke brought him a golden cup filled with
sweet water. After the boy had drained the goblet, a

soldier tossed him a scratchy blanket. Duke Coren's saddlebag made a poor excuse for a pillow, but Reade was fast asleep before he could complain.

And so it went for a week. Every morning, the duke roused Reade from a deep sleep. Reade would drink from the golden cup, swallowing every drop of the sweet water. He would chew the dry bread. He would be lifted up to sit in front of Duke Coren.

If he ever thought of complaining, ever thought of asking for Mum, he remembered Crusher's intent gaze and the dog's dripping tongue. Duke Coren had saved him from Crusher. Reade should not bother Duke Coren. He should go with Duke Coren and be good, even if that meant riding away from the People, away from Mum.

The days passed in a haze.

They left the forest behind and made their way across open land. In the rare moments when he was awake, Reade began to see signs of people. Individual fields were defined by fences as high as his head. A clear road stretched beneath the horses' hooves.

One evening, when the taste of the sweet water had faded from the back of Reade's throat, he sat up in front of Duke Coren, looking out at the road that snaked before them. They crested one especially long hill and looked down on some whitewashed houses gathered together like eggs from one of Mum's hens. The cottages were so crowded against each other that there was scarcely a patch of ground for growing herbs. The village green was striped with footpaths, and a small herd of milk-cows stood in the middle of the grass, chewing their cud.

Reade cried out when he saw an actual smithy on the far edge of the green. He recognized the anvil from Da's stories. The gigantic metal block stood by the ashes of an open fire. Looking behind him, Reade swallowed audibly. He could not see the first houses they had passed when they entered this village—no, this *town*. "Please, Your Grace, are we going to your castle now?"

"My castle!" the duke barked in the twilight. "We're nowhere near any castle, Sun-lord. We'll be another fortnight on the road before we reach Smithcourt." The duke laughed again. "Just for you, though, we'll stay at the King's Horse for the night."

The words confused Reade until he looked at the building where Duke Coren had reined to a sudden halt. A great sign blew in the wind—a horse's head picked out in bright paint, with fiery eyes that flashed at the young boy. A golden crown rested on the magnificent beast's ears.

Duke Coren snorted at the sign and muttered under his breath as he lifted Reade down from his flesh-and-blood stallion. "Damned fools! Still, this is the best of the lot in this backwater—supposed to have the only drinkable ale in the entire cursed village." There was more, but Reade could not catch the words as he trotted to keep up with the scowling duke.

Reade quickly forgot Duke Coren's fascinating curses as he stared at the tavern's strange patrons. Every face he could see was male; each was half covered with a bushy beard. Clouds of pungent smoke filled the air. Most of the men sucked on intricately carved pipes. Every pipe, though, was removed from brown-stained lips as the men gaped at the soldiers and their two golden-robed charges. Reade drew back from the staring faces, backing up until he felt the strength of Duke Coren's legs against his spine. His hand crept to the bavin about his neck, his fingers closing tightly about its black points.

A huge, red-faced woman came out of the crowd of awestruck villagers. Her face was puffy, like dough that needed to be punched down. She hesitated for a moment before dropping a rough curtsey to the duke, and then she twisted her chapped hands in an apron that might once have been white. "Good evening, m'lord. I—" She stopped pretending to be polite. "Who *are* these children?"

Before Reade could answer, Maida broke free from Donal's grip, darting toward the fat woman with a cry. "Please!" she sobbed as she buried her face in the dirty apron. "I want my mum!"

Reade stared at his sister in awe. How did she dare to run to a stranger, to a woman she'd never seen before?

As Reade watched, he saw that the woman looked afraid, but her hands started to smooth Maida's tangled hair. The woman whispered something to Maida, and some of the men in the smoky room started to grumble. Two or three climbed to their feet, but they didn't move any closer to Duke Coren after a dagger flashed into the nobleman's hand.

Reade saw the firelight glint on the blade, but Maida did not. She kept her face buried in the fat woman's skirts. Her words were muffled as she sobbed, "We've been on the road for days! They took us away, and they put us in these robes, and they made us ride and ride and ride. . . ."

Maida sobbed as if she'd lost the last of her rag dolls, and the red-faced woman folded the girl closer against her padded hip, clucking meaningless noises as she stared in shock at Duke Coren. As Reade heard his sister, tears welled up in his own eyes. He *did* want his mum. And he *did* want to be back home. Duke Coren hadn't answered any of his questions, and Reade still didn't know why they were going to Smith-court, or why they had to leave the People behind.

"Good lady," the duke crooned, and Reade remembered how the man had spoken to Alana Woodsinger, back home. The thought made him feel all strange inside. His belly flipped over, and he took his own step toward the red-faced woman, trying to duck away from the nobleman's hand on his shoulder. Duke Coren, though, tightened his fingers, keeping Reade firmly in place. The duke went on, pitching his voice just above Maida's sobbing. "Good lady, we have ridden hard, traveling from Land's End in just a single week. You can see that these children are exhausted."

"I can see that this bairn is terrified!"

"And well she might be, after the horrors that we witnessed in her village. On the Headland of Slaughter."

The name of home made Maida wail even louder, and Reade could barely make out her words. "I want to go home! I want my mum!" Reade took a deep breath, ready to cry out, too. Maida was right. They were so far away from Mum and Sartain Fisherman, from Alana Woodsinger and the Tree. Things were scary here, with Duke Coren, and with Donal, and with Crusher, the dog that was probably waiting outside even as the people in the tavern stared.

Before Reade could start to wail, though, Duke Coren sighed and shook his head. The nobleman made a show of setting his dagger on the long wooden table. When he looked up at the drinking men, his face was exhausted, pale behind his dark beard. "I beg your indulgence, goodwife, honest men. These children are the only ones we were able to save from the Headland of Slaughter, and our journey has been hard. Even now, we haven't dared to tell them the full story of what they left behind. Perhaps my men can put them to bed, abovestairs, and then I can tell you the truth of what happened on the Headland."

The red-faced woman started to reply, but Maida interrupted, shrieking, "No! Don't let them take me away! Don't let me go! Help me!"

"Easy, child." The woman smoothed Maida's hair like Mum would, but Reade saw the careful look she gave to the dagger that Duke Coren had set upon her table. The woman was afraid, too. "No one is going to take you away. We'll hear the lord out, though. Hush, girl. Stop your crying."

Duke Coren waited until the woman looked up again, and then the nobleman shook his head. His face was sad, like Sartain Fisherman's when Da went fishing with the Guardians. The duke sighed, and said, "I'm sorry to bear this horror into your house, good woman. But certainly you've heard rumors of the . . . strange habits out that way, on the Headland of Slaughter."

A squawk of protest rose in Reade's throat. The People weren't strange! Before he could say anything, though, Duke Coren tightened his grip on Reade's shoulder. Each of the man's fingers was a separate little spade, digging into his flesh. Reade wasn't stupid. He understood an order, even a silent one. Reade was not supposed to talk. He could listen, but he could not talk.

His heartbeat began to throb beneath Duke Coren's fingertips, and he knew he would have a bruise beneath the golden cloth. Duke Coren continued, though, as if he weren't pinching Reade's flesh to the bone. "You see, good woman, any mention of the horror among those people is painful to this boy."

The duke lowered his voice, and each of the villagers leaned a little nearer. Reade was reminded of the People, gathering around the fires in their cottages, eager for the news that Duke Coren had brought when he arrived at the Headland. "A new woodsinger holds sway at Land's End, good folk. She . . . she has convinced her people that the Guardians must drink blood before the summer sun can rise." As Reade gasped in disbelief, Duke Coren dropped his voice to a dark whisper. "They will soon come on raids to the inland, come to steal away your newborn babes. I trust no one has been taken yet?"

"No, my lord." The red-faced woman was clearly frightened by Duke Coren's story. "No one."

Now, Reade was more than a little frightened himself. He'd always been afraid of Alana Woodsinger, and Sarira Woodsinger before her. There was something scary about the patched cloak the woodsingers wore, the swirling colors of brown and red, blue and white. They were always busy with the Tree, ordering people around to help them bring water, to help them bring fresh fish to lay in the earth. They could be so mean, telling Reade what he could and couldn't do. Alana Woodsinger was much stricter than Mum, especially than Mum was now, now that Da was gone.

But Alana Woodsinger meant to kill him? She meant to give his blood to the Guardians? That made no sense at all!

"We haven't lost children, m'lord, but I've had two newborn lambs taken in the past fortnight!" a shepherd shouted from the back of the room, and there was a low rumble of agreement. Other men cried out, too—four more lambs had been taken. Reade wiggled his fingers—four lambs and two lambs—*six* had been taken altogether.

Six lambs. That was a lot. Even Reade knew that didn't happen by accident.

Maybe Duke Coren *wasn't* making up stories. Maybe he had just misunderstood everything. The People did not want to give the Guardians the blood of children. They wanted to give the blood of *lambs*. It was easy to see how the duke could be confused. After all, Mum had called Reade a poor little lamb, the day that Da disappeared fishing. She had said often enough that Reade and Maida were her poor lost lambs, her poor fatherless lambs.

The People would sing their Song of Sacrifice, like they did every year, because they were grateful for the spring. The spring Song included lambs. Maybe Duke Coren thought that the Song of Sacrifice was real! Maybe he thought that the lambs in the song were real children!

Even now, the duke was nodding slowly, as if he had expected to hear about the inlanders' missing livestock. His lips were thin with a grim smile. "It is as I feared then. The cursed outland raiders have come this far."

Maida cried out, "My people don't have any raiders!"

Reade saw the look that Maida cast at him across the room, saw her demand that he stand up for the People. He swallowed hard and tried to think of something to say. It was all so confusing! Duke Coren was saying one thing, and Maida understood another thing. The people in the tavern room would not know whom to believe, and Reade could not begin to figure out how he would make them all understand.

Before Reade could speak, though, Duke Coren tightened the pincers of his fingers even more. This was clearly not the time for Reade to speak, to clarify things for Maida and the men and the fat, red-faced woman.

After all, what did it really matter? Six lambs *had* been stolen. The inlanders had no reason to lie about that. And Mum had been talking just the other day about how she looked forward to the spring, to making stews with something other than salt fish. Who knew what had happened to those lambs?

In any case, Reade could not doubt the message that Duke Coren was sending through his fingers. It was exactly like when the bigger boys told Reade not to tattle, when they glared at him just before the elders came to stop whatever they were doing. The older boys were always threatening the little children. Only the other day, Reade had been forced to lie and say that *he* had trampled the new plants in the communal field. He took the blame because that bully Winder had threatened him, threatened to twist his arm behind his back and break it. Goody Glenna herself had punished Reade, but even her ear-boxing was not as bad as Winder's punishment would have been.

Reade understood what Duke Coren's fingers meant.

Even if the People *didn't* have raiders, even if they hadn't stolen the lambs, Reade must stay quiet.

"You see," Duke Coren was saying to the red-faced woman, "that poor girl denies her people's raiders because she is terrified by what she has seen. She's been frightened to the point that she will lie outright. You can imagine how shocking it must have been for her, for both these poor children, to learn that the parents they had trusted, the People they had loved"—the duke lowered his voice, whispering his last words as if he meant for Maida not to hear him—"the People they had loved intended to slit their throats like new-born lambs."

No! That wasn't it at all! The inlanders were missing six lambs. Mum had said that she wanted to cook something other than fish. Mum loved lamb. The People might have come to take the inlanders' meat. But hurt Maida and Reade? Slit *their* throats?

Reade would have to explain to Duke Coren. Reade would have to let him know that the woodsinger did not *really* collect children's blood for the Guardians. She threatened a lot of things, but most of them she never followed through on.

Reade would tell the duke the truth. But he would wait until later, until the people in the tavern were no longer listening. After all, Reade wouldn't want them to laugh at Duke Coren, to think that the duke had been foolish. Not when he had been so kind to Reade and Maida. Not when he had saved Reade and Maida from Crusher.

Duke Coren continued talking to the people in the tavern. "My men and I longed to carry all the children away, for we feared their fate if the outlanders could not find enough innocent lambs to slaughter. Alas, these were the only two we could save."

Only two? Now Reade was more confused than ever. He was the Sun-lord, Duke Coren had said, and Maida was the Sun-lady. Had the duke's men tried to take other children from the seashore? Had they tried to bring other children with them, into the inland? Were there other lords and ladies among the People's children?

"These were the only two," Duke Coren repeated and his voice shook with emotion. Reade looked up and saw tears in the man's eyes—tears! Then the duke pulled Reade close, putting his strong arms around the boy's shoulders. For just a moment, Reade held back, certain that he should wait, that he should explain, that he should make everything clear. Before he could speak, though, he realized that Duke Coren's embrace felt familiar. It felt safe.

For just an instant, Reade thought that he was back in Da's arms. Without thinking, he threw his own arms around Duke Coren's waist and buried his face against the soldier's hip. The man smelled different than Da— he smelled of leather and horse, not of sea and fish. But all the same, when the duke pulled him close, Reade thought he would burst into tears.

The fat woman's voice trembled, and she clucked like one of the goodwives back home, like a woman fussing over Reade's skinned knees after one of his countless accidents. "Sit down, you poor souls! Let me bring you something hot from the kitchen."

She hesitated only a moment, clearly wondering what to do with the still-sobbing Maida, but Donal stepped forward at a nod from Coren. As the soldier awkwardly gathered up the little girl, Reade saw that his sister was red-faced and exhausted, as if she had run a footrace or climbed the cliff to the Tree a dozen times. Her sobbing faded away as the soldier drew her to a bench, and she collapsed in her crumpled golden finery as if she were ready to fall asleep immediately.

The aproned woman was only gone for a few moments, and she was still shaking her head as the duke and his men tucked into great bowls of lamb stew. The men tossed back ale as if they were at a feast.

Reade did not enjoy the meat nearly as much as he had anticipated. With every bite, he thought of the stories the duke had told. Stories? Or truth? After all, Duke Coren had *cried*. Reade had never seen a grown man cry before, not even when Sartain Fisherman came to tell Mum that Da had gone.

Were there bad things happening back home, back at the Headland of Slaughter? Was Alana Woodsinger evil? Were Mum and the other People in danger— even more danger than he and Maida? Reade swallowed his stew and tried to believe that everything would be right in the end.

4

The next morning, Reade's shoulder still hurt where the duke had pinched him. It wasn't fair. He had only wanted to help, to explain that Duke Coren did not understand the People. Reade rubbed his arm through his golden robe and sulked as he drank from Duke Coren's cup.

They left the inn just after sunrise. All the villagers gathered to see them on their way, and more than one person muttered about riding west to "root out" the People's threat. As the village disappeared behind them, Duke Coren looked down at Reade and said, "You were wise not to speak out last night, Sun-lord. It would have been wicked to lie to your people."

"I wasn't going to lie!" Reade was grumpy. Mum would have said that he needed to go back to bed, that he needed more sleep until the honey in his dreams had sweetened the day. Reade knew that he didn't need more sleep. He just needed his shoulder to stop hurting.

"Ah, but you were! Not because you intended to be bad, but because you did not know the truth. Always remember, Sun-lord. When you speak out of ignorance, you might speak a lie. Your people would have been hurt, if you had lied to them."

"My people weren't in that smoky room. My people are at the Headland!"

"Some of your people are at Land's End." Duke Coren nodded. "But the better part of your people are inland, spread between here and Smithcourt, Sun-lord."

The duke's words were scary. How could Reade's people be inland? How could anyone know him between here and Smithcourt? Reade did not want to think about all those strangers, people like the fat woman and the whiskered men in the tavern. They weren't fishermen. They didn't even grow herbs outside their own homes. They were different from the People. Worried about what Duke Coren might say regarding the strange inland people, Reade asked a different question, one that he'd wanted to ask since the duke first spoke to him. "Why do you call me that? Why do you call me Sun-lord?"

"Because that is who you are. That is who I came to find and free—the Sun-lord and the Sun-lady."

"But I'm just Reade. I'm just one of the People. I don't know anything about your lords and ladies!"

"As you grow closer to your home, you'll learn the true stories."

"My home is behind us! My home is with Mum!" There. That was what Reade had wanted to say all morning, for days, even.

"That was your home of exile, Sun-lord. Your mum was a good woman. She kept you safe until it was time for you to come to your true home. You've grown, now, though. You don't need your mum anymore. You're a big boy, and I've come to take you away from your home of exile, to Smithcourt. To your home of truth."

Reade's voice was very small. "Home of truth?"

"Aye, Sun-lord."

"Then I'll never see Mum again?"

"You'll see many things, Sun-lord. Many, many things."

"But I want to see Mum!"

"Maybe you will, Sun-lord. Maybe you'll see her after we arrive in Smithcourt, after you do your work in the Service."

"The Service? What's that?"

"That's another story, for another day. Sit back now, Sun-lord. We've a long ride ahead of us."

Reade had been fighting the darkness that spread inside him, the fuzzy feeling that always came over his body after he drank from the duke's golden cup. His arms and legs were heavy. He didn't really care what the Service was. It didn't matter that he had to wait to see Mum. He didn't mind that he might be away from the Headland for a long, long time.

He even forgot about the confusing lies and truths and half-truths. He forgot that he meant to explain things to Duke Coren, to tell the lord about the mistakes he had told the people back in the tavern. With the sweet water inside him, Reade stopped caring about lambs and the Song of Sacrifice. Instead, he leaned back against Duke Coren's chilled armor, shifting a little to ease his bruised shoulder.

The duke's gauntleted hands gripped tighter on the horse's reins, and Reade grew sleepy as Duke Coren's arms closed around him. He let his head slump against the nobleman's chest. They rode on for league after league, leading the troop of loyal men over the hills.

That night, they stayed at another inn. Duke Coren asked about lambs again, and told the villagers about the People needing blood. This time, Maida was held tight at Donal's side so that she couldn't run to any of the people in the common room. Donal's hand looked heavy on her shoulder, and Reade suspected that Maida was being pinched as he had been the night before. Even so, she glared at Reade across the smoky room, daring him to speak up as she had at the King's Horse.

Reade remembered that he shouldn't lie, shouldn't

tell a story with half-truths. He remembered that the men drinking in the tavern were somehow his people, and he owed them true stories.

But Reade also knew that he didn't want Maida to be angry with him, and he didn't want her to think he was a coward. After all, she was his twin. She was his only sister, as Mum always reminded him, the only sister he was ever going to have.

And so, Reade interrupted Duke Coren to say that the nobleman was wrong. He said that Alana Woodsinger had tried to be nice to Reade and Maida. He even pointed out that the woodsinger had honored him, that she had given him his branches when he was the huer. She could never have planned to kill him, not after she had let him cry *hevva*.

Duke Coren tightened his fingers into a fist as Reade spoke. His jaw got hard, like he was going to spit something onto the tavern floor. All of a sudden, Reade remembered how the duke had looked back on the Headland, how he had held a knife and glared at Reade when he came riding through the harvest festival. Reade remembered how Duke Coren had upset the first harvest, on top of his roan stallion, leading his dogs. Dogs like Crusher.

Reade's heart pounded, and his face flushed. He didn't want Duke Coren angry with him. He didn't want to be in trouble. He tried to be good, really he did! Sometimes he just forgot! Sometimes Maida *made* him forget!

After a moment, Duke Coren got a sad look in his eyes, just like he had at the King's Horse. He shook his head and said that Reade was only a child. A child could not truly understand anything about the outlanders. Reade was really just a very little boy.

And then, before Reade had a chance to say anything more, before he even got to finish his supper, Duke Coren had him carried upstairs, to the sleeping room. For good measure, he sent Maida upstairs as well. The soldier who guarded them did not let them speak to each other.

Reade was still awake when Donal came in to make his last report of the night. Most of the soldiers were sleeping in a long hall beneath the eaves of the roadhouse, but the duke and the children shared a small room. Maida had already fallen asleep, and she was breathing heavily through her mouth. Reade lay beside her, his eyes closed, but his ears open.

"Your Grace, may I speak freely?"

"Of course, man." Duke Coren's voice was cold, like Mum's when Reade made excuses. Reade did not think he would have had the courage to go on, the way that Donal did.

"You let the boy say too much. Song of Sacrifice? Lamb stew? These villagers won't know what to make of the boy's tale. If an outlander walked into the common room tonight, he'd be welcomed with a full tankard."

"You exaggerate, Donal. These backwoods fools might not treat the outlanders as child-killers, but they'll still rise up against thieves. Don't forget that they live by their flocks. Lost lambs are lost gold."

"You need to unite your people, Your Grace. You need to show that you can keep them safe, even against bloodthirsty ravagers who would murder their own children, murder stolen children for a tree!"

"I know what I need, man." Coren's voice sounded like his jaw was hard again. Reade lay as still as he could, terrified that either man would notice he was still awake.

Donal continued, as if he didn't hear that the duke was angry. "That boy is going to cause problems—mark my words. He should respect his elders, not contradict them. The girl was bad enough, at the first tavern, but at least those countrymen just thought she was hysterical. That boy is going to cause us a lot more trouble, if you let him go on and on."

"The boy is no fool. He knew I was displeased, and he went to bed hungry. He'll hold his tongue now." The duke's voice softened a bit, and Reade could tell that he was smiling. "Don't worry, Donal. They'll both be fine. We'll train them properly, once we're back at Smithcourt. They'll be ready to play the Sun-lord and Sun-lady in time for the Service."

"The Service is not my concern, Your Grace. It's the journey to Smithcourt that worries me. You're supposed to be raising the countryside on this trip. You're supposed to be gathering support."

"We haven't lost that support, Donal. People saw the Sun-lord in that room tonight."

"They saw a child in golden robes, a child who contradicted you."

"Are we going to have that argument again, about the robes?" The smile was gone from Duke Coren's words.

Donal answered quickly. "No, Your Grace. I understand why you want them in their finery. You want your duchy to remember the Sun-lord and the Sun-lady, and for the legend to spread, even after you've gained Smithcourt. It's just that if they say the wrong things when they're wearing those golden robes, we could have an entire village rise up against us. Your claim to the throne will hardly be advanced if you have to burn one of your own villages."

"You worry too much, Donal. The boy will hold his tongue. If he doesn't, we'll teach him a sharper lesson than an empty belly." Duke Coren sighed. "This is the hardest time for us, Donal. This is when we need to take the gravest risks. You and I both know that my claim to the Iron Throne will die altogether, if I can't produce the Sun-lord and the Sun-lady in Smithcourt, alive and ready for the Service."

Donal was silent for so long that Reade thought he

wasn't going to answer. Then he finally said, "I'm just saying that you should watch him, Your Grace. Watch him closely."

"I do, Donal. With every step we take closer to Smithcourt, I do just that."

Donal bowed then and left the tiny room. It took Reade a long time to fall asleep, even with the sound of Maida breathing on his right, and Duke Coren snoring in the great bed above.

The next morning, Reade thought about the men's argument. He decided he would let Duke Coren say whatever he wanted, even if he was wrong about the lambs and the Song of Sacrifice. That way, Duke Coren wouldn't be angry with him. He wouldn't be angry, and Reade would get to eat his supper. He'd get to share a bench with the nobleman, sitting in the tavern common room like a big boy.

After all, what did it really matter if Duke Coren told some stories about the People? Lambs were sacrificed in the Song of Sacrifice. Was that so different from pouring lambs' blood on the Tree? And no one could *really* believe that the People would pour a child's blood on the Tree.

Duke Coren must be telling a scary story, like the Men's Council did on the longest night of every year. Grown-ups told stories all the time, and most of them were confusing. Confusing, or outright lies. Da had lied, when he'd said that he'd take Reade fishing.

Besides, Reade was having an adventure that would make all the boys jealous back home. Even Winder, who always made Reade wait on the edge of the green while the big boys chose their teams. Reade would lead those games when he and Maida returned to Land's End, after they journeyed to Smithcourt. After the Service, whatever that was.

Every day for a week, Duke Coren pushed them hard. He knew all the best taverns along the way, and he always arranged for rooms upstairs. Maida was taken away whenever she cried too much or got too mouthy. Reade, though, remembered to hold his tongue, and he got to sit at the duke's right hand. He was proud, even if he was still a little scared.

After a week of listening to Duke Coren talk to people in common rooms, the line between truth and story was completely blurred in Reade's mind. Over and over, he heard stories about the People. He learned that Sartain Fisherman had been training men for months, teaching them to steal inland children. Duke Coren explained that the People had always hated the inlanders. The People were jealous. They wanted fine fields and rich harvests. They wanted iron. They would kill for gold.

Reade was glad that he wore his bright robes, glad that the inlanders could see that he and Maida were different from the People. After all, the twins had left their home. They hadn't done the horrible things that Duke Coren talked about! They had never hurt anyone, for harvests or iron or gold or anything at all!

Sitting in the taverns, listening to the duke's stories, Reade pulled his golden robes closer about his shoulders and reminded himself of all the lessons he had already learned. He remembered to sit quietly. He remembered to eat his supper. He remembered not to confuse anyone with his own stories about life on the Headland.

At night, Reade dreamed of the ghosts who walked the beaches of Land's End. He dreamed of inland traders who were killed for their goods, and children who were drowned so that their parents did not go hungry. He dreamed of the branches of the Tree, spreading out across the sky like a spiderweb, waiting to catch bad boys, waiting to punish them.

When he woke, he almost believed that Sartain Fisherman *had* meant to slaughter him over the Tree's roots. After all, Reade had been chosen as the huer, hadn't he? He'd been recognized as the smartest boy in the village, the fastest and the loudest and the best at spying out schools of fish. What would keep Sartain Fisherman from offering up Reade, Reade *and* Maida both, as sacrifices to the Guardians? Surely the Guardians only wanted the best.

Reade also kept remembering Alana Woodsinger's face. She was always yelling at him to stop some harmless fun. She was very strict, and she had that funny knife that she carried with her everywhere. Maybe that was the knife she would have used to sacrifice Reade. Maybe that was the knife she would have used to slit Maida's throat while Reade watched, helpless.

One night, thinking about Alana Woodsinger's sharp, iron knife, Reade stepped closer to Duke Coren. He raised a hand to the woodstar that swung from his neck. Certainly, the duke had given him the bavin, but the thing had been sung by the woodsinger. It was part of the Tree, the same Tree that wanted to drink his blood. Maybe he should throw away the woodstar. Maybe he should take it from his neck and walk over to the hearth. He could throw it into the flames right then and there.

Before Reade could act, though, Duke Coren settled a reassuring hand on his shoulder. Then, for no reason at all, the duke gave him a bite of meat from beneath the steaming crust of his pie. The duke shared his ale as well, pouring from his pewter tankard into a small leather cup. Reade's eyes grew heavy as his stomach grew full. He was almost asleep when Duke Coren stood and picked him up, moving toward the stairs.

"Allow me, Your Grace." Donal pushed back from the table and reached out for Reade. He was still chewing; he had taken Maida upstairs earlier in the evening, when she had refused to touch the kidney pie. Maida said the pie smelled funny.

"Stay, man," Duke Coren said easily. "Finish your meal."

Donal bowed and returned to the table. Reade put his head on Duke Coren's shoulder as the tall man carried him up the stairs. He could feel the duke breathing, feel warm hands across his back. The nobleman needed to stoop low to enter the room at the top of the stairs. Da had needed to duck to pass through the door of their cottage.

A serving girl sat beside the bed. She bit off a small shriek as Reade and the duke entered the chamber. "Begging your pardon, Your Grace," she said, and she dropped a curtsey. "I was just watching the little girl, as your man ordered."

"Very good," Duke Coren said. "You may go now."

"Aye, Your Grace." She bobbed up and down again. "Is there anything I can be getting you?"

"Nothing. I'm just putting the boy to bed."

"I'd be happy to do that, Your Grace. You can return downstairs. Have another mug of ale."

"I'll attend him myself." The girl ducked out the door without another word.

Duke Coren helped Reade out of the cloth-of-gold. Every night, Reade was stripped to his smallclothes. It was hard to fold the golden fabric. It kept slipping on itself, and it was hard to make it stay in a neat pile.

Maida's golden robe, though, already rested at the foot of her pallet, and Reade could just make out her white linen shift, poking out at the top of her coverlet. She was breathing deeply. Maybe Donal had given her some of the sweet water to drink. Thinking of the golden cup, Reade remembered a question he wanted to ask Duke Coren.

"How much longer until we get to Smithcourt, Your Grace?"

"Still many days, Sun-lord."

"When will we stay at another inn that has venison?"

"I don't know, Sun-lord."

"Didn't you like the venison stew we had last night?"

"It was good, Sun-lord."

"Why do you send Maida upstairs each night?"

"Because she asks too many questions, Sun-lord."

Reade heard the warning, and he fell silent while the duke folded up the last of his golden cloth. Without planning to, Reade opened his mouth and yawned so broadly that he heard his jaw pop. "I'm not ready to go to sleep yet," he protested, as Duke Coren pulled a linen shift over his head.

"You're barely standing on your feet," the duke said, laughing.

"Tell me a story!" Reade begged. Da used to tell stories every night. Reade and Maida would huddle on the pallet they shared by the hearth, and Da would sit close to the fire, his hands working his nets as he spoke. Da would tell of wondrous things—about the Guardians of Water and their towns beneath the sea, about the age before this one, when there were no people, but only talking animals. "Tell me a story," Reade repeated, whining a little as Duke Coren forced his head back onto the heavy bolster.

"Very well," Duke Coren said, and he smiled as he pulled up the coverlet. Reade smiled, too. "Lie back. And close your eyes. And no talking while I speak."

Reade opened his mouth to agree, but the duke shook his head. "No talking," he repeated. "None at all."

Reade settled his head on the bolster and closed his eyes, stretching his arms and legs out straight. There was a pause, and he heard Duke Coren swallow. Then, the story began. "Years ago, before the boyhood of your father's father's father, there was great unrest in all the land. Brother raised arms against brother, father against son, and crop after crop failed because the fields were watered with too much blood."

What type of story was this? Da never told a story with blood! Da never told any stories about people fighting. Reade started to ask a question, but he stopped himself just in time.

"In the midst of that chaos, there was a great woman, the Queen of the Cave, who wed a great man, the Smith of the Skies. The Smith led foray after foray against his enemies, always emerging the victor. When the Queen was heavy with child, she pleaded with her husband to stop his battles, for she feared that she would die in childbed, and she did not want her child to be an orphan. The Smith, though, was scornful of the Queen's fears, and he was far afield when his wife collapsed in labor.

"For two full days, the Queen cried out in childbed, and only when a soldier brought her news that the Smith had indeed been slain in battle did the Queen bring forth not one child, but two, a boy and a girl. The Queen looked upon them and blessed them with their names—Lord of the Sun and Lady of the Sun. Then, she foretold their terrible future.

"Their lives would be hard and dangerous, and their own children would rise up in arms against them. Even as the Queen spoke those words, she knew that her death was upon her, and she ordered her trusted maidservant to take the two perfect children and slay them, lest they suffer the dolorous fate that she foresaw."

Reade thought of those two little babies, with their mum and their da both dead. His throat tightened. He was about to open his eyes, about to tell Duke Coren that he didn't want to hear *this* kind of story, a scary story. Before he could speak, though, Duke Coren settled a hand on his belly. Heat flowed through the coverlet, heat and weight, like a magic blanket, protecting Reade.

The duke continued: "The maidservant grieved so

at the passing of her lady that she could not do as the Queen commanded. Instead of slaughtering the innocent babes, she took them to the woods and left them on a bed of softest moss beneath a tree.

"Before night fell, the twins were found by a doe. The deer raised the two children as if they were her own fawns, and the twins learned grace and beauty and how to flee the hunter. And when they were of the proper age, the old doe took the Lord of the Sun and escorted him to the far northern edge of her forest, and she took the Lady of the Sun to the far southern edge of her forest, setting them on the road to make their way in the world.

"The Sun-lord traveled and his adventures were many. He married and had a dozen children, strong men and women all, who became great warriors and led scores of heroes into battle. The Sun-lady traveled as well, and had adventures as well. She, too, had a dozen children, and they, too, were great warriors, who led scores of warriors into battle.

"But the day came when a son of the Sun-lady all unknowing lay with a daughter of the Sun-lord, and she grew heavy with child. She became ashamed that she could no longer lead her warriors, and she told her family that she had been taken by force.

"The children of the Sun-lord grew hot in fury and rode against the children of the Sun-lady, all the while not knowing that they fought their own kin. Village after village was burned to the ground, and field after field was sown with salt.

"Only when the Sun-lord and the Sun-lady faced each other across a field of blood-red mud did they learn that they had fulfilled their mother's bitter prophecy. The twins fled their embattled children, riding until they reached the end of the earth, where the sun last touches the land before dying every night."

Reade's mind whirled. The Sun-lord and the Sun-lady had ridden to Land's End! They had come to the

People! Reade could not help but slit open his eyes, looking up at the duke. The nobleman smiled and nodded.

"Aye," Duke Coren continued, and his eyes were for Reade alone. "The Sun-lord and the Sun-lady settled among the People on the Headland of Slaughter, intending to live out their lives in hardship to atone for the bloodshed they had brought to the inlanders.

"Every month, though, as the moon reached its fullness in the sky, people came to Land's End to call back the Lord and Lady. All of their children had died on the bloody battlefield, and the kingdom had no one left to guide it. Nevertheless, the twins remembered how fate had driven them to destroy what they loved best, and always they refused.

"Finally, after five years, a pair of children arrived at the distant point of land. They were clothed in robes of gold, and they walked hand in hand. They were of an age, and the Sun-lord and the Sun-lady knew that these children were twins like themselves. When questioned, the children said that their father had died on a great battlefield, and that his body had never been recovered from the bloody mud. Their mother had died at their birthing, cursing the day that she had started the great war that had destroyed her land. As soon as the twins could walk, they had been driven forth from the sorrowful castle of their childhood, accompanied only by a single guard, the faithful Culain.

"Then the Sun-lord and Sun-lady knew that the twins were their own grandchildren, and they welcomed the boy and girl with open arms. The old twins knew that they had wasted valuable years trying to flee their own destiny, and they left Land's End. They traveled back to Smithcourt, the old twins and the young, along with soldiers gathered from the countryside to accompany them, all led by the honorable Culain. Upon their return, there were more sorrows and more prophecies, but in the end Culain himself took the throne, one thousand years ago, and the days of chaos were finally ended."

Reade struggled to sit up, but Duke Coren shook his head. The duke's hand was still heavy across his belly, and Reade settled for whispering, "Why did Culain become king? Why didn't the Sun-lord and the Sun-lady rule the People?"

"Those are other stories, Sun-lord, for other times."

The duke had so many wonderful stories to tell. Reade was missing so much as he slept through day after day. He flushed and gripped Duke Coren's arm. "Please, Your Grace. Tomorrow, I don't want to drink from the golden cup."

"The ride is long yet. We have to cover more ground every day, until we reach Smithcourt."

"I don't care." Reade smiled his best smile. "The ride was long for the Sun-lord, too, and Culain would never have made *him* drink."

Duke Coren stared at the boy. All of a sudden his eyes were dark, sharp. "Ah, Sun-lord, you're probably right at that. Once you set aside the golden cup, though, I'll not let you change your mind."

"I won't. I swear it."

"The Sun-lord's oaths are not casual things," the duke warned.

"I'm not a baby!"

"No, Sun-lord. You most certainly are not a baby."

"Then you won't make me drink tomorrow?"

"I won't, Sun-lord. Just remember that you are the one who asked for the privilege."

A shiver crept down Reade's spine. He remembered how much his legs had hurt on that first day, when he rode without drinking the sweet water. He remembered crying, even when he was trying to be brave. His nose had run, no matter how much he wiped it on his arm.

For just a moment, he thought that he would tell

Duke Coren that he had made a mistake. Maybe he wasn't big enough to ride without the golden cup. Maybe he needed to break his oath.

Then, Reade remembered the Sun-lord in the duke's story. *He* would have been brave enough. He would have been strong enough. Even if it hurt like a stinging eel, the Sun-lord would keep his promise.

Reade would be brave and strong, too. Sitting on the stallion in front of Duke Coren, Reade would act just like the Sun-lord.

5

Irritation pricked Alana's eyes as she stepped into her empty cottage. Of course, not a single villager had thought to set a fire on her hearth. Not one person had thought to bring her supper, despite the fact that she'd spent the entire day at the Tree, stretching her powers landward, struggling to commune with the oak's earth-power, harnessing the air-power that hovered between the Tree and its woodstars. She sighed in exhaustion, even as a swirl of thoughts drifted into her consciousness from other woodsingers, from the women who had gone before her.

"The People never realize the sacrifices I make," whispered one old crone, her tremulous voice captured forever in the woodsingers' communion with the Tree.

"Would it be so hard for them to lay a fire?" asked another of Alana's predecessors.

"Couldn't they set out some food? I don't need fresh-baked bread—anything, really, after a long day tending the Tree. . . ."

Alana took some grudging comfort in the fact that she was not the first woodsinger to be slighted by the People. In fact, she managed to think in a moment of lucidity, the People were not mean, or even lazy. It most likely never occurred to them that the woodsinger would *want* her privacy invaded. Nevertheless, the cottage was chilly and dark, and Alana had to comfort herself with a tough heel from yesterday's loaf of bread.

She sighed as she collapsed onto the low stool by her hearth. This landward business was draining. In the past fortnight, Alana had taught herself to extend her powers into the Tree's roots, to feel the rich earth beneath her. She had felt the Tree gather up the land's rich, dark energy, the nutrients that stretched across the earth from the western edge of the Headland of Slaughter to Smithcourt. The Tree's earth aspect, though, was bound tighter than its familiar, watery soul, and Alana's jaw ached with the power of concentrating on her new skills. She had ratcheted up her concentration until she felt like a child's top. By the end of each day, she ached to spin free.

And reaching through the air was no easier. Alana felt the breezes blowing in the Tree's leaves, she absorbed the free and lithesome energy of the Guardians of Air. It was hard to focus that force, though, hard to keep a single gust blowing all the way across the Headland, over the land to swirl around Reade's bavin. Over and over, Alana caught her own breath, starving her lungs until she gasped with the effort to guide the wind.

Even when she was away from the Tree, even when she had set aside her efforts to harness earth and air, she did not find much relief. Each night, when she managed to stagger back from the Headland, she was confronted by the dusty shelves of journals in her cottage. The moldering leather volumes were filled with the cramped notes of all her predecessors. The journals captured words that had never been spoken to the Tree, information that she could not glean by focusing on the swirl of voices inside her mind. It took concentration to read, though, concentration in the stillest part of the night, when her eyes were grainy for lack of sleep. A few of the accounts were written in a strong hand, the words easily made out, but most sprawled like spiderwebs, spun out across the page with gossamer strands lost to aging parchment and fading ink.

So far, Alana had not deciphered anything useful. There were meticulous accounts of the Tree, of course, of its growth from year to year. Her sisters recorded the springtime ritual of bringing water from the Sacred Grove to fortify the Tree's roots against the corrosive ocean air. Alana read how she could harvest the Tree's acorns to make a sustaining bread that would take months to go stale. She could weave the Tree's autumn leaves into thatched roofs to keep water out. So many pages, so many secrets, yet nothing to instruct her further about stretching the bavins' power over land.

Alana's tightly wrapped tension had sprung loose only the night before, when Goody Glenna stopped by to check on her progress. "There's so much here!" the woodsinger had exclaimed. "How am I supposed to learn it all?"

"By doing what you're doing. By reading and studying."

"It's not fair! Woodsingers are supposed to be trained by the women they replace."

"Who ever said that the Guardians are fair?" Goody Glenna's face drew into a scowl as she wiped thick dust off one of the journals. "We all encouraged Sarira Woodsinger to take an apprentice, but she refused. She died before we had a chance to change her mind. But you know all that—that's why *you* were chosen. The Women's Council, the Men's Council, and the Spirit Council all agreed that you had the urge to learn, that you could regain the wisdom we lost with Sarira."

"But—" Alana began, but Glenna shook her head.

"Back to work, woodsinger." When Goody Glenna

had left, Alana forced her way through another three years of journals, reading, hoping, and all the time rubbing her tired eyes.

Her conversation with Goody Glenna had made her even more tense. Maybe that was why she had fought with Teresa that morning. The day had begun like every other since the children had been taken. Alana had awakened just before sunrise. She grabbed a handful of dried apples, remnants from the winter stores, and then she made her way to the Tree, losing her thoughts in the crunch of frosted grass beneath her feet.

When she arrived at the Headland, she found everything as she had left it the day before. The oak had completely healed from giving its bavins, but Alana could sense the power of the lacy wooden knots, power that grew stronger as she settled her hand over the gnarled bark. She had scarcely leaned against the great oaken trunk when Teresa appeared on the path, floating toward the Tree like a ghost.

"Woodsinger!" the mother called, her voice as harsh and urgent as a gull's.

"Teresa."

"How are the children? What is Reade thinking today?"

"I don't know yet, Teresa. I need to check on Maddock."

"Maddock! He doesn't need you! You have to help Reade—he's just a child!"

"Teresa, I know that." Alana tried to keep her voice even, tried to forget that they had engaged in the same debate every morning for the past two weeks. "Teresa, today I have to check on Maddock. That was the whole reason I sang the second bavin. Let's see how close he is to the children."

"You can't! Check on Reade first! Tell me about Reade and Maida! Don't abandon my babies!"

"Teresa—" Alana began, but the young mother threw herself at the woodsinger, clutching at the hem of Alana's patched cloak.

"You promised! You have to! Please, watch my babies!"

"Teresa, no!" Alana loaded her exclamation with anger, fighting to pull her cloak from the woman's claws.

Teresa's sobs crested into a high-pitched wail. Without warning, the woman convulsed and arched her back, her arms stiffening into boards. Her teeth locked around the guttural howl that knifed from her belly, and her legs began to thrash. White foam blossomed at the corner of her mouth.

Alana stared in horror. "Teresa!" she managed after a moment. "Teresa, stop it! Teresa, it's all right! I'll look to Reade! Stop it, Teresa!"

But the young mother was beyond hearing. Her eyes stared into the Tree's branches, and her limbs continued to twitch. Alana ran for the village.

Goody Glenna stood on the edge of the green, as if she had expected Alana to return from the Headland so early. The old woman listened to the woodsinger's horrified gasps and then nodded her head slowly. She raised a commanding claw to summon two brawny fishermen. "Carry Teresa to my cottage."

"That's all?" Alana asked, shocked into calmness.

"What else would you have me do? I'll brew her some lionsmane tea. Get back to your work, woodsinger"

"But Goody—"

"Go and do your job, woodsinger. I'll do mine."

And so Alana had climbed back to her Tree, hardly acknowledging the two fishermen that she met on the path, Teresa's now-limp body strung between them. For just an instant, she thought that she *should* check on Reade. She should be ready to report on the boy when Teresa came to.

But then Alana realized she must exploit the small reprieve she had been given, she must check on Maddock's progress as she had not been allowed to do for the past several days. Besides, whatever Alana learned from Maddock's bavin, it couldn't be worse than watching Reade's confusion, watching the child bounce back and forth between terror and bravery, between calling for his mum and challenging Duke Coren.

Alana did not want to linger in the boy's thoughts. She did not want to lose herself in the mind of a child who had lost all the things he held dear.

She especially did not want to think about how desperately Reade sought a man to be his father. The boy's sorrow on that count was too close to Alana's own. The five-year-old might be more vocal about his loss, but he could not miss his father more than Alana did hers. She knew Reade's ache; she knew his rage. She knew how it felt to mourn a father who had been safety and security, gentleness and wisdom, all spun into one good man.

Setting aside her sorrow, Alana took a deep breath. She exhaled slowly and drew on the tricky powers of the Guardians of Earth and Air, reaching for Maddock's bavin across the landlocked leagues.

"Bogs and breakers!" Maddock swore loudly as his horse stumbled in the dim twilight. Fourteen days since they'd ridden from home. Fourteen cursed days of rising before dawn and riding hard until dusk, but still the kidnappers were well ahead of them. Maddock had more ability in his left thumb than that damned tracker Glenna had chosen to accompany him.

Of course, Maddock would have been forced to admit in a moment of sane contemplation, Landon wasn't a bad man, and his skills *had* been useful until their prey had reached the cursed hard-packed earth of the Great Road. It was just that the tracker was so blasted negative. Every decision Maddock made was questioned minutely, held up to scrutiny as if Landon were the Men's Council, Women's Council, and Spirit Council all rolled into one.

Bracing himself for the challenge he was certain to receive, Maddock reined in his horse and waited for Jobina and Landon to come up on either side. "I think we'd better leave the road for tonight." He gestured toward the carefully laid out fields to either side. "We're obviously getting near a village, and I'd rather not have some farmer armed with an overactive imagination and a pitchfork decide that we look like highwaymen."

Jobina nodded, arching her back as she stretched for a more comfortable position in her saddle. The movement strained the fabric across the front of her riding dress, and Maddock let himself be distracted for a moment. Landon, of course, did not spare the healer a glance as he busily scanned the horizon. "Over there." The tracker gestured toward a smudge in the distance. "It's a line of trees. There must be a stream running through there."

"What I wouldn't give for fresh water to wash in." Jobina made the wish sound like a promise. Rather than trust himself to answer steadily, Maddock dug his heels into his gelding's flanks. The horse took off like an arrow, hurtling across the unplowed field.

They reached the line of trees as the last bruise of sunlight faded behind them. As always, the cursed tracker was right—there was a stream, and a convenient clearing between the trees and the riverbank. The rivulet, though, proved too shallow for bathing, and Maddock smothered his disappointment by ordering Landon to build a small fire. When the tracker started to protest, Maddock cut him off, acerbically noting that they had not seen anyone for the entire day, and they had purposely ridden this far from the road to enjoy some privacy.

Landon finally had the fire crackling when a lamb wandered into the clearing.

The animal was little more than a newborn—some shepherd and his dogs had been lax in their duties. The pitiful creature was mewling when it reached them, long ears bobbling about its face as it stumbled from one person to the next, trying futilely to suck on their fingers.

Jobina was the first to suggest that they dine on meat that night. The thought of fresh food was as tempting as the Guardians' gold, and Maddock had his dagger unsheathed before Landon could frown. The blade was level against the creature's throat by the time the tracker made himself heard. "Maddock, you'd better not do that."

The warrior felt the tight woolen curls shudder beneath his left hand. "And why not?"

"We're guests in this land. That lamb belongs to someone, and they're certain to realize it's missing."

"We're travelers who are dying of hunger on the road. What sort of people would forbid us hospitality?"

"Shepherds who rely on lambs for their livelihood! Maddock, these people live by their animals. Besides, we're not starving."

"Then we'll buy the cursed thing, if anyone asks."

"Maddock, we're likely trespassing on someone's land right now, someone who could summon the sheriff and enforce the law."

"If you're afraid, Landon, just say so."

"Dammit, I'm not afraid!" The men stared at each other across the flames of the fire. Without a word, Jobina drew her dagger, sitting back on her heels to strip green bark from three long sticks. Maddock could imagine the aroma of fat sizzling into the open flames.

"If you're not afraid, then act like a man." Maddock gathered up the squealing lamb, avoiding the hard lit-

tle hooves as he passed his wriggling victim to the
tracker. "Be quick about it."

Landon stared at him with a look close to hatred.
It had been like this for all of Maddock's life. Ever
since he was a child, since he was first called to be
the huer on the cliff face, he had been the fastest, the
strongest. The village boys had always hated him, and
most were afraid of him. He had learned to take a firm
hand with his playmates, never hesitating to enforce a
little respect, even from older boys. His strategy had
paid off—all the village youth, boys and girls, had
known who was the leader.

In fact, Maddock mused, that might be why Landon
was making every step of this cursed journey so difficult. Maddock remembered the look in Alana Woodsinger's eyes as she put the bavin in his care. Surely,
no one could have blamed him for casting a triumphant glare toward the rival tracker.

After all, everyone knew that Landon had brought
the woodsinger mistletoe berries as a pledge at winter
solstice, and she had declined to accept his gift of
intention. It wasn't surprising—Landon should have
made his move before Alana was called to be woodsinger, before she was sworn to the Tree. Even if he'd
spoken up early enough, there was no guarantee that
Alana would have accepted the tracker. Alana as
comely as she was, and Landon with his awkward
lope, his balding pate . . . Maybe if the man stood to
his full height he wouldn't make the girls run in fright.
But instead, he stooped over, unsuccessfully masking
his size and looking like one of the walking undead.

Now, though, Landon's eyes looked nothing like the
undead. Maddock watched bitter emotion flash across
the other man's face, but the tracker silently gathered
up the lamb. One quick slash of his blade, and the
animal was reduced to hot meat. The tracker's steady
hands held the little corpse upside down for a moment

as blood pumped out of its severed arteries, and then he set to the messy job of skinning the beast.

Jobina's face was impassive as she skewered the proffered meat and placed it over the flames. Landon rolled up the sodden pelt and strode into the woods, heading toward the shallow stream.

"You're hard on him," Jobina said.

"Don't you start in, too, Jobina."

"Start in?" She feigned innocence as he caught her green eyes, but two spots of color highlighted her pale cheeks, reflecting the glow of her flame-red hair.

"Aye. Sartain Fisherman made me the leader of this mission."

"And who would challenge you, brave soldier? With your strong muscles and your voice of command?" She batted her long eyelashes, and he took an un- planned step closer to her.

He growled, "You mock me, Jobina, but can you sit there and say that your belly doesn't want the lamb?" The aroma of the cooking meat was already heavy on the air, and juices flowed into his mouth as he spoke.

"I won't tell you that, honored leader. I won't lie to you." She turned the roasting meat on the green sticks, but one of the pieces overbalanced and fell into the flames. Maddock reached for it without thinking and saved his dinner at the cost of singeing the hair on the back of his hand. He caught a flicker of a grin on Jobina's lips before the woman managed to swal- low her amusement. "Here, worthy soldier, you keep an eye on supper, while I get some salve from my bags."

His hand didn't hurt very much, but he let her go, following her swaying hips with his eyes. When she returned, she brandished a wooden box of green- tinged cream. She didn't need to tuck his arm by her side as she massaged in the soothing ointment, and she certainly didn't need to linger over the task for quite so long. Still, Maddock did not pull away until Landon crashed back from the stream, making an uncharacteristic amount of noise.

The three ate in silence, and rolled up in their blankets when they had finished. Maddock was closest to the fire, then Jobina, then the tracker. Maddock could hear the healer breathing beside him, and the sound might have been arousing, if not for Landon's unnerving stillness at Jobina's other side. Maddock's last thought as he fell asleep was that the dispute with Landon had been worthwhile. For the first time in days, his belly felt full.

Perhaps that fullness kept him from moving quickly when they were discovered. A dog came crashing through the underbrush with a snarl on its black lips, foam flecking its bared teeth. The beast was as fierce as the gigantic hounds that Coren had summoned to the beach, and it commanded all of the mystical power that the People feared.

Reflexively, Maddock grabbed for his sword. For the first time in his life, he was using the weapon for something beyond the elaborate training rituals he had set for himself. His fingers closed on the hilt with grim determination, his muscles flowing into the fighting patterns with well-practiced ease.

The dog was attracted to Maddock's sudden movement, or maybe to the smell of the lamb's blood still soggy in the earth. The powerful muscles in the animal's haunches bunched together, and Maddock saw the fur ruffle down its back. His own adrenaline surged in response. Then the mad creature was in the air, slathering jaws flinging foam into the dancing fire.

Maddock forbade himself to imagine the damage those jagged teeth could inflict. He ordered himself not to picture the ravaged corpses of men, women, and children that had once littered the Headland of Slaughter. Instead, he instructed his body to stand firm, to transfer his energy through his shoulders, down his arms, into his locked wrists.

The sword connected with a sickening crunch. The animal's trajectory was cut short, and the blade passed through the thickest part of its body. Blood sprayed from severed vessels. The canine corpse seemed to hang in the air for a moment, as if Maddock had cast a spell on it. Then, the body fell squarely in the fire, scattering half-burned logs and immediately yielding up the smell of scorched hair.

It took Maddock a long minute to realize that the roar in his ears was his own pounding heart. Somehow, he remembered to suck air into his aching lungs, and then he managed to kneel, to poke at the dog's gruesome head until he was certain that no life remained in the bloody thing. He reached down and wiped his sword in the spring grass, stripping off the shimmering, magical blood.

Only then did he become aware of Landon, the tracker glaring at him accusingly from the edge of the clearing. "You bloody fool!" Landon hissed, and Maddock could only squawk his outrage at the unwarranted attack. "You stupid, bloody fool! Don't you know some shepherd sent that dog? Some villager is waiting for him to come back, leading a new lamb home. You might as well have rung a cowbell to let them know we're coming."

"Sharks and fins, man! What was I supposed to do, let him eat me alive?"

"You might have thought with your brain instead of that cursed sword! He wasn't going to attack you, not until he saw you move like that." Landon swore. "Come on, let's get back to the road before his owner comes and finds him."

"Is that an order?" Maddock's voice shook with fury.

"It's a statement. I'm *telling* you that we should get back to the road. We're going to have a cursed hard

time explaining how we mean nothing but good if anyone finds us here—lamb bones in the fire and a sheep-
dog killed."

"That dog was a threat to all three of us! I won't
go slinking about in the dark like a common thief."

Landon's voice was bitter as he surveyed the chaos
of the clearing. "You were more than willing to act
like one when your belly was empty. Let's go."

"Sartain said that *I* lead this party."

"You'll be leading a party of one, then." Jobina's
voice was even as she sheathed her unblooded dagger.
Maddock whirled to face her, exclamations about her
betrayal rising in his throat. Jobina's eyes were dark
in the scattered firelight, but disapproval was patent
on her pale face. "We are guests in a strange land.
I'll not stand by to explain this."

Maddock almost bellowed his protest—the dog had
been about to kill her! Jobina, though, ignored him as
she gathered up her own meager belongings. Landon
had already retrieved his horse's tether from a low-
hanging branch.

Maddock managed to hold his tongue, but it was
more than he could bear when Landon started to lead
the way back to the road. "Hold, man!" His voice
was loud in the still night, driving away the chirrup of
crickets. "You're not the leader of this party."

He shouldered past the ungrateful, too-tall oaf and
mounted before the others had the chance, setting a
fast pace through the night. Once, he thought he heard
Landon admonish him to slow down, but then the
tracker's womanish concerns were lost in the darkness
and the distance.

It was not long before Maddock realized that he
was heading in the wrong direction. The ground they
had traveled at twilight had been hard-packed, the
only water the stream that had cut along the horizon.
Now, there were little flows that cut across his path,

and the earth had a spongy feel underfoot. The farther the horse galloped, the softer the land became, until Maddock was unable to say whether he rode across earth or water.

Bogs and breakers! he muttered over and over. Their gallop should have brought them to the road by now. Even in the moonless night, even if the mire were caused by some cursed inland dew, he should have felt hard-packed earth beneath the horse's hooves long ago. He angled more to the left, intending to pick up the line of the road that way, but the changed course was no better.

Once, his gelding stumbled into watery mud up to its knees. As Maddock heaved impotently on the reins, the terrified beast scrambled for footing. Reaching out to grab onto saplings at the edge of the boggy sinkhole, Maddock bit back a curse as he realized that the narrow trunks were actually a cow's crow-picked ribs.

Another sodden hour passed, and they were no nearer to their destination. As if the mire underfoot were not enough, the storm clouds that had been threatening at sunset loosed their attack. Maddock was drenched in seconds.

It was a gift of the Guardians when a flash of lightning illuminated a dilapidated shack just ahead. Maddock encouraged his weary horse onward, pulling up in the lee of the crumbling building to wipe his dripping hair out of his eyes. That movement gave his companions the opportunity to come even with him.

Jobina's usual sultry pout was dissolved in the rainwater that streaked her pale skin. Landon sat tall and silent in his saddle, his eyes dark with condemnation as he stared at his leader. "What?" Maddock asked. "What would you have me do?"

"Whatever you desire," Landon said.

Jobina spoke before Maddock could spit out a bitter

reply. "Come. We'll get no further tonight by arguing. Let's wait in the shed until morning, and then we can find our way."

The roof was half gone, and the walls stank of mildew, but the shack offered a semblance of dryness, at least in the back corner. The horses, though, had no hope of a gentler bed, and they whickered softly under the dripping ruins of the roof, protesting the injustice as their riders huddled beneath damp blankets.

Dawn came a few hours later, blowing away the worst of the rain and leaving behind a chill mist. Maddock rose before his companions and went to stand in the shack's canted doorway.

Sharks and fins! He never should have let Jobina convince him to slaughter the Guardian-forsaken lamb. Even after that mistake, he should have stopped the foolishness there. The cursed nighttime plunge through the bog had given him ample time to replay the moment of shock when the blasted dog appeared in the clearing. Maybe he *could* have tamed the damned beast without killing it.

It was just that things were so different out here. Maddock closed his eyes, breathing a humble prayer to the Guardians that he might be back in Land's End soon, back amid the familiar safety of the People, the Tree, and the woodsinger. Back home.

"It's still raining?" Jobina's whisper slipped into his thoughts, returning him to the misty field and the mission at hand. The woman passed dangerously near him as she gazed out at the field.

"More like mist," he managed to say against the sudden swell of desire in his throat. The healer clutched her blanket about her shoulders, but Maddock could still make out the delicate lines of her bared throat. She was like an alabaster carving, and Maddock's hand rose unbidden to trace the flawless curve of her flesh. He watched Jobina measure his intention, felt the woman's pent energy as the tip of her tongue touched her lips.

What was it that made her so desirable? What was it that made Maddock's blood heat over any of the village women? Maddock had reached his full man's growth early, and he'd spent years practicing the rakish seduction that brought the village girls to his fisherman's cottage. His desire was natural, he often reminded himself. It couldn't be helped. No one was harmed by his games. He hadn't offered mistletoe berries or black currants to any one of his conquests, and none of them had expected such a bond. They all knew the rules. They all knew that he was just a man, not a suitor. A healthy man. With healthy appetites.

Landon chose that moment to emerge from his dusty bed, groaning as he got to his feet and made a show of stretching his lanky limbs. Maddock bit back sharp words and ordered himself not to watch as Jobina turned back to her own corner of the hut, bending low to gather her few belongings. He told himself that there was no way for her to collect her comb and her boots without such stretching, but he doubted his assessment when he glimpsed her sly grin.

"Come along, Landon," Maddock vented his irritation as the tracker was slow leaving the hut. "Sartain sent you to help us find our way. You might as well earn your keep." Landon favored him with a penetrating stare before saddling his unhappy horse and setting out at an unlikely angle through the stream-crossed bog. As if by magic, the field dried as they rode, and it was only a matter of minutes before the road materialized on the horizon, a smooth snake rippling toward the east.

Only when Maddock saw the well-worn mile markers did he realize that his headlong dash from the stream had sent them traveling in the wrong direction, *toward* Land's End. In fact, they spent the better part of a long morning working their way back to the fateful place where he had chosen to leave the road the night before.

Maddock did not trust himself to speak civilly to the tracker as he dug his heels into his horse's flanks. Instead, he drove his companions hard all day, scarcely letting the horses catch their breath while the sun still hovered in the gloomy sky. It was just after sunset when they arrived at a small village, the first they had seen since leaving Land's End.

Maddock should have been suspicious of the deserted street that crept along the feet of the dripping buildings. He knew enough to question the blind shutters that covered the houses' windows. He should have been warned by the uneasy silence that rippled through the mist. He was tired, though, exhausted by the long day, and he was determined to show no further weakness to Landon. Or Jobina.

Maddock reined his gelding into the yard of one building that was larger than most. He thought he recognized the tavern from his earlier trading mission inland, and he squinted to make out its swinging sign in the gloom. A horse glared at him with dramatic red eyes, its muscled neck arching beneath a golden crown. The King's Horse, that was right. He had stayed there before, had met with the king's census counter in the tavern's common room.

Then, the King's Horse had been a hospitable place, with excellent ale and a warm fire. Maddock looked around expectantly, for there had been grooms to service a weary rider's mount. No servants appeared now, though, and Maddock was forced to loop his reins around a nearby post.

The heavy wooden door swung open on a room that filled the entire ground floor of the building. A roaring fire blazed on the huge hearth, and a score of men sat at rough wood tables, surrounded by tankards and trenchers. The heady aromas of hot bread and hearty stew mixed with pungent ale. Laughter filled the air, and a number of voices fought for supremacy in the crowded room.

When the door flew open, though, all conversation stopped. Laughter died, and the fire flickered lower on the hearth. Maddock saw half a dozen men reach for daggers at their waists, and other fists shifted on heavy metal tankards.

Maddock's own hand fell to the cross-hilt of his sword, and the motion brought more than a murmur from the crowd. There was a long, balancing moment, and then Jobina pushed past Maddock, her flame-colored hair striking a contrast with the pacifying tone in her voice.

"Good folk, we thank you for your greeting on this cold, wet night." Maddock thought she might have been received like a queen for the gentleness of her words. "We come from Land's End, seeking warm beds and supper for ourselves and our mounts."

Her words produced openly hostile grumbling, and it was only with reluctance that the burly men at the front of the room gave way to a large, red-faced woman. She spat: "We've no rooms left."

"No rooms?" Maddock began, indignation spiking his words, but Jobina laid a stilling hand on his arm.

"No rooms, good lady?" the healer countered. "We've ridden hard today, and had hoped that we might sleep in a bed. All of Land's End has heard of the hospitality at the King's Horse."

A flash of fear crossed the woman's crimson face, and she muttered through stiff lips, "There're no rooms for you here."

Jobina lowered her voice to a cajoling tone. "Perhaps we might stay in your stable then, good lady, any place that is warm and dry against the miserable rain on the road. We were forced to sleep last night in the fields, and we pray not do so again."

The red-faced woman started to spit, "I told you—"

but before she could finish, one of the brawny men rolled to her side. Carefully turning so that he could keep one eye on the travelers, he whispered something to the woman, his voice low enough that Maddock could not make out the words.

The woman pushed at her hair nervously, her eyes darting to each of the large men on her hearth before she framed a response to Maddock. "You can stay in the barn, then. If you've money, there's hay for the horses, and we can probably find the butt end of a loaf or two for you."

Her words were grudging, and Maddock started to answer with the bile that rose in his throat, but Jobina gentled him one last time. "Many thanks, good woman. We are grateful for your hospitality." If the healer's words shamed the innkeeper, the red-faced woman made no sign.

The only animals in the barn were two large workhorses and a pair of sleepy cows. Maddock swore as the wind slammed the door behind him. If there were empty stalls here, there must be empty tavern rooms to match. Before Maddock could grumble his complaint, though, Landon started to settle his horse for the night, lifting off its heavy saddlebags and uncinching its girth. Maddock swore fluently for another minute before following suit.

The horses were contentedly munching their hay by the time a man thrust open the barn door. While he stood on the threshold, his hairy hand ostentatiously resting on the hilt of a large iron dagger, a terrified woman dashed into the barn, almost tripping as she set a tray at Maddock's feet. The pair were gone before anyone could speak, and Maddock swore anew when he saw that the innkeeper had been true to her word. The tray held nothing more than three dried crusts of bread and a short flagon of ale.

The three travelers made short work of the meager victuals, supplementing the food with their own dried goods. There was no making sense of the inland folk, Maddock grumbled as he pushed together a pallet of hay.

His belly no longer ached with hunger, though, and he ordered his muscles to relax, to release the tension in his arms and back and legs. He sighed and burrowed deeper into the hay, ignoring the prickle of dried grass that poked through his clothes. At least he was warm. And dry.

He was teetering on the cliff edge of sleep when the barn door crashed open like a thunderclap. Before he could leap to his feet, he was blinded by flaring torches, unable to see anything but murder reflecting off a dozen iron knives.

The men who had filled the common room looked even larger as they hulked in the barn's shadows, dark faces contorted into terrifying grimaces as the leader brandished his torch. The first sweep of the flames, clearly intended to intimidate the outlanders, swung wide and caught at the loose straw dusting the floor of the barn.

A few wisps of fire skittered across the dirt floor, coming up against the wooden stalls, and Maddock found himself on his feet, clutching the edges of his blanket to his chest, as if the wool could protect him from those hungry tongues. From the corner of his eye, he saw that Jobina and Landon were also standing, and the healer had drawn her dagger. He was surprised to find his sword unsheathed, hefted with familiar ease, as if he had planned on fighting for his life on this cold, dark night.

"You misbegotten curs." There was something slippery about the man's words, and Maddock knew that this was the man who had spoken to the inn's red-faced proprietress, the supposedly merciful villager who had gained them a bed for the night. "Coming amid good folk with blood on your hands."

"I don't know what you mean, good man." Maddock tried to diffuse the tension. "My companions and I are merely traveling to Smithcourt, to see the world and offer our humble services to the king."

"The king is dead, fool." The man spat in the straw, targeting Maddock's feet and missing by the barest of margins. He seemed oblivious to the snakes of fire eating their way through the manger. "And what sort of services would you offer, in any case? All three of you butchers?"

"We're simple folk, from Land's End. You've no right to question what my companions and I do on the high road!"

"It's not the road we're worried about, son. It's what you do off the road!" The man's words were like oil flung on the fire of his fellows' rage. The seething knot of men surged forward, their ale-soaked anger matching the heat of the flames growing at Maddock's back.

"I don't know what you mean," Maddock spluttered, and he would not have believed himself if he'd been on the other end of the torch.

"What was your plan, son? Did you figure to sharpen your blade on our beasts before you took our children?"

"Your children!" The accusation was so preposterous that Maddock actually laughed, even though adrenaline shook through his sword arm. "I don't know anything about the children in this village. Listen! Some men, some evil men, came to my home. They traded with us as friends, but then they took our people, our own children, twins. My friends and I, we ride to save a little boy and girl."

The reasonable explanation only kindled the maddened crowd. Steel flashed in the torchlight, and cries of "Traitor!" were mixed with "Murderer!" and "Liar!"

With a curious calm, Maddock realized that he was not likely to leave the barn alive. Glancing across at his companions, he saw that they had reached the same conclusion. He nodded once, and Jobina's hand shifted awkwardly to grasp her dagger in something approximating an offensive stance. Sickened, Maddock realized that the woman had probably never used her blade as a weapon. She had treasured her smith-precious knife for healing, for cutting flesh in order to *save* men's lives.

Landon was scarcely better trained. The tracker had not even thought to draw his borrowed blade. Instead, he had turned a fraction of his height closer to the stalls where their horses moved restlessly. As if in response, the animals nickered above the growing crackle of open flames.

"To Land's End!" Maddock bellowed, and he plunged among the inland villagers before they could react. He leaped as far from his fellow outlanders as possible, trying to carve a path of escape for his companions and their mounts.

The villagers had not expected an outright attack, and Maddock had a better reach than the village leader. The brawny man reacted in surprise, parrying automatically with the most convenient weapon—his torch. Maddock heard the fire sweep toward him, and he reflexively knocked the brand away with his sword. The torch roared hungrily as it fell in the next stall, feasting on the manger's dry straw. Maddock did not have time to worry about fire, though, because two of the burly villagers closed behind their leader, and the trio moved forward with a grim determination.

Maddock's body settled into the familiar stance that he had practiced for so long on the village green. Raising his sword, his arms moved with the confidence of a learned response. Before Maddock could measure his actions, his attackers' stocky leader was bellowing in frightened rage, staring at a stump that pumped crimson blood where his hand had been.

There was a deceptive pause while the villagers

gaped in shock, then Maddock was besieged on all sides. He swung his sword as he was backed farther into the burning stall. Craning his neck, he could not see if Jobina and Landon fared any better.

The villagers' blades could get nowhere near him, not past his singing curtain of sword strokes. He was tired, though, exhausted by long days on the road and poor sleep at night. The muscles in his shoulders protested each time he raised his heavy weapon. The heat from the fire behind him was abominable, and he began to cough as heavy black smoke billowed from the well-caught stalls. His chest heaved impotently to carry precious air into his lungs.

"Maddock, look out! To your left!" He began to whirl even before he identified Landon's hoarse voice, but his foot slipped in a pool of blood. He came down hard on his knee, and pain shattered up his leg. Even the white flash of that agony, though, was not enough to block out the grimacing villager who stood before him—the villager who had just thrown the longest, sharpest dagger Maddock had ever seen.

6

Alana Woodsinger gasped for breath, struggling back to consciousness like a near-drowned fisherman. "Maddock!" she cried, and then she hurled her thoughts back toward his bavin, down the confusing paths of the Guardians of Earth and Air, toward the startling tangle of fire that threatened her grasp on his distant woodstar.

Even as an ache blossomed behind Alana's eyes, she struggled to teach herself how to harness the Guardians of Fire. Water, she knew. Earth and Air, she had learned over the past fortnight. Fire, though, remained alien, threatening, terrifying in its destructive force. She caught a glimpse of how the element worked, how it danced above Air and Earth, how it set itself opposite Water, but she was unable to gather together the strains of that knowledge, unable to focus past her fear for Maddock's life.

Frantically, she shoved her awareness back toward the Tree, past her woodsinger sisters to the smooth rings of oaken knowledge. She chased her thoughts around several circles, scrambling for a grip, trying to pry up an answer, to learn about the fourth element.

There was nothing there, though, nothing that would help her in this crisis. Rather, she found the burden of potential, the weighty knowledge that the Tree *could* come to know the Guardians of Fire, *might* yield

up all its strength to those flaming beings. Could . . .
Might . . . What good was that to Alana now? What
good was that, as Maddock was threatened in a burning barn, halfway across the land?

She heard the hovering swarm of former woodsingers inside her mind, sensed their agitation at the edges
of her consciousness. She shut them out, though, ex-
cluding them so that she could better concentrate on
the horror at hand. What had happened to Maddock?
To Landon and Jobina? Had all three of them been
cut down? Were they, even now, engulfed in flame?
Were they already dead?

Silence. Darkness. Nothingness.

Alana tried to remember how the bavin had felt
inside her mind, how the woodstar's power had spun
its web across the land. Closing her eyes, however,
and reaching for that pattern left her empty-handed,
empty minded. Each breath daggered through the pain
that now pulsed beneath her skull. She could barely
make out swirling clouds where the bavin should have
been, like ocean water tainted by a squid's ink.

Against the darkness, she could see the flash of fire
on iron, see the threat of the villager's thrown knife.
Panic overwhelmed her, and she hurled her body
against the Tree, pressing against its rough bark with
her hands, her cheek, as if she would crawl inside the
trunk, as if she would become one with the ancient
oak.

"Great Mother!" she gasped in despair. "Great
Mother!" She tried to force her consciousness through
the Tree, through the bavin to the trio of rescuers.

Children called on the Great Mother. Not grown
women. Not woodsingers schooled to recognize the
power of all the Guardians, of the complex world
around them. Children, who were desperate and frightened and alone in the night.

"Great Mother!" Alana sobbed, and the sound
brought back the last time she had called on the an-

cient goddess, when she had knelt on a sodden beach beside a bloated corpse that could not be her father, that had to be her father. The image made Alana retch, and she fell to her knees, trying to forget the stench, to forget the frozen finger of certainty that had walked down her spine as she identified the body from its carefully knotted rope belt.

She had lost so much. She had forgotten so much. She had failed to learn so much. She was so alone.

And now, to have lost Maddock and Landon and Jobina, as well. . . .

"Great Mother," she moaned again.

As if in response to her plea, the woodsingers' voices stirred again in her mind, shifting beneath the throbbing pain. She let them speak to her now, now that there was no longer any way for her to reach across the land for Maddock's bavin.

"The Great Mother won't help, you know."

"She can't help you."

"This is all beyond her. The Great Mother only *planted* the Tree. She watered it, and she spoke to it, but she never *knew* it. Not the way that we do."

Alana interrupted the swirl of voices. "Leave me alone! If you don't have anything useful to tell me, leave me alone!"

"Prithee, sistren," said one of the woodsingers, her tone folded softly around ancient words. The voice was tight and small, as if it were encapsulated in one of the rings closest to the Tree's oaken heart. The words were wrapped in long-lost sounds, guttural vowels and harsh consonants that scraped the back of the speaker's throat. "Puir bairn such a strangething desireth, finding the spiritforce of a lost bavin. Such a strangething, but a strangething can be done. With the heartpower of the Tree. With the bonestrength of the fairsister."

Alana was not certain that she could make out the individual words, the specific meaning of all those ancient sounds, but the overall sense was clear. There *was* a way for her to reach Maddock. There was a way to snare the distant bavin.

As if drowned in Alana's shock, the swirl of wood-singers quieted. Alana, fighting to hear her own thoughts above her pounding heart, dared to speak to the one voice, to the most ancient woman she had ever heard in her woodsinger thoughts. "Thank you, sister," she said gratefully.

"Thank not this puir vocet, fairsister woodsinger. Ye should not timewaste with fairsister thanks. Ye should trace the seekerswordsman. Thoughtgrasp his bavin."

The ache behind Alana's eyes as she focused on the slippery words was so sharp that she was certain she would retch again. She struggled, though, to pull meaning from the strange sounds, to twist the soft voice into a guiding rope. "I— I don't know how to fight, how to, to thoughtgrasp. I can't *reach* him. I can't find Maddock. And even if I could, I don't know how to help him." Alana's fear and frustration broke her voice, breaching the wall that had held back her tears. "I knew it was wrong for him to slaughter the lamb, but I couldn't reach out to change what he was doing. I couldn't stop him. I couldn't help!" Her entire body began to shudder as she sobbed, quivering in reaction to the pain that lanced behind her eyes, to her exhaustion, to her surrendering hope.

"Fairsister, ye have the puissance to changefate the woodstar." The voice was slightly scornful, as if the ancient woodsinger could not believe Alana was so ignorant. "Vocet ye can be, like any fairsister. Thought-words can landbridge. Ye can thoughtspeak to the seekerswordsman. Make him bodyact. Make him body-save himself."

"How?" Alana was so surprised, she blurted the one syllable aloud.

"Thoughtgrasp the woodstar."

"I don't know what that means!"

"Mindcloak the woodstar. Spiritsend your thoughts."

"I don't know what you're saying!" Alana wailed.
The ancient woodsinger used words as if they were
the People's tongue, but the words made no sense.
Alana could babble, too. She could throw together
phrases and pretend that they were words. She could
pretend that she had the powers of all the Guardians.
She could pretend that she knew what she was doing,
play-acting as the People's woodsinger.

"Become a vocet, fairsister. Become a vocet for
the Tree."

Alana sensed that the other woodsinger was frustrated as well.

"What in the name of all the Guardians is a vocet?"

"A *vocet*," the ancient woman repeated, as if by
stressing the word all would be made clear.

Alana's frustration leaked out as a wail. The other
woodsinger visibly shrugged, and began to move away,
back to the core of the Tree that had been her only
home for time out of mind. Alana stumbled to her
feet, reaching out a trembling hand as if she could
stop a living, breathing woman from walking away.
"Wait!" she cried. "I want to understand you! I want
to learn!"

The other woodsinger lingered, floating just above
the dark core that was the very center of the Tree's
essence. Alana went on desperately. "What is your
name, fairsister? Let me read your journals, try to
understand you that way!"

"Parina," the voice whispered at last. "Parina
Woodsinger." The words faded away, sinking back
into the unknowable depths of the Tree's inner
knowledge.

Alana stumbled down the path, rushing to her cottage. She built up her fire, almost smothering the
banked coals as she piled on too much wood. Looking
down, she saw that her hands were scratched, that her
arms were bleeding. As if in a dream, she remembered

surrendering to the Tree, pushing against its bark as if the pain would let her break through to Maddock and his fellows.

What did it matter, though, a little blood on her hands? She lit a reed lamp and threw herself at the wall of ancient journals, peering at their leather-bound covers. She did not need to study the newer volumes, the smooth, supple leather of Sarira Woodsinger's life, or Sarira's teacher, or that woman's teacher. No. Alana needed the very oldest of the tomes, the most ancient, the most faded.

Alana shifted the heavy books, stretching to reach the back of the top-most shelf. At last, she found the one she wanted, small and cracked, and so dry that she thought the parchment pages would crumble to dust before she could carry it to the fireside. Nevertheless, she was able to make out scrawling words on the first page: Parina Woodsinger.

The woman had lived a long and productive life; she had filled page after parchment page with a scrawl that made spiderwebs look coarse. Parina was not the very first woodsinger, but she was the first to have written down her observations about the Tree. Parina had tended the oak when it was scarcely more than a sapling; the woodsinger had just been able to encircle the Tree with her arms when she began to serve it.

Hours passed, and still Alana read, trying to find the answer, searching desperately for some way to save Maddock. Three times, she returned to her shelves, stretching for other buried volumes, for more of Parina's journals that had been pushed aside through the centuries.

After the first few hours, the woodsingers inside Alana's mind slumbered, apparently exhausted by her passion. More than once, she thought that she would take a moment to sleep herself, or sneak a few breaths to splash cold water across her aching eyes. She would just take a brief break, chew on a few dried apples, stretch her aching back. . . .

But every time she started to step away from the fireside, she was overwhelmed by the sense of loss that had capsized her at the Tree. For the first time, she realized what a hole a lost bavin created. It was one thing for a woodstar to lose its power gradually, to fade away as it aged outside the Tree. Alana was already accustomed to the light tug of a decades' old bavin, to the whispery mental impression left by the dried-out husk of a completely faded woodstar.

The gap inside her thoughts now, though, was completely different. Maddock's missing woodstar ached, like an abscessed tooth. It dragged her back to the journals, over and over again, even as she longed to pull away.

Was this the pain a bavin left when it was lost at sea? Was this what Sarira Woodsinger had fought against as she stood on the Headland, trying to sing home Alana's father, and the twins' da, and the two other fisherman? Was this why Sarira had given her life, because she wanted to stop the ache inside her head, inside her heart?

For the first time, Alana began to understand how a woodsinger would risk almost anything to avoid the aching emptiness that spread through her now. A woodsinger would abandon food, abandon drink, abandon the health of her own fragile body, if she could keep from feeling this break with the Tree. Sarira had. Or at least she had tried.

Since donning her woodsinger's cloak, Alana had avoided Sarira Woodsinger, avoided the woman who had let her father die at sea. In her heart, Alana knew that she was being unfair, that she was punishing the older woman for failing at an impossible task. Still, it had seemed that Alana had no choice. She could be angry with the woman who had failed to sing her fa-

ther home, or she could be angry with her father, for
venturing out too far, for staying out after a storm
came up, for failing to find a way back to the
Headland.

Flinching from the ache of Maddock's lost bavin
once again, Alana started to search her mind for Sarira Woodsinger, started to pull together a thought of
peace. Before she could complete the action, though,
she was ambushed by a memory of standing on the
beach, breathing in the stink of her father's bloated
corpse. She remembered her growing anger as she
counted the knots on his belt, her rage at being left
alone, left behind.

Little Reade still felt that anger. Reade, who was
even now selling his small soul to Coren. Reade, who
needed to be rescued.

If Sarira Woodsinger had done her job properly, if
she had sung home the four fishermen, Reade would
be a different child. He would not be so desperate for
Coren's approval. He would not seek out a father in
a kidnapper, in an evil man. He might even have been
brave enough to escape, to wrangle his way free from
his captors.

And Alana? Her life would be different as well. If
Sarira Woodsinger had not died on the Headland,
Alana would be free. She might have found a husband. She might even now be sitting with him beside
her hearth, heavy with their unborn child.

No, Alana was not yet ready to make her peace
with Sarira Woodsinger.

Instead, she harnessed her anger and turned back
to Parina Woodsinger's journals. She forced her way
through endless accounts of the Tree's size, of its wa-
tering, of its progression through the seasons. Parina's words were strange, odd combinations of
familiar words and phrases, and Alana often had to
stop to puzzle out their meaning. Some of the words
were entirely new—"vocet" and "fairsister" and

other, stranger words that Parina had not spoken inside Alana's mind.

Twice, Alana dove back inside her thoughts, stretching toward the shadows where Parina had disappeared. She wanted the ancient woodsinger's assistance, wanted to know where she should look in the ancient parchment volumes. The ghostly presence remained still, though, buried deep beneath the centuries and the circles of the Tree's growth. Alana did not know if she had offended her sister woodsinger, or if Parina had merely exhausted herself by swimming to the surface of Alana's thoughts, by pressing communication for as long as she had.

Exhaustion. Swimming. Alana longed to close her eyes, to rest her head across her arms. She sobbed as she read, recalling Maddock's bravado, transmitted through his woodstar. He might be foolish; he might be rash. But he was so *alive*. Or he had been. Before his bavin winked out of existence.

So alive . . . Alana kept returning to her shock when she first sensed the man's attraction to Jobina. A blush had spread across her own cheeks as she felt the warmth of his speculation. And Maddock had thought of *her* as well, of Alana. He had criticized Landon for not acting quickly enough, for not securing Alana as a helpmeet and a bride. Did that mean that Maddock thought of *her* that way? Did that mean that the handsome fisherman desired her?

The woodsinger shook her head, dragging her attention back to her search. Parina Woodsinger. The ancient journal. Thoughtgrasping, whatever that might be. Mindcloaking.

The sun was high in the sky when Alana finally found the passage she sought.

"This morn, I spiritlearnt another power of the most puissant Tree, which left me fair astonished." Parina's writing was hurried, as if she had rushed to get all her words recorded before she could forget them, before the energy of her discovery could dissipate. "As I wrote before, I woodsang a bavin for Tarin Fisherman to guidelight him and his fleet in the nightdark spring storms. Tarin Fisherman, though, did not return the bavin for woodhoming when he came back to the People. Instead, he gave the woodstar to his bairn Merinda, as if it were a childguard, a gamepiece. I was most displeased at the affront to Our Tree, but I spirit-talked to my Tree-bound fairsisters, and I held my tongue because the woodstar's heartpower was even then fading, in the lifeseep way of all woodstars."

Alana stumbled over the passage, forcing her way through Parina's complex phrasing. The woodsinger had been tending the Tree in an ordinary fashion, bringing it water from the Sacred Grove, singing to it about the latest happenings among the People. She had been recounting a squabble between two of the village goodwives, when the oak had suddenly thrust into her mind, hurtling her attention toward Merinda's bavin.

Even as Parina reeled at the Tree's initiative, even as she tried to shake off her startled dizziness from having her mind thrust in an unplanned direction, she glimpsed what was happening back in the village. Tarin's daughter slept in her cradle, the bavin strung around her pudgy infant neck. Merinda slept in her cradle, but her breathing had stopped. Her heart still beat; her mind still sent child-thoughts along the woodstar's thread. But her breathing had stopped.

Parina realized that it was hopeless to run all the way from the Tree to the village. The distance was too great. The child would be long dead by the time the woodsinger could alert anyone. Even as the wood-singer cried out in anguish, though, an idea sparked deep inside her mind, an idea that seemed to come in equal parts from the Tree itself and from the scant handful of woodsingers who had lived before Parina.

"And so," Alana fought to make out the excited scrawl, "I thoughtgrasped the bavin. I called upon the most glorious, most puissant Tree, reaching into its core of cores, where the greenest heartwood runs deep. I harnessed the powers of all the Guardians, air and earth, fire and water, as they are woven together in the Tree's green heartwood. I spun those powers into a thread of whitelight, of purest thoughtlight, and I cloaked those powers around the bavin. I drew the Power of the Tree into mine own thoughts, and I touched puir Merinda, thoughtgrasped the still-breathed bairn. Through the bavin, I acted on the child. I made her awaken and breathe. Blessed be the Tree and all its puissance."

"Great Mother," Alana breathed. She had never made any attempt to touch the Tree's heartwood. It was so distant, so deep, buried beneath so many lifetimes and generations of the People. Now, though, with Parina Woodsinger's words sprawling like a map, Alana gathered her thoughts to try.

Reaching toward the Tree on its promontory, she felt the hordes of awakening woodsingers like soft cobwebs strung across the path to the Headland. She sensed their concern about the trio of pursuers, about the mission Alana was attempting to guide. She sensed their goodwill, and their wishes that they could help. But she also sensed their lack of knowledge, their contentedness with the aspects of the Tree they had always known, had always loved. If any of them had ever known Parina's thoughtgrasping, they had forgotten it lifetimes ago.

Taking a deep breath, Alana pushed herself deeper, to the threshold where she had left Parina Woodsinger the day before. The weight of the Tree hulked above her, the burden of greenwood and bark and heavy, leafy branches. Alana fought for another breath, pushing against all that weight, all that ancient history.

Now, she could scarcely make out the whisper of the other woodsingers, far above her, closer to air and water, earth and fire, to the Guardians and the People.

Alana hovered for another dozen heartbeats, afraid to take the next step, afraid to wait, near the Tree's very core. Then, envisioning the extraordinary words she had seen scrawled across the ancient parchment page, she caught her breath and pushed across the border, across the ring of ancient bark that had long since been compressed around the Tree heartwood.

"Fairsister!" Parina Woodsinger exclaimed. "Well met!"

Alana reeled at the force of the greeting, amazed at the strength of Parina Woodsinger's voice in her own peaceful home. "Fairsister," she managed to whisper, and her own words sounded as if they were drenched in honey, made heavy by centuries of sap and wood.

Parina laughed, a throaty sound that made the space around Alana tremble. "And are ye ready to thought-grasp, fairsister?"

Alana managed to say a single word. "Yes."

"Then let me show ye about the heartwood. Let me guidelight ye to the thoughtgrasp path." Parina stepped toward Alana and extended one long-fingered, impossibly ancient hand. Alana grasped it tightly and caught her breath, watching as Parina showed her the last step she needed to take, the last step into the core of the Tree's ancient heart.

Even with Parina beside her, Alana was panicked by the changes in her body as she gave herself up to the heartwood. Her own heart slowed its beating, matched its pumping to the impossibly slow convulsions as the Tree sucked water and sustenance from the earth. Her breath sighed away, spread thin as the Tree gathered precious air from its leaves, from the new morning sunlight.

Before Alana could panic, though, before she could

step back from Parina's "thoughtgrasp path," she saw what the ancient woodsinger had discovered. She saw a different bond between the Tree and its bavins, a different thread spun out across time and space. The line was brilliant white and so fine that, even from the heart of the Tree, Alana could only see it if she cocked her head at a particular angle. Standing in the core, though, Alana understood how she could tug on that impossibly fine thread, how she could twist the fibers of earth and air, the balance of fire and water. She saw how she could touch the woodstar at the end of the filament, how she could nudge it to return her action. She could make the holder of that bavin move. She could find Maddock and manipulate him through his own bond to his woodstar, through his own incredibly thin-spun thread of white light.

Now that Alana had made her discovery, though, she could hardly recall why she'd been searching. It took all her thought to remember to expand her lungs, to let her heart beat deep within her chest. She needed all her concentration to remember life and living. It was too hard to think here, too hard to remember the world, the People. Too hard to think of anything other than the Tree, the Tree with its golden sap, its green-leafed light, its heavy, comforting bark.

Alana barely managed to think a question at Parina.

"Yes," the ancient woodsinger answered, a puzzled smile in her voice. "Ye can thoughtgrasp from the surface. Now that ye mindknow the whitelight, ye can heartfind it whenever ye must. But why would ye ever want to leave the heartwood?"

Alana tried to think an answer, tried to explain why she could not stay in the old world, in the ancient times, back at the beginning of the Age. She tried to explain, but she found she had no words left inside her mind, inside her heart. She fought to remember Maddock. Maddock and Landon and Jobina. Reade and Maida. All the People. They depended on her.

Alana fought for words, for thoughts, for explanations, but she was reduced to vague pictures, blurred images, distorted by the weight of time and distance and heavy, oaken wood. There was a man who wore a bavin, a man whose woodstar had gone missing. A man who must be found, who must be helped. . . .

Even as Alana struggled to remember the name of that man, even as she tried to remember why she needed to reach across the land, she felt Parina sigh. The ancient woodsinger shook her head, and her laughter was sad. "Go, then, fairsister," she said, or maybe it was the Tree that spoke, or maybe Alana only said the words to herself.

Then Alana felt herself pushed away, shoved through the heartwood's thin and ancient barrier. The shock of life outside the Tree's core hit her like an icy wave, and she was too stunned to move, too startled to swim back toward the bark-covered surface. She marveled at her fingers and her toes, her heart and her lungs. She felt her body like a miraculous invention of the Great Mother, the shaping of all the Guardians.

"Farewell, fairsister!" Parina cried, and the words brought back more thoughts to Alana's mind. "Good luck!"

She remembered that she had a mission. She had a goal. She was supposed to find a thread, one single, white thread in all the world. . . . She began the long swim through the Tree's rings, but not before she twisted back, twisted around to gasp at Parina, "Thank you!"

"You're welcome, fairsister." Parina's laughter rolled through the Tree's rings, bubbling to the surface, helping Alana float past the other woodsingers, back to her village, back to the People.

Alana came to her senses in her cottage, as stunned and disoriented as if she had been far beneath the sea. Her heart pounded inside her chest, thundered with a regular rhythm that was almost painful. She felt a new awareness of her body, of her trunk and her limbs, and of the fine muscle and bone of her fingers.

And beneath it all, around it all, *through* it all, she felt the shimmering white thread that the Tree had spun to its bavin, the thread that she could pull and weave, the thread that stretched from the Headland to Maddock's woodstar. She felt it like a physical force, a knotted thread that pulled her across the land.

Alana needed to anchor herself, though, before she ventured along that shimmering path. She needed to secure herself to the Headland so that she did not get lost across the distance. With bark beneath her fingers, with wood beneath her hands, she would remember the long road back to the People. She would remember why she reached out to Maddock, to his bavin, why she reached out to guide his actions and lead him in his attempts to rescue the children.

Alana scarcely remembered to extinguish her smoldering reed lamp before she tore off to the Headland and the Tree.

Gasping at the force of her newfound knowledge, the woodsinger collapsed across the giant oak's roots. She ignored the earth that stained her patchwork cloak, and forced herself, instead, to focus on the power Parina had shown her, on the fine white line that linked the ancient oak to its farflung bavin. Closing her eyes to cut out distractions, Alana stretched her thoughts across the land, across the powers of the Guardians of Air, the Guardians of Earth. She sensed the strength of her new weaving, the force of her recent discovery. She was ready to pull Maddock's woodstar, to haul the man to safety.

But she could not thoughtgrasp Maddock's bavin.

She could not find the woodstar, not with the shining white filament. She could not bridge the distance with that narrowest of threads. The line stretched from the Tree across the land, but then it frayed to nothingness, to emptiness. Alana retraced her steps and tried again, then a third time. No matter how carefully she followed the thread, though, how carefully she stretched the white light toward the trackers, she could not reach the distant woodstar.

Maddock's bavin remained as lost as it had been the day before. After all of Alana's struggling, all of her stretching and learning and daring, she could not reach the tracker's woodstar with the precious white thread that would have let her reel him in to safety. Try as she might, Alana could do nothing more than sense a dark upwelling in the Guardians' forces, a swirling of black, like cold water seeping up from the farthest ocean depths. She could not thoughtgrasp the bavin. She still could not sense Maddock.

It was not fair! She had journeyed deep and studied hard; she had read through the night and trusted herself to the heart of the ancient Tree. She had learned to see the white thread of thoughtgrasping, but all to no avail. The tracker was as lost as if she had spent the previous day laughing and sleeping and flirting with the village boys.

Maddock was lost. The rescuers were gone.

Alana fought to swallow a cry of disbelief. Her incredulity was chased by a wave of fury. The old words were *useless*. Hopeless. As ridiculous as sending a trio of fisher-folk to do battle against all the arrayed might of Smithcourt.

Even as Alana raged against the injustice of the world, though, she heard her own furious thoughts. The People had sent a *trio*. They had sent Landon and Jobina, along with Maddock. Even if Alana could not reach Maddock's bavin, she did not know that Landon and Jobina were lost. They might have survived the attack on the barn. They might have survived the flung knives, and the fire, and the fury of the village folk. Jobina might have lived to sing the Song of the Dead for Maddock; she might have led the warrior's soul to rest with the Guardians. Landon might have dug a grave for Maddock.

Jobina and Landon might, even now, be riding after Reade and Maida, more intent on rescuing the children than ever before. Exhausted, possibly wounded, strangers to the land beneath their horses' hooves . . . And if that was the case, then the rescuers would need all the help that the Guardians could give them, all the assistance that Alana could manage.

Alana might not be able to reach Maddock's bavin, but she could try to touch her first-sung woodstar. She could stretch across the land to Reade. And if she could harness Parina's tricks with the boy's bavin . . . If she could make Reade understand that he was being followed, that he would be saved. . . .

Alana dashed her tears from her cheeks. Very well, then. Even if Maddock were lost, even if the rescuers' first battle had been a rout, the war was not yet decided. Alana could fight with other weapons. Gritting her teeth, the woodsinger muttered to the Tree and any of her ancient sisters who might be listening, "Fine, then. I'll reach for Reade."

She found the new white thread and stretched across the land.

7

"Here's your food, Maida." Reade caught the tip of his tongue between his teeth as he balanced the tin plate that he carried to his sister. When he made it to Maida's side without spilling, he glanced at Duke Coren, hoping that the nobleman would notice Reade being polite to his twin. He was trying to remember that he must act like the Sun-lord. He was trying to be good. It was just so hard, with so many different things, so many strange places and people and things to do as they journeyed farther and farther from the Headland.

And Maida didn't help. Even now, she screwed up her face into an awful frown. "I don't like this bread."

"There's nothing wrong with the bread, Maida." Reade reached out and tugged a bite from the hunk that balanced on the plate. He put it in his mouth and chewed hard, bobbing his head as he swallowed. "See? It's fine. It's just made with salt. That's the way they make it here. That's all the lady had at the inn, when we left this morning."

Maida shook her head and pushed the plate away. "Mum makes good bread, not like this."

Thinking of Mum made Reade uncomfortable. That morning, when he'd woken up, he had tried to remember the exact shape of her face. No matter how hard he tried, though, he could only see the woman who ran the inn. Oh, he could still remember how Mum yelled at him when he did something wrong, and he remembered that she always made him do his chores. But she was fading away, becoming part of his life from before Duke Coren came, from before Reade became the Sun-lord and Maida became the Sun-lady.

He tried to tell himself that he didn't need Mum here, anyway. He was a big boy. He had been the huer in the spring harvest. He didn't need his mum at his side, as if he were a little baby. He didn't need his mum to protect him.

Even as Reade lined up his arguments, though, even as he made his thoughts as neat as knots in a net, his lower lip begin to tremble. Maida must have seen him, because she leaned forward and grabbed his arm through his golden robe. "Let's run away, Reade. Let's go back home."

A strange light glowed in Maida's eyes. She looked like old Goodman Jendo, after the horse kicked him in his head. Jendo had sat up in bed, screaming at Guardians who weren't even there. Reade wasn't supposed to have seen Jendo; he had promised Mum that he would not go near the cottage on the edge of the village. The older boys had dared him, though. They told him he wasn't brave enough to creep up to the hut and look between the chinks in the wall. He couldn't refuse the big boys, not without Winder calling him a coward.

He knew he was lucky he hadn't been there when Jendo actually died. The Guardians might have carried Reade away if he had been, dragging him back to their home, along with Jendo. Even without watching the Guardians take the old man's soul, Reade had been afraid that Jendo's spirit would haunt him. Winder had said that it would; he said that the Guardians would punish Reade for looking through the holes in the cottage's wall. Sometimes Reade still had dreams that Jendo had come for him, come to take him to live beneath the sea with the Guardians and other dead fishermen.

Maida tugged at Reade's arm, breaking into his thoughts. "Reade. Listen to me." She looked about to make sure that Duke Coren's soldiers weren't listening. When she whispered, Reade had to lean close so that he could hear her. "Do you remember Mum?"

The question was so close to his own thoughts, to his own fears, that he forced himself to laugh out loud. Ha! he made himself think. This was like Maida telling a joke. She was making up a story about some boy who was too stupid to remember his own mum. "I'm not a baby, Maida. Of course, I remember her."

"I dreamed about her last night. I dreamed about how she prayed with us every night before we went to bed. I held my Great Mother, and Mum put her hands on top of mine."

Unconsciously, Reade reached for the metal charm that hung about his neck, his own Great Mother. His hand brushed against the woodstar that Duke Coren had given him. Of course, the woodstar was powerful, more important than any gift he had ever received. His Great Mother, though, was special for a different reason. He couldn't remember a time that he had not had the iron charm strung about his neck.

He had asked Mum about it once. She said that she'd given him his Great Mother the day that he was born. He and Maida both—they had the iron charms to watch over them, even when they were so little that they shared the same cradle.

If Maida had dreamed about her Great Mother, then she must be afraid. Again. It seemed like she had held on to her charm the whole time they rode toward Smithcourt. She acted like she was on Da's boat, tossing on the sea, and the Great Mother was her anchor.

Reade was a little scared when he thought of Maida's

dream. It reminded him of how far they were from home, of how frightening this whole journey was. He covered up those bad feelings by making himself laugh again, like Winder, back home. "That must have been a pretty stupid dream," he said.

"It was a good dream!"

"Only babies dream about the Great Mother."

"I am *not* a baby!" Maida shrilled, and a number of the soldiers looked over at them. Reade shushed his sister, afraid that Duke Coren would get angry.

"All right, Maida, you're not a baby. By all the Guardians, stop squealing like a stuck pig."

"I'm going to tell Mum that you swore!"

"You're never going to see Mum again for the rest of your life!" Reade said the words before he could even think if they were true. Maida burst into tears, so suddenly that even Reade was surprised. Her wail was cut short as Reade clapped a hand over her mouth. "What are you trying to do? Duke Coren will *kill* us if you screech like that!"

She tossed her head free from his hand, but at least she remembered to whisper. "You're bad, Reade! You're breaking all the rules. You use bad words, and you don't pray to the Great Mother, or the Guardians, or anything."

"No one's here to make me!"

"That's not it, and you know it! You're bad because you're afraid. You're afraid of what Duke Coren would do if he caught you praying to the Great Mother!"

"I am not afraid!"

"You are, too! You're as scared as a lamb. You're a coward!"

"I am not a coward! I was the huer, Maida. The huer has to stand on the very edge of the cliff. I couldn't have been the huer if I was afraid!"

"Who cares about being the huer, Reade? There

aren't any cliffs here. There aren't any boats, and the duke doesn't need a huer. No one cares about a stupid *huer*."

There. That was it. Maida was still jealous of him. When Sartain Fisherman had made Reade the huer, Maida had cried for an entire day. She'd still been sulking the day *after* Reade had been chosen, even when Mum had let her stir the porridge, and add an extra portion of honey. Maida was such a baby.

Before Reade could tell her that, though, she got a strange look in her eyes, like Winder when he was planning something mean. "If you're so brave, Reade, if you're so important, then why don't you just get rid of your Great Mother? Why don't you just leave it on this rock?"

Without thinking, Reade raised his hand to the metal charm. "I'm not going to do that."

"See! It's true! You are a lamb! Coward!"

"I am not! It's just that—"

"What? It's just what?"

Reade couldn't think of a good ending to the sentence. He *wasn't* afraid. Not exactly. But he didn't want to give up his Great Mother. Not when Mum had given him the charm. Not when he had no idea when he would see Mum again. But he would never be able to make Maida understand. He sighed and looked up at her miserably. "It's just that you don't have to be very brave to leave a Great Mother on a stone." She snorted, and he said, "I'll get rid of it! But you have to promise you'll never call me a coward after I do."

"What are you going to do?" Maida asked, suspicion filling her voice.

Reade started to say, "I'll drop it in the bushes, the next time I piss," but he didn't want to fight with her about the dirty word. Instead, he just said, "I'll get rid of it. That's all you need to know. Promise, though. Say you won't call me a coward."

"That's easy to say. You'll never get rid of your Great Mother."

"Say it!" Reade insisted, but Maida only frowned at him. "Say it!"

"Fine, Reade. If you get rid of your Great Mother, I won't call you a coward."

"Ever."

"Ever."

Reade nodded, pleased that he had won. Now he just had to figure out a way to get rid of the charm, a way that would make Maida remember forever that he was brave.

Before he could come up with a plan, the duke's man, Donal, walked over to him. "Come along, Sunlord. You shouldn't keep the duke waiting."

Donal always said "Sun-lord" like he didn't mean it. Reade wanted to tell the soldier that he should be nicer. Reade wanted to say that he had heard Donal talking with Duke Coren that night, back in the tavern. Donal had been bad. Donal had made the duke angry.

Every time, though, that Reade started to talk back to Donal, he saw the anger in the man's own eyes. And when Donal was angry, he was much scarier than Duke Coren. He didn't just fold his hand into a fist. He reached for the hilt of his dagger.

Reade decided not to explain that he *wasn't* keeping Duke Coren waiting. Instead, he tucked his Great Mother back inside his golden robes and let Donal hoist him up on the duke's tall stallion. Reade settled down in front of Duke Coren and reached out to grasp the pommel on the high saddle.

The first day that he had ridden without the duke's sweet water, he had regretted his oath. The horse had gone on and on without stopping, each step jarring until Reade could not keep tears from streaming down his face. Duke Coren had kept such a tight grip around Reade's waist that the boy thought his back would always be dented from the metal studs on the duke's armor.

Reade was stubborn, though. He remembered Duke Coren's stern warning. No matter how sore he was, no matter how long the afternoon lasted, Reade had not asked for the golden cup. After all, the Sun-lord would not have complained. Da would have been proud of him.

Besides, Reade had not wanted to back down in front of Maida. That first morning, when the duke prepared to let Reade ride without drinking, Maida had thrown a tantrum. It was funny to watch his sister, screaming and kicking and biting, all because she wanted to do what Reade was doing.

It was funny, that was, until Duke Coren knelt down beside Maida. Reade couldn't hear what the duke said, but Maida certainly did. She cut off her scream mid-wail. Casting a tear-sharpened look at her brother, she said, "It's not fair! You call him Sun-lord, and you call me Sun-lady. If you don't make him drink, then why should I have to?"

The duke had gazed at her for a long moment, his brown eyes as dark as Da's. Reade got a twisty feeling in his belly, and he thought that he should step forward, that he should help his sister. He should try to explain things to Duke Coren. Maida was *always* trying to copy Reade. She had wanted to be the huer. She had wanted to go out fishing with Reade and Da. She had wanted to do all sorts of things that girls should not do.

Before Reade could explain, though, Duke Coren straightened up and put the golden cup in his saddle-bags. "Fine then, Sun-lady," he said, and his voice was as serious as when he spoke to Reade. "I'll tell you the same thing that I told your brother, though. I won't let you change your mind. If you make this decision, you can't go back."

"I won't if Reade doesn't." Maida had glared at him as she settled into the saddle in front of Donal.

Reade wondered if Maida regretted her decision now. He knew that *he* did. Not only was the ride painful, but it was boring.

Well, it *had* been boring. Today would be different. Today, Reade would prove that he wasn't a coward, no matter what Maida said. No matter what names she called him.

The duke kept them riding very fast. Reade heard one of the soldiers say that they were only seven days from Smithcourt. Sometimes they passed people on the road, walking or riding toward them. Those people always stepped to the side, giving lots of room to Duke Coren and all his men.

Once, Reade saw a giant farmer knuckling his forehead, just like he was a child, just like he was honored to be near the riders. The sight made Reade want to laugh aloud, and he glanced up to see Duke Coren eyeing him with an open smile. Just by sitting on the stallion, just by wearing the Sun-lord's golden robes, Reade made the duke proud.

No, Reade wasn't a coward. He wasn't a frightened little sheep. Maida didn't know what she was talking about. Reade thought about the farmer, staring in awe at the Sun-lord, and he sat even straighter in front of Duke Coren.

Throughout the long morning, he watched and waited, knowing that many of the soldiers would fall back as the afternoon dragged on. Duke Coren even loosened his grip around Reade's middle, and Reade leaned forward to catch the stallion's reins. He had a plan, now, a plan that would prove that he was brave. He glanced back at the duke, but the nobleman did not seem angry or alarmed. He was no more watchful than he ever was along the road.

Reade thought about how strong the horse was, and

he realized that he was being foolish. Foolish and bad. Duke Coren would be furious with him. Donal would glare at him, and the duke might even say that Reade would get no supper.

Maybe it would be wiser just to hold on to his Great Mother. Let Maida say what she wanted. *Reade* knew that he wasn't a coward. He knew that he wasn't afraid. It was just that following Duke Coren's rules was the right thing to do. The safe thing. The thing that the Sun-lord would do.

Uncertain, Reade leaned back against Duke Coren's chest, resting his head against the armor. Afraid to touch his Great Mother, afraid to remind Maida of what he had promised to do, he shifted his hand to his bavin instead.

The woodstar was prickly beneath his fingers. He turned it over and over, running his hands across its points. Maida didn't have a woodstar. She had a Great Mother, but she didn't have a woodstar. Duke Coren had given the bavin to Reade. He *could* have given it to Maida, but he gave it to Reade instead. Duke Coren liked Reade better than he liked Maida. That's why he let Reade ride in front of him, instead of making Reade ride with Donal.

Duke Coren had chosen *him*. Duke Coren wouldn't have chosen a coward. As Reade repeated that thought, he looked down at the woodstar in his hands. The sun was high in the sky, and the bavin picked up the bright light. In fact, the woodstar seemed to glow with a light of its own, a bright whiteness that leaked around Reade's fingers.

The white light didn't frighten Reade, though. Oh, no. He wasn't a coward. He could do anything he wanted. He was brave enough to be the huer, on the very edge of the cliffs. He was brave enough to go out fishing in the nighttime. He was brave enough to walk to the Guardians' Sacred Grove all by himself. He was brave enough to take Duke Coren's reins and pull the horse from the road. He was brave enough to throw away his Great Mother, now that he was a big boy. Now that he didn't need the Great Mother's protection.

Before he even knew that he was ready, he let the bavin fall back on his chest. He was distracted for just a moment as the woodstar flashed white against his golden robes. Then, he leaned forward, jerking half out of the saddle. He pretended that the horse had caught its foot in some unexpected pothole. As he fell forward, he pulled hard on the reins, jerking the stallion from the smooth road.

For one instant, he felt the horse hesitate, not quite turning from the road. Reade knew how to make the stallion move, though. He leaned forward as far as he could across the beast's neck, screaming like the wind in one of the great Land's End storms. After one scary moment, when Reade thought the horse would rear up, the stallion leaped across the rough-plowed field, tossing its head.

That first jump threw Reade backward, almost making him drop the reins. He swayed on the edge of the high saddle, and his woodstar flew up and hit him in the face. It wasn't glowing white anymore. It was just an ordinary bavin, a black, prickly piece of the Tree that scraped his cheek.

The horse jumped again, and Reade was slammed down on his tailbone. He opened his mouth and gasped like a fish caught in a net, unable to breathe in air. Duke Coren swore and leaned far forward to grab the reins. The horse was even more frightened by the duke's motion, and Reade was certain that he was going to be crushed. Duke Coren would smash him from behind, and the horse would jump up from below. Reade shut his eyes, terrified by the commotion he had made. His hands flew up, closing over his bavin.

The woodstar reminded him of the Great Mother

that also swung around his neck. The curved iron burned against his hand like a brand. Before he could think, he pulled the charm off his neck. He cocked his arm back and threw the Great Mother with all his might, the breath grunting out of him as he let it go. He could not see it land.

There! Let Maida say that Reade was a coward now! Let her say that he was afraid of anything!

Before the horse could jump another time, Duke Coren gathered up the reins. He pulled back on the leather so hard that the stallion reared up. Reade whooped in surprise. He wasn't a coward just because he was glad Duke Coren grabbed him around his belly. That was only smart, the way he clutched at the duke's sleeve. Any smart boy would have done the same thing.

At last, the stallion stood still in the middle of the field. Its sides moved in and out like the bellows Mum sometimes used on the fire back home.

Duke Coren swung down from the animal's back and tugged at Reade's arm, pulling him off the horse so hard that the boy stumbled. "What in the name of the Seven Gods are you trying to do, boy?"

Boy? What had happened to Sun-lord? Duke Coren must be furious! He always called Reade Sun-lord.

Reade could hardly explain what he had done. He barely understood himself. What a stupid idea, trying to leave the Great Mother in the field so that Maida would think he was brave! Duke Coren would never understand!

The duke's fingers clawed into Reade's arm, hauling him upright and pinching his flesh against the bone. Reade's head was thrown back with enough force that his neck popped. When he looked up, he could see Donal riding across the field. The man was swearing as he pulled his horse to a stop. Maida stared at Reade, her eyes wide and frightened.

"I asked you a question, boy!"

"N— nothing, Your Grace. I wasn't doing anything! The horse was running, and I slipped forward. I tried to grab the reins to keep from falling, and that must have scared him. P-please, Your Grace, I didn't mean to do anything!"

The words tumbled over themselves, and Reade tried to swallow the sob that rose in his throat. This wasn't fair! Maida had made him do this! She was the one who had said he was a coward. She was the one who had said he was a lamb!

She should be the one trying to explain to Duke Coren. This was all Maida's fault, just like when Mum punished him for not finishing his chores when *Maida* had tracked dust across the hearth. He craned his neck about, trying to see if Maida was going to speak up. Before he could find her, though, the duke twisted his arm sharply.

"Are you lying to me, boy? You've never had any problem keeping your seat before."

"Your Grace, I would *never* lie to you!" Before Reade could say anything else, he thought about the times that Mum had yelled at him, the times that Reade had gotten into trouble for hurting Maida by playing too rough. He knew how to make Mum forget the bad things that he'd done. He knew how to distract her. He made his voice sound all trembly, like he was afraid. "I—is the horse all right? I wouldn't want him hurt because I was stupid."

This type of question usually worked. He would sound frightened and sad and sorry, all at the same time. Sometimes, Reade was so good at asking the question that Mum didn't even punish him. She would say he was a good boy for watching over Maida, for worrying about her.

Duke Coren was not as easily fooled. "I don't know what you thought to do, boy. Every minute we waste in this field is one more minute you won't sleep to-night. Nothing is going to keep you from arriving at Smithcourt."

"I *want* to go to Smithcourt, Your Grace. I want to see the Service!"

"You act like you want to stay a peasant in the fields, boy. You can't be part of the Service, if you're going to shame me like this. You're as willful as a cat, only not so well-mannered!"

The duke's voice was hard and cold as iron. Reade's heart began to pound with shame. Why had he ever let Maida tease him? Why had he ever thought of riding out into the field?

"But—" Reade began, not even certain of how he would defend himself.

"*But* you obviously have no sense of what it means to be the Sun-lord, what it means to rule over your people. If I bring you to Smithcourt, it's so that you can restore *order* to your people, not ruin their lives. Look at the mess you've made of this field! Look at how the horse has torn up the farmer's careful rows! Do you think it fair that a hardworking man's labor was destroyed by your games?"

"I didn't think—"

"Precisely, boy. You didn't think at all! You acted like some foolish *child*. If you're going to be the Sun-lord, you must leave behind your silly games. You have your people to think about now. Your people will depend on you for fairness and justice. Perhaps I chose the wrong person; perhaps you aren't truly the Sun-lord. Maybe we should just ride back to the Headland now."

"Please, Your Grace, it won't happen again!" Reade had been so stupid! Why should he prove to Maida that he was brave? He was riding to Smithcourt, by all the Guardians! That should be enough to prove to anyone that he wasn't a coward. "Please, my lord, don't keep me from going to Smithcourt!"

In a flash, Reade realized that his words sounded

like a grown man's. He sounded *noble*! Reade knew how noblemen acted; Mum had told him stories. Nobles knelt down before people who were more important than they were. Reade sank to his knees in the muddy field, ignoring the squish of water through his golden robes.

From the ground, he could see his Great Mother. She had fallen in the mud, far to his right. Her head and the top half of her body stood up out of the earth, just like she'd been planted. Reade quickly looked away. Duke Coren must not realize that Reade had *intended* to ride into the field. Trying to distract the duke, Reade said quickly, "Your Grace, I didn't think of the farmer who works this field, or the people who ride with us. I'm sorry! I'll do anything to show you that!"

"Anything?" Reade swallowed hard. Duke Coren's voice was shivery, like when he'd spoken to Donal in the small tavern room. Reade was afraid to look at the duke's face, but he managed to nod his head once. The grown-up waited for a long time, so long that Reade thought he might have decided never to speak to Reade again. Finally, though, he said, "Very well, Sun-lord. Your words are spoken like those of a nobleman, and so you shall be treated as one."

Sun-lord! That was better than "boy"! Maybe Duke Coren *would* forgive him. Reade kept his voice very small as he asked, "Please, Your Grace, what are you going to do?"

"No more—and no less—than Culain himself. When the Sun-lord wronged Culain, he was treated as a grown man. The Sun-lord chose his own punishment."

"Ch—chose his punishment, Your Grace?" Reade dared to sneak a glance at Duke Coren's face. He couldn't read anything there, though, couldn't tell if the duke was really angry, or if he was just angry like Mum was when she thought Reade needed to learn a lesson.

Choose a punishment. There were lots of horrible punishments. He could be forced to give back his golden robes, give back even his smallclothes and walk around naked. After all, he had acted like a baby, breaking rules, so he should be treated like a baby. He blushed as he thought about how all the soldiers would laugh at him.

Or he could be kept from eating dinner. Duke Coren could make him go to bed that night, without any food. But Duke Coren had done that before, when Reade had just *said* bad things. This punishment would be worse, now that he had *done* something wrong. Reade realized that his hands were trembling, and he clenched them into fists.

He could be forced to feed Crusher. Duke Coren could make him cut up pieces of raw meat and hold them out to the dog. The dog might even decide that he wanted fresher meat, that he wanted to chew on little boy bones instead of his own food. Reade swayed on his feet, imagining Crusher's hot breath, and he curled his arms across his belly.

His lips started to quiver. Before he could actually begin to cry, though, Duke Coren's stallion snorted at a fly, stomping one mud-covered hoof in the muddy field. Reade felt almost weak with relief as he thought of another punishment. "Tonight, when we reach our camp, I'll brush your horse."

Duke Coren shook his head firmly. "I have a groom to tend my horse. You would gain nothing for the beast, for me, or for yourself." Reade wasn't going to gain anything for himself, no matter what punishment he chose. He shouldn't say that to the duke, though. Choose his own punishment—this was the type of thing that Mum would think up.

"I'm waiting, Sun-lord."

Reade shook his head, pretending that he could not think of any other punishments. "Please, Your Grace. What punishment would the Sun-lord choose?"

Duke Coren's lips curved into a hard smile. "The

Sun-lord would have recognized that his punishment should fit his deeds. If he played with the reins frivolously . . ."

Reade felt the words pulled out of him. He could not raise his head, could not lift his eyes from his muddy knees. "Then the reins should punish him. He should be struck with the reins."

"How many times?"

How many? If Duke Coren asked, then once would not be enough. "Twice?"

"The Sun-lord would have asked for five."

"Five." When Reade said the word, he got a bitter taste in his mouth, like he'd been sick. He wanted to spit out the taste. He wanted to spit at Maida. This was all her fault. *She* was the coward! She should have spoken up by now. She should have told Duke Coren that it was her fault Reade had ridden out into the field.

Maida wasn't speaking, though, and Duke Coren remained silent. That meant that the duke expected Reade to say something else. Swallowing hard, he forced himself to look up again. "Please, Your Grace. I ask that the horse's reins hit me five times." Even though he tried to be brave—he knew he wasn't a coward!—he had to whisper the last two words.

"Spoken like a true nobleman, Sun-lord. Like a man who can fight for order and peace in these troubled times." The duke nodded and waved his hand. Reade realized that he was supposed to march across the field, back to the road. With every step, his belly turned over, and his heart jumped in his chest so hard that it hurt to breathe.

When they reached the road, Duke Coren told him to stand still. The nobleman undid his golden robes without saying anything. When Reade was standing in his smallclothes, he started to chatter. He took a deep breath, but his teeth still clicked together. He wondered if his lips were turning blue.

Duke Coren took the golden sash from the robe and wrapped it around Reade's hands. He pulled it tight, tugging until Reade's fingers tingled. Reade fidgeted until Duke Coren passed the sash to Donal. Then, the duke walked away, crossing over to the horses. Reade started to turn his head to watch Duke Coren, but Donal yanked on the golden sash.

Reade waited, then, for Duke Coren to come back. When the duke stepped in front of him, he held a long, narrow strip of leather, a replacement rein. The man looked at him steadily, like Da had when he taught Reade a lesson, like how to clean a fish or how to build a fire. "The correct response is 'All praise to the Seven Gods.'"

Duke Coren snapped the leather between his hands and doubled it, then doubled it again. He flexed the rein one more time, and Reade heard the leather slap against itself. The duke nodded and walked away, moving to where Reade couldn't see him.

Reade's whole body was shivering by then. His legs felt as though they wouldn't let him stand, like he'd been on Da's boat for an entire day and then jumped onto the shore. Reade opened his mouth to say something, to say anything, to make Duke Coren stop. Before he could speak, though, Donal pulled at the golden sash, forcing Reade to look straight ahead. Then, there was a scream in the air, like an angry bird screeching for a fish, and fire burned across Reade's back.

The pain was more than he had imagined, more than he had ever felt, even the one time that Da had set a stripe across his bare bum with his grown-up leather belt. That was because Reade had called Maida a name, a filthy word that he'd heard Winder use. Mum had bit her own lip when Da hit him, and then it had all been over. *Maida* had started crying, and Da had looked sad before he shrugged his shoulders and left the cottage.

Now, Reade could not see the duke's face, and the nobleman did not walk away after one blow. Donal tugged the golden sash hard, and Reade remembered that he had to say something, that he had to speak, or it wouldn't be right. The punishment wouldn't be good. The words got all mixed up with a sob in his throat. "All praise to the Seven Gods."

There! Maida couldn't call him a coward now! Maida couldn't call him any names at all, not when she was standing behind Donal, with her golden robes pulled up nice and warm under her chin!

Before Reade was ready, there was another scream in the air. He didn't mean to pull away, he didn't mean to flinch, but he couldn't help himself. The rein found him anyway, hot and sharp. Donal tugged hard, and Reade shouted, "All praise to the Seven Gods."

Another scream, another slice, and he praised the gods again.

Maida's mouth was open now. He could see her behind Donal. He could see her breathe in, see her get ready to say something. But if Maida admitted now that Reade's ride was her fault, she would take away the power of the whipping. She would take away the brave thing that he had done, getting rid of his Great Mother. If Maida spoke now, she would make him a coward. She would be disappointed in him, and Mum would, and Da. Especially Da.

Reade heard the whip scream again, and he called out his words as fast as he could. One more slice, fast, before Maida could do anything, before she could speak, and Reade yelled as loud as he could, "All praise to the Seven Gods!"

And then it was over.

Duke Coren knelt in front of him. Reade was shivering so hard that he could not lift up his hands, but the duke managed to untie his wrists. Tears were hot on his cheeks, but Duke Coren wiped them away, using the golden sash. Gently, carefully, he helped

Reade back into his robes. The fabric hurt where it touched his back, and the duke tied the sash very loosely around his waist.

Reade took a step forward, and he stumbled. His legs had turned to honey, flowing down the road. Duke Coren caught him before he could fall, holding on to him for a moment until he wasn't shaking as hard. Reade opened his mouth to speak, but he couldn't think of words, couldn't think of anything at all to say. The duke nodded, though, as if he'd said something brilliant. "Aye, Sun-lord. You did well. You were very brave. When we stop for the night, I'll rub ointment on your back, little man."

Brave! Reade *was* brave! Even Duke Coren realized that! The duke swung up on his horse and waited as one of his soldiers helped Reade get settled at the front of the high saddle. Reade sat very straight, because it hurt to lean back against Duke Coren's armor. It hurt, but the duke's words were better than any ointment.

"Little man," the duke had called him. Not a boy. Not even Sun-lord. Little *man*.

Reade was brave. He was forgiven. And Duke Coren knew he was a man.

8

Alana gasped for breath, feeling each slash of Coren's leather rein like a brand against her own flesh. She pressed herself against the Tree, trying to diffuse the blows through the oak's thick bark. The wood, though, only amplified the pain—the pain and the startlement and the betrayal of a small boy who had never been so treated.

Parina's journal had made it seem so simple—reach out through a bavin, save a dying infant. Reade, though, was no newborn, open and receptive to the woodsinger's thoughts. Instead, he was a thinking, feeling child, confused about Duke Coren, about his mother, about his poor lost father. Whatever Alana's good intentions, she had scarcely been able to plant the seed of rebellion, and it had taken all of her strength to force the boy to lean forward, to scream in the horse's ear.

Now, the Tree resonated with the punishment that had resulted from her clumsy efforts. The boy's pain and shock, spoken inside Alana's mind, were overwhelming. He had never been beaten this way among the People. He had violated all sorts of rules, even rules set by Alana herself, and he had never been required to pay any real physical penalty. Things were different in the wide world, different once a child was carried beyond the Headland. Alana tried to make sense out of that world, out of the strange customs that she was observing. She tried to make sense out of the pain and the fury and the stinging brand of a lash across her back.

But even while the Tree showed her Reade's pain, it magnified the boy's growing determination. With horror, Alana sensed Reade's vow that Coren would never be disappointed in him again. Reade was becoming less and less from the Headland, and more and more of whatever the duke wanted him to be. Rescuing the twins was more important now than it had ever been before.

Even as Alana swallowed her frustrated anger with the child, she heard someone approaching the Tree. Forcing her eyes open, she watched Goody Glenna struggle up the rise. Alana barely waited for the old woman to approach before she exclaimed, "Those old woodsingers don't know what they're talking about!"

"Which woodsingers?" The old woman lowered her head, wheezing for breath. "And what are they talking about?"

"The ones in my mind, Goody Glenna! The ones that you've told me to listen to, to learn from. They come to me when I'm waking, when I'm sleeping, when I'm serving the Tree."

"Aye. You're a woodsinger. They're supposed to come to you."

"But they're not supposed to tell me half-truths! They're not supposed to tell me part of the story and leave me to discover the rest, when I'm playing with Reade and Maida's lives!"

"I suspect they do the best they can," Goody Glenna said wryly as she tried to straighten, resting a hand against the Tree's trunk and sucking in a wheezing breath. "Well, what have they taught you?"

"Nothing! They haven't shown me how to do anything except get poor Reade whipped! I had the power, but I didn't know how to use it. Why didn't you warn me?"

"Woodsingers warn woodsingers. You have all those voices inside your head, girl, not me. Learn what *they* have to tell you." Alana harrumphed, and the old woman tilted her head, raising one eyebrow. "Besides, girl, I wasn't certain what was possible, what you'd be able to work through the Tree. Sarira told me once, when we were both girls, that the ancient woodsingers could reach through their bavins, make people act, but she thought the skill had been lost. That was one reason she kept her knowledge to herself, afraid to admit how little was left to her."

"Afraid!" Alana spluttered. "Goody Glenna, you have me playing with children's lives, and I don't know the first thing about what I'm doing!"

"The first thing? That's easy, woodsinger. The first thing is the Tree. Listen to what it tells you. Go where it takes you." The old woman shook her head, as if she were telling a child that fish swam in the sea. "Oh, and it's not just children's lives in your keeping, Alana. What do you see through the other bavin?"

For the first time since she had listened to Parina Woodsinger, Alana let herself think about the inky darkness, about the loss that surrounded Maddock's woodstar. She clutched her arms about her, trying to hold in her fear, and she almost succeeded in keeping her voice from quavering. "Goody, I think they're gone."

"You *think*? What is that supposed to mean?"

"I lost Maddock. They were in the barn, and it caught fire, and someone threw a knife. . . ."

"Did you see him die?"

"No! I couldn't see anything! The bavin must have burned."

"Fool!" Glenna spat the word, and Alana's eyes blinked open as if the old woman had dashed cold water across her face. "Bavins don't burn. Even *you* know that. It wasn't fire that destroyed your vision."

"Then what was it?"

"I'm not a woodsinger, now am I? I'm just an old woman who got up too early in the morning. Stand up, Alana. Use the Tree. Check on Maddock."

"I can't." Having felt the power of Reade's beating through the oak, Alana recoiled from the rescue party's pain. Even if she succeeded where she had failed before, even if she managed to reach through to Maddock's woodstar, would she have the strength to take on the pain that he had suffered in the attack on the barn? Could she handle the slashing and the cutting and the burning, seething pain?

"You don't have a choice, woodsinger. Get to work." Glenna sounded like she was ordering a woman to sweep her hearth, but then she added grudgingly, "Here. I brought you some bread. I thought you might want to stay with the Tree."

Alana took the loaf without thinking. Before she could speak, she was startled by Goody Glenna turning back to the village. "Goody!" she called and then, when the older woman turned around, "I tell you, I can't do this. I don't know how."

"You're learning, Alana Woodsinger. You're certainly learning."

Alana bolted the still-warm bread, surprised by her ravenous hunger. Could Goody Glenna be right? Could there be some hope left for Maddock's bavin?

The woodsinger circled the Tree to the invisible scar where she had sung the second woodstar. Knotting her hair against the wind's prying fingers, she muttered another prayer to the Great Mother. She was so afraid that she would reach out and find nothing—an emptiness worse than the swirling ink that had driven her away before. How would death feel through a bavin? How would she recognize it, in her mind, in her body? Sighing, Alana mustered her thoughts and stretched across the miles, grasping for the bavin's core.

She feared that she would fail. She feared that she would succeed.

*   *   *

The trio stared at the muddy field, ignoring the tender seedlings they had trampled. Maddock knew that he should dismount, that he should look about more closely at the clues in the earth, but the mere thought set his knee to throbbing once again. That morning had been the first that he could swing up on his gelding's high back without visibly steeling himself first.

Of course, he reminded himself, he was lucky to have fallen when he had, back in the barn. The cursed iron dagger that had been aimed at his chest had sailed over his head, sheathing itself in one of the burning barn's upright supports. A good handspan of the blade was swallowed by the wood before it came to a quivering halt, and Maddock knew that he would have been dead if he had not slipped, if Landon had not warned him.

He had scarcely had time to contemplate that fact, though, because the dagger had bitten to the heart of the burning post. For one instant, the weakened wood was whole, and then it was split in two, its fiery heart glowing orange before the air in the stifling barn fed its hunger. As the wood exploded into flame, Maddock was deafened by a monstrous crack. Men screamed around him, the wounded adding a note of horror to their moans. The bellowing cows reached a new frenzy as the roof crashed to the ground, covering the beasts with a cruel blanket of orange and yellow.

From the corner of his eye, he saw a heavy beam falling, and he whirled around. He did not move quickly enough, though, and the upright struck a glancing blow across the back of his head. In a heartbeat, he was submerged in an inky darkness, foul, like the shadows beneath a capsized boat. He fought for air, fought for breath, but it was easier to slip into the stinking darkness.

"Maddock!" The voice came from a distance, burbling as if through water. "Dammit, man!" He realized that Landon was calling to him, dragging him up from the cool, dark depths. "Maddock!"

He forced his eyes to open. He was still in the barn. The cursed heat was unbearable. Flames gnawed at his back.

Bogs and breakers! He could not make his screaming leg move. He could not force himself away from the fire, away from the burning death. Instead, he ordered his fingers to stretch for the sword at his feet. He'd fight off the villagers, even if he couldn't escape the burning barn. He'd use the sword to prolong his life for another dozen breaths.

Maddock found, though, that the weapon was clutched by one of his attackers. A villager's fingers were wrapped tightly around the hilt, and Maddock tightened his fingers around the other man's, ready to pry them off. His desperate bravado changed to revulsion, though, when he realized that the hand beneath his did not belong to a living man. He had found the claw of his first assailant, the hand that he had severed when this nightmare began.

Maddock slipped back toward the inky horror, toward the chittering beasts at the corners of his thoughts. Pain screamed in his leg as he tried to steady himself, tried to stand straight and uncurl his fingers and pry loose the lifeless hand beneath his own, but he could not make himself move.

As the fire surged above him, he felt a strong shoulder beneath his arm, hoisting him up when he was unable to put his weight on his injured leg. He let himself be half carried, half dragged to the flaming doorway of what had once been a barn, and then there was a dash across open space, and a pain-crazed torture as he was made to crouch in the shadow of a distant wooden building.

Air. Blessed cool air. Night. Well lit by a fully risen

moon, a moon that was cold and distant and pearly white.

And outraged cries from villagers, bellows from the men and shrieks from the women. Maddock heard shouted commands, one deep voice demanding all available buckets, ordering a brigade to carry precious water to quench the flames that had begun to show at the barn's door.

"Come on, then," Landon hissed. "Before they realize we've escaped. I'm not going to carry you all the way to Smithcourt." Landon's voice was tight as he guided Maddock away from the inferno, away from the village. They stumbled through new-plowed fields without regard for sprouting crops. Jobina waited for them on the far edge of the plot, holding their restless horses.

Maddock remembered little of the next three days; he had passed in and out of a swirling midnight haze of unconsciousness. Landon had somehow gotten him up on his horse, he knew. The beast looked mangy, with its singed mane and charred remnants of a tail. The outlanders rode as if they were chased by the Guardians themselves, for the rest of that night and all the next day. Landon decided when they would rest, and which copse of trees would be their shelter. Landon decided what they would eat and when. Landon decided when they would pull up for the night, shivering, exhausted, and starving.

And Maddock gave way to the tracker in all things, and to Jobina as well. The healer's compounds gradually worked their magic, and he found that he could breathe without coughing after the first day. He could place some weight on his bad leg in two days, and the throbbing behind his eyes had subsided to a dull ache by the third morning. By the fourth day from the hapless village, he was able to limp a few steps unassisted.

Each time they stopped, Jobina tended to him with

her lips pressed tight, her flirty ministrations as dead as the lamb he had butchered a lifetime ago, in the clearing.

It had been shortly after noon on the seventh day when Landon pulled his horse to a sudden halt. The tracker drew to attention like a hunting cat, his grim face conveying an unexpected hint of excitement. Eyes glued to the field, he led the trio off the road, across the rutted furrows.

"They were here." Landon shaded his eyes to squint along the horizon, and Maddock tried to make out what had caught the man's attention. The earth was gouged and pitted, but it didn't look any different from any other cursed field they'd ridden past. Maddock started to make a sly comment about the tracker's vision, but he managed to swallow his frustration.

Landon nodded impassively, as if he'd heard the words Maddock did not speak. "Look how the earth is still moist at the bottom of these footprints. They can't be more than a day ahead of us."

"Not more than a day!" Maddock exploded. "We've been pushing ourselves until we can't see straight, and we can do no better than that?"

"Apparently not." Landon ran one hand through his thin hair, shrugging his narrow shoulders. He ignored Maddock's implied criticism of his tracking. "The real question," he mused, "is why they came into this field at all. If you look there"—he pointed at a mess of hoof- and boot-prints in the drying mud— "you can see that only one horse came this far from the road. One horse that carried a man and a child."

Now that Landon was explaining, Maddock could just make out a child's print in the mud, a surprisingly small shape cradled in the drying earth. "I'd say it was Reade," the tracker continued. "Maida tends to shift from foot to foot when she's standing in one place."

"Look here!" The two men turned at the shout. Jobina was a few paces away, her gaze intent on a patch of muddy earth. Her hand was extended as if she were casting out a fishing net. Maddock could not see what her trembling fingers indicated, but Landon turned immediately, circling around the spot like a cat snuffling the burrow of its prey.

"Is that what I think it is?" Jobina asked.

"If you think it's a Great Mother amulet." Landon ignored the healer's batting eyelashes, apparently unaware that she was enthralled by his tracking ability.

Maddock edged his horse closer to the woman. "I'm impressed that you spotted it," he said chivalrously, and he warmed at the grateful smile that she shot in his direction. A twist in his words managed to condemn the tracker as well, for if the unskilled Jobina had found the little metal object, the trained Landon should have done at least as much.

The other man ignored him, though, lost in his intent inspection of the dark statuette. Landon circled around the amulet, viewing it from all angles, pointedly leaving a wide circle of undisturbed earth. Bogs and breakers! There were obviously no footsteps near the thing. The tracker's care was absurd. Maddock sighed his impatience, but Landon still circled another two times before he finally strode forward and plucked the iron charm from the earth.

"I thought you were waiting for it to sprout." Maddock sneered, but—as always—Landon refused to take offense.

"This belonged to Reade," the tracker said, hefting the piece of metal as if he were about to set it on a scale. "See how the leather thong has been chewed? He does that when he's nervous." Landon looked from the trampled crops to the Great Mother, measuring the distance with his eyes. "He must have thrown it from horseback, from that cluster of prints there. The distance is far, for a child, but the angle is right. Reade must have created a diversion, ridden from the road and left the amulet here."

"Don't you think that plan is a little sophisticated for a five-year-old boy?" Maddock could not keep the sarcasm from his voice.

"The only other possibility is that Coren dropped it himself, and that makes no sense at all. Reade must have figured out that someone would come after him. He forced Coren's horse from the road and left this for us, as a sign."

"You don't even know that the duke rode out here!" Maddock flavored his disbelief with a touch of anger as Jobina nodded, eagerly accepting the tracker's evaluation. The healer was growing a little too impressed with Landon.

"I can't be certain," the tracker agreed, either ignoring or unaware of Jobina's rapt attention. "Someone may have taken his horse for some reason, but the animal that rode out here was Coren's stallion."

At Jobina's renewed look of respect, Maddock sharpened his voice. "And I suppose the Guardians of Earth whispered that little secret to you."

"Of course not." Landon's voice tightened a fraction. "I noticed the stallion at Land's End. He has a curious gait—his right hind leg scuffs along for just a fraction of a second. See? In the mud, there. It might be correctable by a good farrier, with a proper shoe."

"It certainly hasn't kept him from outpacing us every step of the way!"

Landon shrugged, managing to indicate that their pace had been hampered by Maddock's injury. Maddock tightened his hands into fists and forced his mount to take a menacing step toward the tracker. Clenching his knees about the beast's girth, though, made his leg twinge, and he settled back into his saddle.

So, Maddock thought, grimacing, Reade had stood in this field yesterday afternoon. Assuming that the child's escapade had not evoked reprisals (and there were, thank the Guardians, no signs of bloodshed in the field), then at least one of their quarry was well enough to rebel against his captors. Maddock clenched his teeth and turned his horse back to the road. They were not entirely too late.

After they left the trampled field behind, Maddock resisted the urge to push through the night, to ride hard until he reached the duke, no matter what the cost. He was not so prideful that he believed he could best a cursed company of warriors who had been trained since childhood to kill men like him. At least not when he had ridden for hours, without proper rest or food, in a strange and dangerous land, with a throbbing, unhealed knee.

A small village spread halfway between the three travelers and the horizon. This one had no walls. Just as well, Maddock thought. Gatekeepers were twice as suspicious when long shadows fell across a man's face.

Full dark had settled in the narrow streets by the time the three riders made their way into the hamlet. Despite the late hour, though, the lanes were filled with people, small children running and calling to each other in the darkness, men and women walking together through the moonlight. A festival air whipped through the town, scarcely pent excitement surging along the dirt roads. All of the stir centered around the trampled yard of what appeared to be the only inn in the village, and Maddock and his companions followed the stream of people, urging their tired mounts forward.

Maddock did not even bother to glance at the sign that swung in the nighttime breeze. He had had enough of clever taproom names to last a lifetime. The three travelers stooped under a low doorway and found themselves in the midst of a quiet room, strangely hushed after the excitement outside.

There were close to a hundred villagers crowded into the space, and the smell of sweaty bodies was overwhelming after the cold night air. All eyes were glued to the wooden stairs leading up to the inn's second floor.

Maddock glanced about until he had located the innkeeper, a stout man whose bulbous red nose hinted that he enjoyed a good bit of his own brew. Even if a white apron had not announced the man's status, the carved wooden tray in his hands would have done the same. While the crowd remained spellbound by whatever spectacle had moved upstairs, the ostler bustled about his business, refilling an empty mug here, bringing a fresh meat pie there. When he noticed the three strangers, he paused long enough to leer at Jobina's lithe form beneath her travel-worn clothes.

"I'll not be having rooms for the lot of you," the innkeeper huffed. "We're all full upstairs. I can give you a mug or two, though."

"Who's up there?" Maddock asked, dropping a coin on the wooden tray and indicating that he and his companions would like food and drink.

"It's the duke himself," the innkeeper whispered. "Duke Coren and his men."

Maddock's breath caught in his throat. After these weeks of travel, to finally be under the same roof as that cursed bastard. . . . Maddock scarcely heard the innkeeper continue. "They'll be here through the night, you can mark my words, and probably tomorrow as well. It will take that long for the little girl to die."

"The little girl!" Maddock gasped, barely swallowing Maida's name.

Landon cleared his throat pointedly before asking, "What ails the child?"

Before the tracker's words were out, though, Jobina had pushed her way forward. "Perhaps I can be of assistance. I have some small knowledge of herbs."

Sharks and fins! Maddock wanted to scream aloud. Jobina could not help Maida! Duke Coren had spent weeks among the People; he had certainly noticed the healer. There was little chance he could have *missed* her, with her taut calves flirting beneath her skirts.

Maddock almost did not hear the innkeeper's life-saving response. "Thank you, good lady, but the duke has said his own men will care for her. He wants none of the townfolk abovestairs." The ostler made a short bow toward Landon, setting down his tray and wrestling his hands dry on his apron as he acknowledged the man's question. "The girl suffers from a fever, goodman, from fear and hard riding."

"But how did a little girl come *here*? And with Duke Coren?" Maddock managed to ask.

"The duke saved her, that's how. Her and her brother, twins." The trio of outlanders listened to the tale that had become painfully familiar, swallowing their indignation against the unfair lies that Coren had sown in the innkeeper's fertile imagination.

Maddock heard how the Tree demanded the annual sacrifice of human children—fresh blood poured upon its roots by a priest and priestess, a brother and sister coupled in an unholy alliance. The blood of twins, like the vulnerable Maida and Reade, was more potent, more valuable to the craven Tree.

The tale was so twisted, so incredible, that nausea swirled through Maddock's gut, as if his people actually *did* perform such abominations. Unbidden, Maddock's hand crept to the woodstar beneath his tunic.

The ostler must have seen something of his guests' disgust, for he wrapped up his tale quickly. "Enough of such horrors! You'll still sup with us, even if we can't give you a room for the night?"

Swallowing hard, Maddock said that the three of them would indeed dine in the common room. The innkeeper brought them food without delay. As Maddock's companions dug into a stew that was more broth than meat, he tried to calculate a plan. If only there were some way that he could spirit a disguised

Jobina upstairs, some way that she could bring her
healer's craft to the feverish Maida. . . . All the time
that Maddock thought, he could feel his bavin burning
beneath his clothing, its prickly points rubbing his flesh
like new wool. More than once, he shifted the woodstar, uncomfortably aware of how the villagers would
react if they saw this relic of the Tree, if they recognized a bavin carved from the blood-starved nightmare of Coren's lies.

Even as Maddock contemplated taking off the woodstar altogether and hiding it, he was interrupted by a
soldier clattering down the steps, his armor rattling
like death. "Innkeep!" The roar cut through the uneasy mumbling in the room, and Maddock recognized
Coren's aide-de-camp, Donal. He also remembered
that Donal was the soldier who had stolen Maida from
the beachhead, the one who had wrapped his mailed
fists around the little girl's throat and bundled her
onto the back of a horse, barely keeping her toes from
his dogs' slavering jaws. Without conscious thought,
Maddock found himself on his feet, reaching for the
sword that was half swathed in his cloak.

Only Landon's hand on his sword arm kept him
from crying out his challenge then and there.

Landon's hand, that was, and the vestigial memory
that Maddock did not want to fight Donal. No, *Coren*
was Maddock's man. Coren was the one who had
masterminded the attack, who had tried to seduce
Alana Woodsinger, who had wangled a woodstar from
her. The duke was the power behind the fear he heard
in every voice, the tales of horror that were muttered
like filthy jokes in every village that they passed. A
deep breath managed to clear the scarlet fury from
Maddock's eyes, and he was able to listen to Donal's commands.

"Innkeep, do you have any sort of healer in this
miserable excuse for a village?"

"Begging your pardon, my lord," the ostler muttered, bobbing an awkward bow. A flush of exertion mixed with fear on his face, and his fleshy nose glowed with renewed color. "Begging your pardon. There's only the midwife, Goody Rina, and she's out to her son's farm, helping with the calving."

"The calving!" Donal bellowed, and Maddock braced himself for the inevitable smack of flesh against flesh. "We've children here, man, a girl who is dying! Perhaps you forget that you have a duke abovestairs!"

"Please, my lord, how could I forget that?" the fat innkeeper pleaded. "I forget nothing at all, nothing requested by any of my guests! If it please your lordship, this lady is passing through, and she has offered her assistance." The ostler nearly tripped over his feet in his effort to get to Jobina. "She says she knows herbs and the ways of healing."

"Then what are you wasting my time for, fool?" Donal turned on his heel without even glancing at Jobina. "Get her upstairs now. Before it is too late!"

Maddock bit back a curse. Jobina, though, merely smiled with satisfaction before she gathered her cloak closer about her body, swaddling her curves in disguising cloth. Her hands flashed to her face like sparrows' wings, and in a flash, she wove her hair into a single, unbecoming braid. Maddock shook his head as he handed over her herb-filled satchel. He could only hope that two weeks on the road had worked some alchemy, and the healer would not be recognized.

As Jobina disappeared up the stairs, Maddock told himself that the safer course lay in letting the healer go alone. One person from Land's End had the faintest chance of not sparking a deadly connection in the duke's mind. Two would almost certainly invite disaster. He did not even notice the innkeeper looking at him oddly when he let Jobina climb the stairs by herself. Did not notice, that was, until the bavin on his chest seemed to shift entirely of its own accord. As clearly as if Alana Woodsinger were sitting next to him on the trestle, Maddock heard the woman's voice prompt him to look up at the astonished ostler.

He barely resisted the urge to pull out the bavin, to stare at it outright. Of course, Alana was watching him! Of course, she was tracking everything that had been done by all three rescuers. Maddock had no time to dwell on that uncomfortable thought, though, as the innkeeper asked, "Sir?" and looked toward the stairs in obvious amazement that Maddock would abandon his ostensible wife.

Bogs and breakers! Every eye in the room was trained on him now. Whether he had a plan or not, he had to climb the stairs. Sighing, and indicating with a pointed glance that Landon should remain at the table, Maddock settled a hand on the woodstar beneath his clothes and followed the healer to the sickroom.

Looking through the door of the crowded bedchamber, Maddock thought that Maida had already died. The child was stretched out on a lumpy mattress, her arms pulled into unnaturally straight lines beside her narrow chest. Maddock dragged his cloak across his face, as if he feared catching some deadly plague. The motion brought his wrist to rest against the edge of his woodstar, making its points dig into his chest.

Of course, he'd known that Alana Woodsinger would be watching what happened along the road. He'd just managed to block that surveillance from his conscious thoughts. Uneasily, he shifted from foot to foot, the nagging pain in his knee reminding him of *all* that the woodsinger had witnessed. She would know that he had let Landon lead the rescuers for days. She would know that Maddock had failed in his first pitched battle. Even now, she might be recounting his failure to the Women's Council. She might be saying that he was a coward and a fool, that he had let Jobina walk into a snake pit by herself.

Biting back a curse, Maddock edged past an ocean

of golden cloth that frothed about the mattress, clear remnant of some ornate gown or tunic. He stepped near enough that he could make out Maida's frail chest rising painfully. Her lungs seemed barely to expand with the supreme effort of breathing. Even as Maddock strained to hear the faintest rattle of air in her throat, he made out the sound of soft sobbing.

Reade knelt beside the bed, his head lowered to the pallet. His narrow shoulders shook as he wept. Gone was the mischievous child who accepted any dare, the proud huer who had guided grown men to their first fishing harvest of the season. Reade was a forlorn child, a waif far from home.

"If you can't quiet your sobs, Sun-lord, I'll dose you from the cup."

Maddock glanced at Duke Coren, bristling at the steady tone of command that ignored the child's distress. The man wore the same cursed armor that had fascinated the naive villagers on the Headland of Slaughter, the golden sun dripping with blood from a crimson-sheathed knife. The same beard framed his thin lips; the same eyes glinted like steel in the warrior's lean face. Now, though, there was a bared intensity in the man's visage, a ravenous focus. If Coren had dared to show such a vicious gaze to the people of Land's End, he never would have been welcomed into their hearts and homes.

Maddock closed his fist over his bavin. How had Alana come to sing a woodstar for the duke? How had the People been taken in by a handful of beads and a few slivers of glass? What were they thinking when they sold themselves so cheaply?

At least Maddock was spared watching the duke carry out his threat. At Coren's even words, Reade fell utterly silent. For a moment, Maddock thought it odd that the child did not look up at the newcomers, but then the warrior felt Alana's presence, felt the woodsinger's thoughts brushing across his own bavin as she focused on the woodstar still strung about Reade's neck. The power of the Tree resonated across the knot of its heartwood, and Maddock sensed the pressure on Reade to keep his face buried in the dingy sheets.

Unnerved by the woodsinger's invisible power, Maddock forced his own gaze back to Maida. Her face was much thinner than he remembered; she had clearly missed meals along the road. Her hair was matted, tangled in sweaty strands against her face. Red blotches stood out on her skin, as if she had rolled in fevergrass, and her breath remained shallow.

"How long has she been like this?" Jobina's words were twisted by a fair approximation of an inland brogue.

"One full day," one of the warriors answered at a nod from the duke. "The fever came on suddenly; she woke with it this morning. She's had a hard journey— she hasn't eaten well since we saved her from the beasts at Land's End."

With awkward hands, the soldier moved to bathe his patient's face. Jobina, though, clicked her tongue and stepped forward. "You'll only give her a chill with that filthy water. Innkeep!" The fat man oozed into the doorway, keeping as much of his corpulence from the room as possible, as if he feared to contract Maida's illness. "I'll need hot water, as hot as you can get it to me. And soak some bread in milk. She'll need the sustenance if she pulls out of this."

The ostler waved a fat hand toward a half-seen servant girl, and the child went running, the echo of her small feet underscoring the urgency of Jobina's commands. The healer bit her lip and shook her head. Gone was the vixen of Land's End, the flirtatious wench who had treated Maddock's burns. Cloistered behind her braided hair and close-gathered cloak, Jobina was another woman entirely.

Maida had only suffered through a half dozen breaths when the hot water appeared. Jobina had already rummaged in her bags, extracting some dried, crumpled leaves that were bound tightly in white linen. When she tossed the dusty greens into the water, the smell was immediate and sharp. The leaves contained the memory of salt on wind-seared grass, and the odor prickled the back of Maddock's throat.

The soldier-medic who had tended Maida jerked back from his charge, and Reade's raven head burrowed deeper into the sheets. Jobina leaned over her patient, her movements tight and controlled.

She held the fragrant bowl beside Maida's head, watching as the steam curled around the child's bleached face. For one moment, the little girl remained oblivious, apparently lost in her merciful dreams. Then, her nose twitched at the familiar ocean harshness; her lips trembled. Jobina moved the herbs closer, forcing the steam into the child's next labored breath. Every watcher in the room caught his own breath in fear and wonder, and then Maida was coughing—deep, hearty coughs.

Jobina waited until the child had caught her breath, and then she brought the potent bowl forward again, forcing the smooth edge against her patient's parched and broken lips. She tilted the liquid with an expert's hand, simultaneously cradling the semiconscious neck with confident fingers. One labored swallow, another scarcely managed, then a third and fourth in rapid succession.

Jobina barely stepped back before Maida broke into renewed coughing, a body-deep hack that shook the pallet on which she lay. Each gasp brought color back to the child's face, forcing blood into her chilled fingers and toes, curling her limbs into living appendages.

Maida began to thrash about on the bed, moaning and crying out. Maddock caught the words "whipping" and "Reade." Even as he wondered what terrors she must have witnessed, what horrors had driven her into her fevered world, Jobina forced more of the healing potion down Maida's throat. As Maddock stared in astonishment, the little girl's eyes snapped open, and she cleared her throat twice before croaking, "Food."

Jobina's hand was soothing on her brow, and if the healer was relieved that Maida did not recognize her, she gave no sign. "Aye, little one. You shall have your supper." And then a tavern wench materialized with milky bread in a wooden bowl. Jobina reached for the watery stuff, ready to feed her patient, but Coren put out a hand to stop her.

"Sun-lord." The duke spoke with a stunning intensity. Reade looked up, blinking tears from his eyes. "Sun-lord, the Sun-lady needs you now. She needs your help."

Reade got to his feet shakily, keeping his attention fixed on the duke. For one incredulous instant, Maddock felt power surge over his bavin, rush past him to Reade's woodstar. He sensed Alana Woodsinger pinning the child's gaze on the nobleman, giving the rescuers a chance to escape undetected. Maddock caught his breath, as if even that slight motion might be enough to disrupt the bavin's power. Reade, apparently unaware of Alana's energy stretching through the carved woodstar, waited until Coren jutted his chin toward the bowl that Jobina held. The child turned to the healer, and he reached for the milky bread.

The boy blinked as if emerging from a trance, and a frown creased his brow. His free hand rose, ghost-like, to the leather thong about his neck. He shuddered, and then he dropped the woodstar. "Jobina!" His clear soprano cut through the room as his eyes darted toward the door. "Maddock! Have you come to take us back?"

Coren's soldiers were well trained. They may have just witnessed a miracle in Maida's salvation, but there was scarcely a heartbeat of hesitation before they grabbed Jobina. Bread and milk spilled over the bed, splashing across Maida's chest. The healer twisted like a whirlpool, screaming, "Run, Reade! Run to Maddock!"

The child hesitated, though, glancing at Duke Coren. Maddock read volumes in that one look. Reade was asking for permission, looking for leadership. Maddock swore a foul curse and grabbed the boy's arm, jerking him across the bed and heading toward the stairs. Reade was startled, but he managed to fight back with teeth and pummeling fists. Maddock continued to swear as he bustled the desperate child down the steps.

The crowd in the common room looked up in astonishment as the pair hurtled into the room. Maddock's curses turned to a bellow as Reade caught the man's fingers between strong teeth, breaking the warrior's skin as he ground his jaws together. "Wind-cursed bastard!" Maddock hollered, even as he heard Coren's men behind him on the stairs, even as he recognized the ominous scrape of steel on steel, of swords clearing their sheaths.

Landon waited at the foot of the stairs, and Reade tumbled into the tracker's arms as Maddock leaped clear of the steps. The gangly tracker fell backward beneath the child's twisting weight, and man and boy alike were tangled in golden cloth. Maddock glimpsed the soldiers pulling up as each tried to distinguish a safe opening for his thirsty blade. The snarls in the soldiers' throats were like the angry roar of a pack of dogs.

Maddock drew his own sword, pivoting painfully on his injured knee. The common room had turned to chaos. Townsfolk cowered under tables, desperate to avoid the flash of iron weapons. Reade's screams were piercing, and Landon wrestled with the child as if the boy were a sea serpent. Coren's soldiers searched for room to swing their weapons.

Above the chaos, Maddock locked his eyes on

Donal, saw the man hook his fingers in the corners of his mouth. The common room was filled with a series of piercing whistles. "Crusher!" the soldier bellowed. "Thunder!"

Maddock heard the dogs before he saw them. One howled like a wolf, and others set to baying as they ran. There was a scrabble of claws on wood, and a huge beast crashed through the inn's door, ripping leather hinges and sending the oak planks crashing back against the wall. While Donal had only named two of the creatures, they came as a pack, the same snarling beasts that had terrorized the People on their beach.

Conditioned to terror, Maddock's heart froze beneath his bavin; his fingers grew clammy and weak on his sword hilt. These Guardian-forsaken animals were killers. They would tear him limb from limb. He still had the smell of the ostler's stew on his breath; the dogs would rip out his throat where he stood.

Even as one of the dogs tore its way toward Donal, another leveled red eyes on Maddock. The beast slung its belly low to the ground and tensed the tremendous muscles in its haunches. Its growl was deep in its throat, almost below the level that Maddock could hear.

He could smell the animal, though, and he could imagine those knife-teeth ripping at him. Even as he sensed strength pouring through his bavin, even as he felt Alana Woodsinger tugging at his mind, Maddock threw himself past the dogs, hurtling through the tavern door and into the velvet night.

He did not realize that the dark air was cold as his lungs screamed for mercy. He did not realize that his horse was shuddering as he pulled himself onto the gelding's back. He did not realize that the road was rutted as he spurred his mount into the dark. The sheltering night closed in upon him, cutting off the noise of the embattled inn and the howling dogs and the bellowing soldiers and the high-pitched scream of a terrified young boy.

9

Alana fought not to wrinkle her nose against the odor in Goody Glenna's hut. The still, stale smell whispered of death. "Over here, child," the old woman greeted her, summoning her to the hearth.

Teresa lay on a pallet beside the open flames. Alana caught her breath, shocked at the change in the woman. The young mother's skin was a pasty white, her lips almost purple in her pale, pale face. Like her daughter leagues away, she had been perspiring with fever, and her hair straggled beside her cheeks in desperate tendrils. Even now, she gasped for breath, and her teeth chattered as if she were caught in a snowstorm in the dead of winter.

"Teresa!"

The young mother grasped at the woodsinger's skirts, pulling her nearer to the fire. "Please! Tell me about my children! How are my Reade and Maida?"

Alana glanced at Goody Glenna just long enough to catch the old woman's tiny shake of her head. Not the full story, then. "I've been watching them, Teresa."

"And are they safe?" The mother sounded like a starving woman begging for a crust of bread.

It was wrong for a woodsinger to lie, to offer up false words to the People. Alana reached quickly for her sister woodsingers, asking them what she should say.

"Woodsingers do not lie," confirmed one of the voices in her mind immediately.

"*I* did not lie, even when I told three women their husbands were lost at sea."

"Aye, you did not lie, but one of those women hanged herself in her cottage, and another lost the babe she was carrying."

"That was not my fault! Woodsingers do not lie!"

Alana wanted to cry out at the squabbling hordes in her head, scatter them as if they were a flock of clucking chickens. Instead, she drew a deep breath and forced a smile into her voice, even as she crafted a story for Teresa. "Your children are fine. Reade and Maida are safe and sound."

"Don't make up tales!" Teresa's claw closed around Alana's ankle, grasping until the woodsinger was embarrassed enough to kneel beside the pallet, to fold Teresa's hands in her own.

"I'm not making up tales, Teresa." Alana forced her voice to be steady, firm like the Tree. She had to focus her response past the suddenly silent woodsingers in her own mind, past the surprise among her sisters as they apparently remembered that Alana had real problems to confront—living, breathing people who needed her guidance. Alana chose her reassurances carefully, making sure that every word was true. "The duke has been caring for Reade and Maida as if they were his own children. I swear by the Guardians, Duke Coren acts as if the twins are royalty in his inland court."

Teresa collapsed back onto the pallet, her breath coming in short gasps that might have been either sobs or grateful laughter. "Thank the Guardians for that. Thank the blessed Guardians." She muttered a prayer to the Great Mother, her voice scarcely audible as it rattled over her chapped lips. "And Maddock? Will he bring my babies soon?"

Alana swallowed hard, certain that the truth about

Maddock's cowardice would destroy this poor woman. Before she could pick out the threads of another deceiving truth, Goody Glenna stepped forward. "Teresa, you demanded to speak with Alana about the twins, and I gave way to you in that. You must sleep, now. You promised me that you would rest after we got the news." The old woman produced a mug from somewhere and dosed her patient with sweet-smelling tea. "Sleep, Teresa, and let the woodsinger return to her post."

"Sleep . . . Yes, that would be good," Teresa murmured, her eyes already closed, her face relaxed. "My brave Reade . . . My sweet, sweet Maida . . ."

Goody Glenna guided Alana toward the door. Pulling the woodsinger's cloak closer about the younger woman's shoulders, Glenna bit back a sigh. "It's as bad as all that, then?"

"Worse, Goody Glenna," Alana whispered. "Maddock ran like a child—"

"Hush. I don't want Teresa to hear." Glenna pulled Alana outside the cottage.

"Goody, I managed to reach Maddock. He felt me through his bavin, when I reminded him to climb the stairs. I've become better at this, but I still didn't know enough."

"Enough for what?"

"Enough to give him courage. Goody, he deserted the others! He was afraid of the dogs, and he fled the inn! He left the twins, and Landon, and Jobina, even though I tried to keep him there. I tried to make him stand and fight! I tried, but he ignored me. Goody, I *hate* him! I hate him, and his cowardice, and his running away like a child!"

Goody Glenna's lips tightened, and for an instant, Alana thought the old woman would have no response. Then, she shook her head, stepping quickly into her cottage. When she came out, she handed the woodsinger a small packet, bound up in cloth. "Make a tea with this, child, and drink it tonight. Drink all of it, even the dregs, before you reach out for Maddock's bavin. It will help to clarify your thoughts."

"*My* thoughts are perfectly clear! Didn't you hear anything I said? Maddock, the man we've pinned all our hopes on, is a coward!"

"Listen to your elders, woodsinger!"

Alana's retort was on her lips, heated by her anger, by her fear, by her nagging guilt that she had not done right by the rescuers. Before she could speak her hurtful words, though, the other voices chorused in her head: "She's only afraid herself, woodsinger."

"She speaks out of fear, not anger."

"She works for the good of the People."

"She works for the good of Teresa."

Alana heard her sister woodsingers' soothing voices, and she let those crooned words calm her own rage. She could not bring herself to speak, though. She could not humble herself in front of Goody Glenna when she knew that *she* was right.

The voices in Alana's mind tsked and scolded. Before she could make herself give in to Goody Glenna, though, the old woman softened her own voice. "Get back to the Tree, Alana. Check on the children. Teresa does not have much longer to wait."

Alana clutched the sack of herbs that Goody Glenna had thrust upon her, and she walked directly back to the Headland. As she climbed the path to the Tree, she wondered at Goody Glenna's words. Did Teresa not have long to wait because the twins were about to be freed? Or did Teresa not have long to wait because the deadly pallor of her skin hid a darker tale?

The woodsingers inside her mind, though, had no answer to those questions. No answers to Alana's questions, and no advice for the young woodsinger. The only thing the ancient women whispered was that nobody could live with the fever that pulsed behind Teresa's pained, crystal eyes, not for long. . . .

Even before Alana was comfortable beneath the Tree, she stretched her consciousness toward Reade's bavin.

Reade watched Maida stretch beside Donal's horse. They'd left the inn at sunrise, and now the sun was halfway to noon. Maida had been awake all that time. She was still weak from her strange fever, but she hadn't cried all morning. She hadn't even asked for a special break. Mum would be proud of her.

It had been four days since Maida's fever had broken. They had spent an extra day at the place where Maida had gotten sick, waiting and waiting and waiting while Duke Coren ordered his men to track down Maddock. Other soldiers tied up Landon and Jobina, making sure that Reade and Maida were safe. Even knowing that the outlanders could not harm him, could not carry him back to the Tree, Reade had had nightmares that night. He thought he saw his own blood poured over the Tree's twisted roots.

Even now, in the middle of the day, it was hard to remember that those nightmares were not real. He was safe from his dreams. He was safe from Landon and Jobina. The duke would protect him from Maddock. Duke Coren would protect him from everything, protect both Reade and Maida.

Reade was a little embarrassed that the People had fooled him for so long. Of course, they had fooled Mum, too. Mum could not have known what Alana Woodsinger planned. She could not have known that Reade would be tied to the Tree's roots, that the woodsinger would come after him with her iron dagger. . . . That was why Da had left! He must have found out what Alana Woodsinger was going to do. He'd been ready to fight to save Reade and Maida, to stop the Tree from drinking the twins' blood. That was why the Guardians had taken Da away.

Reade was grateful that Duke Coren explained things. He answered Reade's questions, even when Reade forgot and asked the same things twice, or even three times. Over and over, the duke told how Maddock and Landon and Jobina were very evil, rotten to the core like a sick tree. That was why the three adults had disguised themselves, sneaking into the inn. If the People had had good intentions, they would have walked upstairs like everyone else, spoken with the duke like other grown-ups, shown some respect. The People should never have drawn steel inside a roadhouse, threatening to harm innocent villagers. They shouldn't have forced Donal to call the terrible dogs.

Once, Reade pointed out that Jobina had come upstairs to *save* Maida. Duke Coren, though, had only shaken his head and sighed. Reade realized that he had disappointed the duke. After all of Reade's questions, after all of Duke Coren's answers, Reade should have understood. Luckily, the duke had the patience to explain one more time, to tell Reade that Jobina had meant to *hurt* Maida, had meant to poison her.

Duke Coren's voice stayed quiet and calm, even though Reade was being stupid. Even Da had not been patient like Duke Coren. And Mum . . . Well, there was no need to think about Mum. Not now.

Now, stretching his own legs after their morning of riding, Reade realized that he was thirsty. He wandered away from the soldiers to the stream that ran beside the road. He had learned to drink upstream from the horses, above the mud that the animals churned up with their feet. He had to lie down on the riverbank to get close enough to cup his hands. The water was very cold.

When he wasn't thirsty anymore, he turned around to find his sister. Maida had already curled up against a boulder. She was fast asleep. That wasn't right!

Maida was acting like she had drunk from Duke Coren's golden cup. She shouldn't be tired yet! Maybe Reade should find Duke Coren and ask whether Maida was still sick.

Before he could find the duke, though, Reade saw Landon. The tracker looked like a ragged bear. He didn't have a lot of hair, but what he had was sticking out from his head at all angles, as if he'd never even heard of a comb. His beard had grown in, but it came in patches, scraggly like plants that tried to grow beneath oak trees in the forest.

A large bruise stood out across the tracker's cheek, and Reade remembered that the soldiers had needed to beat Landon into silence that very morning. If they weren't punishing him for speaking at the wrong times, they were beating him for *not* speaking. Just the day before, Landon had refused to tell Duke Coren the color of the horse that Maddock had ridden from the Headland of Slaughter.

Landon wasn't very smart. He didn't realize that when Duke Coren asked him to do something, he should do it, well and quickly. Reade was smarter than the tracker. Landon only thought he was smart, because he was friends with Alana Woodsinger.

Alana Woodsinger! Duke Coren had told Reade that the woodsinger was only a girl pretending to be a priestess. Reade had listened when Duke Coren explained that the woodsinger did not have as much power in her entire body as the High Priest of the Seven Gods had in his beard. The duke had even promised that Reade would meet the priest, once they got to Smithcourt.

Reade realized that his fingers had closed around his bavin when he thought of the woodsinger. He let go of the woodstar with a snort of disgust. What was he, some sort of baby? He didn't need a silly piece of wood to protect him. He should just throw the stupid thing away, get rid of it, like he had his Great Mother.

He reached for the leather thong, but just as he lifted it over his head, Landon opened his eyes. For a moment, the tracker just looked tired. Then, Reade saw something else in his gaze. He looked . . . sharp. Like he was plotting something evil.

"What are you doing, Reade?"

"I'm the Sun-lord," Reade said. "You have to call me that." His fingers closed around the bavin. He didn't want the tracker to look at it.

Landon snorted. "Aye, Sun-lord." How did one conspiring rebel make Reade's title sound so silly? "Conspiring rebel . . ." Reade liked the sound of that—he had heard the duke call Maddock and Landon and Jobina all conspiring rebels. It sounded worse than anything Mum had ever called anyone in the village. Now, Landon refused to mind his tongue: "But what are you doing?"

"Why do you care?" Reade scuffed his toes in the dirt. "You're not my da."

"No, Reade. Your da was a brave man who went to the Guardians too soon."

"You don't know anything about my da!" Reade started to raise his voice, but realized that the soldiers would hear him, would order him to step away from the prisoner. Well, Reade was smart enough to talk to a prisoner. Reade wasn't just a stupid child from the Headland. He was the Sun-lord, and he could talk to any prisoner he pleased.

"I know about your da, boy. I know that he would be ashamed of you, wearing those golden robes, parading around like a Smithcourt prince."

"My da was *proud* of me! My da was going to take me out on his boat. We were going to bring in pilchards, all in nets, more than the People had ever seen in one haul!"

"You won't be doing any fishing now, will you, Reade?"

Anger hit Reade like an ocean wave. What did this

stupid man know? What did a chained prisoner know
about Reade's da, or what Reade would do when they
got to Smithcourt? What did a conspiring rebel know
about anything?

"I know one thing, boy," the tracker said, as if he
had read Reade's mind. "I know that your da would
not want you wearing that woodstar. He'd be ashamed
that any son of his defiled a bavin, a woodstar sung
by Alana Woodsinger herself. If he were here, he'd
pluck it from your neck himself, and send it down that
stream, rather than see it wasted on the likes of you."

Reade screamed without words, and he jumped on
top of the tracker, kicking and biting and trying to
pull his hair. It took only a moment for Duke Coren's
soldiers to come running, and then Landon had new
bruises all over his face, all over his arms and legs.
One of the soldiers smashed Landon's nose, and bright
blood splashed across the tracker's face.

As Duke Coren himself led Reade away, the boy
laid a triumphant hand on his woodstar. He'd show
Landon! He wouldn't let the woodstar out of his sight.

Later that morning, Reade caught the tracker staring at him. The man smiled crookedly, a smile that
was scary because of the bloodstains on his face. Stupid man. He didn't even know when he'd been beaten
by his betters. Reade kept his fingers on the bavin
until they stopped for lunch, well after noon.

As Reade brought Maida her bread and cheese, he
could not help but laugh at Landon. The man's hands
were tied so tightly that he had to lower his mouth to
his fingers to eat. Reade pointed out the tracker's
problem to Maida. She did not find Landon quite as
funny as Reade did. Well, Maida never understood
the true meaning of things. She never knew what it
meant to be a grown-up. Duke Coren had never called
her a little lady, the way he'd called Reade a little
man.

One of Duke Coren's soldiers came to take away

Reade and Maida's tin plates. "Give those here," he growled. The man was not Mikal, their usual guard, and Reade almost decided not to give back his plate. Maida did, though, but before the man could walk away, she screwed her face up into a pout and crossed her arms over her narrow chest. "Where's Mikal?" she demanded.

"He's gone back along the road. His Grace told him to find that mongrel from your home."

"What's a mongrel?"

"A dog. The cursed fool who ran away from the inn."

"Maddock?" Maida shook her head. "Mikal won't catch him. Maddock will be riding a very fast horse."

The soldier turned on Maida very fast, making Reade think of a gull swooping down to catch a fish. "A fast horse? And what color would that horse be?"

"I don't know." Maida shrugged. Reade watched the soldier clench his hands into angry fists. Maybe Reade would have to step in and save his stupid sister. Again.

"What do you mean, you don't know?" the soldier snarled. "How many horses do you outlanders own? You can't have so many that you don't know what color *his* is."

"Maddock doesn't own *any* horse." Maida rolled her eyes. "Not like you do. None of the People own horses."

"What do you mean, you little . . ." The soldier took a step closer, but then Reade saw him remember that he was talking to the Sun-lady. The man swallowed hard, breathing out for a long time before he knelt before Maida. "What are you trying to tell me, girl? Will he be riding a fast horse or not?"

"Maida—" Reade realized that he needed to interrupt. He needed to keep Maida from answering the soldier. He grabbed at the woodstar around his neck. Even though it was on a long thread, even though it was nowhere near his throat, it felt like it was choking him. He held it tight in both his hands. "Maida, don't—"

The soldier went on, ignoring Reade's protest. "How can Maddock ride a fast horse if he doesn't even own one?"

"Maida!" It was *wrong* for Maida to talk to the soldier. She shouldn't tell Duke Coren's man about the People's horses. Reade had to stop her. He had to keep her from explaining, from saying anything else to the soldier.

"We *share.*" Maida glared at Reade as she emphasized the word. She sounded just like Mum, teaching Reade a lesson. "Maddock will have the fastest horse of all the People."

"And what color is that animal?" The soldier leaned forward.

"Maida—" Reade warned again, squeezing his bavin with urgency. She had to stop! She had to keep the People's secrets! Reade had to stop her from talking!

Maida, though, ignored her brother. She squinted across the clearing until she found Landon and Jobina's horses. "If Landon has the black stallion, and Jobina has the grey mare, then Maddock must have the bay gelding."

"Ha!" the soldier exclaimed, and he pounded his fist on the ground. Before Maida could say anything else, the man stood up and ran across the clearing to Duke Coren.

At the same time, Reade glared at his sister. "You shouldn't have said that, Maida."

"What? I'm allowed to talk to the soldiers, too! You may be the Sun-lord, but I'm the Sun-lady."

Reade wanted to explain to her. He wanted to tell her that she was wrong to talk about Maddock's horse. The more he thought about it, though, the less he could remember about why they should keep that secret. He let go of his woodstar, and he was surprised to see tiny spots of blood on his hands. He raised a finger to his lips, sucking at the hurt.

Reade had been silly to worry about Maddock's horse. What was so special about a stupid old horse? Besides, why should he try to protect Maddock? Duke Coren had told Reade all the terrible things that the outlander had done. Maddock had stolen from the peasants in the villages. He had threatened to kill boys and girls.

Reade wished he still had his Great Mother, so that he could pray for Duke Coren's men to *catch* Maddock. As the duke had said many times, the People could only be shamed by a common criminal like Maddock. *If* the People were able to feel any shame at all, the duke always added. After all the terrible things that they had done, that they planned to do. . . .

Even knowing that Maddock rode the bay gelding, Duke Coren's men weren't able to catch the outlander that day. Reade was disappointed. He wanted Maddock to be caught. He wanted Maddock to be punished for frightening him, for dragging him down the stairs in the tavern, for leaving him surrounded by Duke Coren's dogs in the common room.

As the days went on and the riders got closer to Smithcourt, Reade watched the soldiers punish Landon more and more often. He broke so many rules that the soldiers finally refused to untie his hands for anything. Anything! Reade felt a rush of power pump through his chest when he saw Landon's stained leggings. Served Landon right, for trying to talk Reade into throwing away his bavin, back on the riverbank.

At least once a day, Landon broke another rule. He talked back to the duke, or he refused to get back on his horse after a rest stop. Each time he was bad, he was punished. Reade shook his head, wondering how the man could be so stupid. Didn't he know that he'd be beaten? Didn't Landon know that Duke Coren was in charge?

Jobina Healer understood the rules. She did exactly as she was commanded, every time one of the soldiers issued a gruff order. When one of the men told her to kneel before he would give her a bit of bread, she fell down on her knees immediately. She twisted around, though, moving in a way that Reade had never seen before, certainly not the way Mum moved, when she knelt to put wood on the fire back home. When another soldier told Jobina to get on her horse, she immediately crossed to her grey mare. She couldn't grab the high pommel, though, not with her hands tied together. Three men stepped forward to help her mount.

Reade was a little surprised at how much help Jobina got from the soldiers. Every one of the men—even Duke Coren—took the opportunity to guard Jobina, even Donal. Because she minded her manners, she was treated better than Landon.

There was even one afternoon when Jobina called out for the company to halt. All of the soldiers reined in their horses. As Reade looked back, he saw the healer point out a stand of herbs, growing just beside the road. She blushed bright red, and her voice was soft as she told the soldiers it was called "sailors' jig." She told the men that it would bring them new life, and she even offered to brew the herbs at their next stop.

Reade didn't understand why Duke Coren laughed at her words. The other men were excited; some of them poked their friends in the ribs as they helped the healer dismount and mount again. Reade didn't understand, but he enjoyed the break in riding.

Once, they pulled into an inn's stable yard, and Donal came back from negotiating their rooms with a grin on his face. He announced that the innkeeper had an extra chamber, a tiny closet down the hall, too small for sleeping. One of the soldiers called out that there'd be no sleeping done in that room, and Jobina laughed with the men. When Landon was hustled past Reade and Maida, though, he was muttering under his breath. He sounded like old Goodman Jendo, like a man gone mad, and Reade caught a word his mum would never let him use. Once again, the tracker was beaten into silence. Landon was stupid.

Unlike the tracker, Reade enjoyed their days on the road. He almost forgot they were riding to reach Smithcourt. One morning, when they left their tavern, the men were telling lots of stories, laughing at lots of jokes. One soldier told how he was going to spend the silver coins that Duke Coren was going to give them. The group got to the top of a hill as the road curved. When Reade looked up, he was so surprised that he shouted out loud. Without thinking, he reached down to clutch at Duke Coren's mailed arm.

"Yes, Sun-lord?" There was a smile in the duke's voice.

"It's gigantic, my lord!" There was a city spread out before them on the plain. Not a village, not even a town. It was a *city,* with walls and towers and endless buildings, stretching on and on and on.

"It's the most magnificent city in all the world," Duke Coren said.

Crystal sparkled in the morning light. Some of the towers were much taller than the Tree, stretching up into the sky. The city walls were built of giant stones, and the tops of the walls marched up and down, like stairs. Smithcourt was bigger than anything Reade had imagined, than anything he'd ever dreamed of.

Reade ducked his head, feeling as shy as when the Spirit Council quizzed him on the Guardians' ways, back at the Headland of Slaughter. "Do we have to go there, Your Grace? Do we have to ride into the city?" Reade looked up at Duke Coren and tried to smile, tried to pretend that he had just had a brilliant idea. "Why don't I just stay with you out here, outside the walls?"

Duke Coren looked down at him, his eyes suddenly serious. "This is why I saved you, Sun-lord. This is why I took you and the Sun-lady from your home of exile. To bring you to Smithcourt, your home of truth."

"Please, Your Grace," Reade whispered. "I'm afraid."

Duke Coren caught Reade's chin between his fingers and leaned close enough that Reade could feel the ends of his beard. "Listen to me, Sun-lord. You must never be afraid! Fear is a luxury for people too weak or too stupid to rise above their emotions. You are destined for great things, Sun-lord. Your story was told at the dawn of this age, and it will be spoken by men and women far into the next one. If you wish to attain all your power and glory, you must not be afraid."

But I *am* afraid, Reade wanted to say. I'll get lost in your city, and I'll say the wrong things. I'll do something wrong, and people will laugh at me. Grown people, like your own man, Donal. I don't want to be the Sun-lord. I just want to be Reade, from the People. I want my mum!

"Do you understand me, Sun-lord?" Duke Coren stared into Reade's eyes. He was angry, almost as angry as he had been when Reade had thrown away his Great Mother. Reade remembered the lash across his back, the stinging pain as the duke punished him. He had been able to stand that pain. He'd been very brave. He'd been a little man. Duke Coren pinched his fingers closer around Reade's chin and shook the boy's head. "You must answer me, Sun-lord! Your answer is more important than anything that has gone before, than anything you have yet said or done. Do you understand me? The Sun-lord must show no fear!"

"I understand, Your Grace." Reade pulled his head away. The motion made his woodstar flop on his chest, and he caught it in his right hand. As he closed his

fingers around the bavin, he remembered stories that
Mum used to tell him, stories where men swore oaths
after putting their hands on the most valuable thing
they owned. "Your Grace, by this woodstar that was
given to you by Alana Woodsinger, I understand what
you said, and I will not be afraid." The words were
like magic—Reade felt powerful and strong as he
said them.

Duke Coren reached out to tousle Reade's hair.
"By your woodstar . . . Now there's an oath your
woodsinger would love to hear."

There was something scary in the way Duke Coren
spoke the words, like he was growling. All of a sudden, Reade thought of Winder, one day when the
older boy had been caught by Goody Glenna, pouring
oil over a mangy cat. Winder had been about to light
the oil, to set the cat on fire. When Goody Glenna
dragged Winder to the common, all the boys had come
to watch. All the People heard Winder argue with his
elders, explain that he hadn't meant any harm. Reade
had seen the fire in Winder's eyes, though. Reade
wasn't fooled.

Now, Duke Coren blinked, and Reade wondered
what he could have been thinking. He was talking to
Duke Coren, not to some silly boy in a village on the
edge of the sea. Duke Coren would never harm a cat.
Duke Coren would only help the Sun-lord, and the
Sun-lady, too.

The duke smiled tightly. "You will not be afraid,
Sun-lord. And to remind yourself of that fact, you
might repeat, 'By the power of the Sun-lord, by the
faith of the Sun-lady, by the strength of Culain, I will
not be afraid.' "

" 'By the power of the Sun-lord . . .' " Reade began,
liking the rhythm of the words. He couldn't remember
all of them, though.

" 'By the faith of the Sun-lady,' " Duke Coren repeated. " 'By the strength of Culain.' "

" 'I will not be afraid.' " Reade nodded as he completed his pledge. The words felt good. They felt right. They made him want to sit straight in the saddle. He grinned at Duke Coren; then the entire company of soldiers began to ride down to Smithcourt.

Reade chanted Duke Coren's magic words to himself many times that day. First, Duke Coren dug his heels into his stallion's sides. The horse galloped down the hill, faster than he'd ridden anywhere on the road, faster even than when Reade had pulled him into the farmer's field.

After that terrifying ride, Reade had to pass through the Smithcourt gates. Fierce guards glared down at him, their eyes looking cruel beneath their iron helmets. Some of the men wore armor with Coren's knife on it, and they smiled at their lord and cheered. There were other soldiers, though, soldiers who did not smile at all. The scariest ones wore blue armor, and they had silver dragons that twisted across their chests.

Even after they entered the city, there were frightening sights. Crowds filled the streets, pressing in close to Duke Coren's men. Reade told himself that he should not be afraid of the cheering people. Many of them waved golden cloth above their heads, cloth like the fabric of Reade's Sun-lord robes. Those people called out Duke Coren's name, as if he were the first fisherman to bring in full nets.

There were frightening people in the crowd, though. There were men and women with burns on their faces, brands that puckered their skin. One man bellowed without a tongue in his mouth. There were children, too; children who were even scarier than the grownups. Reade saw them huddled in doorways, like piles of rags that someone had left behind. One girl, hardly older than Maida, shivered in front of a building. Her dress was torn off her shoulders, and Reade saw blood on her legs, creeping past her dirty fingers. Reade looked away fast, but then his eyes fell on an old woman who was stealing a crust of bread from a little boy, from a child even younger than he was!

I will not be afraid, he reminded himself. The Sunlord is not afraid.

It was also frightening, though, to hear the cheers change after Reade and the duke, after Maida and Donal rode by. The people started shouting at Landon and Jobina as they were dragged through the streets.

The tracker and the healer were forced to walk beside their horses because Duke Coren had said that he could not trust them if they were mounted. Their hands were tied to the pommels on their saddles, making it awkward for them to walk. Sometimes, Jobina stumbled because her horse walked too fast, and she was dragged for a pace or two. The healer's brown robes were stained and torn, almost as dirty as Landon's clothes.

Reade thought it was a little strange that a nobleman, a *duke,* would not stop to help a lady. He soon learned, though, that a little dirt was nothing. As the group rode through the streets, Reade smelled rotten vegetables. When he craned his neck to look behind Duke Coren, he saw that both Landon and Jobina were pelted with brown, slimy cabbages, spoiled from a winter of storage. The smell got worse as women leaned out of high windows above the street, emptying slop buckets that splashed on the cobblestones, on the horses, and on Landon and Jobina. Reade breathed a prayer to the Guardians, grateful that he did not need to walk through the stinking, rotten mess behind him. He tried to breathe through his mouth.

By the time they arrived at Duke Coren's palace, Reade's eyes burned with the effort to open wide, to stare at all there was to see. The palace gates were of the blackest iron, thick as tree branches. Reade gaped as a soldier stepped forward, wearing red and gold. The man had Duke Coren's sign on his chest, a giant knife that dripped blood on a golden sun. The guard lifted a tremendous sword, the largest weapon that Reade had ever seen. The man had to use both hands to hold it, and his arms trembled with the effort. Duke Coren accepted his soldier's salute from horseback, clenching a fist across his own mailed chest.

"Your Grace," the guard said. "All Smithcourt rejoices at your safe return." Then, the guard turned to Reade. "Sun-lord. Be most welcome in Smithcourt. Know that I and all my brethren will keep you safe from harm."

Reade could feel his cheeks burn bright red as everyone stared at him. Then, the man turned to Maida and repeated his greeting, honoring her as the Sun-lady. The soldier was so serious, he sounded like he was *praying*.

When the man turned back to Duke Coren and bowed low, Reade swallowed hard. He wanted to show the duke that he understood how special it was to be the Sun-lord. He made his hand into a fist, like he'd seen Duke Coren do, and he put it on his chest, right above where his heart beat. He looked down as the soldier straightened up, and he said, "Thank you. The Sun-lady and I thank you for your welcome and . . . and your sword."

Duke Coren put his hand on Reade's shoulder, squeezing gently. Reade thought that his heart would burst, it pounded so hard. Duke Coren was proud of him! Reade had said the right thing!

The duke nudged his heels against his stallion's sides, and they rode through the gate, into the palace courtyard. White sand stretched out in a large square. There were soldiers standing everywhere, row after row. Everyone wore swords and armor. Coren's dripping knife was painted on the men's chests, and it was carved into one of the walls. A flag waved above the courtyard, the bright red knife snapping in the wind, along with a golden sun.

Duke Coren dismounted, but he didn't reach up to help Reade. Instead, Reade sat alone in the saddle. He felt like a baby on top of the giant horse, and he clutched the reins. He didn't know what he would do if the stallion decided to run away, but his fingers wanted to do something, anything.

"All hail the Sun-lord!" Duke Coren suddenly proclaimed in a deep voice, and Reade jumped. "All hail the Sun-lady!"

"Hail the Sun-lord! Hail the Sun-lady!" The soldiers shouted all together, as if they had practiced for days. Reade's ears rang with the sound of swords on shields, as the soldiers pounded their weapons in time with their shouts.

What was Reade supposed to do? Was he supposed to just sit there? Or was he supposed to make the stallion walk around the courtyard? Should he lead the men back out into the streets of Smithcourt? Were they all supposed to walk past the smelly mess from Landon and Jobina, back to the city gates with the silent, angry dragon guards?

Before Reade could decide, Duke Coren stepped forward and reached up for Reade, helping him down from the horse. Donal helped Maida to the ground.

Then, they walked through a cold, black arch, into a long hallway. Coren led the way, and Donal followed the children. Reade had never seen halls as long as this; he had never seen any building larger than a tavern.

The palace was dark inside. There were only a few torches that smoked against the walls and narrow windows at the very end of each hallway. The stone walls smelled like smoke and water, water that had been left standing for too long. As Reade turned one corner, he felt a small hand grasping for his own. Maida stepped up beside him, looking very pale.

"Reade, where are they taking us?"

"Wherever they want to," he responded. Maida's

lips trembled as she squeezed out a pair of tears. Reade sighed at how frightened girls could be. He was glad that he wasn't crying. Glad that he wasn't that afraid. "It's Duke Coren, Maida. Don't worry. He'll keep us safe."

"I'm scared," she whispered.

"You shouldn't be. You must have the faith of the Sun-lady."

"But, Reade—"

"The faith of the Sun-lady, Maida. I already have the power of the Sun-lord. And you know that Duke Coren has the strength of Culain."

Maida did not look like she believed him, but she stopped crying long enough for them to turn one more corner. Duke Coren stopped in front of a heavy wooden door. He bowed as he opened it and waved his hand so that the twins walked in. "Welcome, Sun-lord. Sun-lady. Welcome to Smithcourt. This will be your nursery. This will be your new home."

10

Alana lifted her mug of steaming tea and gazed out the door of her cottage into the night, wondering why she bothered to watch after the children, why she bothered to fight any longer.

She had not felt this hopeless since she'd been called upon to serve as woodsinger. Then she'd been reeling from worry and fear, knowing that Sarira Woodsinger had died, but not yet certain that her own father was lost. She'd been overwhelmed by the Spirit Council, the Men's Council, and the Women's Council, all making her come to the Tree, all pushing for her to become the next woodsinger. She had argued that she wasn't ready, that she wasn't qualified, that she wasn't right for the post, but they had ignored her. They had told her that the Tree would choose her or reject her, and she would have no say.

That was how she felt, watching Reade arrive in Smithcourt. She had no say. She could do nothing to stop the child, to make him step back from Coren, to make him remember the People who loved him, who missed him, who needed him here on the Headland.

She raised the mug to her face and breathed in the steam from her tea, trying to take some comfort from its warmth. As seen through Reade's eyes, Smithcourt was overwhelming. It was a sprawling city, so different from Land's End that Alana could scarcely comprehend its existence. The streets, the buildings, the hundreds of people . . . What could one woodsinger do against all of that? What could the Tree, the Guardians, even the Great Mother do against Coren's might?

Reade had fallen completely under Coren's sway, dragged into the duke's court by an unholy combination of lies and fear and awe. Maddock, who should have been the People's greatest hope, had fled in terror. Both of them were lost, despite her attempts to work through their woodstars. Reade and Maddock gone, and Landon and Jobina as well, who had not carried bavins. She should be grateful that she could not experience directly the tracker and the healer's decline.

The woodsinger stretched her aching back and raised her mug to her lips. As the fragrant steam swirled across her skin, she could smell mint, a traditional soothing plant. There were other things in the brew as well, things that she could not identify by scent. Shrugging, she swallowed Goody Glenna's gift.

Part of the mixture was expected: the tiny flowers of everwhite for clear sight and bitter acorn for strength. But there was a surprise as well—redshell for wakefulness. The tea contained so much of the ground nut that Alana knew that even now, even with her bone-deep weariness, she would not sleep for the rest of the night. And hidden beneath all those familiar flavors, lurking under the canopy of mint, there was a darker taste. Alana rolled it around on the back of her tongue and dipped her head to the mug twice more, yet still she could not identify it.

"Heartswell," whispered one of the woodsingers in her mind.

"Aye, heartswell," confirmed another. "Heartswell for passion."

"Heartswell for love!"

"Heartswell for a long night on rumpled sheets!"

The chorus of voices dissolved into laughter, and Alana felt a blush rise on her cheeks, hotter than the steam from her cup. These were *woodsingers* speaking to her. They were holy women. They weren't supposed to know of such things; they weren't supposed to joke.

Besides, she thought, purposely turning away from the good-natured chortling inside her thoughts, why should Alana need passion? What could Goody Glenna have been thinking? It was the woodsinger's fate to *sacrifice* passion, so that she could serve the People and the Tree with clear sight.

Even as she asked herself the question, Alana thought of her current responsibilities, of Maddock and his bavin. She saw the man standing on the village green, swinging his sword with his well-muscled arms. . . .

"Aye, fairsister!" One of the woodsingers teased, twisting ancient Parina's curious name for Alana until it sounded like a lewd promise. "Have another swallow! Drink down your tea and see what you can learn about the People you serve! Or people you would have serve you. Or should I say *service* you?"

The musky heartswell coated Alana's tongue, and her belly clenched in rebellion. How many times had Goody Glenna told the village girls that they must not pay attention to the boys, to Maddock in particular? How many times in the past year had Alana herself told giggling young women that they must concentrate on their stitchery, their gardens, their maidenly duties? Heartswell was the last herb she needed, the last distraction she should have as she tried to channel strength through the Tree. She turned to set the mug on the rough table by her hearth.

"Now, now," chided one of the woodsingers, a voice that Alana had always associated with motherly common sense. "You mustn't set aside the tea. We all heard what Goody Glenna said. You must drink the entire draught. Even the dregs."

"But—"

"We'll brook no arguments, young one. Drink up!"

"But I'm the *woodsinger*!"

"Aye. And heartswell grows in the woods. It's an herb like any other, and there's no shame in brewing it for a tea. Besides, you made a promise to one of your people. Would you be forsworn to her? Are you so afraid that you'd back away from a pledge, all to avoid a few swallows?"

Afraid? Alana? No—she was no coward. She was not like Maddock, who had fled at the sight of dogs. She was strong. She was brave. She was the woodsinger, not a mindless, giggling maid. She could swallow her medicine like a woman. That last thought made her think of Teresa, the young mother almost too weak to take any medicines at all.

Alana muttered a prayer to the Great Mother to watch over Teresa, to bring her peace and comfort. With a renewed determination, she realized that she *must* use the gift that Glenna had given her. She must use the wakefulness from the redshell tea to track Maddock, to find him in the wilderness and feed him strength. She would just ignore the heartswell.

She tilted her head back as she drained her stoneware mug, purposely not listening to the ribald chorus of woodsingers inside her head. The tea spread through her limbs like the warmth of a flesh-heated coverlet on a bitter winter night. Alana rolled the still-warm mug against her cheeks, held it against the pulse in her throat.

Only when the stoneware was cooler than her burning flesh did she settle her patched cloak about her shoulders. She could not pass the night indoors. Not in her woodsinger's hut, alone with a stack of dusty journals. She needed air. She needed to move her body. She needed to stretch and bend, to arch her back. . . .

By the time she reached the Tree, the tea's throbbing warmth had uncurled inside her fingers, her arms, in the depths of her belly. She leaned against the oaken trunk and gasped at the roughness of the bark, at the pull of the oak's woody fingers. She threw back her cloak, so that more of her body touched the Tree, pressed against its solid strength. She laughed out loud at one wry suggestion from a sister woodsinger— surely no self-respecting fisherman would ever let his nets be used for _that,_ even if one of the men ventured to the Headland on this moonless night!

Swallowing the musky aftertaste of heartswell and redshell, Alana fought to still her mind. She was certainly awake now, more awake than she had been in weeks. She could look across the land for days now; her body could not remember what it felt like to be lazy with sleepiness. She _wanted_ to look across the land; she wanted to stretch for Maddock's bavin.

Maddock . . . Alana caught her lower lip with her teeth, grateful that her thoughts could only be heard by her fellow woodsingers. Any other woman would cry out with shame, to hold such thoughts for a coward, for a man who had abandoned his fellows. Cry out . . . Alana could hear her own voice, coaxed from her throat, seduced by a long, hot kiss. . . .

The woodsinger forced her thoughts to stillness, forced her mind to stretch for the white thread that bound her to Maddock's distant woodstar. After all, she reminded herself, she had a mission here. She had business to complete. She needed to reach for Maddock's bavin, to find how the warrior fared, now that he rode alone. . . .

She made herself ignore the remembered rhythm of riding on horseback, ignore the sea of thoughts that crested in her mind, ignore the fire that burned beneath her flesh.

She must reach Maddock. She must check on the warrior, for the People. Not for herself. For the People.

"So, what'll it be, boy? Are you going to try your luck again?"

Sharks and fins! Maddock gritted his teeth as he clutched at the cloak that slid from his shoulders. His fingers caught in the leather strand that held his bavin about his neck. Alana Woodsinger might be watching him even now. He had not sensed her energy through the woodstar for several days now, but he did not trust his own knowledge. Maybe she had watched him all night, seen him dice away the last of his money and the clasp for his cursed cloak. Maybe she had watched him flee from that Guardian-forsaken inn, running from the pack of hounds that Coren's man had summoned.

Flushing, Maddock could see hunger in the ring of men that surrounded him, read it in their lean faces as they waited for him to decide. A pile of coins glinted in front of Wilson, the cursed rogue who had just spoken, and Maddock could not keep his eyes from the brooch that the other man had already attached to his own garment. The piece was fashioned from a fist-sized shell, and it spoke to Maddock with the People's loud condemnation, berating him for abandoning his fellows in the roadhouse, for skulking through the countryside, for squandering the coins that the People had entrusted to him on his mission.

As if to underscore the message, Wilson caught the silver in one large fist, feeding it coin by coin to the low wooden table. Next to the glittering pile were two dice, carved cubes with malevolent eyes that mocked Maddock, tempting him, luring him, even now. He had watched men dice in the taverns on his inland trading trips, but he had never tried his own luck before. He'd been a fool to try now—a fool and a cursed coward.

It was just that he was caught, stranded outside these Guardian-forsaken city walls. After fighting his way through the hostile countryside, dodging Coren's hunting soldiers, skulking like . . . like a dog . . . Maddock had arrived after dark, too late to sneak inside Smithcourt, to rescue the children and Landon and Jobina.

Mere luck had brought him to this particular campfire, to this huddle of soot-faced men who had offered him a friendly mug of ale and a spiced sausage. After an evening of their hospitality, Maddock began to understand how miserable old men could sit at tavern tables for hours, throwing pieces of bone as if the future of all the Guardians depended on the next cast. What did a little dicing matter, when Maddock had failed at everything else?

Even now, ominously certain that he had no coins left for food or drink or bribes, Maddock itched to toss the bones just one more time. Once more, and his luck might turn. He could gain back all the wealth he had lost, and more. He could come back to the People with Reade and Maida, Landon and Jobina, and an unlooked-for bonus—more silver than the People had ever seen in one place.

"I don't have anything else to wager," Maddock responded at last.

"No more coins, perhaps." Wilson smiled easily, picking up his cubes of bone. He rolled them around in one hand, caressing the smooth surfaces with a knowing thumb. Maddock had to force himself to look away from the creamy, compelling cubes, to gaze into the other man's sharp eyes. "No more coins, but you surely have other things to offer in trade. That mangy beast you call your horse, for instance."

Maddock glanced at the bay gelding, which stood

at the edge of the firelight. In the gloom, the horse's singed mane looked even worse than in daylight, and the animal's eyes gleamed red.

Sharks and fins! Even the horse was gazing at him with condemnation. When the beast snorted, Maddock almost believed that he could hear Sartain Fisherman demanding to know why he had left his fellows behind in the roadhouse. Once again, Maddock was aware of the bavin weighing against his chest, and now he was certain that Alana Woodsinger was watching him.

"I can't wager my horse!" Maddock protested.

"Of course you can," Wilson said. "Explain it to him, Lila."

Lila was Wilson's lady companion. She had watched the men all evening, scarcely taking her eyes from Maddock. At first, he had flushed under her frank inspection, but he had gradually grown accustomed to her hungry eyes. When she had refilled his borrowed leather mug for the third time, Maddock had been certain that she smiled just for him. Smiled, because she didn't know that he was a craven coward.

"Yes, Maddock," Lila spoke now. "It's your turn to have a little luck. It's your turn for the . . . dice to come your way." She hesitated only a moment, but he read volumes into her words. As if to confirm his thoughts of dice and more, the woman padded around Wilson, scooping up the bones on her way.

"It's just that the horse isn't mine. . . ."

"Isn't yours?" Lila crooned, and the threat of a frown creased her brow. "Whatever do you mean?" Lila held out her slender hand, and Maddock automatically reached for the carved cubes. He caught a whiff of sweet perfume from her hair as he closed his fingers over the trinkets of bone. She purred, "Have you made a habit of taking things that don't belong to you?"

"I—" He had to stop and clear his throat. "I borrowed him from a friend."

"Ahhh." Lila sighed, and she smiled softly before she looked across at Wilson. Maddock resisted the urge to reach out for the woman, to reclaim her attention for himself. "Well, if you haven't any more to gamble, then you must be on your way. What a pity, though. Just as your luck was certain to change. The horse would have been worth ten pieces of silver. But come along, Wilson." Lila reached out to take back the dice.

"No! Wait!" Maddock protested, and he was rewarded by Lila's gentle smile—her smile and her hand closing on his arm. Ten pieces of silver . . . "One more toss, then."

Lila's fingers pressed into his flesh, her eagerness barely restrained. Her words were so soft that he had to lean down to hear. "One more toss." Her repetition sounded like a promise.

Maddock squatted beside the flat board, closing his fist around the bits of bone. Breathing a prayer to all the Guardians, he shifted the bavin beneath his shirt, forcing himself not to think of Alana, not to think of the People waiting for him back at Land's End. Instead, he tried to forget all that had gone wrong, all of his mistakes since leaving the People. Exhaling explosively, he flung out his fingers, letting the dice soar. They clattered onto the board and spun for a moment before two eyes glared up at him, cursing him like a cancer from the smooth white bone.

"Too bad, boy." Wilson barely swallowed a chortling laugh. "What's the horse's name, so that he doesn't feel too lost away from home?"

The question inspired rough laughter from the ring of onlookers, and Maddock bristled.

"Aye, boy," one of the ruffians jeered through a greasy beard, "we wouldn't want the beast missing his master too much." The leering drunkard tugged at his trews suggestively.

Maddock glanced at Lila, embarrassed that she had to hear such vulgar jests. When a pretty flush stained her cheeks, his anger rose like high tide. His hand fell on the cross-hilt of his sword, and he stood to his full height. "Here, now! No need to be crude in front of the lady!"

"Lady!" Another of the rogues spluttered. "There's no lady by this fire! At least there wasn't till you arrived."

Laughter hooted among the ruffians, and Maddock's sword cleared his scabbard before he could measure the danger.

"Easy, boy," Wilson spoke into the sudden silence. "You're new to Smithcourt. You don't want trouble."

"I've had trouble enough, with you stealing my money and my horse."

"Those are harsh words, boy. No one has stolen anything. You chose to play a game or two, and the Seven Gods weren't watching over you tonight. Don't turn spilled grain into a famine, boy."

"I'm not a boy!" Maddock barked, and the gamblers cringed when he swept his sword around the semicircle.

"Certainly not." The two words came from Lila. "You're man enough to know when to set aside childish things."

Maddock's determination wavered as Lila took a step toward him. The firelight glinted through her skirts. "They're the ones who are childish," he muttered.

"Certainly," Lila said. "And there's no reason for us to waste any more time with them. Come along, Maddock. Come along with me, away from all these folk."

Maddock heard the promise in her voice, and he let her words pull him around the fire. Her fingers settled in the waistband of his trews, and his passion stirred, even as he leveled his sword against the gamblers. "Aye, Lila," he cast a challenge toward Wilson. "I'll take you away from the likes of these."

He kept the sword level as they backed away from the firepit. Lila's fingers became more insistent, and she scarcely waited until they had ducked behind a rough stack of hay bales before she was doing disturbing things with her fingers, her mouth, her hungry, hungry flesh. The woodstar began to burn against his chest, but its heat was quickly lost amid Lila's attentions.

Maddock twisted beneath the woman, managing to slide his sword into its scabbard. "Lila," he breathed, and she shook her head, her hair cascading about his face as she silenced him. Hay pricked through his shirt, and he closed his fists amid her skirts.

As he felt her willing flesh beneath his hands, he heard a clatter on the other side of the haystack. The bay gelding nickered nervously, and Maddock started to stand upright. "Wait," Lila gasped, and she emphasized her command by shifting beneath his stiffened fingers.

"My horse," Maddock said, fighting his distraction.

"He's not yours any longer." Lila knelt and reached for the lacing on his trews. Her hands were on his thighs, and then he felt her lips, hot and smooth. He threw his head back against the haystack and gave himself up to her ministrations.

His breath caught in his throat, and he forgot that he was miles from home, forgot that he was on a mission to save the twins, forgot that he was watched over by Alana Woodsinger. He forgot everything except the fact that he was a man, a trained body of tempered flesh and heated blood. Pulsing, pounding blood.

As crimson waves crashed behind his eyes, Maddock's gelding screamed in terror.

Panting, he put his hands on Lila's shoulders and thrust her away, ignoring her mewed protests. Scrambling at the lacing on his trews, he settled a hand on his sword hilt and peered around the hayrick to spy on the gamblers' firepit.

The scene was chaos. Soldiers had surrounded the gamblers, two armed men to every rogue. The captain of the guard bellowed over Wilson, "On your feet, outlander!"

Wilson clutched his right arm with his left; firelight glinted on the blood that spurted from a deep cut. The gambler said, "I'm telling you, man, I'm not the one you're looking for."

"Oh no," the guard snarled. "I can see that. You're wearing a brooch made of shell, you're counting coins from the outlands, and you've got a mangy dog for a horse. You couldn't be our man."

"I won them from the man you seek!" Wilson practically scraped the ground with his belly, he was so eager to please the captain. "Please, your honor, I diced with the man and beat him." As if to prove his point, Wilson edged a pair of bone cubes from the pouch at his waist, almost losing a hand to the guard's suspicious blade. "See! Look here, if you don't believe me!"

The captain gestured to one of his underlings, and a soldier came forward to take the dice. The man gave Wilson a sneering glance as he hefted the bits of bone, and he threw them three times in quick succession.

"So, you're a cheat and a liar, that's clear enough. These are trick dice," snarled the captain.

"A man's got to earn a living," whined Wilson, even as Maddock's rage snapped in his chest. Curse them all to a storm-tossed crossing! He'd been bilked out of his property, and he hadn't even suspected Wilson's duplicity. Maddock took a step toward the firepit, but Lila's hands grasped at his waist.

"You can't!" she whispered urgently.

"Whore!" He bit off the word. "You knew the entire time!"

"You can't go out there! They'll cut you down before you say two words, and then they'll come after me!"

Before Maddock could retort, the decision was taken from him. "Come along, the lot of you," the captain ordered. "You'll be enjoying Duke Coren's hospitality now."

It happened so quickly that Maddock was not certain who made the break for freedom. One moment, the gamblers were being driven toward the city gates, the captain manhandling the restless bay gelding on a short tether.

The next instant, someone bolted. The soldiers responded like the trained fighting men they were, leaping for their captives. When the frightened gamblers resisted, the soldiers used their blades. The smell of fresh blood maddened the already jumpy horse, which reared up and brought its sharp hooves down near the captain.

The fighting man swept up his sword reflexively, catching the gelding's well-muscled neck. The horse screamed once before falling to its knees, its blood pumping across the rough earth like a river broken through a dam.

Wilson was promptly sacrificed in the soldiers' desperate attempt to restore order, his body slit from groin to throat like a gutted fish. Another man forfeited a hand, and a third was hamstrung by a blade as sharp as any butcher's. Several of the men were knocked senseless by the iron hilts of swords and daggers.

Then, almost before Maddock could register what had happened, the remaining gamblers were hastened away. Four soldiers were appointed to watch over the wounded, the dying, and the dead. The horse shuddered for a few minutes and then lay still in a pool of spreading night-black crimson. Maddock felt his own blood drain from his face.

If not for Lila, he would have been dead or captured.

The woman seemed to realize the same. She stared at him with horror. "Who are you?" she whispered.

"I'm a boy from the outlands," he growled, forcing his eyes away from the destruction.

"What do Duke Coren's men want with you?" Her words trembled, and her full lips stood out against her flesh as if they were painted on.

Grimacing, he reached for the dagger stashed in his right boot. "Better that you not know that. You'll be able to claim innocence once you get me past the city gates."

"You're wanted by Duke Coren!"

"The duke got the body he wanted," Maddock answered with a grim satisfaction that he did not feel. "Let's move, before the soldiers come back to clean up." She stared at him for long enough that he had to raise his dagger, setting the blade against her quivering neck. "Come along, Lila. See me through the gates, and then you'll be free to go."

The woman had shifted her gaze to Wilson's corpse, and Maddock finally stepped forward to block her line of sight. Only then did she seem to become aware of his blade, of the bitter threat in the man she had duped. She came back to life with a disbelieving shudder.

A cry broke from her lips, and Maddock hissed as he pulled her close, covering her mouth with his own. He glimpsed the four remaining guards turn toward them as he whispered, "I'll gut you as easily as they did that thief. To the gates, and not another word."

Lila's eyes flashed in terror, but she managed to speak. "Your sword. The night guard will never let an armed man enter. Leave it here, in the hay."

Maddock was washed with misgiving—the sword

was his greatest possession, more valuable even than the People's horse that he had squandered. Nevertheless, he could see the logic in Lila's words; an armed man was certain to be questioned, especially in the dark of night.

"Do it," Lila urged. "I don't have the powers of the Seven Gods. I can't work miracles."

Forcing himself to act with more decisiveness than he felt, Maddock burrowed into the hayrick, nestling the sword in a dry, cushioned bed. He could retrieve it later, he justified, in the morning even. Once he knew his way through the city streets, once he could come and go with other travelers, anonymous in the light of day. Once he had gotten past this cursed night.

He sensed Lila pulling away from him, recognized a tension in her muscles that told him she planned to flee. "Not yet," he whispered, and reckless courage filled him. Nestling his dagger against the small of her back, he stepped out from behind the hayrick, simultaneously pulling her close for a struggling kiss.

As the soldiers looked up, hands on their own weapons, Lila settled her arms around his waist, leaning toward him in a credible facsimile of lust. To Maddock's surprise, she barely glanced at Wilson's cooling body as they made their way to the gate, winding between other folks who had been drawn by the nighttime commotion. If he had not felt her tremble beneath his fingers, he would not have known that she had any reaction to the bloody camp.

The heavy gate was locked for the night and the portcullis lowered, but a pair of soldiers stood alertly at a narrow doorway built into the wood-and-iron defense. Without a conscious thought, Maddock stiffened, and his fingers slipped inside the waistband of Lila's skirt. His precious iron dagger seemed hot enough that it would shine like a beacon through the soft fabric, shine like the bavin that was swaddled against his chest.

"Halt!" one of the soldiers cried out, but Lila merely stumbled forward, pulling Maddock with her.

"Evening, your honor," Lila slurred, cascading the words as if she had drunk a barrel of ale. Maddock let himself be carried along by her charade, and he purposely stumbled as they approached the uniformed man.

"The gates are closed for the night."

"But, your honor," Lila protested, and she lurched forward, displaying a generous bosom, "you wouldn't abandon a lady outside the walls, would you?"

"A lady!" snorted the guard, but he reached out to steady the woman. Maddock tightened his own grip on Lila's waist, determined to remind her who was in control.

"Aye, your honor. A lady who got surprised by nightfall. Surely you have other disturbances to look toward?" Lila smiled sloppily with her words, and she slipped her hand down the guard's arm. Maddock stiffened and started to intervene, but then he saw a glint of metal coin pass between the pair.

"Aye, I suppose," the soldier grumbled, and made a show of crossing the portal to talk to his fellow. Lila merely dropped another curtsey, flashing her chest once again.

Maddock stumbled over the raised threshold with her, pulling her close and miming his supposed lustful intent. He gripped her tightly as they wandered down the middle of the thoroughfare, staggering like the drunken lovers they pretended to be. He let her guide them into a side street, but he was not surprised by her sudden vehemence as she pushed him away, scarcely waiting until they were out of sight of the guard.

"There! Let go of me, you animal!"

"Keep your voice down," Maddock hissed.

"I did what you ordered. Let me go!" Before Maddock could comply, Lila twisted like a salmon caught in a net. Her long neck curved, and her teeth dug into the flesh of his shoulder. He bit back a curse as he dropped his knife. She took advantage of his confusion to spring away, her footsteps already fading by the time he recovered his blade.

It would take her only a few seconds to summon the guard. Maddock bolted down the night-still street, taking turns at random until he was lost in the heart of Smithcourt.

Maddock stood in the shadows, looking out at the postern gate of Coren's palace. The cursed building was impregnable. Maddock had studied it from all sides, at every hour of the day and night. Coren had simply been too careful. He had too many guards.

The duke needed those soldiers, Maddock had discovered. Smithcourt did not yet belong to him. Rather, Coren was locked in a bitter battle for the Iron Throne, basing his claim on the massive sums of gold that he had pumped into the royal treasury. That same gold permitted him to purchase the most ruthless mercenary soldiers.

Nevertheless, Coren was being challenged directly by Bringham, the Duke of Southglen. Bringham was a young man, much beloved by his own people. He'd been a confidant of the dead king, and while inexperienced, he had much potential. So far, he had managed to escape Coren's attacks, slithering to freedom repeatedly, like the dragon that was his coat of arms.

Bringham's popularity had apparently grown in Smithcourt while Coren was on his journey to the westlands. Coren felt more and more pressure to consolidate his position, to win over the people of Smithcourt, and all the rest of the kingdom. The city folk could all too easily throw their support to Bringham, making it impossible for Coren to take the Iron Throne.

So, Coren worked to curry favor among the Smithcourt folk. He paid his soldiers to keep some semblance of peace in the streets. He hosted a three-day festival to welcome the arrival of Reade and Maida, the Sun-lord and Sun-lady, complete with fireworks and sweetmeats for everyone in the streets.

Nevertheless, gangs of young men roamed the streets at night, fighting each other and building nasty rivalries. Three times, Maddock had seen fresh-blooded bodies lying in the streets—one with a crude knife carved into his chest to show that Coren's men had been at work. The other corpses had been little more than boys, and there had been no hint who had murdered them.

At first, overwhelmed by a city that could have swallowed thousands of Land's End villages, Maddock had wandered aimlessly through Smithcourt. The first people he'd dared to ask for directions had run in fear, apparently thinking him a lawless cutthroat. A second group had roared at his outlandish accent. The third cluster of rogues had attempted to steal from him, kicking him in the ribs when they found that he had nothing left to take, nothing but an odd, pointed star made of blackened wood.

It was not until that horde attacked him that he realized Lila had stolen the pouch that had hung at his waist. Even now, he grimaced at her pretended passion outside the city walls, at his gullibility in responding to her. In the end, though, the joke had been on her—the leather sack had been empty.

Of course, she had probably gained a pretty penny for his sword. As expected, Lila had spread the word that an outlander was on the loose, and the entire city of Smithcourt seethed with suspicion. No matter how much Maddock cursed to himself, he had been unable to exit the city gates to retrieve his weapon. The chances were simply too great that he would never regain entrance into Smithcourt.

Trapped inside the city walls, he'd been forced to figure out some sort of disguise. He put his dagger to good use, chopping off his hair in an approximation of a soldier's helmet-sculpted cut. He had contemplated stealing other clothes, but figured that theft would likely result in additional unwelcome attention. Besides, his doublet and trews were so filthy, they could hardly be named a color. Nothing he wore would betray him.

Trying to believe that he blended in with Smithcourt's turbulent population, Maddock had tracked down Duke Coren's palace. The duke was a cautious man, however, and Maddock soon learned that there was no easy way into the massive stone edifice. Both gates were manned by heavily armed guards. Every visitor was inspected, and no one was permitted to enter without a pass.

Still, in Coren's ongoing efforts to keep his name in the people's prayers, the postern gate was opened each morning. Coren's kitchen wenches came out, bearing remnants of food from the palace kitchens. Butts of bread, flat ale, fruit starting to turn—Maddock found that he could fill his belly without missing the coins that Wilson had stolen from him. More importantly, on a few occasions, Duke Coren's guard had handed out jobs as well, small missions that were worth a copper or another meal—and a day's pass into the palace compound.

Maddock cleared his throat as he joined the day's hungry horde. During the past fortnight, he had learned that his voice would betray him to these city folk. Looking at his face, no one realized that he was from the outlands—his beard had grown in heavy, and his hair was short enough that no one would confuse him with a fisherman. But try as he might, though, he could not consistently reproduce the rounded vowels of the city folk.

That was fine. Begging did not require speech. He could hold out a pitiful hand, grunt and push like the Smithcourt scum who'd been born to this life.

There were more hapless fools than usual today. Soldiers stood at attention to either side of the heavy metal portcullis, hands resting ominously on their weapons. As Maddock jostled for a good position, the postern gate opened, and a scowling soldier came forward with a pair of women.

The crowd surged as the kitchen maids handed out heels of bread. Grasping hands scrambled for apples that had gone soft, and a squabble broke out over a pile of roasted bones. Amid the cursing, Maddock remained silent, remembering to fight for his portion without saying a word.

Just as he laid his fingers on a roasted rib, he felt the prick of a dagger in the small of his back. "Take the bone," a voice growled. "Take the bone and come with me." If Maddock had given any serious thought to disobeying, he changed his mind at the blade's sharp reminder. "Don't turn about. Just walk."

Maddock did as he was told, feeling foolish as he clutched the cold, greasy rib bone. His unknown assailant guided him away from Coren's palace and down a dark side street. Just as Maddock concluded that he had no choice but to confront the man, three shadows leaped from a nearby doorway.

Maddock fought, but he never truly had a chance. A rough burlap sack was tugged over his head, and his arms were pinned behind him, his hands lashed so tightly that he dropped even the silly weapon of the roasted bone. Blind and weaponless, Maddock cursed himself for a fool as he was marched through chilly, winding streets.

His captors took him to a building that stank of standing water and rotted meat. Maddock was forced up rickety stairs and then shoved to his knees on a rough wooden floor. He heard men walking around him, heavy men, but he could see nothing through the burlap sack. He started to crane his neck wildly, but then froze, determined not to give the men the satisfaction of seeing his fear.

Maddock's lashed hands were suddenly grabbed be-

hind his back, and some strong man pulled up sharply.
His shoulders stretched to the point of pain, but he bit
off a curse. One man set a knife against Maddock's
pounding jugular, and another leveled a dagger at his
groin, pricking through his trews so that he understood
his danger.

"Speak, man! Name yourself, or you'll find you're
missing some valued equipment."

Maddock gasped for breath, struggling to break
away from his captors. His throat worked, but he
knew that he must not speak; he must not reveal his
identity through his accented words.

"Cat got your tongue, man?" the interrogator taunted,
and he must have given some silent command, for the
other captors tightened their grips. Maddock's shoulders were nearly ripped from their sockets, and he
could not help but moan at the pain. Moan, but not
speak. Not give them the satisfaction of defeating him.

The pain crested to a red wave behind his eyes, and
Maddock fought to catch a breath against the knife
that still flickered at his throat. He might have kept
his silence even then, but he felt the other blade cut
through his ragged trews, felt the cold iron against his
cringing flesh. "Who are you bastards?" he bellowed
at last, casting prudence to all the Guardians. "What
do you want?"

The captors were still for a moment, and then the
leader must have given another silent signal. The
knives withdrew. Maddock gasped for breath, but his
relief was short-lived.

"You *are* the outlander, then." The man barely
hinted that his statement was a question.

There seemed no advantage in refusing to answer.
"Aye."

"The one Coren seeks."

"Aye."

"Then you'll fight against the duke, once we get you
into his palace."

"Wh—what?"

"Come now! You may come from the outlands, but you must understand plain speech."

"Why would you help me get into the palace?"

"We've been watching you, lad. We know you try to hide your speech, but you don't always remember, and you don't do it well. We know you lurk by Coren's postern gate every morning, every night. We've seen you study the walls, trying to find another way in."

"Why is that any business of yours?" Some of Maddock's bravado returned, stung to life by the man's criticism of his accent.

"I think we've got the same goal, lad. Neither one of us wants to see Coren on the Iron Throne." The man spat, and there was a general rumble among the other captors.

"So what do you propose?" Maddock's heart was pounding.

"We have a man on the inside, a guard at the postern gate. Go beg tomorrow, and he'll see that you're chosen for one of Coren's special details."

"And then?" Maddock could not believe entrance to the palace would be so easy.

"And then you look around. You do whatever Coren asks. You do whatever you planned on doing when you get behind those walls. And you report back to us, about what the bastard's planning. If you make it out."

"It's as easy as that?" Maddock's skepticism bought him another tug on his bound arms, but the unseen leader laughed harshly.

"Not so easy, lad. Have you seen anyone return from working inside the palace? Have you seen any of your beggar friends leave Coren's stronghold, once they've selected for service?" Maddock's silence was sufficient answer. He had not thought about the matter before; he had been too intent on getting into the palace to think about leaving it. The brigand in front of him continued speaking, apparently unaware of Maddock's thoughts. "We'll give you the chance to try, though, to help yourself and us."

"But if you already have someone inside the palace, why do you need me?"

"You ask a lot of questions, lad." For an instant, Maddock thought he'd get no further answer, but then the man continued. "Our man is just a guard. He's not allowed into some parts of the palace—the parts where Coren is plotting something, something that will cement his claim to the throne."

"Then send in another one of your men. Let *him* do Coren's . . . special task, and your work besides."

"We have sent our men. Three of them. Each has been selected by our guard. Each has been taken to the inner keep. None has returned. We don't have enough men to continue the sacrifice."

A prickle of fear walked up Maddock's spine. "Why do you think I'll fare any better?"

"You have your own reason to try, whatever it is. You've managed to stay alive in the city streets. You might succeed. And we don't have any other option."

"Who *are* you?" Maddock asked again. "Why should I trust you?"

"If you don't know my name, you can't betray me. Suffice to say I think Duke Bringham is the best man for the Iron Throne."

"But—"

"Enough!" The man stomped his foot on the floor, and the crumbling room shook. "You have two choices. Accept our offer. Or refuse."

Maddock felt cold iron kiss his jugular. "I'll help!"

"I knew you were a wise man. A brave one, too." The leader's voice was sardonic.

Maddock's voice rang out in the small room, loud enough and steady enough that he heard Bringham's men take a step back. "I'm brave enough to do your job. Your job, and my own as well."

11

◆≈◆∞◆≈◆

Alana stood beside the Tree, gulping the cool breeze that came off the ocean. Her palms were slick with sweat, and her heart pounded inside her chest. It had been days since she had drunk the heart-swell tea, but her body still remembered the herb, still remembered the fever it had planted deep inside her. Even now, her flesh yearned for the sensations that Maddock had experienced by the gamblers' fire. Her vision blurred as his breath—her own breath—came short, as Lila's lips settled on his, on hers.

Sick with embarrassment, Alana settled her flushed cheek against the Tree's rough bark. The oak's rings pulsed outward, calling to her with their living force. The Tree wanted her to sing. It wanted her to tell it of the People, near and far.

Alana resisted, though, as she had ever since drinking the heartswell tea. She was afraid that she would sully the oak with her new knowledge, her new memories. She quavered at the thought of what the other woodsingers would say, how they would treat her when they learned about the intimacy she had shared with Maddock. For days now, she had cut herself off from her sisters and the Tree, drowning in her shame as completely as her father had drowned in his ocean storm.

Still, Alana lingered on the Headland. She did not

want to leave the Tree. She did not want to retreat to her cottage, to her musty journals and her cold hearth and her lonely, narrow bed.

Maybe she *should* reach out to the other woodsingers. Maybe one of them had been tricked in a similar fashion, fooled into drinking heartswell and sharing a fisherman's thoughts, a fisherman's flesh. Maybe one of the women would know how to drive the heartswell dreams from her mind, from her body.

And if Alana asked her sisters, then she could live those feelings one more time. She could feel hot lips on hers, urgent fingers fumbling at her waist. She could remember heat and warmth and blood pounding. . . .

Desperate, mortified, Alana threw her mind open to her sisters.

"So!" The woodsinger's exclamation startled Alana into a wordless cry. "You've learned the power of heartswell!"

"I didn't mean to, sister! It's just that Goody Glenna . . . She gave me a tea. She told me to reach for Maddock. I didn't know that I would . . . I didn't think. . . ." Alana trailed off, blushing. There were tears in her voice as she asked, "Why would Goody Glenna do such a thing?"

"Goody Glenna thought to help you." The woodsinger's voice surprised Alana. It was gentle, kind. There was no trace of scorn or revulsion. "She knew that you were disappointed in Maddock, ready to abandon him and his bavin. You needed to remember that there was a *man* you were watching, not just a coward."

"But to think of him *that* way!"

Another sister chimed in, teasing. "What better way to think of a man? Stop your blushing, girl! Do you think you're the only woman who's ever felt the call of flesh to flesh?"

"But I'm a woodsinger!" Alana protested.

"Aye, you're a woodsinger." A third woman joined

in the discussion, scarcely restraining her laughter. "Does that make you special? Does that make your flesh colder than any other woman's?"

"I'm not supposed to think about such things," Alana moaned. "It's unnatural."

"Unnatural?" All three of the woodsingers pounced on Alana's word.

"The Tree does not allow its woodsingers to wed!" Alana cried.

"Aye," agreed the first sister, the calm one. "The Tree does not want you to shift your loyalties, once you're sworn to it. It doesn't want you torn."

The third voice, the laughing one, went on. "But the Tree is still part of the natural world, sister. Look at the birds in its branches, the squirrels collecting its acorns! The Tree understands hot blood!"

"Besides," teased the second woodsinger, "you've hardly decided to *wed* Maddock. You merely thought of him as a man. Your feelings weren't shameful or bad. They're natural."

"Aye," the laughing sister said. "They're part of the world the Guardians shaped, part of the world the Great Mother birthed."

"I should have been stronger, though," Alana said miserably. "I should have held myself apart. And now that it's over, I should be able to make myself forget."

The first woodsinger answered, and Alana could picture the woman shaking her head. "You demand too much of yourself. Ask the Tree if you won't believe us."

For the first time since she had become a woodsinger, Alana cringed at the thought of embracing the Tree's essence. She was not worthy. She was unclean. Before she could refuse, though, she felt the Tree's awareness ripple along the edges of her thoughts. Once again, it was asking for her to sing. It wanted her to talk to it, to share with it, to let it know her thoughts.

Sighing, Alana gave herself up to the oaken essence, letting it pull her in, slip her past the other woodsingers. She was drawn into the Tree's sheltering embrace, into its smooth, even rings. She ran her mind around those circles, gliding over them as if she were meditating.

As she touched the Tree, she immediately sensed its calm acceptance of her heartswell thoughts. It embraced her passion; it understood her body. The Tree had lived for centuries. It had seen far greater folly in all its years; it had witnessed greater mistakes. One woman's stirrings for one man were like a single drop of rain amid the oak's green leaves.

Alana felt the Tree's love for her, its endless, depthless forgiveness. She remembered seeing that emotion in her father's eyes before he went to sea, before he was taken by the Guardians. She had thought there could be no such love left in all the world, not after her father's bloated body had washed onto the sandy beach below.

But she'd been wrong.

Alana opened her mouth and filled her lungs with cool ocean air. As she began to sing, as she began to tell the Tree of Maddock and heartswell and all that had happened in Smithcourt, she knew that the Tree already understood. It already accepted her. It already loved her. It already welcomed her safe return.

She sang louder, then. She gathered together the heat in her blood and wove it into her wordless song. She explained to the Tree that she had never meant to reach out for Maddock in that way; she had never meant to invade his body. She had not known how it would feel to kiss a man, to be kissed by a man. She had not known how it would feel to have her blood rise, throbbing throughout her body. . . .

But then Alana realized that she *should* have known. She could have known. Any time that she had wanted to learn, she could have reached inside the Tree, plumbed the oak's deep memories. Other wood-singers had sung of love. They had sung of men and women. They had sung of pure and burning lust.

Alana was not alone. She was not flawed.

Her song faltered, frayed into silence by the Tree's wordless acceptance, by the oak's simple love. Before she could begin her chant again, though, a question emanated from deep inside the oaken core. Thoughts vibrated through the wood as if the Tree were a musical instrument.

The oak asked her if she wanted to be released. It asked if she wanted to leave, to return to the world of the People, to fishermen and warriors, to men and women. To ordinary, fleshly pleasure.

The Tree spiced its question with some of the memories planted in its rings. Blood pounded again through Alana's veins, heated with the musk of heart-swell, throbbing with the memories that chased each other through the Tree's concentric depth. Alana gathered the oak's question in her body, collected it in her flesh. She studied the pounding bass notes until every fiber of her body understood what the Tree asked.

And then she sang her answer.

She was no mere animal, mating and moving on through the forest. She was anchored to the Tree. To the Tree, and the People, and her life as a woodsinger. Alana filled her lungs and sang her way up through the Tree's encircling rings. She did not want to leave the Tree. Her passion had served a purpose; she *had* forgiven Maddock's cowardice. She had accepted him back into the People's fold.

Maddock's passion had had a purpose as well—it had spared him the swords that slew Wilson and gained him entrance into Smithcourt. Other passions, from other people, might give way to love, and love might lead to children. As Alana circled the Tree's bark with her mind, she sang that last line again. Love might lead to children. Children like Reade and Maida.

The woodsinger took a deep breath. She had wasted enough time with her foolishness. Let her look to the children, as she should have been doing these past few days. Let her turn to Reade's bavin, to see how the twins fared. Alana ceased her singing and reached through the Tree for the thin white thread that stretched across the land.

Reade sighed and shifted his bottom on the hard wooden stool. This was stupid, all of his tutor's questions. This was as bad as the day when Da had taught him how to tie a sharkstooth hitch.

Then, Da had found Reade and Maida playing on the beach. Reade had been pretending for Maida, showing her how well he could tie a knot. He convinced her that his sharkstooth held fast, and he laughed when she could not imitate his loops around a driftwood branch. It was all very funny, until Da tugged at the rope and made it come loose. Da had laughed at Reade, and Maida had laughed with Da, and Reade had burst into tears.

Da had sat next to him then, on the sand, beneath a setting sun as red as cow's blood. Da had put strong arms around him and guided his hands, over and under and around and around. That had been the first time Reade had tied a real sharkstooth, and his heart had pounded like pilchards turning over in the bottom of a boat. The second time was less interesting, though, and by five repetitions, he hardly cared if he ever tied another knot again.

"This is important, Reade," Da had said. "Someday your life may turn on whether you can tie this knot. You wouldn't want to be caught far out at sea, depending on another man's work."

"This is important, Sun-lord." The echoing words made Reade blink, and he found himself staring up into an old man's wrinkled face. "Pay attention!"

It wasn't fair, old Kenwald scolding him. Reade *had* been trying. He'd been trying all morning. Kenwald hadn't let him eat a sweetcake, or even duck into the garderobe. The old herald was worse than Da had ever been. Worse than Mum even. Reade clenched his hands into angry fists. "*Why* is it important? Why do I have to know all these things?"

"You wouldn't want to depend on a herald, Sun-lord. Not when all the glory of the Iron Throne might depend on your remembering a noble's proper title."

Just like Da, Kenwald was. Well, the old man *looked* different, with his wrinkled face, and his shaking hands, and his long white beard. Da had never had a beard. But Kenwald made Reade learn things just like Da had done. Da had made Reade learn where the pilchards swam, the names of all the winds, the times that the tides rose and fell. . . .

"Who are the four dukes, Sun-lord?" Kenwald asked.

Reade sighed and said, "There are four dukes in all the land: the Duke of Norvingale, who is called Ferin; the Duke of Southglen, who is called Bringham; the Duke of Eastham, who is called Lymore; and the Duke of Westmarch, who is called Coren."

Reade was startled by a crashing sound. He whirled toward the door of the solar and saw Duke Coren leaning against the stone arch. The duke's strong hands came together again and again, slowly, like Sartain Fisherman applauding the largest catch of the season. Reade's cheeks flushed hot, as red as Coren's doublet. "Well done, Sun-lord. Well done."

Reade wriggled down from his high stool and tugged his robes into place. "I've learned all the dukes' names, Your Grace, just like you told me I

must. And I've learned the names of the Three Kingdoms, and the Four Seas, and the Five Marches. I've
learned so much my head has grown!"

Duke Coren settled a hand on the boy's head, tou-
sling his hair. "So, is it true, Kenwald? Has the Sun-
lord been a good student?"

The old herald bowed deeply. "Aye, Your Grace.
He's learned all that. It took him a few days to grasp
the difference between a duke and a king, but once
he caught on, he had no trouble memorizing the lists."

Reade flushed. He wanted Duke Coren to smile at
him again. "I would have learned it faster, Your Grace,
but I kept thinking about the dragons in Southglen."

Duke Coren knelt in front of Reade, grabbing his
shoulders. His eyes flashed bright. "Dragons? What
have you been told about dragons?"

Reade glanced up at Kenwald. That was funny—the
old man was gaping like a salmon plucked from the
ocean. "Kenwald told me all about the dragons in
Southglen, about how Duke Bringham's da slew the
last one, when the duke was the same age that I am
now. Duke Bringham has a dragon painted on his
shield, to remember his da."

"So Kenwald has been telling you about Bringham,
has he?"

The old man answered before Reade could. "Your
Grace! The boy is making up tales! Someone else
must have told him about Southglen!"

That wasn't true! Kenwald *had* spoken about dragons. And the dragons had kept Reade from concentrating, from learning the names of all the dukes
yesterday. Yesterday, and the day before, and the day
before that.

Duke Coren's hand was heavy on Reade's shoulder.
His lips were so thin inside his beard that they almost
disappeared. "Sun-lord, I ask you in the name of
Culain. Did Kenwald speak to you about Southglen?"

"Yes, Your Grace."

"And what precisely did Kenwald tell you about that . . . about Bringham?"

"H—he told me about the dragons, Your Grace. He said that Bringham's da was a brave man, and that Bringham wears a coat of arms to remember his da. It's silver, his shield is, silver with a dragon azure. That's blue, Your Grace."

"Yes, Sun-lord. It is."

Reade barely swallowed his smile. There! Now let Kenwald tell the duke that Reade was slow to learn! But when Reade looked up at the old herald, he saw that the man was gripping the table with his brown-spotted hands. The teacher's head was bowed, and his breath came in funny little pants, as if he'd been running. The old man licked his lips, and he swallowed, loud enough that Reade could hear.

Reade was surprised to find that his own palms were slick with sweat. He said, "Please, Your Grace. I *like* stories about dragons. I like Duke Bringham's coat of arms."

Duke Coren nodded, but something shifted behind his eyes. Reade thought of the sharks that the fishermen sometimes brought up in their nets. "Kenwald distracted you from your studies, didn't he, Sun-lord?"

"I liked the dragons," Reade whispered. Duke Coren's burning eyes forced him to add, "But I was distracted."

"And would you change that, Sun-lord? Are you man enough to remove distractions and learn the lessons you need to serve your people?"

His people. Reade needed to learn so that he would not disappoint his people. A thrill plucked his spine. If Reade learned all of his lessons, he could spend the rest of his life here in Smithcourt. He wouldn't have to be a fisherman. He wouldn't have to go out in a boat and get caught in a storm and never come home to a family that loved him. But only if he learned. Only if he didn't let Kenwald distract him.

"Oh yes, please," Reade said, when he realized Duke Coren was waiting for an answer.

"Very well, then. Watch, Sun-lord, and learn." Duke Coren stepped toward the old herald. "So, Kenwald. You've been tutoring the Sun-lord as you were commanded?"

"Aye, Your Grace. He's been studying hard. He's a smart boy."

"A smart boy? Then why did it take him three days to learn the names of the kingdom's dukes?" Duke Coren's voice was as cold as sea foam in winter.

"He's young, of course. Too young to learn the politics of the kingdom. Too young to understand a struggle for power."

Too young! Reade wasn't too young to do anything! He was the Sun-lord! "That's not true, Your Grace! I am *not* too young! Kenwald is lying! It was Kenwald's fault. He told me about Bringham and Southglen and the dragons!"

Duke Coren moved even closer to Kenwald. "It sounds to me as if the Sun-lord understands a great deal about politics. He understands everything about power."

"Your Grace, he's just a little boy!"

Reade glared at Kenwald. Everyone always said that he was just a little boy. Da had said it all the time. Da would make Reade scale fish and hoe the garden, all because Reade was too little to go fishing. It wasn't fair. But things were different here in Smithcourt. *Reade* could make his own rules. Reade was the Sun-lord. "I'm not too young!" he repeated.

"So, Kenwald. The Sun-lord thinks he's not too young to learn your lessons. *All* your lessons."

"Your Grace—" Kenwald sank to his knees.

"Perhaps I was wrong to trust you, old man. Perhaps you're too old to remember who holds power in this palace." The duke towered over the herald. "What precisely were your orders, old man?"

"To teach the Sun-lord?" Kenwald turned his answer into a question, like Reade did when Da had asked him impossible things, questions that had no good answers. "To teach him the Table of Lands and the Lists of Nobles."

"And what else?"

"To see that he is fit for the Service."

"And what else?"

The old man trembled, and then words spilled out of him, as if he were a boy called to task by his own da. "Nothing else, Your Grace?"

"Precisely." Duke Coren smiled slowly, and his fingers flexed inside his leather gloves. He pointed at Reade. "And did you teach him anything else?"

"I-I did not think it mattered, Your Grace." Kenwald glanced from the duke to Reade and back again. "Sun-lord, if I have given you any displeasure—"

Before Reade could marvel that the old man was apologizing to *him*, Duke Coren's hand shot out, closing around Kenwald's throat. Duke Coren pushed the old man back toward the table. Kenwald's fingers scrabbled at Duke Coren's fist, and his feet kicked the air, catching at his dusty robes. "Please, Your Grace—" he managed to croak.

"You betrayed your liege, Kenwald! That's not the way to settle into a life of leisure in your twilight days at court."

"Ask the young lord!" Kenwald gasped. "Ask him if I said anything about Bringham's claim to the throne!"

Reade stared in shock. He had wanted to show Kenwald that the Sun-lord was special. He had wanted Duke Coren to pay attention to him. He'd never meant, though, for Kenwald to be *hurt*. Reade did not care about dragons that much!

Duke Coren glared at Reade across the old man's body. "So, Sun-lord? Did Kenwald tell you anything about Bringham's claim to my throne?"

"I—" Reade started to say. Before he could answer, though, the old man began to choke. He twisted onto his side, trying to escape from Duke Coren's hand. Reade could not think of an answer to the duke's question. He could not even remember what Kenwald had said, what Duke Coren wanted him to reply. "Please, Your Grace!"

"It's a simple enough question, Sun-lord. If Kenwald has not even taught you how to answer a simple question, then I know that he has failed *me,* regardless of whether he failed you."

The old herald thrashed on the table, like a fish caught in a net. Reade tried to remember why he had thought it would be fun to taunt the old man, why he had even mentioned Duke Bringham's dragon. "Please, Your Grace. You must have misunderstood me!"

"Misunderstood you? Then once again, your teacher has not served his function. The Sun-lord should never be misunderstood, not about something as basic as whether a servant has done his job. If Kenwald has not taught you that much then, again, he has disappointed me."

The old man's legs stopped jerking in the air. He was giving up.

"Please, Your Grace. Kenwald taught me well! I have no complaints against him!"

"But did you not say, when I came into this room, that you had been distracted—"

"I wanted you to be proud of me! I was just telling a story!"

Duke Coren stared at Reade across Kenwald's body. *"Just telling a story?"*

"Yes, Your Grace. I'm sorry! I just wanted you to listen to me! I just wanted to share a story with you, something special, like the Sun-lord and Culain! Please! It's not Kenwald's fault! Let him go!" Reade's words poured out of him, desperate, begging. He didn't think that he could ever say enough, speak quickly enough.

"So, Sun-lord. Are you still telling stories? Are you lying now? Or were you lying when you said that dragons kept you from learning your lessons?" Duke Coren gave Kenwald one last shake and threw him onto the table.

The herald crawled onto his side, gasping for air. He slid to the ground and hit the floor hard, still choking. Reade's legs began to tremble, and he saw the trap that Duke Coren had built for him.

"It wasn't a lie," he whispered, but his lower lip trembled, and he could not keep his voice steady. Kenwald began to retch, bringing up a disgusting mess onto the flagstones. "Please, Your Grace, you must have misunderstood—" At Duke Coren's arched eyebrow, Reade quickly tried again. "*I* must have been confusing. Me, it's *my* fault, not Kenwald's. Your Grace, I did not want him punished. I only wanted you to tell him not to talk about dragons during my lessons."

"Well then, Sun-lord. Your desire has been granted. Kenwald will not speak of dragons again." The duke dug one booted toe into the old man's side. "Isn't that correct, Kenwald?"

"Y-yes," the herald gasped. He retched again before he managed to add, "Your Grace."

Duke Coren nodded at his title. He started to turn for the doorway, but he stopped himself. Looking at Reade, he settled his black boot across the back of Kenwald's neck. For just a moment, he stood perfectly still, and then he shifted his weight. The crack of breaking bones was loud in the room. Kenwald struggled for another dozen breaths before the chamber was silent.

"Well." Duke Coren stepped back, flexing his hands inside his leather gloves. "It's time for you to work with a new tutor, Sun-lord. You mustn't fall behind in your studies."

12

❦

"I hate him!" Reade exclaimed, as soon as he found Maida in the small garden attached to their nursery. She was sitting beside the small pond in the middle of the green grass.

"Prithee, dear brother, of whom do you speak?"

"Stop it, Maida! Talk like a regular person!"

"But, dear brother, a regular person in the duke's court speaks as I do. We must prepare for the day when our lord, the duke, takes the Iron Throne."

"Stop it!" Reade choked back tears, dashing a fist across his face so that Maida would not see the drops in his eyes.

"Dear brother, you must take your studies to heart. Elsewise, Duke Coren might take offense."

The "elsewise" was too much. Maida's curls had been woven into two braids and bound together at the nape of her neck with a length of crimson ribbon. Reade dug his hands into the nest of hair and tugged hard.

"Ow!" Maida howled. "Why did you do that, Reade? I'm going to tell!"

"Quit yelling, Maida! In the name of all the Guardians—"

"You swore!" Maida gasped. "I'm going to tell Mum—" She broke off her own threat.

Reade sat down beside the pond. He waited a long

time before he said, "I don't think we're ever going
to see Mum, Maida."

"Yes, we will. After the Service."

Reade didn't even bother to answer. Instead, he
picked up a pebble and skipped it across the water. It
only made three jumps before it skittered onto the
grass at the far side of the pool. "Sharks and fins!"
Reade cursed, the way the fishermen swore back
home.

"Reade!"

"I can say what I want to, Maida. They don't care if
I swear. It's just their stupid lists I have to memorize."

"The lists aren't stupid! Nurse was talking just this
morning to the girl who brings our breakfast, and she
said—"

"Nurse was talking to Cow-girl?"

Maida laughed, but she hid her teeth behind her
palm, like all the grown-up women in Smithcourt.
Reade wished that Maida had not learned that lesson;
it made him feel very alone. Maida said, "That's not
nice, Reade!"

"What did Nurse say?"

"She was telling Cow— she was telling Jamela that
there isn't much time before the Service. She was worried that you wouldn't learn the lists, and she said
you'll need to recite them in the Service."

"All of them?" Reade thought of Kenwald trying
to teach him everything he needed to know. Maybe
the old man had only pretended to be hurt. Maybe that
was just another one of the lessons. Maybe Kenwald
had just waited for Reade to leave the solar, and then
he got to his feet. Maybe Kenwald and Duke Coren
had planned the whole thing, so that Reade would
study harder.

"I think—" Maida began.

"Ach! There you are!" Reade jumped at the harsh
voice. When he looked up, Nurse was rushing across
the garden. Following the rules of Smithcourt, she

wore huge skirts that wrapped around her ankles, like
a cat that wanted to trip her. By the time she reached
the children, she was out of breath, and her hands
fluttered over her heart. She snorted as she tried to
fill her lungs.

"You naughty children!" she finally wheezed. "Terrible children! Who said you could come to the garden?" She kept on scolding before Reade or Maida
could make up an answer. "Well, don't just stand
there like two buttons on a gown! Hurry up! Duke
Coren is waiting for you. You mustn't keep His
Grace waiting!"

Her breathless snorts turned to a cry as Reade stood
up. "Ach! Look at you!" Reade looked down. Mud
streaked the front of his doublet. Nurse swatted at the
dirt with the flat of her palm, hard enough to rattle
his teeth. His bavin dug into his chest.

"Come along, both of you. There's no time to
change your clothes. Oh, you dirty children, what have
you done to me . . . ?" On and on she went, grabbing
Reade's hand in her left and Maida's in her right. She
dragged the twins out of the garden, back to the nursery and through the tangle of dark castle hallways.
With every turn, she fussed a little more, telling them
that they must not keep Duke Coren waiting, that
they needed to hurry, that they mustn't be late.

Finally, Nurse dragged them to a stop in front of a
pair of high, carved doors. "Oh, you wicked children . . .
here we are."

"Where?" Reade asked.

"Why, at Duke Coren's chapel!" Reade started to
ask another question—he'd never heard of the
chapel—but she just repeated, "The *chapel*. Where
His Grace prays to the Seven Gods. Don't tell me you
poor lambs have never been in a chapel before!"

Why would the duke pray inside a *building*? Prayers
were supposed to be said outside, under the branches

of the Tree, or in the Sacred Grove. The Guardians
didn't like buildings. They'd listen to prayers much
better if they were comfortable, if they were outside.

Before Reade could ask any questions, Nurse grimaced and licked a finger. She rubbed at his face,
scrubbing as if she would remove the skin. He tried
to squirm away, but she held him in place with her
other hand. "Just a moment, young lord. You'll not
be seeing His Grace with garden dirt on your face."

"I've seen Duke Coren lots of times."

"Don't talk back to me, young lord." Nurse darted
a glance at Maida. "And you, young lady. Straighten
your hair." Nurse fussed for a moment longer, and
then she stepped back, still wheezing. "Well, there you
go. Into the chapel."

"What?" Reade asked.

"Aren't you coming with us?" Maida said.

"Oh no. Not Nurse." The old woman huffed. "His
Grace was quite clear. I'm to wait for you here. Only
the two of you go into the chapel."

Reade swallowed hard. He didn't want to see Duke
Coren again today. He didn't want to be reminded of
Kenwald. Maybe he should beg Nurse to come with
them. Before he could say the words, though, he pic-
tured the old herald lying on the solar floor. No. Better not ask anyone to break Duke Coren's rules.

"You'll be *fine*, children. You're only seeing the
duke. You don't need to be afraid of him. And just
remember, I'll be out here the entire time." Nurse
smiled, and then she stepped to one side. "You can
do this, little ones. You're my Sun-lord and my Sun-
lady." She nodded, as if she saw some response that
she approved of, and then she pulled at the heavy
door, grunting out loud.

Reade hesitated for a moment, and then he reached
down for Maida's hand. He should help her into the
chapel. He should hold her hand so that she wouldn't

be afraid. He took three steps forward with his sister, and he tried not to jump when the door clanged shut behind them.

Smoke. Fire. An aisle that was grey with sweet-smelling fog. Maida sneezed twice.

Reade squinted through the gloom. There were benches on either side of him, marching across the stone floor. Metal pots sat at the end of each bench, pouring out sweet smoke. Against the walls stood iron posts covered with candles, so many that Reade could feel the heat like little ocean waves. Beeswax dripped from some of the posts, sounding like heavy raindrops as it hit the floor.

At the front of the room, barely visible through the fog, Reade could just make out Duke Coren. He stood on a platform, on top of four steps. An altar was behind him, and on the altar sat a wooden box.

Duke Coren still wore his crimson tunic. His black boots were invisible in the fog, so that it looked like he was floating above the stone stairs, in front of the altar. He raised a gloved hand and beckoned with one finger. "Sun-lord," the duke said. "Sun-lady."

Reade understood the order, and he dragged Maida forward. All the smoke made Reade's eyes water. He raised his free hand to wipe his face. When he looked up at Duke Coren again, he was surprised to see the man shaking his head. Instead of talking to Reade, though, the duke spoke to Maida.

"Sun-lady. I suppose your brother told you about his lessons this morning."

"Yes, Your Grace." Reade could feel Maida's hand shaking in his.

"And I suppose he told you that I was very, very angry."

"Yes, Your Grace."

"And he told you that I punished Kenwald, for failing to teach the Sun-lord properly."

"Yes, Your Grace."

"And how have your own lessons gone?"

"Your Grace?"

"Have you been learning from your own tutors? Have you been learning everything that you need to know for the Service?"

"I-I think so, Your Grace."

"You think so." Duke Coren repeated Maida's words. Reade knew that it was hot in the chapel. He knew that sweat was slipping down his backbone. But he felt chilled by the duke's voice; gooseflesh rose on his arms. "You *think* so. And therein lies our problem."

Maida was shaking so hard that she could not have answered Duke Coren if he had asked her a question. Reade put his hand on his chest, settling his fingers around his bavin, and then he stepped forward. After all, Mum had said that he must protect Maida. He had to be like Da. He had to clear his throat, though, before he could be heard. "Wh—what problem do we have, Your Grace?"

The duke pinned Reade with his eyes, like a stinging eel grabbing its prey. "I was thinking, Sun-lord, after I left the solar. It occurred to me that for all your studying, for all your working with your tutors, you and the Sun-lady still don't know what is expected of you at the Service. You don't know what you will be called upon to do, and so you do not realize how important your studies are."

"We've studied, Your Grace!" Reade *had* studied. He'd learned the names of all sorts of nobles and all different places. He'd even come to understand the difference between a duke and a king. Surely that was good enough.

"You've studied. But you're not prepared." Duke Coren took a step toward the twins, and Reade's belly turned over as the man's boot heel echoed on the stone platform. "I thought it was time to rehearse the Service. We thought it was time that you learned exactly what your people will expect of you."

Reade barely managed to ask, "We?"

"Aye, Sun-lord. High Priest Zeketh and I." Duke Coren lifted one gloved hand and gestured toward the altar. Reade followed the duke's finger, and caught his breath as a man appeared from out of the shadows. Maida was even more surprised—she cried out loud and grabbed at Reade's arm.

Appeared from nowhere. That was impossible. Even the Guardians couldn't appear from nowhere. They needed songs to make them become visible. They needed prayers.

"Sun-lord, Sun-lady, I present to you High Priest Zeketh."

The high priest took another step toward the twins, and Reade realized that he had not just appeared behind the altar. No. High Priest Zeketh was wearing black robes, all the way from his neck to his feet. Even his curling dark brown hair was underneath a black hat, a funny hat with four sharp corners at the top of it. High Priest Zeketh had been standing behind the altar the entire time, with his back to Reade and Maida. The twins had not been able to see him until he turned around, until his face and his hands stood out against the black cloth in the dark, foggy chapel.

Figuring out the man's trick made Reade a little braver, and he managed to say, "Good afternoon, Your Grace."

He tugged on Maida's hand until she whispered, "Good afternoon, Your Grace."

"Good afternoon, Sun-lord. Sun-lady. I am honored by your presence." The high priest's voice was deeper than any person's Reade had ever heard. It sounded like thunder rolling far off the Headland, like the storm that had brewed the night that Da disappeared forever. Reade remembered Duke Coren saying that the high priest had more power in his beard than Alana Woodsinger had in her entire body.

Well, it *was* a very long beard, curling halfway down

the man's barrel chest. Without thinking, Reade pulled his woodstar out of his dirty tunic. The bavin pricked his fingers, but Reade felt better holding on to it. The high priest might be stronger than Alana Woodsinger, but Reade welcomed any power he could get.

Duke Coren stepped forward. When he stood beside the high priest, Reade realized just how tall the new man was. Duke Coren only came up to his shoulders— shoulders that were as broad as any fisherman's. Duke Coren waited for Reade to swallow hard, and then he said, "High Priest Zeketh wants to ask you some questions, questions that will be a part of the Service."

Reade forced himself to look into the priest's eyes. They were as black as the man's robes, and they were set close together on his face. They narrowed as High Priest Zeketh stared first at Reade, then at Maida. It seemed like he was looking inside of the twins, seeing past their robes and their hair and their skin. Reade swallowed hard and tried not to take a step away.

The high priest finally nodded, and he raised a hand—a hand as big as a ham—to gesture at the chapel. "Welcome to this house of the Seven Gods, Sun-lord, Sun-lady. We light your way with candles and send your prayers skyward on the breath of incense." Incense. That must be the name for the sweet fog, the smoke that made the back of Reade's throat itch. "Do not be afraid. You'll find the Service is not frightening. I'll only ask you a series of questions, questions that you must answer from the truth that is at the bottom of your hearts."

"Questions?" Reade repeated. He had *tried* to learn. He had tried to study hard. He had tried to memorize everything old Kenwald taught him. Old Kenwald, whose neck had sounded like chicken bones when it crunched against the floor. . . .

Reade wanted to turn around and run for the door of the chapel. He wanted to leave behind the smoking pots, and the dripping candles, and the fog that tickled his nose. He wanted to leave High Priest Zeketh and Duke Coren and even Maida. Nurse was waiting for him outside. She would take him back to the nursery and feed him milk-sweets. She would give him bread and honey. She would fold him against her hip, and smooth his hair, and tell him that everything was going to be fine.

But Reade had to stay. He had to prepare for the Service. He had the power of the Sun-lord. Maida had the faith of the Sun-lady. Duke Coren had the strength of Culain. Reade would not be afraid.

"Aye, Sun-lord." The high priest took a step forward, towering over the twins. "You must listen to my questions and answer with your heart of hearts, for you and the Sun-lady are special. You are powerful and glorious to all the land. You are peace for Smith-court. You are the power of the Iron Throne."

Reade's head whirled as he listened to High Priest Zeketh. Reade knew he wasn't special. Da had always said that Reade was just one little boy, and he had better learn to live with that.

The People didn't plant their gardens just for him, Da had said when Reade wanted an extra serving of stew. The People didn't hunt just for him, Da had scolded, when Reade carried his bow and arrows to the Upper Pasture with the men, but got lost on the way back. The People didn't fight the sea just for him, Da had hollered when Reade got trapped on White Rock, when the tide came in while he was catching stinging eels.

Well, Da was wrong.

Da had gone off without Reade, leaving him alone. Da was gone, but High Priest Zeketh was here. High Priest Zeketh and Duke Coren. They understood that Reade was special. Reade was the Sun-lord.

Reade realized that he was gripping his bavin even tighter than before. Its pricks hurt his hand, but he did not want to set it aside. It was his, because he was special. It belonged to him, not to any of the other boys back at the Headland. Not to Maida, or even to Duke Coren, not anymore.

"Are you ready to answer some questions?" High Priest Zeketh asked. Reade nodded, and he felt Maida move her head up and down beside him.

"Sun-lord and Sun-lady, will you freely join Duke Coren and me, leaving behind your false home and false faith?"

False home? That must be the Headland. And false faith? That would be the Great Mother and the Guardians. And the Tree, which wanted to drink their blood. Reade squeezed Maida's hand, and they answered at the same time, "Yes, Your Grace."

As Reade answered, he felt the woodstar stir a little beneath his fingers. The bavin moved, as if it wanted to pull him back toward his false faith, back toward his false home. The woodstar wanted him out of the chapel and away from High Priest Zeketh, away from Duke Coren. Reade held the bavin tighter, as though to control it, as High Priest Zeketh nodded.

Then the man asked his second question. "Will you work with us for good and not for evil?"

That was an easy question. Maida almost answered first; Reade had to rush so that he said at the same time, "Yes, Your Grace."

The woodstar shifted again. This time, when Reade closed his hand around it, he could see a white glow between his fingers. He felt the bavin pull at his mind, whisper to him about the People and the Tree. He lifted it up a little, to stare at it, and he heard Duke Coren and High Priest Zeketh catch their breath.

The high priest went on, though, as if he were used to seeing glowing woodstars in his chapel. His words were faster, as if he needed to finish all his questions before the bavin got brighter. "Sun-lord and Sun-lady, will you lead your people in the ways of righteousness for however long you shall live? Will you rise up against the shadows of your past and lead your new people? Will you fight to save your new people from the unholy power of the Tree and the Guardians and the false god of the Great Mother? Will you offer up your souls to all the Seven Gods?"

Before Reade could answer, the light flared high from his bavin, cutting through the incense fog and the candlelight. It was wrong to answer "yes!" It was wrong to agree to what the priest demanded.

For one instant, Reade thought that he could take his burning woodstar and turn his back on High Priest Zeketh, on Duke Coren. He could walk down the aisle. He could leave the chapel. He could stop being the Sun-lord and go back to being just Reade. Everything seemed so simple in the white light, everything seemed so easy.

Before he could turn away, though, Maida said, "Yes, Your Grace."

Her words made Reade look away from his woodstar, look away from the blinding white light. Maida was staring at the high priest, looking right in his black, black eyes. High Priest Zeketh, though, was looking at Reade. The priest was, and Duke Coren was, too. All of a sudden, Reade was afraid that he had disappointed the duke, that he had ruined everything by missing the right response. Duke Coren leaned forward, eyeing him like a snake watching a baby mouse. Reade swallowed hard and answered, more loudly than Maida had, "Yes, Your Grace."

The woodstar flared as he spoke, so bright that Reade's fingers looked like stripes of blood across its prickly surface. Duke Coren darted a glance at the high priest. The men seemed to have some secret conversation; they shared some grown-up words that Reade was not allowed to know. Then, High Priest Zeketh stepped forward and pointed at the bavin.

"What is that trinket you wear, Sun-lord?"

"It's called a bavin, Your Grace. It's from the Tree."

"From the *Tree*?" High Priest Zeketh roared. "From the Tree that lives on child-blood?"

"Y-yes," Reade whispered.

"And you wear it here? In the house of the Seven Gods?"

"I-I thought . . . Duke Coren gave it to me."

"Duke Coren *gave* it to you." The priest glared at the duke, his white face turning red beneath his long, curling beard. Then, the high priest pulled himself up even taller, taking a step to tower over Reade. Reade had to crane his neck back to stare up at the man's face. "It was a fine gift, Sun-lord. A fine trinket for your journey to Smithcourt. Now that you are home, though, it does not serve as well."

"Does not serve, Your Grace?" Reade knew what the priest was going to say. Reade was going to have to give up his woodstar. Even now, the bavin seemed to sense what was going to happen. Its light began to fade, streaming away into the dark chapel as fast as it had grown.

"Sun-lord, you must set aside your past if you would serve as Sun-lord to all your people. You *do* wish to be the Sun-lord, don't you?"

Of course, Reade wanted to be the Sun-lord. That was why he had come all this distance. That was why he had studied so hard. That was why he had fought to prove that he was brave. "Yes, Your Grace."

"Very well, then. Why don't we exchange gifts, then?"

"Exchange gifts?"

"Yes, Sun-lord. I have brought you a present, a token of my appreciation for your hard work in preparing for the Service. You give me your woodstar, and I'll give you and the Sun-lady the thing in that box."

The high priest nodded to the wooden box on the altar.

"Do I have to share it, Your Grace? Do I have to share the thing in there?" For just an instant, Reade thought that High Priest Zeketh might actually laugh. He defended himself. "The woodstar was given to *me,* not to Maida. It's not fair that I have to give it up, and then share what I get for it."

"The woodstar is old, though. See, even now its light has faded." Reade looked down at the bavin. It looked like an ordinary piece of wood now. Its prickly points were cold and black, without a hint of the white light.

"But—"

"Here's a bargain. You give me the woodstar. Then you get to open my gift for you and the Sun-lady."

"That's not fair!" Maida cried.

High Priest Zeketh looked at her and smiled coldly. "Do you have anything to trade?"

Reade could see Maida try to think of something, try to dream up a gift for the high priest. She had nothing but the gown on her body, though, and the ribbon in her hair. At last, she was forced to shake her head. "No, Your Grace."

"Very well, then. Sun-lord? Do we have a deal?"

Reade did not want to give up his bavin. Fishermen got bavins. Da had had a bavin. But there was a present sitting in the wooden box. If Reade did not hand over his woodstar, then Maida would certainly get to open the wooden box. High Priest Zeketh and Duke Coren might even let her keep that gift, all for herself.

Slowly, carefully, Reade nodded. "We have a deal."

Before Reade could change his mind, before he could say that he wanted to keep his woodstar, and Maida could have whatever was in the wooden box, High Priest Zeketh nodded to Duke Coren. The duke retrieved the casket from the altar and held it out toward the priest. Zeketh took it and turned back to the twins. "Sun-lord. Sun-lady. The first twins who bore your name, at the beginning of this age, had a special friend."

"I know," Reade interrupted. "They had Culain." Reade realized that he had cut off the high priest, and he caught his breath. The towering man only smiled, though, his cherry lips curling in his black beard.

"This was a different sort of friend." The high priest nodded toward Duke Coren, who lifted the lid off the wooden casket.

For just an instant, Reade could not figure out what was inside the box. He could see fur—black and tan and white—and he could pick out a long, straight tail. Only when the creature squirmed did Reade see the muzzle and the whiskers. The animal yawned, and Reade saw down its throat, past its black gums and blood-red tongue.

"A dog!" He gasped and jerked backward, hitting Maida and almost falling down the stairs.

"For you, Sun-lord." The high priest nodded, and his own white teeth stood out against his red lips, his black beard. "For you and the Sun-lady."

Reade could not catch his breath. He could not fill his lungs. He could not tell High Priest Zeketh that he needed to escape, needed to get away from the dog. Dogs killed people! Dogs tore at bodies on the beach! Dogs were unclean! Even Da was afraid of dogs. Reade clutched his woodstar against his chest. It wasn't fair! They were trying to fool him! They were trying to get him to give up his woodstar—for a *dog*!

Duke Coren smiled and reached inside the casket. He lifted out the puppy carefully, turning it around so that its head was toward the twins. He held it out toward Reade.

The dog was actually very small. It barely filled the duke's hand. With its mouth closed, the puppy was not nearly as frightening. Duke Coren held out the ball of fur, and his lips curved into a smile. "He belongs to you, Sun-lord. You can touch him."

"No!" Reade exclaimed.

"The first Sun-lord and Sun-lady had a hound named Greatheart who stood by them through fire and flame." Duke Coren's voice was calm and gentle. Da had sounded like that when he first showed Reade how to take a fish off an iron hook. Reade had been scared of the fish, scared of its teeth and its glassy staring eyes. But he had been even more afraid of losing the precious iron hook, of disappointing Da and all the other fishermen.

"Just touch the puppy, little man. After all, you have the power of the Sun-lord!" Reade could remember sitting in front of Duke Coren, could remember the comforting feel of the man's arm around his belly, holding him on the horse, keeping him safe and secure. The power of the Sun-lord, the faith of the Sun-lady, the strength of Culain. Reade was not afraid. Reade was a brave boy. Reade could do anything. Duke Coren stretched his arm toward Reade, reaching out through the incense fog and the smoke. "Touch him!"

Reade could not stop his shaking. He felt as though he'd just been fished out of the ocean, like he stood on the beach in the middle of winter with a full gale blowing. Still, he swallowed hard and forced himself to take a breath. He made himself lean forward. His hand looked as if it belonged to someone else, to another boy, a brave boy. One trembling finger brushed against the puppy's fur.

The animal did not move at all. Reade caught another breath and found the courage to touch the dog again, this time with three fingers. Duke Coren smiled and nodded, beaming down with pride. Relief crashed over Reade, like a wave breaking on the beach.

Duke Coren was proud of him. The duke would keep him safe. Duke Coren would not let him be hurt.

This was a *puppy* after all, not a grown dog. Swallowing hard, Reade started to reach out with both hands.

He'd forgotten, though, that he still held his woodstar. The bavin swung around, came dangerously close to swatting the puppy across its nose. Reade caught the bavin awkwardly and looked up at the two men, embarrassed by his clumsiness.

High Priest Zeketh stepped forward and put his hand on Reade's shoulder. "Here, Sun-lord. Give me that bauble. In fact, why don't you put it here, in this box?" He gestured toward the casket that had held the puppy.

Reade hesitated for a moment. He *had* promised, though. And the woodstar's white light had completely faded away. It even seemed that the bavin had shrunk. It didn't want him. It didn't want him to own it.

What did a woodstar matter, anyway? It was just a piece of wood. A piece of dead old wood. Duke Coren was giving Reade something much better. Duke Coren was giving Reade a living, breathing puppy.

Reade felt the animal squirm beneath his palm. He had not even realized that his fingers had been stroking the puppy's back, rubbing against its soft, soft fur. The puppy yawned again, and then it wrapped its warm tongue around one of Reade's thumbs. He laughed out loud, squirming a bit because the tongue tickled.

What did it matter if Reade wore some stupid piece of carved wood? Shifting his hands to pick up his puppy, Reade dropped his bavin into High Priest Zeketh's wooden casket.

13

A lana shoved her precious iron knife to the bottom of her rucksack before glancing around the cottage. She had little to take on the road. Her patchwork cloak belonged here, with the People. For the next woodsinger, if she did not return.

She sighed and kicked ashes over the last embers on her hearth, then turned for the doorway. "Ai!" she exclaimed, jumping before she recognized Goody Glenna's shadow across the floor. "You frightened me near to death!"

"You'll be nearer, soon enough. What do you think you're doing?"

"I'm riding to Smithcourt." Alana's chin jutted defiantly.

"So much for relying on the power of the Tree, eh?"

"It's no use! Reade's lost to me now. Goody, now that he's given up his bavin, I can't even *try* to help him make the right choices." Alana heard the rising panic in her voice, and she swallowed hard. "Maybe if Sarira had taught me, maybe if she'd introduced me to the Tree, to the other woodsingers, while she still had her power. . . . As things stand, though, I don't have the strength to use the Tree, to guide Reade or Maddock through their bavins." Alana fought for a calming breath. "Goody, I wanted Maddock to be brave, and he ran away. I couldn't even make Reade keep his own bavin. He chose a *dog* over me."

Alana's deep breath threatened to turn into a sob, and she tried to distract herself by gesturing toward her own new-sung woodstar. Its sharp points still pulsed against her flesh, prickling through her bodice. The voices of her sister woodsingers prickled as well, sharper even than Goody Glenna's silent gaze.

"Going off and leaving us, you are." Alana could not identify the individual speaker in her thoughts, but the voice was only one in a swirl of agreement.

"Afraid to work through the Tree, hmm, like a proper woodsinger? Afraid to rely on your sisters?"

"Oh, she's not afraid of us," complained another voice. "It's just that she thinks she's better than we are!"

"Not better, sister," crooned a peacemaker. "She's young, and the blood still beats hot in her veins. She *can* ride, and so she will."

"Aye, she can ride, but does that make it right to do so? She can throw herself off the Headland to swim with the sharks, but does she think that will save the children?"

"Stop it!" Alana cried aloud, and she was surprised that the other woodsingers fell silent. Alana flushed beneath Goody Glenna's scrutiny. "Goody, I've sung myself a bavin so that the Tree can follow me. When . . . if the Councils choose a new woodsinger, she'll be able to find out what happened to me. The other woodsingers will know."

"You've become so wise," Goody Glenna said dryly. "And to think you've only been a woodsinger for two seasons."

"Don't laugh at me, Goody! I'm doing the best I can!"

"Laugh at you? I'm not laughing, girl." The old woman sighed. "Have you spoken to Sartain yet? Which horse are you taking?"

"I-I don't know. The bay, I suppose. The bay mare."

"Very well." Goody Glenna nodded, as if she were crossing items off a list. "I've brought you some herbs."

Reflexively, Alana reached out for the packets, raising each leaf-bound bundle to her face and breathing deeply.

Chamomile, for sweet dreamless sleep.

Redshell, for wakefulness along the road.

Mint, for clear vision.

Heartswell.

"I don't need these, Goody Glenna." She did not need the heartswell. The other woodsingers began to chatter in her mind, reminding her of her embarrassment when she had last consumed the herb. Alana gritted her teeth.

The old woman snorted. "You don't know what you need. Take them. If you never use them, so much the better. I won't be able to sleep nights, knowing you have nothing to help you on your journey."

"Nothing!" exclaimed one of the woodsingers, but Alana thrust down the voice, saying instead: "You knew all along that I was going!"

"I knew that what you were trying here wasn't working." Glenna snorted with an old woman's disdain. "Finish closing up your cottage. I'll fetch the mare for you."

Alana nodded, not trusting herself to speak, and then she was alone in her home, alone but for the sisters who prowled beneath her thoughts. Who was *she,* a woodsinger, to ride across the country, as if she could help the People's best warrior and tracker and healer? Who was *she,* a woman from the People, a young woman at that, to think that she could stride into Smithcourt and change things? Who was *she,* to try to succeed where three trained rescuers had already failed?

Taking a deep breath, Alana settled her fingers over her bavin. "I'll leave you here," she warned. "If I must, I'll leave this bavin behind. I'm riding after Reade and Maida. I'm trying to save Maddock, and Landon and Jobina. You won't stop me." The woodsingers in her mind fell silent.

The sisters must have finally heard the iron in her voice, the tempered metal that was stronger than wood, stronger than the heart of the Tree. For just an instant, there was a flurry of surprised whispers; then the woodsingers settled into watchful silence. Clasping her bavin, Alana could feel the Tree's power beat through the woodstar, shining with an ancient force that warmed her against her sudden chilling fear.

Smiling grimly, she trailed her fingers across her folded patchwork cloak, bidding the garment farewell. Then, she reached out with her mind, stretching through her bavin to another woodstar.

For just an instant, she feared that she would not be able to cross the double bridge, that she could not span the gap from her bavin to the Tree, and from the Tree to Maddock's woodstar. Before she could falter, though, she felt the assembled woodsingers shift, felt their minds fall into neat, orderly place beside hers.

Her sisters were prepared to bolster her power, to give her the strength that she needed for this new feat. Alana could use the double trail of bavins. She could track and ride and reach Smithcourt in good time. And all the while, she could watch Maddock, see what impossible hurdles awaited her in the distant city. She would watch with her sisters, and she would have a plan by the time she arrived in Smithcourt.

Maddock woke slowly, blinking at four white walls and trying to remember where he was. The walls were whitewashed, and cold sunlight leaked through a glazed window. Maddock's eyes fell on a small table.

A golden pitcher glinted dully, partnered by a matching goblet. Memory began to seep back

Maddock recalled the guard selecting him at the postern gate, flicking cold eyes toward him without a glint of recognition. Before Maddock could even be sure that the soldier was Bringham's man, he was hustled through the gate and dragged across a white sand courtyard. Coren's men forced him into hallways so cursed dark that he navigated them better with his eyes shut. He recalled being thrust into a dingy chamber, a room that backed against a kitchen, if the heat and mouth-watering smells were any hint.

His suspicions had been confirmed when a new guard kicked open the door, swaggering in with a heavy platter. Starving after his encounter with Bringham's men and determined to have his full strength as he faced whatever Coren planned for him, Maddock had grabbed a capon leg and stuffed it into his mouth, washing the bird down with warm ale. Only as he bolted half a loaf of bread had he noticed that both the platter and the pitcher were gilded.

All of Maddock's wariness surged back to the front of his mind, and he stood to examine the metal in the meager light from the hallway. When he swallowed again, he could taste a metallic tang at the back of his throat. He sniffed at the ale left in the golden pitcher, and there was a heavy note beneath the drink, a sharp taste that made him swallow hard and fight to bring up the food he had downed. He stumbled to his knees, trying to clench his belly, but he was struck by a wave of dizziness. The disorientation was strong, worse than any wave he'd battled as a fisherman. The golden platter and pitcher clattered onto the floor, and he remembered nothing else, nothing before waking in this strange, white room.

Curse Bringham's men for getting him into this mess! If only they had let him eat the roasted bone that he had gleaned from Coren's leavings! Better yet, if they had fed him, given him the meanest sustenance before sending him to work their labors in Coren's palace! Bogs and breakers! Would it have been so much for them to give him a cup of water?

Maddock dared not drink from the pitcher in this white prison room, even if he could command his drugged body to reach for the gilded ewer. Who knew what potion awaited him beneath the golden surface?

He'd had such strange dreams while he slept—visions of Alana Woodsinger on horseback, bent low across a bay mare's neck. Once, he thought he'd glimpsed Reade and Maida in some sort of ceremonial hall, surrounded by mist. *That* vision must have been a dream—a nightmare—for Maddock had seen Reade touching a puppy, petting a *dog* as if it were a tame, loving beast.

Sharks and fins! If he'd dreamed such visions, had he cried out? Had he betrayed himself and let Coren's men hear his Land's End accent? As Maddock's heart raced with new adrenaline, he realized that he must have kept silent; otherwise, he'd be in a dungeon. Or worse. He raised a hand to wipe sweat from his upper lip and realized for the first time that his wrists were covered with loops of golden chain, links that glinted as balefully as the pitcher on the side table. A massive lock rested above his hands, heavy and ominous with its empty, keyless mouth.

A quick tug confirmed that the chain was looped around his waist. Staring down, Maddock found that he was wrapped in yards of clean, white samite. Wrapped like a sacrifice to the Guardians. Like an offering for the altar in the Sacred Grove. With an effort, he managed to climb to his feet, staggering a few steps and shaking his head to clear away the fog. Tossing his head made him overbalance, though, and he crashed to the floor.

The chains about his wrists kept him from breaking his fall, and he thudded against the floor, absorbing most of the impact with his chest. That was when he learned that he still wore his bavin. The woodstar's spikes dug into his flesh, sharp as tiny knives. He started to curse, but bit back the words when the door to his chamber crashed open.

A finger of chilly sunlight picked out the dripping red knives that were embroidered across both guards' chests. Maddock snarled deep in his throat, scarcely remembering that he was supposed to be mute. He tried to pull himself into a fighter's crouch, but only managed to tangle himself in his robes. His determination was rewarded by a harsh laugh, like a boat scraping across a rocky beach.

"Who do you think you're going to fight, sewer scum?" Maddock could only glare as the older man spat on him. "Let's go, boy." The younger guard wrestled Maddock to his feet and prodded him into the hallway.

Sharks and fins! Maddock was as awkward as a fish on land, flopping against the corridor walls as a length of chain snagged between his feet, and his robes caught between his legs. Grimacing as he slammed his shoulder against a stone wall, he swallowed an angry retort. Soon, the guards had herded him to a tower. They wound down endless spiral stairs, round and round, deeper into the palace walls.

A series of narrow windows informed Maddock that he was closer to the ground, at the ground, then under the earth. The stone steps were slick with water, as if rain had blown in the unglazed slashes and then flowed down the stairs. Pits had been dug in the rock by the passage of countless feet.

One of the guards kept pushing at Maddock's back, prodding with his short sword whenever the outlander hesitated. Maddock's head reeled, as if he'd been wrapping fishing nets around an endless spool. He tried to lean into the stairs' stony spine, but the guards kept him moving too quickly, stepping too fast.

At last, just as Maddock concluded that the spiral stairs were some endless torture, the men reached the end of the steps. Now they were far below ground, and as Maddock panted to catch his breath, he could smell the damp. Patches of lichen flaked off the walls, scaly yellow and green beneath flickering torches. The colors reminded him of bruises.

Before his head stopped reeling, the guards pushed him toward an ornately carved doorway. Sea shapes writhed above his head, and he reflexively looked for fish that he could recognize. Even as he picked out a carved squid, tentacles waving through the stone like poisoned streamers, the senior soldier set a heavy hand between his shoulders and shoved him through the doorway. "On your knees before High Priest Zeketh!"

Maddock could not keep from grunting as he fell to his knees on the stone floor.

"I thought you said this one was mute." A voice hissed from the darkness on the far side of the small chamber.

"Aye, my lord." Even as Maddock's heart pounded in his ears, he heard naked fear in the guard's voice. "He's got lungs in his chest and cords in his throat, but he doesn't say words."

"He's a mess! I've told you to bathe the prisoners before you bring them here!"

The soldier stammered, "I-I'm sorry, Your Grace. He was late coming to us. We thought that if he wore the robes and the chains, that would be enough."

"You *thought*!" Zeketh raged. "Did you stop to *think* that this man is here to honor the Seven Gods?"

"N-no, Your Grace."

"Do you *think* the Seven Gods should be defiled by your incompetence?"

"No, Your Grace."

"I haven't time for this foolishness. Get him to his feet! Hand him to me."

Maddock had to bite his tongue to keep from exclaiming as the younger guard tugged hard on his golden bonds, knocking the breath from his lungs. His legs were trembling from the endless stairs, and he looked as if he were quaking when the soldier handed a length of chain to the priest.

"Very well," Zeketh said to the guards. "You may wait by the stairs. Do I need to remind you that no one—*no one*—must know that I am here?"

"No, Your Grace," the senior guard said, even as he and his fellow backed toward the stairwell. The soldiers closed the door behind them, and Maddock wondered how he could already miss their presence, how he could have found the brutes a comfort. Silently, he shivered and reminded himself that he was a warrior. He repeated that admonition more desperately as the high priest unlocked a shadowed door and dragged him into another, larger room.

A fire burned in a pit at the far side of this chamber, sending out tendrils of heat against the chilly stone. The crumbling flue did not draft well, though, and smoke seeped into the room. The walls were blackened to either side of the fireplace, and the floor was dull with soot.

The smoky light glinted off a glass box sitting beside the hearth. As Maddock blinked, he made out thick crystal walls that were as high as his chest and twice as long as his body. Sand gleamed behind the bubbled glass, pure silver sand like the finest stuff on the People's beaches. A bare branch leaned against the glass walls, stark black against the glimmering silver. Thorns as long as Maddock's palm glistened in the firelight.

Before Maddock could wonder at the meaning of such a large enclosure, of such long thorns, High Priest Zeketh reached out for his prisoner's chain, pulling Maddock toward the glass with one sharp tug. As Maddock raised his hands to protect himself, the priest grabbed hold of his wrists, twisting the golden links with thick, strong fingers.

Even as Maddock fought to free himself, the priest produced a knife out of nowhere, an iron blade that barely glinted in the firelight. Maddock thrashed as the weapon drew near; he kicked out and bellowed wordlessly. His timing was off though, victim of the drug that still pumped in his veins. Zeketh's blade found its home easily, slicing through Maddock's palm as if he were simply a boiled fish.

For an instant, Maddock felt nothing, and then the dungeon's fetid air stung his wound like the acid in a sea snail's trail. He sucked air through his teeth and braced himself for further attack, but there was none. Instead, the priest held the knife aloft, muttering some unholy prayer.

"Hail, Seven Gods," the priest intoned. "Accept this offering of blood and sanctify the one who bleeds. Make him most holy, that he may do thy sacred works. Bless the one who bleeds, most honored Seven Gods."

Zeketh twisted the blade in the flickering firelight, and Maddock could see his own blood glistening silver-red on the dagger. He fought down a wave of nausea. Unbidden, he remembered the words of Bringham's man—no one had survived this ordeal. No one had lived to tell whatever evil Zeketh planned. Maddock must find a way to get through whatever the priest plotted, to get through, and to escape the palace, and to deliver his intelligence to Bringham's men.

And to find Reade and Maida. He mustn't forget Reade and Maida. Reade and Maida and Landon and Jobina. Maddock shook his head and silently cursed the drugged food and ale. His thoughts were thick, muffled. He was having trouble remembering his most basic mission, his most basic goal. He needed to concentrate, needed to focus on what was happening to him. That was his only hope to get out of the dungeon room alive.

The priest lowered his weapon and stalked to the fireplace. Maddock swayed and squinted to make out a wooden box that sat beside the hearth. The priest knelt low, touching his brow to the iron clasp, all the while holding the dripping knife above his head. Then, with Maddock's harsh breath the only sound in the room, Zeketh opened the box.

Maddock knew that he should attack the priest. He should take advantage of the fact that Zeketh had his back to him. Maddock should raise the chains that were slung between his wrists, should throw them around the priest's throat, pull them tight. Try as he might, though, he could not make himself move, could not issue the order through his fuzzy mind to his drugged arms.

As Maddock fought down a moan of fear, he blinked hard, managing to clarify the scene across the room. Against all expectation, the priest lifted a rabbit out of the wooden box. The coney trembled in the man's hands, but the priest ignored the creature's obvious terror. Slowly, he shifted his grip to the front of the animal's furry throat. Then, he took his bloody knife and thrust it into the rabbit's neck, piercing the base of the animal's skull.

As Zeketh sawed back and forth with a double motion, the rabbit convulsed. Blood began to well from its wound, but the priest neatly shifted his furry burden, holding the animal so that the crimson pooled against its soft grey fur.

Maddock watched with horror as Zeketh approached the glass cage. For an instant, he thought that the priest was going to impale the rabbit's carcass on one of the long thorns. Instead, the holy man laid the animal on the silvery sand, passing a hand over it with apparent gentleness.

For ten heartbeats, there was nothing, not even the sound of Maddock's ragged breathing, for he caught his breath and waited for something to happen. Then, the sand exploded upward, grains of silver flying through the air, spattering the glass walls, showering the black branch.

Maddock jerked back and his eyes blinked in reflex, but he still made out the horror in the glass cage. He saw the long, scaly body, the yawning mouth, the razor fangs that glinted in the dim light, dripping with a poison that glistened like pearls.

In seconds, all was over. The coney's belly was shoved against three brutal spikes, suspended above the floor of silver sand. On either side of the priest's knife slash, fang marks gleamed like holes to another world. The flesh already shriveled around the strike marks, boiling into pustules that broke open and filled the room with a rotten stench. As Maddock stared, the coney's body writhed on its spikes, contorting as the corruption spread from the pair of wounds. Great gobbets of flesh fell onto the silvery sand, staining it black with polluted blood.

Maddock's gorge rose, almost distracting him from another motion in the sand. The silver grains began to move, sliding across each other with an audible hiss. Maddock could make out a spiral shape in the sand, swirling faster and tighter. The chunks of rotted rabbit fell toward the center of the vortex, clumping together in a single night-black mess. Before the rotted blood could melt into the sand, the massive snake reappeared, exploding from the bottom of its whirlpool. Jaws agape, the serpent swallowed the entire putrid mass that moments before had been a living, breathing beast.

Only when the snake had bolted its meal did it lie upon the sand. Its eyes glared up at Maddock, daring him to look at the bulge of meat that even now moved down the animal's throat, pulsing slowly toward its acid gut.

"Excellent," Zeketh whispered, pulling Maddock back from his horror. The outlander, still snared in his drugged haze, was captivated by the single word, fascinated by the other man's red, red lips, by the white teeth that glinted against his night-black beard. "So, now you have seen the Avenger's power. You've seen her power, and her attraction to the drug that beats in your veins." At Maddock's confused look, the high priest laughed. "Aye. The capon you ate and the ale you drank were laced with a tempting little potion, a poison that cries out to the Avenger. It summons her from her sleep beneath the sand. It still runs thick enough in your blood to transfer to my knife, to the rabbit."

Maddock clenched his fist, willing his heart to stop feeding the crimson seam across his palm. His fingers were slick with his own blood, and he imagined that the snake was stirring in its cage, even now flickering its tongue, seeking out another fresh meal.

Meanwhile, the priest towered over Maddock, seeming to fill the dark chamber. Maddock looked at the gorged snake and fought the urge to empty his stomach on the sooty flagstones. He closed his eyes and willed himself to stillness.

"You'll look at me when I speak to you!" the priest bellowed, and Maddock's head shot up. "That's better. Now, what is your name?"

Maddock's throat worked as he remembered his assumed muteness, and the priest took a moment before he laughed. "Ah, that's right. The guards said that you were mute. I should have thought of that before—a speechless man tells no tales. Of course, that assumes that you'd ever have someone to tell stories to. None of my other . . . assistants have." The priest darted another fond glance toward the crystal cage. "Very well then. I shall call you . . . Blackhand, for such you shall surely have before your service to Duke Coren is complete."

Maddock was certain that he blanched at the priest's chortle, but he refrained from speaking aloud. He could not keep his sickened glance, though, from falling on the thread of blood that still trickled across his palm. "So, Blackhand," the priest continued. "Here is your mission. Our duke needs the Avenger's poison. One bite, like the coney received, makes her venom flow. The second bite, though, that's the treasure trove. The poison will drip from the Avenger's fangs, more copious, due to the drug that you have consumed. Unfortunately for you, there's only one way to harvest that wealth. I'll collect it from your wounds in the few seconds before . . . it is too late."

Zeketh turned to the mantel over the fireplace, showing Maddock a crystal goblet. "I hope you give us a fine harvest. Time is running short. Your flesh might withstand the poison for a few minutes—you look like a strong man. Better than some of the miserable wretches we've had here."

Maddock shook his head, trying to clear away the cobwebs in his drugged mind. The miserable wretches . . . Of course, those must be the other men that Bringham's followers had mentioned; they must be the rebels who had found their way into Coren's palace, never to escape. What had the men said—three of their fellows had been lost? How many others had been taken to this dungeon, though? How many others who had begged at the postern gate, unnoticed by rebels or dukes? How many men had been offered a meal, drugged, poisoned?

Shaking his head against the gilded potion that still confused his thoughts, Maddock flashed a defiant glare toward the priest. "Ah," the tall man crowed. "You have spirit. Fine. The Avenger feeds best on rebellion. Come then. Let the harvest begin."

Before Maddock could brace himself, the high priest unlocked the warrior's golden manacles with a single twist of a suddenly produced key. The same movement brought the priest behind Maddock, forcing his chest against the sharp upper edge of the glass cage.

The priest caught Maddock so that his still-bleeding hand was levered over the crystal side, hanging dangerously above the sand pit.

Maddock bellowed as the priest pushed him, but before he could fight for his freedom, he felt the telltale prick of the iron knife, steady above his vulnerable kidneys. Realizing that he could not waste time on such a mundane threat, Maddock forced himself to focus on the greatest danger in this room of death.

The Avenger turned toward him, sluggishly flicking her crimson-tipped tongue. The smell of fresh blood apparently excited the beast, and Maddock heard a warning above the pounding of his own heart—the jangle of the animal's scales as she inflated the fleshy collar about her head. The snake began to weave, mesmerizing the outlander. She swayed back and forth as she ignored the absurd bulge in her gullet, the only remaining evidence of the meal she had consumed only minutes before.

As Maddock stared at the Avenger, he experienced the cold shock of a memory relived, a shiver of ancient recollection that cut through the Smithcourt drugs. For just a moment, his bavin burned hot against his flesh, stinging sharper than the knife cut across his palm. He thought of Alana Woodsinger, thought of the woodstars that were lashed to every fishing boat among the People.

And as he remembered those woodstars, he recalled his childhood. As a boy, he had played along the People's rocky beaches. He had challenged other children to capture the stinging eels that nestled in stony crags along the shore. The eels were long and muscled, with a bulge in their throats where they strained shrimps and small fish. They had sharp teeth and a mean bite; the People's children dared each other to venture onto the slippery rocks to snare the creatures. They were not good for eating, but their oil burned bright and clean.

Now, forgetting that he was in a duke's dungeon, forgetting that he was in danger for his life, forgetting that he was an entire country away from the ocean that had nurtured him and protected him and fed him all his life, Maddock took a deep breath against the edge of the glass cage.

Blood had filled his cupped palm, and a single shimmering drop fell to the silver sand. Before Maddock could react, the Avenger darted forward, sinking her fangs into the sand, impaling herself on a single ruby pearl of man-blood. Maddock moved before the snake could discover her mistake.

With his cut hand, he grabbed the serpent behind her neck, using the bulge of digesting rabbit as an anchor for his muscled wrist. Without pausing to think of what would happen if the snake's jaws worked differently from the stinging eels', Maddock clamped his thumb and forefinger on either side of the creature's mouth, forcing the jaws open.

Fangs glinted in the firelight, pearly with poison, and Maddock whirled toward the mantel. He seized Zeketh's crystal goblet and caught the snake's fangs against the cup's edge, bearing down with all his weight. The Avenger had recovered from her initial surprise, and now she thrashed about her cage, sending up sprays of silver sand. Maddock's grip slipped because of the blood that slicked his palm, but he dared not shift to a more secure position. Instead, he crushed the snake against the glass walls, trapping the serpent's head between the sheet of bubbled glass and the crystal goblet's sharp edge.

The snake's venom flowed more freely as she fought for her life. Two drops of poison turned to four and then eight, and Maddock continued to grasp the furious beast. The poison slid down the inside of the crystal goblet like sweetened wine, pooling in the bottom of the cup.

Even as Maddock stared at the opalescent liquid,

he realized that he was not yet done. He needed to release the snake and clear the top of the cage, all without letting the poison touch his own open flesh. He could only use one hand, and he must act soon, or he would have no more strength.

Already, his right arm was beginning to tremble from the unrelieved exertion. Filling his lungs and planting his feet, Maddock used the last of his strength to shift his grip on the massive snake's head. With a flip of his wrist, he thrust her toward the far side of the cage, managing at the same time to pull himself safely over the top of the enclosure. Throughout the maneuver, he kept the goblet steady with its precious pool of poison.

For an instant, the only sound in the room was Maddock's tortured breathing. Then, he became aware of other noises—of something knocking frantically against glass, of High Priest Zeketh crying out to his Seven Gods.

Forcing himself to focus, Maddock made out the cause of the commotion. The Avenger writhed on the spiked branch, impaled neatly on the same three thorns that had caught the rotting rabbit. As Maddock watched, the snake's thrashing increased until the beast snagged her own skin, ripping her flesh in a frenzy to be free. As Maddock stared, the Avenger tore her neck from the branch, twisting enough to sink her fangs into her own tortured side.

The snake's demise was as swift as the rabbit's. The serpent's venom ate her own flesh, boiling the meat into black corruption. Within seconds, the Avenger's only remains were a streak of slime and her own vicious fangs, glinting through the cage like deep-ocean pearls.

Maddock tore his gaze away from the mess, managing to face High Priest Zeketh. As if he intended the motion, he raised his left hand, still grasping the crystal goblet. Just remembering to hold his tongue, he bowed deeply and set the cup in the High Priest's waiting hands.

"Ah," Zeketh said after settling the chalice on the mantel. Maddock read volumes of furious respect in the single word. The priest studied him through eyes that glistened like venom. "Killing the Avenger was a grievous wrong, Blackhand. The Mothersnake will not take well to your action. I'd execute you here and now, but you might still serve the Seven Gods. We still need venom—two more harvests at least. Fortunately for you, we have another of the Mothersnake's spawn. You'll meet the Destroyer tomorrow."

Then, before Maddock could brace himself, Zeketh reached forward and twisted his golden chains, jerking the outlander upright so abruptly that Maddock thought his arms would be pulled from their sockets. The priest ignored his prisoner's wordless exclamation, producing his iron key from some deep pocket and shutting the lock on Maddock's manacles. Before the outlander could struggle, Zeketh forced him out of the snake's room, back to the antechamber and the door at the bottom of the stairs.

Belatedly, the two soldiers sprang to attention, and even through the screen of his drugged, exhausted vision, Maddock realized that they had never expected to see a live prisoner emerge from the inner chamber. The older man recovered first, jumping forward as Zeketh growled, "Remember, men. You have not seen me, not here in Coren's palace. It will be your lives if I hear otherwise."

Both guards assented and bowed their necks, and then they chivvied Maddock up the twisting stairs. Zeketh disappeared back into the smoky dungeon room, shutting the door with an ominous thud.

Maddock could barely make his legs climb the endless steps. Why were the guards to pretend that they had not seen Zeketh? What had happened in that dungeon room? What did Zeketh want with the deadly poison? And what, in the name of all the Guardians, was the Mothersnake?

After a lifetime of climbing, Maddock was shoved into his chamber. "Cursed fool!" the older soldier spat. "Now we'll have to stand guard the rest of the night. You!" the man snarled at his companion. "Keep an eye on him. I'm going to get our evening rations."

The door slammed on the younger soldier's protest, and Maddock sprawled on the floor, trying to catch his breath. What evil did Coren intend to work with the poison? Was he going to murder Bringham, or one of his other rivals? That made no sense—there were easier means of assassination. Perhaps he intended to make an example of Jobina and Landon, to execute them so that they became a hideous lesson to any who would rebel against the duke? No sense there, either. One twist of rope was all he needed to dispatch the rebel pursuers—a good executioner could teach many an object lesson without the showmanship of the Avenger's poison.

Shivering, Maddock pulled himself to his knees and dragged his aching body across the small room. He was thirsty; his throat burned as if he had lived in the Avenger's silver desert for decades.

He lifted the hammered metal to his lips before he smelled the metallic drug. Of course, the water would be tainted. With a prisoner's certainty, Maddock knew that he could slake his thirst, he could drink, and awake tomorrow, and find another snake, the Destroyer. And, if he were strong enough, he'd find another serpent. And maybe even another, even the Mothersnake.

He had to escape. Now.

Maddock glanced at the glazed window. It was too narrow for a man. Besides, he knew how many steps he had climbed—the fall from this height would kill him. Nevertheless . . . If the sea only presented krill, then a fisherman used his tightest net.

Before he could question his own decision, before he could let his bone-shaking weariness win out, Maddock hefted the pitcher in his good hand. The first time he crashed it against the glass, the pane held. Realizing that the older guard might return at any minute, though, Maddock swung again, putting his full body weight behind the blow.

And as he swung, he bellowed, "In the name of all the Guardians!"

The glass shattered. Sparkling fragments caught at the late-afternoon sun, glinting like light on a tumbling wave. Maddock was too high in the tower to hear the glass as it hit the ground below, and he did not waste time listening. Instead, he leaped to the side of the door, setting his chained hands in front of him to protect himself from being crushed when the soldier came to stop his outcry, to silence the secret prisoner. All the time, he continued to cry out, hollering his words into the hinges that held the door fast.

He needed the guard to hear him, to be compelled to act, but he could not afford for any other assistance to arrive. He could not risk being liberated by one of Coren's men who had journeyed to the Headland, who would recognize him as one of the People. He directed his words to the door: "They're keeping me prisoner here! They're holding me against my will! In the name of all the Guardians, help me!"

The wooden door slammed back on its hinges, and all of Maddock's bracing was hardly enough to keep him from being stunned. He barely managed to step clear as the younger soldier tumbled into the cell, set off balance by his own force. "You lying bastard!" the man exclaimed. "You're no cursed mute!"

The guard expected Maddock to be at the window; he thought his prisoner was calling out to the court-yard below. It took him only a moment to regain his footing, to realize that the door had not swung all the way back to the wall. That moment, though, was

enough for Maddock, who brought his golden pitcher
crashing down upon the guard's head, putting all his
weight, all his sick terror of the Avenger, behind the
blow. The man crumpled to the floor like a child's
plaything.

Maddock closed the door to his prison room, panting hard as he stared at the soldier. He dared not
waste time; the older guard should be returning soon,
and someone might actually have been summoned by
the falling glass, by Maddock's bellows. Fumbling, he
dug out the key to his chains. It took him longer to
unlock the clasp than it had taken Zeketh, and then
he had to find the strength to unwind the golden links.
The yards of slippery samite were an even greater
challenge to his trembling hands, and he was slicked
with sweat by the time he had finished. His belly
turned as he saw that the wound across his palm still
bled, and the snowy cloth was stained a brilliant
crimson.

For an instant, Maddock contemplated escaping in
his familiar garments, filthy though they were. Then,
he realized that he might have need of further disguise. He paused for a moment to lift the bloodied
samite to his teeth, and his head jerked back as he
tore free a length to use as a bandage. He wrapped it
around his palm several times, making sure to cover
his wound completely.

After he was certain that he would not bleed over
his new clothes, he turned back to the still-unconscious
guard. It took almost all of his remaining strength to
lift the man, to tug free the man's trews. By the time
Maddock jerked the soldier's particolor doublet into
place, he was breathing hard, snorting as if he'd run
a footrace.

Still gasping for breath, Maddock hesitated when he
saw his bavin dangling over the embroidered bloody
knife that now decorated his chest. He dared not leave
the woodstar, not when its presence would signal to

Coren exactly who had lain inside this room. Instead, he muttered a prayer to the Guardians and tucked the bavin inside his soldierly doublet. The Guardians and the Great Mother had watched over him so far. He could only hope that his luck held.

When he stood, though, black streamers floated in front of his eyes, and he had to take several deep breaths to stay upright. Even as he told himself that he had no time, that the other soldier could return at any moment, that strangers could appear, Maddock could not remember how to make his legs move.

Shaking his head, he was nearly overwhelmed by a vision of snake-rotted flesh falling from bones. Resting one trembling hand over the bavin that was now hidden beneath his uniform, Maddock drew a deep breath.

The woodstar remained cool beneath his touch, but it steadied his thoughts, gave him an anchor as he drifted in his strange drugged sea. Ducking out of his cell, Maddock staggered down the castle corridor before he could think about how lost he was. How lost and alone and desperate. . . .

14

❖❖❖❖

Alana trudged along the road, wishing that she could mount her bay mare, that she could gallop up to the Smithcourt gates and be done with her long journey. Instead, she settled her fists into the small of her back, trying to stretch her exhausted muscles as she cautioned herself to patience. Just a little more patience . . .

She had ridden from Land's End for days, crossing the restless land without incident. It was only as she'd neared Smithcourt that she'd realized she would need a disguise, some excuse for making her way into the city. Alana had watched through Maddock's bavin, and she knew just how difficult it could be to gain entrance to Smithcourt. Even armed with the fisherman's experience, she still had no password for the city gates.

Unable to solve the puzzle of breaching the Smithcourt walls, she had reached for the woodsingers in her mind, talking to them across the leagues.

"You could act like an evening companion for the guards," one of the voices cooed. "Like Lila. She made her way in without problem." Alana hoped that her distance from the woodsingers, the stretched thread of her thoughts through her bavin, would dull some of her sharp surprise. When she heard her sister woodsinger's trilling laugh, though, she knew that her thoughts were just as clear as if she had spoken them in the same room.

"You could be a pilgrim," another woodsinger suggested, "intent on honoring their Seven Gods."

"You could be a madwoman."

"You could be a widow, coming to the duke for justice. Justice for your slain husband."

Alana grabbed at that suggestion. She *was* coming to Smithcourt for justice. She *was* coming to make demands of Duke Coren. A few more silent conversations with her sister woodsingers, and she had settled on her disguise: she would be exhausted, terrified, and pregnant.

She wasted nearly a day watching various folk on the road before selecting a family of merchants to be her companions for the last, crucial leagues. The traders had a boisterous swarm of boys who ranged in size from sprouts to saplings. The father hunched miserably on the driver's bench of a wagon loaded down with wooden goods—tables and chairs, ladders, and stools. Elspeth, the domineering mother, was pregnant herself, and she walked beside the wagon, shouting frequent instructions and admonitions to her brood. Kari, the youngest child and the only girl, walked beside Alana.

"What's in your horse's saddlebags?" Kari asked the question, as if she had not made the demand a dozen times that morning.

"Herbs." Alana was tired of giving the same answer.

"What kind of herbs?"

"All kinds."

"What do they do?"

"Help people who are sick."

"Why did you bring them?"

"To sell at market."

The child ran out of questions, and Alana relished the silence. She plodded on for more than a dozen steps before she became suspicious. When she looked

back at the mare, she saw Kari's hand deep in her
saddlebags, rummaging around. "Don't touch that!"

"I'm sorry," Kari lisped immediately, offering up a
grinning apology for the tenth time since dawn. Alana
resisted the urge to wrap her fingers around the child's
neck. Was this how Goody Glenna felt when she
trained the People's children? Were Reade and Maida
as inquisitive as this girl?

"Of course," one of the woodsingers responded,
speaking through Alana's bavin.

"Maida could be even worse," thought another distant woman.

"But neither of the twins was as bad as Sartain.
When he was a boy . . ."

Alana shook her head, pulling away from the woodsingers' chatter, not trusting herself to listen to the
tales of Sartain Fisherman's childhood. The woodsingers were so far away. No matter how much they cared
about Alana, no matter how much they wanted her
to succeed, they could not wholly understand the danger that she faced. Her sisters could not know the
complete differentness of the land that Alana now
crossed. They were loved and honored, but they could
not help Alana as she now needed to be helped.

Looking up in time to catch Kari with her hands
in the saddlebags yet again, Alana said through set
teeth, "Leave my herbs alone!"

"Ach! Is my whelp of a daughter bothering you
again?" Elspeth waddled up to the side of the wagon,
breathing heavily as she rested her hands on her bulging belly. She grimaced at Alana. "Why do we let men
do it to us, eh? Why do we let them stuff us full?"
Elspeth took a deep breath, as if the air would settle
the child inside her. "Go on, Kari. Run up ahead with
your father. Leave us women to talk."

Kari pouted, but she sprinted up to the front of
the wagon, where her father was driving the team of
spavined horses. Elspeth clicked her tongue. "Let her

father watch her, that's what I say. I've got enough on my mind, with this one coming at the next moon. Kari's father can keep an eye on her for once, don't you know. Only thing men *are* good for!"

Alana struggled to patch together a response from her limited knowledge of men, and Elspeth typically misinterpreted her silence. "Ach! There I go again, stepping in the dung! I'm sorry, Lani! I was forgetting all about your Ronan. How could I be so foolish, Lani?"

How could she be so *loud*? Alana thought. When the woodsinger had changed her name, she'd never imagined she would hear it wailed so often, or so plaintively.

"I *told* him," Elspeth proclaimed, and it took Alana a moment to realize that the carpenter-woman was referring to her own husband, not Alana's putative spouse. "I *told* him I was too far along with this one to come to Smithcourt, but he said that I had to come, that I could argue for a better price for our goods. You never can trust a man, now can you, dear?"

The woodsinger retreated into her own thoughts as Elspeth continued her recitation of woes. Alana was worried about Maddock. Over the past weeks, reaching through his bavin, she had come to know the man like a part of herself. She had lived his shame when he fled from the roadside inn. She had known his lust when he let himself be seduced by Lila.

Since he had confronted the Avenger, though, she had sensed almost nothing but confusion through his woodstar. Horror at the enemy's tools, terror at his role in milking the snake. . . . But overwhelmingly, simple confusion. Alana wondered what drugs they had forced into his body, what they had fed him in his poisoned pitcher of water that could have left him so disoriented. She resisted the urge to raise her fingers to her bavin, to stretch back to the Tree and out again for Maddock, to see how he fared.

It was just as well that she did not touch the wood-star, because Elspeth was peering expectantly at her, apparently misinterpreting the effect of her constant chatter. "Well, tie me to the wagon! I haven't been thinking at all, you poor thing. Lani, why didn't you tell me to shut my fat mouth? Here I am bemoaning *my* troubles, and I haven't given a thought to your own!"

Alana managed a demure smile, trying to look like a young, pregnant widow. She was helped by the quickening breeze, a gust of wind that tugged at her hair. As she brushed the strands from her face, she thought of Landon, of the tracker whose hair had blown in a similar wind, the last time she had seen him in the flesh. Landon, whom she had almost forgotten about on her desperate ride. Landon, with his poor, thinning hair . . .

How would their lives have been different, if she had accepted his mistletoe berries at midwinter? Would Duke Coren still have stolen the children if Alana had not paid him undue attention during his treacherous visit? If she had not accepted his evil gifts? Would she be sitting beside her own hearth, even now, safe and warm and filled with a true child, if she had accepted Landon's intentions?

The wind whipped dust into her eyes and tears welled up without her bidding. "I'm sorry, Elspeth," she choked out, forcing aside an image of the gawky, balding man who had loved her. "It's just that I keep thinking of . . . Ronan. He was such a good man. If only I had told him about our little one that night, that night those outlanders came to our village. . . ." Alana went on with her rehearsed story, ignoring the tears that streamed down her cheeks. For a moment at least, she truly believed her tale. "Burned he was, like a roasted chicken! It took him three days to die, and no one to tend him but me, as all the others rode after the outlanders!"

Alana saw the scene as if it had been real. She hugged her arms against her chest, and her bavin nestled warm against her skin, recalling the fire she spoke of, the fire her Landon had witnessed at the King's Horse in the tiny village. The fire that Maddock had shown her, through his own bavin. Once again, her belly turned over, a queasy reminder of how far she was from home.

"Why do you talk funny?" Kari interrupted her dark recollection.

"What do you mean?" Alana choked out, forcing her mind back to the merchant's wagon and wondering how the child could already be finished pestering her father.

"I mean, why do you say your words funny?" Kari turned to her mother, with every bit of the directness that Reade harnessed when he was focused on some new mischief. "Doesn't she, Mum? Doesn't she talk all strange like?"

"Kari!" Elspeth chided. "Don't be rude."

"But Mum—"

"Go walk with your brothers, Kari."

"I just—"

"Kari!"

The child gave up her protest and darted around the wagon. Shrieks went up from five different voices, and Alana wondered what mischief the child was working among her siblings. The woodsinger kept her eyes on the dusty road, hoping that she could avoid further questions.

"I'm sorry," Elspeth puffed. "She hasn't learned what's right and what's wrong. Her father spoils her entirely too much—her being the only girl, and all." The women continued plodding beside the wagon for a few steps before she cast a sly look at Alana. "Still, your accent *is* a touch strange. . . ."

Elspeth trailed off expectantly, and Alana swallowed a grimace. In the past three days, she had learned that the carpenter-woman would not be put off for long. Alana extemporized: "Years ago, I came from the west. I was only a little older than Kari. My parents left the coastland; they were afraid of the folk there." She laughed and did not need to fake the nervous note behind her words. "I did not realize my speech still sounded of my past. My Ronan always told me he liked the way I spoke. . . ."

Alana let her voice quaver on the last sentence, and Elspeth responded as expected, folding the woodsinger into a nest of acceptances and justifications. They walked a full mile in silence then, as Alana remembered the husband she had never had and the suitor she had rejected, a lifetime ago when she had been a girl among the People.

Later that afternoon, they crested a rise, and all of Smithcourt lay before them, glistening on its plain. "Cor, Mum! It's beautiful!" Kari instinctively reached up for an adult's hand against the city's splayed riches. Alana stifled the urge to pull away from the sticky fingers when she turned out to be the nearest adult.

"Aye, that it is, little one." Elspeth beamed up at Alana as she huffed to catch her breath. "I bet you never thought it would be that large, now did you?"

"Of course, I did," Alana replied without thinking. She had seen the same view twice before, first through Reade's bavin, then through Maddock's. She realized her mistake as Elspeth looked at her queerly. "My Ronan told me, of course. He journeyed to the city many times."

"Ach! Poor man, for all the good it did him. Well you just stay the course, Lani. By tomorrow eve, you'll be requesting your audience with the duke. He'll find justice for you. He'll get you the wergild you deserve. A man's life, and his wife expecting a little one—the duke will pay you your coin, and then he'll refill his treasury come the spring, when he rides to punish those murdering outlanders!"

Alana shivered at the vindictive tone in the woman's voice, hoping that her own horror would be mistaken for grief. What was she doing traveling with these people? What would happen if she were found out? How could she hope to succeed where Maddock, Landon, and Jobina had already failed?

The carpenters swung back into action, Elspeth shouting harsh words to her husband until he got the horses moving in their traces. The road sloped down to the city, and the two rear animals leaned back on their haunches, straining wearily to slow their heavy load. As they reached the long plain before Smith-court, the carpenters fell into an endless line of carts, some even shoddier than their own. Grocers, leather-workers, cloth merchants—all brought their goods through Market Gate.

As Alana inched forward, she watched Elspeth ready the wagon for passage into town. The heavy woman worked side by side with her husband, lashing down goods, tugging at protective tarps. Her sons scampered over the load like squirrels, and Kari whined that she was too little to do the fun work. Once Alana reached up to tug a tarp into place, but Elspeth barked, "Leave that alone! You, in your condition!"

"But you—" Alana began.

"I've been working on wagons my entire life. Kari! Move your fingers if you don't want to lose them! See here, Lani. I bore *that* brat while we were loading up for the spring market five years ago, and I walked to town while she was still looking for my dug to suckle." Kari made a face as she ducked away from her mother's swatting hand, and Alana blushed at the woman's forthright words. Oblivious, Elspeth swore at a tight knot. "Lani, if you want to help, keep an eye on Kari.

I won't have anyone say that you lost your babe on account of us. If we can't handle our load, we have no business coming to the city."

Alana muttered a few more protests, but she already knew that she was not likely to win against Elspeth's carefully orchestrated campaign. Swallowing a grimace, she fell back with Kari.

"Why are we waiting in this line?" the child asked immediately.

"So that the soldiers can inspect the cart."

"Why do they want to inspect the cart?"

"To make sure that your parents pay duty on the goods they're going to sell."

"Why do they have to pay duty?"

"So that Duke Coren can save the land from marauding outlanders."

"Oh."

Alana stared at Kari with suspicion, not quite believing that she had dammed the flow of questions with her bitter answer. The little girl looked at Alana's cloth-bulged belly, then up at the woodsinger's face. She seemed about to speak, but then swallowed her words with unexpected tact. The pair edged forward quietly, one cart length. Another.

"Lani?"

Alana braced herself. "Yes, Kari."

"Will Duke Coren ride for you? Will he kill the bad men who killed your husband?"

Alana's voice was deadly chill, and she hoped the child would accept her warning tone. "Duke Coren rides for whomever he chooses. There's no telling who he'll kill."

Of course, Kari missed the meaning behind the words, and it took her only a moment to launch a new string of questions. Why were the city walls made of stone? Why were there only two soldiers inspecting wagons? Why did they unload all the goods from that wagon over there? Why? Why? Why?

Alana fell into the rhythm of the game, phrasing her answers to provoke new and absurd questions. All the while, Elspeth fussed over the carpenters' load, tightening ropes, shifting goods, trying to make the market wares seem smaller, less important, less worthy of paying a tax.

At last, they approached Market Gate and even Kari fell silent as a tall soldier strode over. With a practiced hand, he tugged at one of the tarps, unveiling a stack of low tables. Nodding to himself, he continued his inspection, kneeling down on the road to view the short stools that were lashed behind the wagon. Elspeth endured the inspection silently, and Alana could imagine the woman counting out coins for each discovered item.

Only after the soldier had circled the entire wagon did he step up to Elspeth's husband. "That will be fifty sous for the duty and one gold crown for lying to the king."

"Fifty!" Elspeth's shriek was as shrill as any ale-wife's. "Do you think my wares are made of gold? And when have I ever lied? And what *king* are you collecting fines for?"

"Pay your dues, woman. You have four ladders hidden beneath your wagon. I'm already being lenient about that table. I can see the fourth leg is broken, but I'll not charge you with shoddy goods. We'll just call it a three-legged stand."

"As if you're any sort of expert on third legs!" Elspeth retorted angrily, turning her rage into a leer and an obscene gesture.

"I could have you unload this entire wagon, here and now," the soldier barked.

"I'd like to see you order that, with all these fine people waiting behind us!" Elspeth planted her fists in the small of her back, forcing her swollen belly out even farther. "I'd like those merchants to view the king's justice!"

Elspeth dripped sarcasm into the word "king," eyeing the restless crowd that wound down the road. Before the furious guard could retort, his fellow glided up to Alana. "And you, mistress? Are you with these carpenters?"

Alana winced. Elspeth had her own troubles now; she wasn't likely to lie for the woodsinger. Even as Alana struggled for some response, Kari chimed in. "Of course she is! Aunt Lani, tell the man who you are!"

The guard waited with a look of scarce-bridled patience. "Aye." Alana managed not to look at Kari with too much admiration. "That is my husband's sister there."

"And where's your man?"

Alana let a little of her nervousness drip into her words, seasoning her tone with a hint of tears. "In the cold ground, kind sir. He was slain almost a month ago."

"My uncle Ronan!" Kari wailed, and real tears coursed down her cheeks.

"Hush, now." Alana fluttered over the child.

The soldier had the good grace to look embarrassed, but he pressed the woodsinger: "You'll be paying the duty, then, along with your kin?"

"You talk to my mum about money," Kari responded through her blubbering. "Aunt Lani, why won't this man leave us alone?"

"Kari, dear! He's only doing his job!" Alana tried to quiet the girl, worried that the child would overplay their meager cards. "Hush and let the soldiers finish their inspection." The woodsinger's humility apparently mollified the guard, and he moved off for a whispered discussion with his fellow. The pair of men glanced over their shoulders at Alana and Kari, and then one of them shrugged. The crowd's grumbling rose in pitch, and the line inched forward restlessly.

Elspeth was still fluffing herself like a wood grouse when the tall leader came back. The woman's feet scuffed the earth beneath her heavy belly as she dug in for a fight. Before the soldiers could launch their attack, a cry came from the line behind Alana. "What's the delay?" a man bellowed from the grumbling ranks. "We've got to set up for market, too!"

The soldiers were quick in weighing their options. It was hardly worthwhile to detain one family of difficult carpenters when the entire restless crowd was surging closer to a riot. "Very well, then," the tall guard said. "Fifty sous, and no penalty for the hidden ladders."

"Forty sous, or we're not moving an inch," Elspeth snapped in response.

"Forty sous from you, and ten from your brother's wife."

"My—"

"Aunt Lani," Kari shrilled, "do you hear that? He wants you to pay ten sous! He wants you to spend Uncle Ronan's money. You won't be able to buy me boiled sweets! You promised you would buy me sweets! You said that Uncle Ronan wanted me to have sweets!"

"Your Uncle Ronan—" Elspeth began, a questioning note behind her words, but Alana interrupted.

"I didn't tell you, Elspeth. That was Ronan's last request, that I buy sweets for the children when I came to Smithcourt. He wanted them to remember him with gladness, rather than as the cause of all your grief."

The last of Alana's speech was drowned out by the scramble of Kari's brothers, who had awakened to the possibility that the tall stranger woman was going to bring them forbidden treasures. The soldiers did their best to ignore the swarm of boys.

"You've got a strange accent to be traveling with these inland folk," the tall soldier said.

"Aunt Lani," Kari cried, ever at the ready. "You *said* they'd be mean to you because of your speech. How did you know?"

"Hush, Kari," Alana tried again, wondering if the soldiers would buy her weak story about leaving the People as a child. Elspeth spoke before she could defend herself.

"And now I suppose you want to tax her *words*? The king—whoever he'll be—can't possibly use all the pennies you steal from us hardworking folk. What are you going to do? Pocket our sous and spend them in the nearest tavern as soon as your shift ends? Which drinking house is it?" Elspeth's eye ran along the row of ramshackle buildings that skulked inside the city walls. "The Dog and Branch? Or do the king's guards go to the Rose and Crown?"

Elspeth must have caught a glimmer in the soldier's eye. "The Rose and Crown, that's it, eh? Well, we'll pay your extortion, but you can be sure that we'll come by tonight. It's a free house, isn't it? What will they say, when two women show up, two women in *our* state appear in the doorway, begging a drink to keep us warm, because we haven't a place to rest our heads the night before market, because our last penny was stolen by the king's men? What—"

"Enough, woman! Take your cursed cart and your sniveling brats and your outlander sister and get out of my sight!"

Swallowing a smile, Elspeth drove her brood through the gates. Just before they passed into the congested city street, the guard cried out one last time.

"Stop!" He directed his words at Elspeth's husband, who had spent the entire debate huddled disconsolately atop the wagon, feeding his reins from hand to hand. "You, man. Stop by the Rose tonight. If you come alone, I'll buy you a drink, out of pity."

Elspeth's face stormed dark, but she bustled her entourage into Smithcourt and around a bend in the road. Only when she could no longer see the gates did she let loose a bellowing guffaw. "*Aunt Lani*! That was a masterpiece, girl! Who would have thought you had it in you!" The pregnant woman clapped a hand on her supposed relative's shoulder. "A stroke of genius, it was."

"But it was Kari!" Alana protested, not wanting to stake claim to the commotion.

"Kari, you, what does it matter? Don't you realize? We got through without paying *any* duty at all!"

Alana heard the cathedral bells toll twice, and she fought against a yawn as she swallowed her ale. She barely remembered to laugh as she leaned against the soldier beside her. There was so much to remember—staring at the guard as if he were the most handsome man in all the Rose and Crown, sighing deeply so that her bodice shifted, smiling seductively when he made a feeble joke. How did the other girls in the village master this art? "So what did you do then? What did you do when you found him?" she purred, burying her accent in a throaty whisper.

The soldier, Brant, poured more ale into her mug from his own. "Drink up, lass. There you go."

Alana swallowed obediently, confident in the herbs she had consumed before coming to the tavern. It had taken her the better part of the afternoon to make both mixtures—the one she had consumed to prevent intoxication, and the other that was stored in a flask hidden in her bodice, held close against her flesh. Twice, she had needed to reach out to her sister woodsingers, to confirm amounts of precious herbs. Each time, she had closed her fingers around her bavin, masking the move with a grimace and a shift of her "pregnant" bulk.

Throughout all of Alana's measuring and mixing, Kari had hovered close, paying far too much attention. Alana had only escaped with tales of traveling to the palace gates, of making her claim for Uncle Ronan's wergild. Even then, Kari would have accompanied her if Elspeth had not demanded her daughter's assistance in preparing supper. Alana had carried her rucksack with her when she left the carpenters' camp, but she had been forced to leave behind the bay mare.

As soon as she had done away with her "pregnancy," she had come to the Rose and Crown, suspecting that most of the city's soldiers frequented the place, not just the guards from the gates. It had not taken her long to comb through her memory and Maddock's bavin visions to identify Brant, the old soldier who had led Maddock down the endless spiral staircase in Duke Coren's palace.

The grizzled old guard appeared none the worse for having let a prize prisoner escape. Even now, the crafty fox was telling her how he had avoided censure. All the while, though, the man kept secret the fact that Zeketh had been in Duke Coren's palace, the omission patently obvious to one who had watched what transpired through a bavin.

Even as Alana flirted to draw out more of the tale, she wondered why the guard did not mention the priest, why the religious's name was being shielded. Hoping for more insight, she shivered and leaned closer to the fighting man. "Tell me!" She tried to spin her words like Jobina. "What did you do?"

"What was there *to* do? I took that idiot guard's knife—my supposed partner's knife—and slashed my arm. Then I picked up the pitcher and drank it down, made it look like the prisoner had forced me to drink."

"And they believed you?" It was not hard for Alana to coat her words with incredulity.

"They were suspicious, but what else could they do? Cursed outland bastard. No one knows where he is now. Somewhere in the palace, or the city. His Grace and . . . and the duke's allies are turning the palace upside down."

"But why did Duke Coren want such a dangerous man in his palace in the first place?" Alana shuddered, as if she were afraid to think about the "dangerous man."

"It wasn't the duke that wanted him at all. It was . . . a very important personage, er, a guest of His Grace."

"Personage." Alana almost snorted in frustration. Zeketh! Just say the high priest's name, and then Alana could demand to know why. Taking a shuddering breath and leaning closer to the guard, she pouted. "But who? Who could command you to risk your life and limb, aside from your sworn liege-lord?"

The soldier preened beneath her attentions. "I'm a fighting man. Risk is my life."

Alana bit her tongue to keep from swearing. The cursed soldier was determined to keep his secret, even if he was a coward and a liar. She let a little of her frustration leak into her words, sounding like doubt. "But this outlander . . . he's just running loose in the city streets?"

"Who knows? He's a mad bastard, pretending to be mute. Cook refused to work in the kitchens without protection, thinks that man'll be jumping out of the larder at any moment. That's why I drew the early shift—they think they're punishing me." Brant laughed and reached out a hairy fist to chuck Alana's chin lightly. "That's punishment, for sure, making me stand near a warm kitchen, where I can duck in for a bite or two. Poor sods. They don't know which side it's buttered on." Brant leered as he made his last statement, and Alana thought that she might never eat butter again. The soldier leaned closer and caught a curl of her hair, twining it around his blunt fingers.

Alana forced herself to concentrate on his words.

Cook . . . the kitchen . . . scullery work was probably her best disguise for getting into Duke Coren's heavily guarded palace. She spoke as if she had just made some brilliant discovery: "I've worked in kitchens myself! I know how nice it can be to have a good man nearby while I'm kneading the bread. It's comforting to know that there's a strong man, a brave man, when the dark night still presses on the windows." She remembered to throw back her shoulders, managing to edge away from Brant's exploring hands, even as she exposed more of her flesh to the soldier. "I wouldn't mind finding a spot of work in the king's own kitchen."

"What can you do, lass?" Brant's drunken eyes were appraising.

"More than you'll have time to learn, soldier." She darted her tongue between her lips and arched an eyebrow.

Brant chortled and leaned back on his rough bench. When he sighed, his hand fell onto Alana's thigh, as if by accident. "I don't need learning, lass. Not much learning at all."

"All the same, we haven't time now. Your shift begins before the next bell." Alana forced her fingers to cover his, to weave between them suggestively. She pouted a little as she looked up at him through her eyelashes. "If I could find a way to earn a sou or two, I could wait for you to finish your watch. Otherwise, I must leave Smithcourt with sunrise. I need to harvest the spring herbs before they flower."

"You *are* an herb-witch, then. I knew it when I saw your satchel."

"Not a witch." She laughed. "I just know how to use a plant or two, how to break a fever, how to make a man . . . awaken. Nothing important."

"Ach, lass, maybe nothing important to you. *I'd* give a pretty penny for that second potion, though."

Alana let her Jobina-fingers travel along the man's trews. "I don't think you need my craft for *that*."

Brant smiled slowly and shifted to give her fingers more room for play. "Nay, lass. Not now. Not knowing that I have a lonely night ahead of me. But when I return to the barracks—now, that's another tale. When I'm needy and tired . . ." He dug into a pouch at his waist. "Would this coin buy what I want?"

The copper glinted dully in the tavern light, and Alana let a little of her true offense seep into her words. "You think to still your needs with a single copper coin?" She withdrew her roaming hands and crossed her arms over her insulted chest. She certainly didn't intend to hold up her end of the bargain they were striking, but she was still insulted that the man thought that he could buy her for so little.

"Copper!" Brant pretended surprise. "I took out the wrong coin, lass, the wrong coin is all." He burrowed deeper for another token, and managed to produce a small silver disk, along with a guttural chortle. "This is what I intended to find."

Alana weighed her options. If she gave in too easily, he was likely to become suspicious. Yet she was about to run out of time; the hour was growing late. "I wasn't playing games, soldier," Alana finally spoke. "I need more than a man's bed, or I'll be leaving the city."

"You'll get more, lass, more than just a bed!" For one horrible instant, Alana thought that he *still* had misunderstood her; his fingers kneaded at her thigh as if he were mixing dough. But then he continued, "Come with me to the kitchens. You can help Cook with bread and the like, and then you can leave with me at noon. The barracks are quiet then."

It was the safest passage into Coren's palace that she was likely to arrange. She might contrive to slip away from the kitchen during her shift. And if she couldn't, there was always the herb mixture in the flask beneath her homespun gown, the tincture she could feed to Brant and then escape.

Forbidding herself to dwell on the bargain Brant thought he was negotiating, the woodsinger reached for the soldier's coin with trembling fingers. The guard snapped it into her palm with a merchant's greedy grin, and Alana barely remembered to smile as she tucked the silver into her bodice, making sure that it did not clink too hard against her herb flask. Brant followed the coin's course, and he licked his lips like a dog. "We'd best be on our way, then," he growled.

Alana let him help her to her feet, let him "steady" her as she left the close tavern. The night air cut through her shift, a sharp reminder of all the risks she was taking. It did not take them long to get to Coren's palace in the middle of Smithcourt, and then it was only a brief matter for Brant to spirit her past the guard, announcing that she'd been newly hired to work with Cook.

Neither Maddock nor Reade had glimpsed the working side of the palace kitchens, so they were entirely new to Alana. Even if she had viewed them through her fellow outlanders' bavins, she would have been unprepared for the blast of heat as she crossed the threshold. A brawny-armed woman looked up as Brant ushered Alana into the dim room, and she nodded shortly at the soldier's words before turning to the woodsinger. "Can you knead?"

"Aye." Alana opted to disguise her accent behind a single word.

"Good enough. There's the dough. His Grace prefers braided wreaths." Alana stared at the mounds of dough, their slick surfaces like a crowd of perspiring faces.

"All right, then," Brant crowed. "You'll work here in the kitchens, and I'll see you when my shift is done. Keep an eye on her, Cook. It'll be my hide if she roams the hallways."

Alana forced another Jobina-laugh from her pounding chest. Cook frowned and waddled back to an iron kettle that was suspended across the great hearth. Brant took advantage of the relative solitude to pull Alana close and snatch a kiss. "You mind your manners, girl. I'll see you after my shift."

The soldier frowned when she did not respond, and Alana forced herself to pay more attention. She needed to pretend that she desired his touch. She needed to act as if *he* were the reason she wanted to be in the kitchen. Not the dark hallways that crept away from the overheated room. Not the tantalizing nearness of other bavins, elsewhere in the palace. "Aye." She rippled beneath his palms. "Make sure you're not left standing too long."

His eyes glinted, and he would have pulled her closer if Cook had not turned back. "I'll mind how I'm standing, you vixen. I won't even need your herbs."

"Out of my kitchen, now," Cook interrupted, before Alana could summon up further banter. "We've work to do." Brant hastened away, and Alana settled into her sentence of hard labor.

By the time the sun rose, her shoulders ached from kneading. When the bells chimed for morning prayers, her eyes were gritty from lack of sleep. As the day's full light pried into the small kitchen windows, she stumbled as she walked, finding convenient walls and benches to hold her upright. She was ordered to fetch water, to keep the fires going, to move, move, move.

Alana Woodsinger accepted the commands, reminding herself of her mission. She needed to stay inside the palace. Even if Cook did not give her an opportunity to wander off, she'd manage to escape once Brant claimed her, once she'd given him her herbal brew. She was confident that she could find Maddock inside Coren's stronghold; the bavin would show her the way. Together, then, they would find Landon and Jobina, and then the twins.

And so, when Alana thought that she could not stand for another instant, she fetched another pail of water, and when she was certain that her arms could not rise again, she turned a spit, roasting a tremendous joint of meat for His Grace's evening table.

By the time Brant returned at the end of his shift, the woodsinger had charmed herself into a sort of dream. "There's my girl!" the soldier exclaimed, and Alana scarcely caught herself from bursting into tears.

She almost did not notice as Brant guided her from the kitchen, barely felt his paws about her waist as he bade her walk in front of him, up half a flight of narrow stairs. She squinted in brilliant sunlight as they crossed a narrow courtyard, only to be blinded when they ducked into a gloomy barracks building. Brant pulled her close as he opened a door, identical to all the others that lined the dim corridor.

"Here's what I call home," he growled, kicking the door closed in a familiar gesture and settling the creaky bar across the oak.

Alana barely took in the rumpled mattress, the high and narrow flyspecked window. She forced herself to focus on Brant's hands, on the increasingly urgent attention he paid to her bodice laces.

"Ho, there!" she cried, as his fingers slipped across the fabric. "Such a man!"

"Aye! 'Twas a long shift, but I stood my ground. I knew what awaited me in the end."

"Then I must live up to my bargain." She forced a laugh. "I told you I'd give you a potion, and I've got it here." She dug out the dark bottle.

"You think I need some witch's herbs to stand for you?"

"I can see that you do not." She made her voice appreciative. "But I've never known a man to pass up an opportunity for heartswell."

"*Heart*swell?" His interest was piqued.

"Come, soldier-man. Drink. I worked as a scullery maid the morning long. I'll not have my reward delayed another minute."

Brant grinned and took the bottle. He sniffed once and then raised the flask, saluting her. She watched him fill his mouth and swallow—once, twice, three times. When the bottle was empty, he tossed it onto the ground, flinging his head about and breathing as if he had swallowed fire. "There, pretty witch. I've drunk your potion."

Alana held out her hand, gesturing for him to come to her. He obliged, with first one step, then another. The woodsinger, exhausted by her stint in the kitchen, was barely able to catch him before he crashed to the ground.

She dragged his great weight over to the bed, rolling him onto the coverlet with a great deal of grunting. More than once, she swore under her breath; she should have manipulated him to be nearer the pallet when he dropped.

Only when his head was turned to the side so that he did not strangle on his own copious drool did Alana pick up her discarded flask. She sniffed at it as the soldier had. No heartswell, alas, for him. She had combined mare's mane and nightdraught for fast, dreamless sleep, adding a healthy dash of thornbuck to force Brant to forget all that had happened. A dose of sweet honey to make the entire mess palatable, and . . .

The victim of her handiwork set to snoring and Alana glanced once more about the room, making sure that she left no incriminating evidence behind. Even as the cathedral bells tolled the first hour after noon, Alana Woodsinger slipped into the shadows, disappearing in Coren's palace as she clutched at the bavin that marked her as an outlander and an intruder.

15

Alana woke slowly, dazed and disoriented as she sat up in total darkness. She shook her head and ran her fingers through her hair, leaning forward to spit a nasty taste from her mouth. By the time she stood, she had remembered where she was, and her resolve rushed back, firm and unshaken.

She had intended to seek out Maddock as soon as she left Brant's quarters, but she had walked down only one corridor before she realized that she was too exhausted to help the warrior. The restorative powers of redshell could only last so long.

Changing her plans, she had sneaked higher into the tall tower in the center of the palace courtyard, the ominous building that hulked over the soldiers' barracks. Scarcely able to keep her eyes open, she had stepped from a dark stairwell into a square room, just as guards' voices rang out on the steps below. Tapestries hung on the walls of Alana's hiding place, blocking out some of the stony chill and the sound of the men. Following her instincts and offering a quick prayer to all the Guardians, Alana had crossed the room to find a short, dark corridor, a hallway that ran the length of the tower.

A tiny storage room opened onto the middle of the hallway. She had to duck nearly double to clear the low door, and she could touch all four walls by reaching out her arms. Dust was thick on the floor, and a mouse's desiccated corpse cracked beneath her foot, yielding up a musty smell of decay. This closet had not been used for years—decades perhaps—probably since the last time the palace itself had been under attack and the guards had needed an extra place to store weapons.

The woodsinger had collapsed in the dark, dusty room, scarcely staying awake long enough to push the low door closed behind her. With her last conscious thought, she had wedged her Great Mother amulet beneath the door, granting herself the illusion of peace and security.

Now, Alana retrieved the metal figurine. She muttered a prayer as she returned the amulet to its rightful place about her neck. The Great Mother had worked with the Guardians to keep her safe these many days and nights; they could not abandon her now. Putting her ear against the oaken door, Alana caught her breath, but she could hear no activity in the hallway. She eased the door open.

The corridor yawned before her, empty and dark. Alana blinked hard and realized that she must have slept for hours. Daylight had fled completely; meager starlight leaked through a window at the far end of the hallway. Fine, she told herself. Better to move under the cover of darkness anyway.

Closing her fingers around her bavin, she felt the gentle tug of the woodstar she had sung for Maddock. She let the Tree's power pull her forward as she edged down the hallway, through the tapestried room, back to the staircase. As if she were summoning fishing boats back to port at the Headland, she let the Tree urge her toward its own heartwood. Her bavin reached out for Maddock's, and she gave herself over to the oaken force, forbidding herself to think about the dark corridors and the guards who might lurk in the shadows.

Round and round she walked on spiral stairs, finding each step in the dark, letting her feet settle into the grooves of centuries. As her bavin warmed beneath her fingers, Alana realized that she was repeating Maddock's steps, passing down the staircase to the stone room that had housed the Avenger.

She almost stopped then. She feared Zeketh, feared his secret chamber and whatever beast he had summoned to replace the venomous Avenger. There was something mysterious at work with the religious leader, some reason that his presence in Coren's palace was meant to stay hidden. How hard would Coren and Zeketh work to protect their secret alliance? What punishment would they mete out if they found her here, tracing their steps, delving into their secrets?

She tried to convince herself that she was misinterpreting the bavin's heat beneath her fingers. She must be caught up in remembering Maddock's earlier passage. Surely the warrior would not return to the chamber where he had been tortured, where he had almost died?

Still, Alana was drawn forward by her woodstar, compelled down the stairs. She paused to dig her iron-precious knife out of her rucksack. Clutching her bavin with the feverish fingers of one hand, she leveled the blade in front of her eyes, pointing downward into the darkness.

Finally, she reached the bottom of the long, long staircase, stepping onto the stone floor. Before she could catch her breath, a claw darted from the pitch darkness. Its clutch about her wrist was frozen, and she could not entirely swallow her scream as her bones were crushed by the cruel grip. Calling upon all the Guardians to give her strength, she tightened her grasp on her knife, ready to fight for her life. Planting her feet on the unseen flagstones, she ducked low and surged forward, knocking her bony shoulder into her assailant's belly.

She heard a tremendous whuff of air, and the clutch on her wrist lessened so that she could pull back. She whirled for the stairs, determined to outrun her attacker, but she took only three steps before she was grabbed from behind. The knife skittered from her grasp as iron-hard hands threw her to the floor, and she struggled for breath against icy fingers that closed about her throat.

She gasped and choked, bucking against the flagstones as her fingers scrabbled against the hands that gripped her neck. She tried to swallow, but the pain was too great, and her screams were cut off by the tightening pressure against her windpipe. She scratched at her attacker's arms, raking icy flesh that only responded by tightening the fingers around her throat. Red lights danced before Alana's eyes in the darkness, and she kicked against the floor in panic. Her heart thundered in her ears, pounding like the most vicious ocean storm against the shoals of her consciousness.

Alana's lungs turned to fire in her chest, and she struggled to pluck at her attacker's hands. It became harder to remember, though, why she bothered, harder to remember what she fought for. A crimson wave crashed against the back of her eyes, and she thought of her father. Had he gasped for his last breath amid a scarlet sea? Had he fought to free his lungs, fought and lost and sank beneath the ocean surface? Was he waiting for her with the Guardians, even now?

The woodsinger's struggles eased as she thought of her father, as she remembered his patient, wind-beaten eyes. He would guide her the last few steps. He would show her the way to the Guardians, the way from the People and the Tree.

The Tree.

Alana Woodsinger heard her sister woodsingers whispering in her mind. No, not whispering. Speaking aloud. Shouting. Ordering her to focus on her bavin, to concentrate on her woodstar. Obediently, Alana's fingers grasped for her bavin, for the last woodstar that she had ever sung. She grasped, but she could not quite reach. Her fingers wanted to curl in upon themselves, wanted to tremble against the stone.

"Fight, sister!"

"Stretch for your bavin!"

"Don't leave us, Alana Woodsinger!"

Alana wanted to make the voices be quiet. She wanted her sisters to leave her alone, to let her sleep. She was so tired, and there they were, making their constant demands. Didn't they remember that she had journeyed far? Didn't they know that she had worked in the kitchens? Didn't they understand that she needed . . . to . . . rest?

"Alana Woodsinger, this is not why the Tree chose you! It selected you because it knew you would fight for it. The Tree knew that you would love it and cherish it and give your last breath to be with it!"

Alana wanted to tell the nagging woodsinger that she was wrong. She tried to form words, tried to structure her argument, but she couldn't. Not without the bavin. Not without the woodstar. She needed to grasp the prickly heartwood, needed to stretch her fingers to the Tree's core. There it was, an arm's length away. . . . One more handspan . . .

Her effort was rewarded by a brilliant arc of blue-red-brown-white light.

The spark leaped from her bavin, bearing all the woodsingers' force in the darkened chamber. Even as Alana realized that she could breathe again, she felt her sisters' strength flowing through her. All the power ensorcelled in the Tree's endless rings blew down her bruised throat, surged into her flaming lungs. Alana gasped at the pain, drawing in more of the sweet, sweet air.

Choking and spluttering, Alana bucked from the stone floor, setting her attacker off balance. The woodstar about her neck burned with a brilliant fire, flickering with all the colors of the Guardians, lighting the chamber without being consumed.

Even as Alana gasped for air, her attacker drew back in surprise. The woodsinger managed to twist beneath his weight, to slide out from beneath the man. Spluttering against the throbbing pain in her throat, she scrambled for her blade, prepared now to fight for her life. She found the knife easily, cold iron sparkling in the multicolored light that continued to flow from her bavin.

Even as she lunged to stab her attacker, she glimpsed his face. She made out his wild eyes and unkempt hair, heard the mad gurgle in his throat and smelled the acrid fear on his flesh.

"Maddock!" she gasped, scarcely able to ease the name past her bruised throat. A quick glance through her gleaming bavin confirmed her horrified discovery. Zeketh's drugs had crazed the warrior, left him terrified and confused. In an instant, Alana saw that he'd been unable to escape the palace, to make his way to Bringham's men. Instead, he had huddled, alone and exhausted, with the remnants of a drugged nightmare whispering to him about defeat and death.

Now, the man panted in the sudden brilliant light, unwanted tears streaming down his grimy cheeks. He raised one scabbed hand to shield his eyes, and Alana could see that he was weighing his course of action. She felt his confusion through her bavin, transmitted from his woodstar to the Tree to the bavin that swung from her own neck. She felt the animal terror of the trapped.

Maddock's stinking breath came harsh in the small chamber, and Alana remembered all that she had seen through her bavin along his long journey—the hopeful warrior who had boasted of saving the children. The would-be lover who had fallen into Jobina's sticky web of seduction. The man who had fled a roadside inn in terror and shame. The creature who stood before her, desperate and frightened and ready to kill.

Alana's own breath rattled in her throat, and she

could still feel Maddock's fingers digging into her flesh. Her blood pulsed hot where his icy fingers had burned, and her head began to spin. "Maddock!" she croaked again, raising her bavin as a symbol of recognition. At the same time, she thought a prayer to the Guardians, begging them to let the warrior recognize her, begging them to let her spare his life.

Maddock cringed at the sound of his name, but Alana forced herself to speak the two syllables one last time. She fought against the horror that pulsed through her rising bruises, the ancient fear of madness.

"Get back, fiend!" Maddock raised his hands in a warding gesture. The stark bavin light turned his hollow eyes into a skull's dark sockets. "Get back to my nightmares and leave me be!" His voice broke on the last word, frantic, desperate, destroyed.

"Maddock, it's me, Alana Woodsinger." Her whisper was harsh in the dank room, but she made herself heard above her thundering heart. Before she could change her mind, she took Maddock's hand, forced herself to grasp his ice-cold flesh. He struggled to fight free of her, writhing as if *she* were the nightmare creature.

Swallowing painfully, Alana reached out toward his bavin, trying to push comfort and awareness through the Tree and into the woodstar she had sung for him so long ago. The other woodsingers added to her thoughts, bolstering her strength along the relay. The man was too frightened, though, terrified by the voices of strange women in his mind, crazed by drugs and exhaustion and evil dreams.

Alana tightened her grip on his hand, but he started to fight her in earnest, started to throw her off with all the power of a warrior intent on saving himself from a mortal enemy. Alana ordered her sister woodsingers to desist, commanded them to drop out of the link that was forged through the Tree. Instead, she reached for the depths of the oak herself, plunging through her own burning bavin until it seemed that she stood beside the giant oak on the Headland.

She drilled into the rings of the People's history and asked the Tree to carry her intention forward, to push her thoughts into Maddock's awareness. Her journey was so sudden, her burrowing so complete, that for a moment she was almost consumed by the Tree. She was lifted from the world of Smithcourt's stone dungeons, from the cage of distance and weariness and cold-forged iron blades. She collapsed into the oak's green beauty, into its quiet, steady power. She breathed in the sea breeze, felt the loam settle around her roots. She felt her sap beat strong in her veins, calming, soothing, deepening her rapport with the People, with the past. She felt the power of earth and air, fire and water.

She almost lost herself.

Almost, but not quite. Alana remembered not to linger in the Tree's orderly rings. She did not permit herself to stay on the Headland, where the fresh wind blew, where she could swallow great draughts of air without the burning, blazing pain in her throat. Instead, she urged the Tree to send her thoughts forward, to leap across all the land with her emotions. She asked the Tree to reach for Maddock's bavin with all its oaken strength, to thrust all her thoughts into his woodstar.

It took a moment, but the Tree complied. Alana felt her own assurance, her own comforting thoughts, her own power sear across the chasm of forest, fields, and city that separated her from the Tree. The giant oak bolstered her warm comfort, poured it into Maddock's bavin. And, after a long moment when Alana did not dare to draw a rattling breath, she felt Maddock absorb the Tree's spirit.

"Alana Woodsinger?" he asked at last, sounding even younger than Reade or Maida.

"Yes, Maddock. I've come to help you."

"How did you get here?" Disbelief carved deep lines across his brow.

"I rode from the People," she answered in a steadying tone, gentling him as if he were a new colt. She tightened her grip on his frozen hand and sent another burst of reassurance through her bavin, to the Tree, to his woodstar. "I've come to help."

"I dreamed about you! I dreamed that you rode the bay mare."

"That wasn't a dream, Maddock. It was the power of the bavin, of the Tree."

"The Tree . . ."

He spoke the two words like a prayer, and she nodded, swallowing hard. Maddock. Proud, boastful Maddock. Reduced to a raving madman in the darkest corner of the duke's palace. What had happened to the cocky young warrior? What had happened to the soldier Alana had watched, had breathed with, had felt inside her mind and body? She forced her voice to sound reasonable. "My bavin spoke to yours across the leagues."

"But who were those others? Who were the other women who were here?"

"They are my sisters, Maddock. Other woodsingers. They are our friends."

"But—"

"Hush, Maddock. Don't trouble yourself with them. I'm here now. We can make our plans. We can defeat the duke."

"Duke Coren," Maddock muttered, and whatever confidence Alana had begun to build in his mind visibly collapsed upon itself. "I haven't even seen Duke Coren. I've only seen the priest, Zeketh."

"That's just as well," Alana assured him. "Coren would have recognized you."

"Not anymore. I cut my hair." Maddock sounded like a child, and Alana's heart twisted inside her chest. Could this be the same man who had swaggered before Jobina? Who had taunted all the village maidens

on the Headland? She reached for Maddock's scabbed
hand to anchor him.

"Yes, Maddock. And if Coren had been here, that
might have been enough. But it was Zeketh whom
you met, wasn't it? Zeketh and the Avenger."

"You know then? The bavin let you see?"

"I saw it all," she answered.

"Then you *did* watch me along the road. . . ." His
words trailed off, and she would have recognized his
shame even if she could not sense his every thought
through his bavin. This creature who cringed before
her was a broken shell, shattered on the hard rocks
of his inland journey. "In the name of all the Guardians," he gasped. "What have I done, woodsinger?
Your throat . . . What have I done to you?"

Alana raised both hands to cup his face. With the
gesture, she forced herself to loosen her link to the
Tree. Maintaining the bond with the giant oak had
left her lightheaded and giddy; she needed to bring
Maddock back to Coren's palace, back to Smithcourt
and the urgent present. As the Tree's presence faded
to the back of her own mind, subsiding to the whisper
of breakers on a distant beach, Alana crushed pity
from her voice. "I am fine, Maddock. I still stand before you. Now we haven't much time. Duke Coren's
Service is tomorrow, in the cathedral." The warrior
stared at the stone floor, defeat bowing his shoulders.
"Maddock, I can't do this alone. I *need* you."

Her ragged tone penetrated, even if her words left
a confused look on his face. "Me? But I—"

"You are still the greatest warrior the People have
ever had. Maddock, you rode all the way to Smithcourt. You stood against Bringham's men. You found
your way inside the palace. You eluded capture when
all the duke's men pursued you."

Each of her declarations forged iron along his spine,
but his words clung to doubt. "I'm just so tired. . . ."

"We're all tired, Maddock." She forbade herself to

sway on her feet, refused to let her sigh turn into a
coughing fit. Instead, she peered behind Maddock
toward the cavern of a room that had housed the
Avenger. "Is there water in there?"

"Nay. But I have the soldier's flask." Doubt drowned
his words almost as soon as he voiced them. "It's only
half full, though."

"Half is better than none." Alana fumbled for her
rucksack, digging deep for Goody Glenna's leaf-wrapped
herbs. A few deep breaths eased a little of the tight-
ness in her throat, steadied her after her drawn-out
contact with the Tree. Her fingers were confident on
the flask that Maddock handed her. She measured out
the dried greenery with a certainty borne of years
among the People. Mint for refreshment. Redshell for
wakefulness. Lionsmane for courage.

After shaking the flask vigorously, she drew her
bavin over her neck, holding the woodstar by its leather
thong. She had held on to just enough of the Tree's
magic to keep the bavin burning bright.

Muttering yet another request to the Guardians and
the nurturing force of the Great Mother, Alana passed
the bavin beneath the flask. She held her link to the
Tree at the very back of her mind now, a comfort, a
song among the green leaves of late spring. She heard
her sisters whispering among themselves, knew that
they watched her, even as she had watched Maddock,
as she had watched Reade. She knew that they were
there if she needed to draw on their strength, but
she was able to summon heat from her bavin without
drawing directly from the women.

The hammered metal grew warm to her touch, but
she only shifted her grasp to its leather-wrapped neck.
The bavin could not heat the water to a proper tea,
but it could bring out some of the herbs' strength.

When she had done the best that she could, she
passed the flask to Maddock. He took it mechanically,

but made no further gesture. She eyed him steadily in the flickering light. "Drink."

"But what good can that do? I can't—"

"I'm your woodsinger, Maddock, and I order you to drink." She put all of her authority into the command, and he raised the flask to his lips.

Perhaps it was the familiar gesture in a strange place. Perhaps it was receiving orders, rather than needing to think of some course of action. Perhaps it was the effect of the redshell and the lionsmane, hitting his blood like alcohol. Whatever the cause, Maddock stood straighter after he had drunk, and the deepest lines eased across his brow. He drew one stout breath, and then another. When he looked up at Alana, she could still make out fatigue and doubt and fear in his face, but she saw another emotion as well: determination.

"Alana Woodsinger," he breathed, lowering the flask and wiping his lips with the back of his hand. "What do we do now?"

"First, we find Landon and Jobina. Then, with the Guardians' grace, the four of us will free the twins."

Hours later, Alana wished that she had saved some of the herb tea for herself. Her eyes were gritty with fatigue, and she caught a yawn against the back of her teeth. Her throat ached where Maddock's fingers had bruised her flesh against her bones. She slumped against the stone wall of her abandoned storeroom, clutching her glowing bavin and struggling to hear Maddock over the pounding of her heart. He was far from Alana's bolt hole; he'd gone down to the dungeons to work the next stage of their plot.

"You cursed idiot," Maddock was swearing at the castellan, the hapless guard who held the ring of keys to Coren's dungeon cells. "You think *I* don't know it's the middle of the night? Will *you* be the one to

tell Duke Coren that you can't be bothered to fetch
the prisoner, or will I have the pleasure myself?"

Even when Alana caught her breath, she could not
make out the castellan's reply. Maddock continued to
berate the unfortunate guard. Alana could sense
through her bavin that he was settling his hands on
his stolen sword, readying himself to fight. "Duke
Coren sent me himself, man. Who do you think issues
orders in the palace?"

Just as Alana was certain that Maddock would have
to draw his weapon, the soldier gave way. The woodsinger could make out the man's grumbling, and then
Maddock was stalking down the dank dungeon corridor. The guard preceded him with a jangling ring of
keys.

The redshell in Alana's tea had made Maddock
jumpy, and he shied away from the prisoners' hands
that reached out from iron bars. Nevertheless, he remembered his role, drawing his short sword as the
prisoners' moans echoed down the corridor. "Quiet,
dogs!" he ordered, making a halfhearted swipe toward
a grasping hand. "Pull your hands back, or I'll give
you something to bay about."

The words, with their casual reference to dogs,
made a chill run up Alana's spine, but she had to
admit that Maddock sounded every bit a Smithcourt
soldier as he sauntered to the dampest, darkest cage
in all the dungeons. "Get him out of there," Maddock
barked at his supposed soldierly colleague.

There were four separate locks on the cage, and
Alana's teeth gritted as each clanged open. Maddock
swore at the delay, cursing the castellan's lineage and
threatening to drag Duke Coren himself down to the
dungeon. Just as the guard succeeded in springing the
last of the locks, Alana yielded to her curiosity, pushing her vision all the way through Maddock's bavin,
stretching her Tree-empowered senses to see entirely
through his eyes.

Bogs and breakers! Landon huddled in the corner
of his cursed cell, filthy and stinking in the ragged
clothes that he had worn from the Headland of
Slaughter. His hands trembled like a foolish old woman's as they curled against his iron chains, and his
head bobbed on his thin neck. His broken nose was
still squashed to one side, and his breath wheezed in
his throat. The castellan's torch flickered in the
Guardian-forsaken cell, and Landon closed his eyes
against the brightness, involuntary tears etching
through the filth on his cheeks.

"On your feet, Outlander," the castellan barked,
thrusting his torch forward, as if the searing flame
would give Landon the strength to stand. The tracker
only huddled toward the back of his cage, sheltering
his head with arms so thin that Maddock could have
broken them like sticks.

Sharks and fins! They were too late. He'd waited too
long getting into the palace; Alana had taken too much
time riding from Land's End. Landon was never going
to rise to his feet. Maddock settled a length of steel into
his voice, barking, "Let's go, you cursed beast."

This time, Landon managed to ease his eyes open,
to squint past the fire's glare. "Maddock!" he gasped,
the word half blocked by his broken nose.

By all the Guardians, was the man that far gone?
It was hard enough for Maddock, trying to disguise
his outland accent for the castellan. He didn't need
Landon pouring ideas into the cursed guard's head. He
reached out to the tracker with a rough hand. "That's
right, you miserable dog. Maddock. You're going to
help Duke Coren find that traitor or die in the trying."
Maddock tugged his comrade to his feet, jostling him
upright despite the tracker's failing muscles and
trembling limbs.

"But, I—" Landon trailed off in confusion.

"You nothing," Maddock snapped, forcing the tracker
to take a step. "You're coming with me, now."

"Hold there," the guard interrupted, and Maddock was forced to turn toward his supposed fellow. The burly castellan gestured with a single curt nod. "Step back from the prisoner."

Cursing silently, Maddock obliged, leaving Landon to tremble like a new fern frond in the forest. Before Maddock could speak, the guard hefted a wooden bucket and tossed icy water across Landon's face and down his chest. Cold and surprise left the tracker gasping for air, swaying on his feet as if he were going to crash to the ground. "You couldn't take him before Duke Coren, stinking like that, could you?" The guard tossed the empty bucket on the floor. "Not that that'll make much difference."

"It's enough," Maddock grumbled, trying to force the note of relief from his voice as he relaxed his grip on his short sword. Instead of gutting the castellan, he used the weapon to harry Landon out of his cell and into the narrow corridor, pausing only long enough to collect the castellan's key for Landon's chains. "Let's go, you bastard. You've kept His Grace waiting long enough."

The tracker's confusion was transparent, but he began to shamble down the corridor, catching his shoulder against another cell's bars when he could not keep his balance. That movement brought a cry of rage from the cell's occupant, and the castellan brought his wooden club down with a muffled grunt. The discipline raised an outcry from still other prisoners, and Maddock hustled Landon out of the dungeon, leaving his supposed fellow guard to quell the incipient rebellion.

Pulling back from the bavin's vision, Alana scarcely managed to restrain herself until the pair of outlanders had reached her hiding place. As they entered the corridor, she swung open the door to the abandoned storeroom, and she reached up with frantic hands to half carry, half drag Landon forward. She caught the tracker as he collapsed to his knees, and she could not keep from crying out as she felt his feather weight in her arms. She let her bavin glow a little brighter so that she could see his face.

"Alana!" he gasped against teeth that chattered with cold. "Then this *is* just another dream."

"No, Landon," she whispered, easing him into a more comfortable position and dabbing her skirts against his soaked rags. "We're truly here. Maddock and I. We're going to fetch Jobina, and then all of us will get the children."

"N-not me." He clutched at her cloak, and his tight grip managed to still his ague for a moment. "Leave me here. You got me out of the dungeon—that's enough. I-I-I'll keep you from reaching the children in time."

"In time for what? Landon, what do you know?"

"Only w-what I've overheard from the guard." His words were faint, and she shifted him to a more comfortable position, cradling his head against her chest, easing the chains that bound him. As the cold stone floor gnawed through his soaked clothes, his teeth chattered so hard that he could only bite off single words. "Tomorrow. Service. Cathedral."

"We're going to stop the Service," Alana said.

Before Landon could summon the strength to speak again, there was a grating at the door, and Maddock ducked into the tiny room. Alana flushed as she realized that she had not even missed the warrior, had not realized that he had left their hideaway. Her surprise sharpened the words that formed at the back of her throat, but she did not get a chance to speak before Maddock thrust a flask toward her, clean water still dripping from its side.

Mollified, she took the canteen and gestured for Maddock to support Landon as she rummaged in her rucksack. The tracker's breath came harsher as Maddock knelt to support him; he whistled through his shattered nose. Maddock bent over the iron lock, turning the castellan's key with a grating curse. Alana fought down her panic, remonstrating with herself to remember all of Goody Glenna's lessons, all of the wisewoman's herb lore.

Redshell, of course, and pungent feverlock to quell his ague. Curly greenleaf for the rattle deep in his lungs, and Guardians' smile for the palsy that shook his limbs. In only a moment, she was holding her bavin beneath the flask to heat the tea, and then she shoved Maddock out of the way, supporting the tracker's spent body with her own.

"Drink, Landon."

"Can't . . . k-keep anything . . . down." He was drifting away from her, back toward the dark regions of sleep.

"You can manage this, Landon. I know you can." She raised the flask to his lips and caught her breath as he fought for one sip, then a second. She forced a confident smile into her words. "See? The medicine isn't so bad."

"This tastes like my dreams," Landon whispered, and Alana looked away so that he could not make out the sudden glint of tears in her eyes. When she had regained her composure, she forced a tremulous smile and reached out a hand to smooth back the tracker's sparse hair. Landon raised trembling fingers to her throat. "What happened, Alana? How did you get those bruises?"

Alana could not keep from darting a glance toward Maddock, but she kept her voice steady. "I'm fine now, Landon. Don't worry about me. What did they do to *you*?"

"Duke Coren is a very determined man." Despite his grim words, Landon's voice grew stronger as the tea took hold, and he paused between sentences to drink more of Alana's mixture. "I tried to convince him that warriors were on their way—"

"But he knows the People too well," Alana completed the thought, sick at heart for all she had taught the duke about the People's true strength, for every word she had given him when he had traveled to the Headland.

"I told him that the other coastal folk were joining us." Landon shifted across Alana's lap, and it might have been a trick of the bavin's light, but color seemed to glint in his cheeks, a blush behind the bruises.

"The other—?"

"I told him that Sartain Fisherman was brother to six tribal chiefs. Seven is an important number to the inlanders. I told them that seven tribes would gather together to come after the twins." Landon had recovered enough that he could put a boastful tone to his words.

"And he believed you?" Alana asked with incredulity.

"He tried to dig deeper for the truth. I had to provide details about the other tribes' forces." Landon set his lips firmly, as if he would speak no more on the subject, but Alana felt his body stiffen. She dared not dwell on the tools Duke Coren had used to draw out Landon's made-up tale.

"What were you thinking, man?" Maddock exclaimed from his place just inside the doorway. "He'll come riding after the People as soon as he finds out that you lied!"

"And why wouldn't he have done that before? He could come and attack us for anything—fish, or oil, or bavins. He decided we were all as docile as deer after you fled the tavern!"

Maddock lunged toward the tracker, his hand clenched into a fist.

"Stop it!" Alana snapped before Maddock could connect. "We don't have time for this! We cannot change what happened on the Headland, or the road, or here." She turned to Landon before Maddock could give in again to his own shame at deserting his fellows. "Do you know where Jobina is being held? Is there a separate dungeon for women?"

"Aye"—the tracker nodded—"or so the guards have said. But you won't find our healer there."

Foreboding knocked at Alana's heart as she forced herself to ask, "Where, then?"

Landon could not bring himself to meet the woodsinger's eyes, and when he spoke, his words were so soft that she thought she must have misheard him. "In the royal apartments." Landon swallowed hard. "Jobina Healer has given herself to Coren."

16

Alana shivered in her stolen uniform. She and Maddock had overpowered an unsuspecting page, leaving the boy to awaken in a chilly garderobe, wearing nothing but his smallclothes, with a lump behind his ear. The high collar of the uniform was tight against Alana's bruised throat. Before donning the boy's clothes, she had hacked at her hair, sending her long auburn curls down the dark garderobe shaft. Now, the back of her neck was bare, and she could not keep from reaching up to touch it self-consciously. She swallowed hard and forced herself to take a deep breath.

Trying to summon up the calm she had last felt standing on the Headland of Slaughter, she found that she could not hear the memory of distant waves above the pounding of her heart. She licked her lips and restrained herself from reaching out to her fellow woodsingers. There was little they could do to help her now, and their distaff chatter might prove a fatal distraction.

Instead, she glanced at Landon, making sure that he was steady enough for what was about to follow. The tracker had rallied a bit, now that his clothes had dried and he'd slept for a few hours. Nevertheless, Alana's heart twisted when she saw how pale he was. His bruises stood out like storm clouds painted on his flesh, and his wrists looked like bare bones where they poked through the manacles that bound them, the chains that had been draped about him in Coren's dungeons.

The weight of the iron might bow his back, but there was nothing to be done for it. Landon had to look like a prisoner. He had to look like a prisoner, and Maddock had to look like a guard, and Alana had to look like a page. A young boy. A nervous boy.

Hunching deeper inside her stolen uniform, Alana raised her fist to knock on the dead, oaken door. Her entire journey to Smithcourt had been based on secrecy, on keeping her identity hidden. Now, it went against all instinct to knock and call attention to herself.

"Go on, then," Maddock hissed in her ear, as if he could hear the conflict chasing itself inside her skull. "The guard's expecting us to relieve him."

Alana nodded once and clenched her hand into a tight fist to keep her fingers from trembling. She glanced again at the men beside her, and then she pounded on the door.

"Aye?" came the terse reply.

"Mather Devane, reporting for duty," Maddock called out, and Alana was comforted by the iron in his words. She doubted that the actual relief guard would have sounded more official. Of course, that man had not had a chance to say anything when Maddock waylaid him in the hallway. Rather, he had only gasped and slumped against the wall, with Maddock's stolen dagger protruding from his ribs. His eyes had looked surprised until Maddock eased them closed with a rough hand. Alana had tried not to notice how the dead soldier's head hit the stone wall as Maddock shoved him into a shadowed alcove, secreting the body behind a wine-dark tapestry depicting the inlanders' Seven Gods. She forbade her eyes to search out the darker bleed of crimson against Coren's livery, even when Maddock twitched the fabric into folds to hide the wet stain.

"It's about time," a voice said behind the door, and then Alana was half ducking behind Maddock, trying to disguise herself behind his soldierly bulk. A guard, dressed in Coren's bloody-knife uniform, glared at them as he peered into the hallway. He jutted his chin toward Landon. "What are you doing with that bastard?"

"His Grace ordered the outlander brought here. He doesn't want to take any chances that Bringham's men will attack during the Service, and try to liberate the outland dog from the dungeons."

"Why not just kill him and be done with it?" The guard reached for his own dagger, running a callused thumb along the blade.

Maddock shrugged and muttered an offhand oath, poking at the swaying Landon's spine. "His Grace thinks the rebel can still be of some use. Who knows? Maybe he'll be executed after the Service. Show the people of Smithcourt what happens to fools who don't recognize their own lord."

"Hardly worth the bother, eh?" The guard snorted, but he let his dagger slip back into its sheath. "It'd be simpler to do it here and now."

"Aye," Maddock agreed, casually reaching down to jerk Landon's chain. The tracker staggered forward a couple of steps, and he raised glaring eyes at his fellow outlander, but he held his tongue. Maddock gestured toward the closed door on the other side of the room. "How's the wench?"

"She's ready for the Service. Been preening for hours." The guard grinned wolfishly.

Alana swallowed the sick taste at the back of her throat, even as Landon's gaze shot up. Maddock's easy laugh, though, matched his broad, shrugging shoulders. "She won't take kindly to the new orders then."

"New orders?"

"His Grace says she's to stay here." Maddock shrugged again. "Bringham."

The guard whistled and shook his head. "She won't be happy about that. She expects to stand by His Grace's side. She's lain there often enough." The guard pumped his fist in an indecent gesture.

Maddock's grin bared his teeth, but there was no humor in his voice. "If the wench intends to stay in Smithcourt, she'd best get used to changing expectations."

"Aye," the guard agreed. "Well, I'll let you tell her. Just watch out for her claws. I'm off to the Service, then." The soldier stood straight and raised his sword arm in salute. "Davil Hunter reporting the prisoner in good stead and the quarters secure."

"Mather Devane accepting the report." Maddock returned the salute.

Alana waited a full count of ten after Maddock closed the door, trying to still the trembling that threatened to seize all her muscles. Then, she asked, "How did you know what to say?"

"I haunted these halls for nearly a fortnight before you found me. I heard enough guards to teach me a few things." He turned his attention to the dazed Landon. "Are you all right, man?"

The tracker shook his head and staggered toward a low chair. "Take—" He had to pause for a moment to catch his breath. "Take off these cursed chains."

Maddock complied with a grimace, working the iron key with a quick twist of his wrist. "I'm sorry—" he began, but Landon waved off his words.

Alana retrieved an earthenware goblet from a table across the room. She sniffed at it before she passed it to the tracker. "Wine," she said.

He swallowed readily as Maddock looked around the room and grimaced. "Not exactly a prison cell, is this? That scheming sow! So, the wench has been preening for hours! Jobina Healer seems to have sold every one of us straight out to sea."

"Coren can be very . . . persuasive," Alana said.

"Are you making excuses for her? That woman would bed her own father, if she thought she'd gain something for her troubles."

Alana just eyed Maddock, remembering the tale the bavin had told her. She had felt Maddock's own interest in the healer, a heat that began to explain his current indignation.

She took a moment to cast away her private flicker of shame, her recollection of her own longing for Coren. After all, *she* had sung the man a bavin! Forbidding herself to reach for her woodstar, to confirm her redemption for that evil with the distant woodsingers, Alana made her voice acerbic. "We've all learned a lot in the past few months, haven't we?" When Maddock refused to look abashed, she glanced about the chamber, settling a pointed look on the exhausted Landon. "Well, there's nothing to be gained by waiting."

"Aye." Maddock sighed, and gestured for Alana to cross before him, casting only a quick glance toward Landon to make sure that the tracker was as comfortable as possible. When the woodsinger reached for the inner door, Maddock hissed, making her wait until he had drawn his sword.

"Surely—" she started.

"You heard what the guard said. She's welcomed Duke Coren into her bed. There's no telling how far she's sunk."

Alana swallowed her protest and reluctantly pulled her iron dagger from her waistband. "Go ahead, then. I'm ready."

She wasn't, though.

She wasn't ready for the darkened room, for the heavy stink of perfume. She wasn't ready for the creature who stood by the shuttered window, stiff in a high-necked robe. Jobina's back was to them, but

Alana could see that the healer's hair was piled in careful curls. Her garment was made of silk, and glinting embroidery picked out a golden sun, along with Coren's bloody knife. Jobina's voice trembled as she asked, "My lord? Have you finally come for me?"

Alana answered quietly, "No, Jobina. Coren has not come."

For just an instant, the other woman stiffened, her straight back changed to stone. Then, she turned slowly, meeting her fellow outlanders with a level gaze. Alana caught her breath when she saw that the healer's face was painted: crimson stained her cheeks and lips, and her eyes were lined with black. The flirtatious village girl was nowhere to be seen in the stern, death-still woman.

Jobina's voice was as cold as the iron bars that had locked Landon into his dungeon cell. "I did not think to see you here, Alana Woodsinger."

"We've come to save you, Jobina. Maddock and Landon and I. We've come to get you, and now we can all fetch the children."

"Landon? Then he lives?"

Alana took one step back so that Jobina could peer into the next room. The healer gasped and moved forward, as if she would aid the weakened man. She was stopped, though, by the vicious glare that Landon cast her way. She had enough good sense to step back, to clench her hands into fists at her side.

The healer's voice was dead as she turned back to Alana. "You're too late, woodsinger. The Service is about to begin. There's nothing you can do to save the twins."

"You lie, woman!" Maddock had tensed when he saw the healer's painted flesh, and now he raised his naked sword. His hand shook, but his eyes stayed riveted on Jobina's face.

The healer only laughed in the flickering firelight, a maddened sound in the close chamber. Her mirth was all the more frightening because she did not move, not even to rustle her long silk gown. "So, woodsinger, you bring the coward with you! Maddock, I must admit I'm surprised to find you in Smithcourt, when you ran so hard to keep away."

"Jobina!" Alana exclaimed before Maddock could splutter his rage. "The Guardians work in strange ways."

"The Guardians hold no sway here, Woodsinger. This city belongs to the Seven Gods. The Seven Gods and Duke Coren. They're the ones who control our fate. They're the ones who decide who lives and who dies. Not your Guardians. And certainly not some self-taught coward from the outlands."

Alana clamped her hand down on Maddock's angry sword arm and spoke before he could. "Jobina, what does Coren plan?" For a moment, Alana thought that the healer would not answer. Jobina held herself rigid, as if she were carved of coldest marble. "Speak to me, Jobina Healer," Alana urged, and she just managed to keep her voice civil. "Tell me what you've learned in Smithcourt."

Jobina finally answered. "I've learned that Duke Coren is the kingdom's best hope. My lord must defeat his rival Bringham, or all of us will pay."

"Fool!" Maddock exclaimed. "*Bringham* is our only hope! Someone has to fight Coren!"

"No one can defeat my lord Coren." Jobina's voice was steady against Maddock's wrath. "You must believe me. I've seen the city, what happened when Coren rode to the Headland. I've seen what Bringham's men call justice. I know what will happen to all the land, if my lord is not crowned king."

"Have you seen what will happen when a kidnapper sits upon the throne?" Maddock's voice dripped with condemnation. "Have you seen a world where a beast rules over men? A kingdom where a man steals children and murders innocent people?"

"I've seen far worse than that." Jobina gazed steadily at her fellow outlanders, her words all the more terrible for her even tone, for her unblinking, painted eyes. "I saw the truth when I was dragged through the Smithcourt streets in a prisoner's chains. There were children starving in those streets. There were girls—children—with blood on their thighs. Bringham's men did that. Bringham's men, when my lord Coren journeyed to the Headland and left them to their own devices."

"But—" Alana interrupted.

"Duke Coren came to me, woodsinger, after we arrived here in Smithcourt. At first, I thought he was a power-crazed madman, and I lay with him so that I could kill him. But he *spoke* to me, woodsinger. He spoke to me, and I learned that his seeming madness was well-reasoned. There is no one else who can hold the kingdom together. Two score men have died in the past fortnight alone. Bringham has hired mercenaries, and they roam the city, threatening to geld any man who is not for their lord. If my lord Coren does not become king, the chaos will continue."

"But Jobina, Coren is not the man you think he is," Alana said. "He brutalized the twins on your journey to Smithcourt. He murdered an old man, Reade's teacher."

Jobina nodded, as if listening to an old argument. "He told me about Kenwald. About how he had no choice. The old man was stirring up trouble. He was inciting Reade to rebel. If the Sun-lord spoke out too soon . . . If the Service does not come off as intended . . . The Service is our only hope."

"What is it, Jobina? What does Coren plan for the children?"

The healer's answer came from a distance, and her fingers began to pluck at a line of gold embroidery on her sleeve. "There is a legend among the people here, about the ancient Duke Culain and twins that he rescued."

"I've heard it."

"Duke Coren has worked out . . . an arrangement with High Priest Zeketh. They'll recreate the old story. They've asked the people of Smithcourt to let the kingdom be handed over to the twins. They've asked the factions—Bringham's men and Coren's men and all the other petty lords who vie for the throne—to set aside their disagreements, to lay down their arms, and be ruled by the Sun-lord and the Sun-lady."

"By Reade and Maida?" Alana laughed incredulously. "But they're *children*! Why would anyone let that happen?"

"It's a way for all to save face. Bringham's men can admit defeat without being embarrassed. The dragon has fought well, you see, but not well enough. He doesn't actually have enough soldiers to defeat Duke Coren, in the long run. He can't afford enough mercenaries. Letting the Sun-lord and the Sun-lady rule is a way for everyone to step back. The kingdom will be controlled by a higher power, by an older force."

"But Coren *brought* the children here. Surely Bringham sees that they'll be nothing but his puppets."

"Coren brought them, but High Priest Zeketh presents them."

"Zeketh, Coren, what difference does that make? They have each other's interest at heart."

"If you know that, it's only because of things you've heard in this palace, behind Duke Coren's walls. Bringham doesn't know that my lord and High Priest Zeketh are united. The people of Smithcourt don't know. They truly believe that Zeketh speaks independently. They believe that this is the will of the Seven Gods, that the Sun-lord and the Sun-lady are the answers to their prayers." Jobina caught her lower lip beneath her teeth, and her hands clenched and unclenched around the stiff knife embroidered on her gown. "And so they might have been."

"Might have been? Jobina! What has Coren planned?"

"In—in the story, Duke Culain brought the Sun-lord and the Sun-lady to Smithcourt. He took them before all the people, so that they could ascend to their rightful place on the Iron Throne. Before the children could be presented, though, a terrible thing happened."

Even as the healer spoke, Alana remembered the cramped tavern room where Coren had told Reade the story of the Sun-lord and the Sun-lady. That tale had ended with a surprise, with the honored *Culain* taking the throne. Reade had asked, Alana remembered. Reade had asked why Culain ruled, but Coren had refused to say.

Jobina would not meet Alana's eyes. "In the story, the Sun-lord and the Sun-lady received gifts, wondrous gifts, from other kingdoms. Coren and Bringham and all the other nobles have made similar presentations. They've put forward their offerings so that the Service can work. They want the Service to cure the ancient wrong." Jobina raised her chin, firming her resolve. "In the old story, one of the gifts was a giant glass cage. It held the Mothersnake, a beast as thick around as a man's thigh. It was supposed to be a symbol of power, a sign that Smithcourt could conquer the world."

Maddock made a strangled noise from where he stood across the room. Alana shot him a quick glance, afraid that his hard-earned distaste would silence Jobina Healer just when they most needed the other woman's knowledge. Jobina, though, had fallen into the rhythm of her tale.

"A sign," the healer repeated, and her restless fingers crept across her belly, writhing over the silk as if they were worms, or maggots. "It was terrible, the thing that happened on that dais. The Mothersnake escaped. She attacked the Sun-lord and the Sun-lady. Poor children . . . To die from the Mothersnake, after surviving so much. They fell on the dais, before they ever had a chance to lead their people to peace. But Duke Culain avenged them—he fought the Mothersnake. He was bitten, but he withstood the poison, and he killed the beast. He survived to lead his people in righteousness and the ways of all the Seven Gods."

"Jobina, we can't let Coren do this!" Alana was desperate to break the healer's enraptured recitation. "We'll kill the Mothersnake before she strikes Reade and Maida!"

Jobina scarcely registered the interruption. "The snake cannot be stopped. She is hungry. She's been without man-blood for all the months since Duke Coren first rode off for the twins."

"But what about the people?" Alana asked. "Surely all of Smithcourt will not stand by and sanction *children* being murdered?"

"They don't know what will happen. They think they come to watch a true resolution, a fair conclusion to the struggle for power in Smithcourt. They've come to watch history change before their eyes. They've come to watch the Sun-lord and the Sun-lady take the thrones they should have taken at the beginning of this age. They think they watch a pageant, complete with a plaything, a snake without true fangs."

"And when the Mothersnake is real?"

Jobina's voice swelled with pride, as if she were speaking about her own children. "The Sun-lord and the Sun-lady will long be remembered for their sacrifice. A traitor—Bringham himself—will be found to have introduced a real Mothersnake into the cage, a real serpent where a toy was expected. Coren will be forced to follow in Culain's footsteps. It will be too late for the Sun-lord and the Sun-lady, and Duke Coren himself will be bitten. But the poison will not kill him, and he will take the Iron Throne."

"How can he survive the bite?" Alana demanded.

"My lord has trained himself. He has taught his body to accept the Mothersnake's poison. Drop by drop, he has inured himself to the venom."

"How?" Maddock cried, and his voice shook as if he stared at a nightmare. "No man could survive that thing!"

"High Priest Zeketh has brought him the poison, one precious cup at a time. My lord has mixed the venom in his wine—first only one drop in an entire cask. Then one drop in a flagon, a drop in a cup. It made him ill, made a fire burn inside his veins. He had visions, and his belly twisted inside him. He cried out to the Seven Gods to free him from the venom's power. But he was not alone." The healer pulled herself to her full height, letting her robe fall straight. "I stood by my lord. I mixed the poison for him, and I held him as he drank. I gave him the strength to conquer the poison. The strength of Culain."

"You traitorous whore!" Maddock's snarl was only half swallowed, and his hand shook on his short sword.

Jobina whirled on the tracker. "Traitorous, Maddock? And who betrayed the People first? Who ran from the inn?"

"I made a mistake, woman! But I never agreed to *help* that bastard! You sold your calling, Jobina! You've given a vicious man the tool to kill children."

"I acted as I could, to save myself, to aid the People. Think, Maddock! If Bringham takes the throne, what bite will our People feel? Coren's supporters will never rest easy under Bringham's heel; they're too strong for that. Bringham will need an army to control his rival, and he'll need to pay those soldiers. Can you see our fishermen impressed to fight these inland wars? Can you see us paying inland taxes for mercenaries? Our lives, the *People's* lives would be forever changed!"

Jobina stood tall. "Scoff all you want, Maddock. I know that I've saved the People. Duke Coren has come to love me, I who served him during this darkest of times. He will make me his queen and spare our people. And our children, the duke's and mine, will extend that protection through the ages. Life on the Headland will be safe." The healer settled her fingers against her belly again, curving in the suggestion of new life.

"You?" Alana asked, before Maddock could splutter a new protest.

Jobina nodded. "I carry my lord's child. His son and heir, if my herbcraft has any power here."

"It's too soon," Alana protested. "How can you know?"

"I'm a healer. I'm trained to know."

Alana fought against the revulsion that choked her, clammy as a kelp-weighted wave.

Landon called out, his voice strangely piercing across the too-quiet room. "Is that the way the old tales go, Jobina? Did Culain take an outland bride?"

The healer's eyes blazed with spite, and more than a little fear. "This is different."

"How, Jobina? Coren has recreated the past. He has journeyed to the Headland. He has stolen our children. He has prepared for a fatal confrontation. He has staged a religious ceremony for his Seven Gods. What bride did Culain take, Jobina? Who bore his children?" Landon was relentless.

"You're jealous! You're angry that the soldiers treated you so harshly on the road! Landon, you're tired and you're sick, and you don't realize what you say!"

"I've said nothing, Jobina. I've only asked you questions. You have told the answers."

"My lord brought me to Smithcourt to be his help-meet!" The healer looked at all three of them, her eyes wild behind their dark paint. "Together, Duke Coren and I will found a new house, forge a new dynasty to ring in the next age!"

"Then come with us now, Jobina," Alana challenged. "The four of us will go to the cathedral. You can stand before Coren and tell him your dreams—before all the people of Smithcourt, before the Sunlord and Sun-lady."

"You think I won't?" Jobina's voice trembled with scarce-bitten fear or anger.

"Oh, no, Healer. I know you will," Alana confirmed. She swallowed hard as she settled her hand over her bavin, as if she were swearing an oath to the Tree and the Guardians. To the People. "I know you will."

Alana stood in the cathedral transept, resisting the urge to raise her fingers to her bare, vulnerable neck. The cathedral was larger than the chapel she had glimpsed through Reade's bavin weeks before—larger and noisier and far, far more crowded. It seemed as if the entire population of Smithcourt had squeezed into the stone building. The throng shifted from foot to foot, lowing like cattle as they waited for the pageant to begin. The sour smell of sweat reeked beneath the pungent bite of old incense.

The outlanders had had an easier time reaching the cathedral than Alana had dared to hope for. They had marched through the near-deserted Smithcourt streets without being challenged. Once, they came across a knot of Bringham's men, swaggering soldiers with silver dragons embroidered on their cobalt sleeves. Alana and Maddock refused to rise to their supposed rivals' taunts, merely chivvying their "prisoners" toward the cathedral.

Both Coren's men and Bringham's ringed the house of worship. The guards were edgy, and many fingered their weapons, but none seemed surprised that two prisoners were being marched in to watch the Service—even if one looked bedraggled and half-dead from Coren's dungeons and the other appeared to be a painted woman from Fishwife Row, however fine her gown. After all, the Service was important. No one wanted to miss the presentation of the Sun-lord and the Sun-lady.

Safely inside the stone cathedral, Alana caught her breath as she maneuvered for a clear view of the altar. Reade and Maida already stood on the dais, swathed once again in their ceremonial robes of gold. Maida looked haunted, her hair pulled back from her too-pale face, her lower lip standing out like blood as she gnawed at it nervously.

Reade, though, showed no fear. He gazed out at the congregation with a fierce look on his face, with the same intensity he had shown as the huer, a lifetime ago on the Headland of Slaughter. Occasionally, the boy broke his perusal of the crowd to glance over his shoulder at the crystal box that stood behind him on the dais.

The massive, clear cage sat on an ornate iron stand. Alana heard Maddock swear softly beside her, and she did not need to reach through her bavin to know what he was thinking. The crystal cage was five times the size of the Avenger's enclosure. The jet-black branch that leaned against the clear wall was a verita-ble tree trunk, its thorns as long as Alana's forearm. The Mothersnake must be a nightmare, a beast so large that Maddock's earlier encounter would seem like a child's game.

Before Alana could swallow her fear, Duke Coren snared her attention. He stood in the first row of wor-shipers, resplendent in crimson and cloth-of-gold. Jew-els glinted from his tunic and his long, flowing cape. The bloody blade that gleamed across his chest was encrusted with dripping rubies, and the sun was em-broidered gold. Within his finery, the duke held him-self as straight as a sword. His hair caught the cathedral light, and his beard was combed and silky.

He looked so noble that Alana might almost have

forgotten the terror that he had wrought upon the People—might have forgotten, if she had not seen Donal standing by Coren's side. The lieutenant looked about the cathedral alertly, as if he sought out ambush or attack. Alana could not gaze at the soldier without thinking of him stealing away Maida, bundling off a terrified child from her family, her home. She shivered as she realized that Donal's sword swung easily at his side.

Also in the front row, but far to Coren's left, stood another man, another warrior, this one tall and proud in cobalt silk and velvet. Alana had never seen Bringham's straight chestnut hair; she'd never looked upon his flat, dark eyes. Nevertheless, she could make out the argent dragon crawling across his chest, and she recognized the hard set to his jaw. This was the nobleman who challenged Duke Coren.

Challenged Duke Coren, Alana reminded herself, but was willing to settle his claims in this farce of a religious spectacle. Bringham believed in peace in Smithcourt; he hoped for peace throughout the land. Whatever accusations Jobina had thrust at him, Bringham was willing to sacrifice his personal ambition for an end to the skirmishing in Smithcourt. Standing before the altar of his Seven Gods, he did not realize that he was forfeiting unjustly the crown that he desired, giving it to a liar and a kidnapper and a murderer.

And up on the dais, High Priest Zeketh stood ready to begin the sham ceremony. The holiest man in Smithcourt was gowned in black, swathed in yards of rich samite. His close-set obsidian eyes glinted as he nodded toward both Coren and Bringham, and then the priest raised a commanding hand high above his head. His fingers were rigid as he directed seven priests to raise the giant censer that sat on the dais.

The massive iron bowl had been pounded out of blackest metal, and it was bigger around than the largest of the People's cooking pots. It was filled with incense, and a priest stepped forward to light the stinking mound. Alana could not keep from wrinkling her nose as the smoke billowed out of the swinging iron bowl. Great clouds wafted toward the ceiling, and tendrils reached down to the dais. As the woodsinger watched, Maida pulled her hand from her brother's, reaching up to rub tears from her eyes. Reade clenched his jaw as if he stifled a cough, but then he sneezed.

The explosive sound made High Priest Zeketh glare, but there was a murmur of good cheer from the assembled people. Reade apparently heard the sound, and he managed a timid smile as he looked out over the crowd.

Clouds of incense began to fog the air, and High Priest Zeketh barked another harsh command. The seven burly priests hefted the massive bowl of incense by pulling on their thick ropes. Each man tied his hawser about his waist, leaning back against the censer's enormous weight. Then, with a symmetry like the People's sailors setting out to sea, the priests began to pull the ropes to and fro, making the censer sway above the transept.

The men began to chant a prayer, and Alana's breath came short with the power of their song. They called to each other across the cathedral, long, low cries that told when to lean back, when to pull forward. Each movement set the censer swaying, coughing out its incense smoke.

The priests kept at their work like a well-trained crew, and Alana shook her head to break the spell of song and incense. She leaned forward to whisper to Maddock and saw that he was ignoring the priests, ignoring the giant censer. All his attention was snagged by the crystal cage, by the still-invisible threat of the Mothersnake. "Now, Maddock," Alana hissed, even as she urged Jobina forward. "It's time."

They pushed their way through the crowd, Maddock pretending to manhandle Landon while Alana kept her hand tight on Jobina's arm. The throng of worshipers resisted at first, but they eventually gave way before Coren's livery.

As Alana drew near the altar, she wished that Reade still wore his bavin. The little boy was standing, awestruck by the finery around him. He was fascinated by the swinging censer, but he kept glancing toward Coren for approval. As High Priest Zeketh began to chant a benediction over the assembly, Coren looked up at his Sun-lord and smiled. Reade returned the attention with his own grin.

If only Alana could snag Reade's attention . . . If only she could make the child turn toward her. Take a few steps away from the crystal cage, a few steps away from Zeketh, from danger.

Her heart pounding, Alana saw a gap in the crowd and forced her way another step closer to the dais. The sudden movement finally made Reade look in her direction, and Alana found herself pinned by the child's gaze.

For just an instant, Reade stared at the woodsinger, his jaw slack with shock. Then, his fingers clutched at his golden robes, at the place where his bavin had hung. The boy's throat started to work, and Alana tightened her grip on Jobina's arm. That motion was enough to make Reade glance to either side. Alana saw the moment the child registered Jobina and Landon, the instant he recognized Maddock.

Reade opened his mouth as he had so long ago, standing on the Headland, when he had been the huer. The sound rang out, high and pure, from the time before he was the Sun-lord, from the age when he had been an ordinary boy among the People. His song was unbearably sweet in the suddenly still cathedral. "To me, guards! To the Sun-lord!"

17

Alana acted without thought, leaping onto the dais even as Reade drew breath for his cry. By the time his words soared across the cathedral, the woodsinger had grabbed Maida, closing her fingers around the little girl's thin arm. Alana tugged hard, and Maida fell forward like a flopping doll, her head lolling back on her neck. Her golden headdress spilled across the dais, spread out like fishnets drying in the sun.

Alana scarcely noticed the web of lace and precious metal; instead, she thrust Maida behind her, into Landon's startled arms. "Hold her!" Alana commanded.

For one heart-stopping instant, the woodsinger thought that Landon would not understand. The man stared at her dully, his eyes glazed with fever, and she could see him struggle to gather up the child. "Landon!" she barked. "Don't you dare fail me now!"

The grim hopelessness in the tracker's eyes lanced Alana's heart, but he responded to her hectoring, and he gathered up the little girl. Even as Maida woke to the horror of her new captivity and fought for release, the tracker pulled her close and hissed, "Be still, Maida!"

Alana watched only long enough to see that Landon was stepping back, falling under the shadow of Maddock's protective sword. Then, the woodsinger plunged back into the maelstrom on the dais.

It was hard to believe that her heart had only beat a hundred times since Reade's cry, that hours had not passed since she had realized the little boy was completely snared by Coren. A hundred heartbeats, though, and then a handful more, and the woodsinger clutched the supposed Sun-lord. Reade was frozen in his golden robes, clearly astonished by the results of his single shout. Soldiers throughout the cathedral were drawing their weapons. Coren's men leaped toward the dais, followed closely by Bringham's soldiers. The woodsinger closed her hands around Reade's waist.

"Come with me, Reade." She tried to keep her voice level, reassuring.

The boy screamed, "Guards! To me! To the Sunlord!" As Alana grabbed him, he kicked her, but his golden robes tangled about his feet. He started to tumble down the dais steps, but Alana snatched him upright, jerking on the billowing cloth around his waist.

The breath was knocked out of his small lungs as Alana scrambled at her own waist for her iron dagger, the precious blade that her father had given her. Her hand was firm as she yanked Reade against her chest, leveling her knife toward the nearest of Coren's advancing men.

The duke had recovered enough from his surprise that he bellowed for quiet, ordering his soldiers to stand down. Bringham called for order as well, causing the blue-clad Southglen soldiers to drop back from the raised dais. The rival dukes glared at each other for a quick instant, each thinking that the other had staged the disruption.

Coren must have read the confusion in Bringham's eyes, though, for he seemed to realize that Southglen did not know what was happening. Bringham clearly did not recognize Alana or Landon; he'd never seen Maddock or Jobina. Bringham did not know the outlanders who disrupted the holy Service. Coren nodded slowly as if making a truce with his rival, and then he turned to Alana.

Taking a single step forward, his coal-black eyes measuring the woodsinger's grip on Reade, Coren clearly calculated the tension in her knife-wielding hand. Smiling tightly through his curling chestnut beard, Coren held his hands out from his sides, auspiciously showing them empty of any weapon. "Alana Woodsinger. Well met."

Alana saw the dark, depthless eyes, watched the hands that had stirred her imagination back on the Headland of Slaughter. She spat at the duke's feet and pulled Reade closer. "Well met for Smithcourt, perhaps."

Above her pounding heart, she could make out Zeketh's scandalized exclamation, the high priest's shock that someone would defile his altar. That outcry, though, was nothing compared to the noise of the panicked congregation. From shouts and cries, it was apparent that Bringham's supporters did not trust Coren; they wanted their own lord to step forward. Swords clashed as the tensions on the dais boiled over to the congregation, and worshipers jostled each other to make room for tight knots of fighters. Coren spoke above the tumult, not sparing his rival a glance. "Lower your knife, Alana. You are not one to shed blood on a holy altar."

"Your altar isn't holy to me! Not when you would sacrifice innocent children upon it!" A rumble went up from the crowd nearest the dais, from Bringham and his closest retainers. Zeketh roared, providing a credible facsimile of a man surprised. Alana raised her voice. "We know the truth, Coren. The real Mothersnake rests inside that cage, and she hungers for the blood of children."

The duke stared at the woodsinger in pretended shock before he turned toward his rival, shrugging a gold-clad shoulder in confusion. Pretend confusion.

He directed his words to Alana, forcing sorrow into his voice. "I would not expect an outlander to understand our ways. Not when you and your people shed children's blood so easily, to feed your Tree. I promise you, woodsinger, there is no threat to the twins here. None at all. Duke Bringham and I, High Priest Zeketh and I, all of us are here to honor the Sun-lord and the Sun-lady from the bottoms of our hearts."

"I'm not a fool, Coren! You plan to slay the children and shift the blame to Bringham."

"That's absurd!" Coren protested, even as the crowd surged forward. Alana saw from the corner of her eye that Bringham held out an arm, restraining his lieutenant, who would have run Coren through with a sword, holy altar or no. Coren must have caught the same action at the edge of his own vision, but he only raised his aggrieved voice. "Who could have told you such lies? What traitor made up such a tale?"

Before Alana could answer, Jobina stepped forward. "It was I, my lord. I told her of your plan."

Coren gaped in mock amazement. "Jobina! What so-called plan could an herb-witch from the outlands have learned in Smithcourt? When you last walked through our city streets, you were chained as a traitor!" Coren spluttered for words as he darted a glance at Southglen. Slowly, he began to nod. "Ah . . ." he said slowly, and Alana could see that he now wove a new plan. "I begin to understand. You hope to cast your lot with Bringham. You support Southglen in his hopes for the Iron Throne."

Bringham needed to bark out an order to keep his dragon-clad men in line. Before the duke could step forward to answer the challenge himself, Jobina countered, "I'd not seen Bringham before this day, Your Grace. You are the only duke I've ever known. The only duke I've ever loved."

"You're mad, woman!"

"Was I mad when you lay with me this morning?

Was I mad when I conceived your son?" Jobina ignored the congregation's shocked gasps.

The duke merely gaped at the healer, not even bothering to justify his reaction for Bringham and the assembled worshipers. "*My* son?" he finally repeated. "Perhaps you bear some bastard, woman, but he surely isn't mine."

Jobina's wail was an animal sound. It rose from deep within her, wild and wordless. Alana tightened her hands on Reade's shoulders, reflexively trying to shield the boy from the healer's terrifying rage. "Liar!" Jobina shouted. "I believed you, my lord! I listened to your stories, and I agreed that it was necessary for the Sun-lord and the Sun-lady to die! I knew that you must do things, terrible things, to save your kingdom from Bringham. I accepted what you said—even the Mothersnake, I accepted. I *loved* you, my lord!"

The healer ran at the duke with a dagger that she produced from somewhere inside her silken robes. The nobleman had no trouble sidestepping her, twisting her wrist sharply and pinning her arm behind her back. "Donal!" he cried as the congregation exploded. The lieutenant sprang to attention, stepping forward with a dozen of Coren's red-clad men. His hands were brutal as he took Jobina from his lord. "Gag her!" Coren shouted to be heard above the tumult, and Donal complied viciously.

As Jobina was wrestled off the dais, Coren inclined his head to Zeketh, then turned to Reade and bowed before he included Maida in a broad gesture. "Holy Father, you must forgive us. I'm sorry, Sun-lord. Sun-lady." The duke spoke directly to the children, in a voice so low that the crowd had to quiet itself to hear. "Jobina Healer has imagined these terrible things. Now she's ruined your presentation to your people."

Alana felt Reade relax in her arms as the duke spoke. "Don't talk to them!" she snapped at Coren.

"Not another word! You've tortured them so much they'll believe anything you say!" There was an outraged murmur from the assemblage, and Bringham stepped forward, but Alana could not know if the man meant to threaten her or Coren. She snarled and took a step closer to the altar, pulling Reade with her.

"Torture?" Coren laughed incredulously. "Look around you, woodsinger. Cloth-of-gold. Jewels. The holiest priest in Smithcourt. Do these children look abused?"

Alana dared not give Coren the satisfaction of gazing at the children's finery, and she knew she would not be able to restrain her anger if she focused on the duplicitous high priest. She could hear Maida's breath coming fast, even across the dais, the little girl panting as if she were an injured animal. Alana barely let her eyes fall to Reade, to his thin neck, to the pulse that beat beneath her palms.

"Tell me, Sun-lord," Coren addressed his words directly to the little boy, "have I ever harmed you?"

"No, Your Grace. You've always done what is best for me." Reade's response was immediate, solemn, and sincere. Alana's heart sank at how readily Reade gave Coren his title, how easily he forgave all that he had suffered. But Reade was not through; he continued to recite his hard-learned lessons. "You've done what is best for me, and best for all the kingdom."

Coren smiled, and Alana's belly tightened as she recognized the true affection between the man and the child. "That's right, Sun-lord. The times are dark, and our people need us."

"There are riots in the street," Reade confirmed, as if he were reciting a poem. "There are bad people who do bad things."

"But you and the Sun-lady can make Smithcourt safe again. You can bring order to the kingdom. You can lead your people."

"The Sun-lady and I can save all the people," Reade completed the catechism.

Coren extended a hand to the boy. "Let us stop this nonsense then, shall we? Come to me, Reade. Let us be done with this foolishness. Let us finish the Service, son."

Alana felt Reade register Coren's endearment. The little boy shifted beneath her hands, ready to move to the duke, to step into his destiny.

Bringham had stiffened as he watched Coren bond with the Sun-lord. Alana saw the moment that South-glen recognized what he should have known all along, the instant when Bringham saw that his own cause was lost, betrayed. She watched the nobleman's dragon-chased sword slither from its sheath. Coren registered the danger and leaped back out of harm's way.

Reflexively, Alana tugged Reade, dragging him toward the center of the dais, trying to move him beyond the reach of Bringham's sword. The boy struggled, though, sinking his teeth into the fleshy part of Alana's palm, and he fought to flee toward Coren. Bringham leaped onto the platform, swinging his weapon. In the middle of the tumult, Alana heard High Priest Zeketh's voice rise. "Now, men! To the left!"

Bringham was so shocked to hear the priest inter-vene that he froze in his fighter's crouch, sword at the ready. Southglen visibly realized that Coren was not acting alone, he saw that the high priest had also lied and cheated to create the Service, to create the facade that all the power in the land was being transferred to the Sun-lord and the Sun-lady.

Even as Bringham's world began to tumble around his shoulders, Alana heard the priests comply with their corrupt leader's order. She heard the ropes rasp against the giant iron censer that hung overhead. She imagined that she could make out the shift of burning incense; she had time to see clouds of smoke billow from the iron bowl. Smoke first, and then the incense came tumbling out.

The embers glowed red, and they fell slowly, as if the priests poured flaming honey. Bringham was frozen in front of Alana and Reade, frozen in a rain of fire, amid the smoldering embers that sizzled on his fine cobalt robes. Even as the swordsman brushed away the coals, Zeketh swore, casting a horrible oath up to his Seven Gods. Clearly, he had expected more from the swinging censer; he had intended to annihilate Bringham. The high priest exhorted his followers again: "Swing hard, men! To the right!"

Alana saw Bringham spring away, and she realized what the men were doing. She commanded herself to move, to drag Reade with her. Her scrambling brain issued the instructions, but her muscles refused to act. She was rooted in terror as she watched the giant iron censer tip above her head, watched the ropes slip along its sides. It was already too late to move, too late to act, too late to do anything but watch the censer fall and hold on to Reade and commend their souls to the Guardians.

And then, she was knocked to the cathedral floor.

Even as she rolled, trying to keep from crushing Reade, trying to keep her dagger from the child's flesh, Alana looked over her shoulder. She forced a ragged breath past her bruised lungs as the censer slipped from its ropes and crashed to the dais where she had just stood. The clang of iron against stone was muffled, though, by a human body.

By Landon's body.

"No!" Alana screamed as time was released, and she watched the censer roll to its side. For one desperate moment, she thought that the tracker had heard her, that he had shrugged off the bowl and was climbing to his feet. The motion, though, was only an illusion. There was too much blood, too much crimson soaking the smoldering, incense-singed carpet.

Landon would not draw another tortured breath in Smithcourt. He would not look again at Alana, stare at her with tortured eyes that said he feared that he would fail her.

Even as Alana registered that Maddock now held Maida, the censer completed its slow roll, clanging to rest against the Mothersnake's giant cage. The iron bowl hit the glass cage hard, making the enclosure shudder and shift on its stand. The sand rolled against the glass wall as if it were a liquid wave. The black branch absorbed the blow and burrowed deeper beneath its grainy silver blanket.

People cried out in the cathedral, for they had heard Jobina's accusation, and now they feared the beast that lurked within the sand. Alana braced herself for the horror, for the serpent in the cage to writhe its way into the cathedral. The Guardians, though, must have heard her silent prayer, for the Mothersnake did not escape. The sand flowed back from the far wall, kissing the top of the crystal enclosure, but the cage held.

Even as Alana realized that the Mothersnake was contained, chaos exploded around her. Women in the congregation screamed, and men bellowed. High Priest Zeketh shouted orders to his priests, exhorting them to seize the Sun-lord and the Sun-lady, whatever the cost. Bringham's men fought to their lord's side, brandishing swords against the treacherous priests. Coren hollered for his own men. Reade sobbed, calling for his da as if his heart would break, and Maida's voice rose in a pitiful moan.

"Hold!"

The single word broke through the tempest like a ray of sunshine. Maddock stepped up to the foot of the dais, tall and fearless. Smoke from the incense-charred carpet rose around him, but he stood tall and true, with a naked sword glimmering in his hands. He thrust Maida toward Alana, and the woodsinger gathered the little girl against her hip, uncertain of Maddock's intention.

"Hold!" the warrior repeated, and an edgy silence fell over everyone in the cathedral. "Coren. Bringham. Fight your own battles, with your own men, but let these children and women return to our home. Let us go."

"My, my," Coren said after a long moment. "If it isn't the People's coward, mewling on my steps."

"Call me names, if that makes you feel more a man." Maddock turned his sword so that it caught a beam of shimmering sunlight. He looked from Coren to Bringham and back again. "Let us go," he repeated.

"And why should I do that, little man? One of you rebels already lies crushed upon the dais. Why should I just step aside and let you take our Sun-lord and Sun-lady?"

"Everyone now knows what you planned to do, Coren. If Bringham doesn't cut you down for double-crossing him, your own men will turn against a child-killer. End the charade and let us go."

"You mean to say that you believe that raving whore?" Coren gestured dismissively toward Jobina, who now stood gagged and broken at Donal's side.

"I believe that you intended Reade and Maida to die." Maddock glanced at Bringham, but he threw his words toward Coren. "You intended to betray your rival, Southglen. You and Zeketh meant to sacrifice the children, so that you could take their place. You wanted to live the old legends, to be Culain."

"To be . . . You're mad!" Coren cast his denial toward his rival. "We spent weeks working out this truce, Southglen. Why would I endanger that by harming the Sun-lord and the Sun-lady?"

Maddock answered before Bringham could reply.

"You wanted all of Smithcourt for yourself, Coren. You wanted to sit on the Iron Throne yourself, whatever the cost to Maida and Reade, to two helpless children."

"You lie!"

"Do I? Then fight me, Coren. Fight to prove that you walk with your Seven Gods on paths of justice."

"Fight *you*?" Coren managed to coat the question in incredulity.

"Aye. Here and now. Single combat, with sword alone. If I win, we outlanders get free passage through Smithcourt's gates, horses for all of us, and we ride home unhindered."

"And when I win?"

"*If* you do, you'll have the children, free and clear."

Coren glared at Maddock for a long minute, as if he were trapped inside a cage. Before he answered, he turned to Bringham, measuring his rival's hungry stare. "Southglen? What say you? If I rid us of this fool, will our own truce hold? Will you stand beside me as we present Smithcourt to the Sun-lord and the Sun-lady in this house of the Seven Gods?"

Bringham looked about the dais, staring first at Maddock, then at Alana. His intelligent eyes came to rest on the giant censer, on the bloody ruin that had been Landon. Slowly, he shook his head and turned his gaze on Zeketh before he said to Coren, "You work with the priest. I will not trust a man who just ordered my death. I will not trust a high priest who ordered his own men to slay me before his altar."

"I was fooled by him as well!" Coren protested. "I thought he would work with *both* of us, that he would help us to build peace."

"Words, Coren," Bringham spat. "You think to seduce me with words."

"Donal!" Coren shouted without hesitation. Coren kept his eyes on Bringham's, steady and unwavering. "Take High Priest Zeketh into custody. Now!"

Donal did not hesitate. He barked orders to a dozen of his men, short sharp cries like a dog in the night. Moving with the same efficiency that he had harnessed against Jobina, against the People, against poor Maida back on the Headland of Slaughter, Donal ordered his men to surround High Priest Zeketh.

Zeketh bolted for the front of the dais, but Donal anticipated the move, snagging the priest's flowing black robes and tripping him. Zeketh fell hard, his teeth catching his tongue. Blood flecked the large man's lips as he struggled for breath, fought to regain his feet. "The Seven Gods will smite you! All of you will burn in endless fire!"

"In your company," Donal growled. Two sharp jabs to Zeketh's solar plexus cut off further imprecations.

A few of the other priests made as if to escape from the dais, but they were rapidly restrained by Donal's men. "Very good, Donal," Coren said when Zeketh was forced to his knees. "Gag him." Donal followed suit. "Now give him to our brother Southglen."

"My lord?"

"Hand the priest to Bringham."

Donal complied without further protest, waiting until the somewhat-surprised Bringham had managed to pass the priest on to his own captain. Coren nodded when the transfer was complete. "Smithcourt has no room for those who would play traitor in the house of the Seven Gods." Zeketh bellowed behind his gag, but he was restrained by the rough ministrations of Bringham's men.

"There," Coren said, when the priest was once again silent. He cocked his head toward Maddock, but he spoke to Bringham. "Are we agreed then? Shall I dispatch this miserable outlander so that we can return to the Sun-lord and Sun-lady's Service?"

Bringham looked as if he wanted to refuse, but he clearly had no choice. Even if he doubted Coren's loyalty, he could hardly argue with the speed with which Coren had handed over the conniving priest. Southglen sighed and stepped down from the dais, gesturing for his lieutenant to drag Zeketh from the fray.

"Very well, then," Coren said, and he bowed stiffly to Maddock. "I accept your challenge, outland dog."

Coren drew his sword for the first time since the confusion had begun, and he handed his rich, brocade cloak to Donal. He made a few passes with his weapon, as if he were getting the feel of its weight. The remaining priests cleared a circle for the two men, encouraged to step lively by Coren's wary soldiers. Maddock moved away from Landon's wrecked body, away from the Mothersnake's glass cage and the charred carpet and all the horror that had already been wrought in this corrupted house of the Seven Gods.

Alana tucked Maida against her side, making sure that the girl could not see the bloody combat to come. She tried to shield Reade as well, but the boy would have none of her comfort. Instead, he twisted like a trout caught on a line, writhing away as if her touch burned him. She barely managed to keep him standing before her.

Reade leaned toward the two men, his eyes dark and distant. His small body tensed, and his throat began to vibrate with a single syllable. The sound was scarcely more than a whisper, but when Alana strained, she could make out one word, repeated over and over again. "Da. Da. Da . . ."

Meanwhile, the men circled each other like nervous cats, and the congregation caught its collective breath. Alana thought of all the times that she had watched Maddock practice his fighting forms, all the times that she had thought he was a foolish boy, a foolish man. Back on the Headland, back on the village green, she had not been able to imagine a time or a place where

Maddock would need his sword skills. Snared by her memories, Alana was not prepared for the brutal clash as Maddock finally rushed at Coren.

Both men used their swords like deadly extensions of their arms, attacking each other with the flats of their blades. They scarcely rotated the weapons to take advantage of their sharpened edges as they crashed and parried, lunging and leaping back.

Coren drew first blood.

Maddock tried to block a blow, but he calculated the angle poorly. In an instant, Coren's sword had slid down the tempered iron cross, rasping toward the outlander's arm. Only by twisting away at the last instant did Maddock avoid losing a limb. As it was, Coren's sharp edge caught him across his bicep, splitting the bright crimson fabric to bare flesh that soon glinted with its own bloody sheen.

Reade cried out at the blow. Sliced free by the sword's brutal path, the boy's emotions were as transparent as if he still wore his woodstar. Alana read terror and hatred, all stirred together with a confused love for Coren. The woodsinger wished again that she could reach Reade through his missing bavin, that she could make him stop rocking back and forth, stop crooning his single syllable over and over.

Even as she longed for Reade's lost woodstar, though, Alana remembered that there was more at stake than a single child's sanity. An entire kingdom hung in the balance. And Maddock wore a bavin, too. Maddock, who even now was bleeding from a cut above his eye, whose sword arm burned as if he'd been attacked by a devilfish. The woodsinger could sense those hurts and more, bruises and darts of pain.

Taking a deep breath, Alana dove back into her own bavin.

"Why haven't you reached for us?" one of the distant woodsingers demanded.

"We've been waiting for you!"

"We wanted to help you!"

Alana thrust her thoughts at them. "What? What can you do?"

The woodsingers hovered, muttering wordless concern. That was the problem, Alana wanted to scream. That was why she hadn't reached for her sisters before. They might miss her, they might fear for her, they might even love her, but they had no support to offer. Not now. Not across a desolate land. Not leagues and leagues from the Tree. Not while Maddock fought for his life.

Thrusting aside her hopeless disappointment, Alana threw her thoughts forward, along the shining thread of Maddock's woodstar. She blazed her consciousness through to where the bavin pricked his chest, to where it nestled beneath his stolen uniform. The lacy wooden points were sharp against his skin, and they leaped with his heart as he failed to deflect a glancing blow from Coren's heavy sword.

Not letting herself think, Alana absorbed the sudden pain, soaking up the agony before Maddock's leg could register the blow. The warrior wasted a precious breath bracing himself for the jagged hurt, and he was so startled by his reprieve that he nearly stumbled.

Alana collected the pain in her own body, in her own mind, and then she thrust it back toward her sisters. For one timeless instant, she thought that they would fail her. She thought that they would not understand what she intended to do, what she needed to do, how she would save Maddock. Then, just as her throat wrapped itself around a bruising sob, she felt one woman reach out.

Sarira Woodsinger. The woman who had sung for Alana's father's bavin, who had given her own life trying to bring Alana's father back to port. . . . Alana felt Sarira catch Maddock's pain through the bavin, gather up the agony and store it away inside the Tree. Then, before Alana could clear her mind, before she could settle herself to receive the next blow, she felt her sister woodsingers throw wordless thoughts across the bavin thread. Devotion. Faith. Support.

They knew what she was doing, they knew what she was asking, and they gave unstintingly of themselves. They took all the hurt and pain and fear from Maddock, all the agony that passed through Alana, and they fed it to the Tree, transforming it into strength and pride and sturdy, oaken love.

All of their efforts, though, were not enough. Even with the collective might and wisdom of the woodsingers, Alana could not harvest every one of Coren's blows. Pain leaked through her grasp, weakening Maddock, distracting the People's only hope. Alana choked back a sob as the flat of Coren's blade landed across Maddock's back—her back—and she almost lost her bond with the Tree.

Almost, but not quite. A voice sang to her across the land, quivering across the white bavin thread. "Fairsister!"

"Parina Woodsinger," Alana gasped. She felt her ancient sister speak from the Tree's very core.

"Prithee, fairsister, fade not your heartstrength now. Listen to the lostboy. Follow his guidesong."

"Lostboy?" Alana barely had the strength to send the question as she gasped against the blinding pain.

"The huerboy. The *hevva*singer."

"Reade."

"Aye. Listen to him. Let the *hevva*singer guide ye. Let him hue ye in."

Alana wanted to argue. She wanted to explain that Reade was only a child, a boy who had been lied to and fooled and used as a pawn. She wanted to explain that she was exhausted, that she was beaten, that she had no energy left for battle.

Instead, she remembered the time that she had first discovered the bavin's white thread. She recalled giv-

ing herself over to Parina's wisdom, descending into
the Tree's sap-heavy, liquid heart. She remembered
that weight in her body; she recalled the drag on
her thoughts. She felt herself pulled into the Tree's
core, into the People's past, into the wisdom of Parina Woodsinger.

She heard Reade's guttural cry, felt him call, beneath her fingers, through her flesh. His throat rasped
across his one word, over and over, "Da, Da, Da."
Each heartbeat drove her deeper into the Tree, each
breath pulled her mind closer to its core. She sensed
Parina beside her, felt the weight of all the Tree's
rings, knew the wisdom of every word that every
woodsinger had ever poured into the oak.

Da, Da, Da. Alana watched Reade presented to the
Tree as an infant, cradled in his now-drowned father's
hands. She saw herself as well, nestled in her own
father's arms. She saw Maddock being offered up. She
saw Jobina and Landon, and Teresa and Goody
Glenna, generations more, all the People through
the centuries.

Da, Da, Da. Storms and harvests, gales and feasts—
Alana Woodsinger flowed through the history of her
People to the roots of the giant oak.

Da, Da, Da. She drilled down to the woven mass
that spread beneath the surface of the Headland, more
complex than any fishnet, holding the Tree stable and
steady and strong, nourishing it, anchoring it.

Almost lost in her dream, Alana clutched Reade
against her side, pressing his head against her stolen
uniform, feeling him shudder, feeling his entire body
gather to cry one last time: "Da!" She held on to that
final syllable, clung to his frantic plea, and she passed
through the final barrier, flowing past Parina Woodsinger into the Tree's deepest root.

Silence.

Silver.

Timelessness.

She could not breathe. She could not see. She could not hear.

Da.

Her body was trembling.

Da.

Her lungs were burning.

Da.

Her heart was pounding, bursting to be free.

Da.

She saw her father, smiling in the silver.

She saw him, and she knew that he was not alone. She knew that he was surrounded by the Guardians, by the Guardians of Water who had stolen him away, and the Guardians of Air who had made him welcome in the land beyond the sea. She saw that he had met the Guardians of Fire and the Guardians of Earth, greeted all of them in the fullness of time.

She saw her father, and she knew that he was with her mother, with *his* mother, with his own fisherman father. She saw him put his arm around the shoulders of another fisherman, and she recognized Reade's lost da. Alana saw all the figures, all the ghosts, all the People gathered in the shimmering embrace of a woman. One woman. The Great Mother.

They were all with the Great Mother.

Alana started to step into the circle of that embrace, started to take her last step into the promise of the endless, silver light.

But then her father turned his back on her.

He was not ready for her to join him. He was not ready to bring her into the silver circle. It was not yet time. She still had work to do, in the living world. Now. Before it was too late.

Alana grasped at the crystal mantle around her, seizing it in her mind, gathering it in her heart and lungs, pulling it into her bones. She filled herself with the essence of the Tree, of the Guardians, of the Great

Mother. And then she cast herself up through the root, back to the surface, to the rings and the bark, across the land, to a warrior who needed her power.

She cried out as she poured her strength into Maddock, cried out in rage and sorrow and disappointment and relief. All of the Tree's white-hot energy seared from her woodstar into his. She surged into Maddock's mind and his body; she felt the warrior melt into her.

For one moment, she was swallowed by the pain of their melding, by the hot, white fire of his separate soul. Then, his thoughts moved with hers; her body moved with his. His breath became her own, and she gave him her arms, her thighs, her lungs, her heart. She pulsed with his being, and the Tree made them one—one blinding, shimmering whole.

She lived Maddock. She breathed Maddock. She *was* Maddock.

At last, she smelled smoke.

Bavins could not burn. The woodsinger knew that in her soul. But the smoke was not in her imagination; it came from the Tree. Alana forced herself to pull back from her warrior being, from Maddock. Separating from his body, from his mind, was like a physical pain, but she felt herself drawn away by her bavin.

With a suddenness that stole her breath, Alana Woodsinger plunged back into the stone and smoke of the cathedral.

She took only a moment to see that Maddock had taken a beating in the furious swordfight. He was bloodied, heaving for breath as he raised his massively heavy sword. She struggled to gather back the strands of his pain, but she had lost her grip on the Tree's power, lost her way to the heartwood. Maddock staggered and cried out against the sudden onset of an entire battle's agony.

Coren, though, was also winded, and he stopped to shake perspiration from his eyes. Even as Alana strove to recapture the bavin's power, she watched Maddock exploit the break in Coren's fighting form. He stumbled forward like a boat grounding on a shallow shore.

Coren saw the threat, and he raised his sword to defend himself. The motion brought him around halfway, and he adjusted his stance so that he could attack the outlander. That shift, though, brought him to the very edge of the marble dais. He flailed his arms for a single, graceless moment, fighting to recover his balance.

And he succeeded. He regained his feet, taking a quick double step to keep from slipping down the stairs. Two small steps. Which brought him up hard against the Mothersnake's glass cage.

The iron-black branch shuddered under the impact, sliding even deeper into the silver sand. The motion was enough to upset the cage's precarious balance, and it finally toppled off its stand. One metal-bound corner crashed to the marble dais, and the stone cracked, as if a massive spider had spun an instant web across its surface.

For one breath, it seemed as if the stone had absorbed all the impact. Then, a deep fissure opened in the glass. Silver sand poured out, like a river into the sea. The black branch lodged against the crack, forcing it wider. As Alana watched in horror, sand cascaded onto the dais, and with it, a deadly iron-black shadow. The Mothersnake writhed onto the platform, thick as a man's thigh, roiling like clouds above a storm-tossed sea.

The massive beast curled upon herself, raising her head above her coiled body. Ripples ran down her flesh like night-shivers in a cemetery, and Alana could just make out the sound of the serpent's scales rasping on the spilled silver sand. As if responding to the woodsinger's horror, the Mothersnake opened her maw and revealed two perfect fangs, each the length of a man's hand. Poison glinted from their needle-tips, iridescent globes that swelled as the snake reared.

Coren flung up his arm to protect his face, but the motion only drew the snake. With a silence more chilling than any roar, the Mothersnake launched herself from the burned and bloodied carpet and buried her fangs in the duke's arm.

Coren's scream echoed off the vaulted ceiling. He thrashed about on the carpet, trying unsuccessfully to dislodge the beast. His legs became tangled in the giant snake's tail, and he arched his back to shift the unholy weight. Through it all, the snake's fangs remained lodged firmly in his arm.

Then, the struggle was over. Maddock stood panting above Duke Coren's twitching body. The sword in the outlander's hand steamed as if the iron had just been forged. As the smell of hot metal grew, Maddock dropped his stolen weapon onto the singed carpet and broken marble, letting it clang beside the Mothersnake's body.

Only then did Alana realize what had happened. Maddock had killed the Mothersnake. He had cut through her swollen body, severing her neck. Her fangs remained sunk in Coren's arm, though, and even from this distance, Alana could see that the duke's flesh was corrupting.

As if to confirm her vision, Coren struggled to a sitting position. He gritted his teeth and pulled with his good arm, forcing the severed head free of his flesh. Blood immediately began to flow from the wounds, dark and clotted.

"By all the Seven Gods!" Bringham managed to choke out the words, his face pale from across the dais.

Before the Duke of Southglen could recover, Reade pulled free from Alana's grasp. The child collapsed on his knees beside Coren. " 'There are bad people who do bad things!' " Reade cried, as if he were seeking reassurance, as if he needed love and support and confirmation of the order he'd thought he understood.

Alana recognized the line from the unholy catechism that Reade had learned from Coren. She saw
the boy hang on the quotation, waiting breathlessly
for his mentor to respond, for the nobleman to make
all right. Coren, though, only shook his head, swallowing noisily as he tried to still the flow of black
blood from his arm.

"'There are bad people who do bad things!'"
Reade repeated. He looked frantically at Bringham,
silent accusation flashing across his face. Alana reached
for the boy, tried to pull him back, but he thrashed
free. "Your Grace!" The boy cried to Coren, and he
started to sob. "There are bad people!"

"Aye," Coren managed at last.

"Say it," Reade demanded. "Say that the Sun-lady
and I can make Smithcourt safe again! We can bring
order! We can lead the people!"

"You can't—"

"I *can*! If you say it, I can!"

Coren reached out a hand toward the raging boy,
but his fingers were covered in muck, blood and bile
streaking his flesh. "I'm hurt, Reade."

As Reade wailed in fury, Coren looked at Bringham,
an odd desperation crossing his face. Alana thought
for a moment that Coren was asking Southglen for
mercy, that he was begging compassion for the child,
pleading that the farce of the Sun-lord might continue.
Whatever was asked, though, Bringham gave no
answer.

Coren drew a shuddering breath and pointed a gory
finger toward Alana. His voice shook, almost as if he
doubted his own words. "Go with your people now,
Reade. You'll be safe." Reade started to protest, but
Coren interrupted him. "Leave me!"

The command deflated the child, who gasped and
scrabbled for Coren's good hand. "Please . . ." Reade
moaned.

Coren pulled his hand back, setting his jaw and turn-

ing away. He whispered, barely loud enough for Alana
to hear, "You don't belong in Smithcourt, son."

"Don't call me that!" Reade recoiled. "I'm not your
son! You're not my da! You never were my da!"

"I—"

"You made me believe you! I thought you were
strong, like Culain!" Reade's anger exploded into
tears, hot and fluid. "I thought you were my friend! I
thought you would stay with me, that you wouldn't go
to the Guardians! I thought you were my da. . . ."

Alana knelt beside the child, gathering him up as
he sobbed with bitter recognition. Reade clutched at
her crimson uniform, burying his face against her
chest. She cradled him, rocking slowly. She whispered
that he was safe, that he was loved, that he was back
among his People.

Coren's foul spell was broken. The Sun-lord was no
more. Reade was a little boy once again, a little boy
far from his home, sobbing like a lost and exhausted
child. Alana managed to pull the boy to his feet, and
then she eased both of them away from Coren, away
from the dais and the Mothersnake and death.

Maddock, though, stepped closer to the fallen duke,
edging his foot into Coren's side. "We made a
bargain."

As if to enforce the agreement, Bringham strode
forward. Coren swallowed hard before he forced
words past his gritted teeth. "Donal will give you
horses."

It cost the duke to pull away from Maddock's
booted toe, to drag his poisoned flesh up higher on
the dais. As if afraid his opponent might yet fight,
Maddock dug his toe in deeper. "Now."

Coren caught his breath against the agony of the
motion, but he managed to speak to his lieutenant.
"Five horses for them. One each."

Alana looked up from where she ministered to
Reade. "We won't leave without Landon."

For a long minute, Duke Coren gazed at her. Even with the pain that stretched his face, even with the pallor that spread beneath his beard, she could sense his power. She could sense the vitality of a man who had trained his flesh to accept poison, to rise above inevitable death. After all, Coren was faring better than the rabbit had, better than the coney that had fallen prey to the Avenger. The duke's flesh was blackened, festering, but he was not yet consumed by the Mothersnake's poison. His preparation, Jobina's ministrations, Maddock's torture . . . all might yet conspire to let Coren live.

Alana remembered how fierce the duke had looked when he stood upon the Headland, months ago, a lifetime ago. She thought about his visit to the People, his cold manipulation as he won over first the woodsinger, then the fisherfolk. She wondered if Coren remembered standing beside her on the promontory by the Tree, if he remembered how the wind had felt in their hair as she told him about the People, about their determination, about their strength.

"Six, then," he finally agreed. "Six horses."

Coren collapsed against the dais as Alana gathered her people and turned for the air and light outside the cathedral. Six people. Herself. Reade and Maida. Maddock and Jobina. And Landon.

18

❖❖❖

Alana stood on the cliff, looking down on the waves that crashed against the rocky shore. The water was frothy and light, but great clumps of kelp had washed up on the beach. The summer months had been hot, and all the sea life had been plentiful—the fish, and the kelp, and the stinging eels that hid among the rocks just offshore. Her father would have rejoiced.

The woodsinger turned to her giant oak and began to sing to it, telling it once more of the rich harvest. A faint breeze whispered from the landward side, and Alana gathered her cloak about her shoulders, wondering again at the sense of comfort she found in the garment's ragged patches of brown and red, blue and white. They were earthy colors, human colors. Not as splendid as silver, but all the more comforting for that.

Weaving that wave of comfort into her song, Alana swallowed hard against the acrid taste at the back of her throat. Whenever the breeze blew from the landward side, she could make out the lingering stink of burned wood. The stench never let her forget the jagged gash that gaped, the blackened wood-flesh that had split on the day of the Service.

Alana almost wished that the Tree's memory of the Service had been among the ones that had been lost, that had been burned out by her desperate grasping

of the oak's strength. She did not want to remember
the power and the glory. She did not want to remember that she was the one who had called the Tree to
make its sacrifice.

Renewing her song, Alana consciously set aside the
panic that was never far beneath her heart. She brightened her words, chanting to the Tree about its People,
about their prosperity, about all the reasons that the
oak should continue to seal off the burned, ruined
part and fight for continued life. She closed her eyes,
the better to reach out to the Tree's calm quiet, and
her song rose high and soft, floating out over the
ocean.

"How much longer before the leaves fall?"

Alana's eyes flashed open, even though she recognized Maddock's voice. Indeed, she realized that she
had heard him approach, heard him in the depths of
her mind. The warrior had come often to the Tree
throughout the long summer months and the turn to
autumn.

Alana lowered a hand to the oak's trunk, ready to
push herself to her feet, but Maddock waved her back
to the ground. When he sank beside her, he settled a
leather satchel against the Tree's roots, and his hands
began an automatic sweep, gathering up something,
anything, to keep from sitting idle.

"We've got another fortnight, at least."

"From this side, looking out to sea, you can't even
tell."

She knew he wasn't referring to color. Instead, he
was apologizing for the iron-black scar that raked the
Tree's other side. She said, "I can. I can tell."

Alana settled the pain between them, stark as the
tide line on the beach below. Even as the breeze died
down, though, she chided herself that she was not
being fair. Maddock had never asked for her assistance. He had never asked for the Tree to give its gift.
Just as she had never asked Landon to give to her,

just as she had never demanded another's life for her continued well-being. "Maddock—" she started, at the same time that he spoke her name.

"You go first." He nodded, and she swallowed hard.

"I know that we did what we had to do. You. Landon. Me. Even Jobina. But I never thought that what we did in Smithcourt would work such damage here." Her voice trailed off, lost on the familiar path to despair.

"But you knew," Maddock said at last, "that if we failed in Smithcourt, it would have an effect here. We needed to save Reade and Maida, to bring them home. The People could not stay mixed up in the sort of madness we saw in Smithcourt. And Jobina was right about one thing—if Bringham had won, he would have sent soldiers. Soldiers and tax collectors and the Guardians only know what other inland grief. Coren would have, too."

"And is this so much better?" Alana's voice cracked on the question.

"Alana, I have to believe that it is. I can't know the pain you feel. I can look at the scorch marks, but I can't know the part of you that is the woodsinger, the part that is the Tree itself."

As if forced by Maddock's words, Alana climbed to her feet, walking around the enormous trunk to the ugly, burned scar. Her throat tightened as she made herself study where the bark was charred away, blasted by a heat hotter than the woodsinger could fathom. The damage went all the way to the heartwood, down through the core to the roots, to the most secret depth of the Tree.

The memories housed in that part of the oak had been scorched, consumed by the People's need, by Alana's demands. The Tree had destroyed part of its past to save the People's future.

Even now, if Alana held her fingers above the scar, she could sense the energy, the pure strength that the

Tree had thrust across the leagues, had poured into her bavin, into her. Her throat closed with the taste of charred wood, and she remembered the pure seductive brilliance of that silver power. Her eyes filled. Again.

"It gave everything for us, Maddock."

"Not everything. The seaward side was spared, Alana. The side of the Tree that looks to the ocean, to the People's lifeblood." Maddock grasped her hand, pulled her back around the Tree, until she stood on the ocean side again. "Look, Alana. From here, you can't see what happened. From here, you can only see the red and gold leaves, the living branches." He paused for a moment, and she knew he was trying to read her face, trying to find the feelings that she had thrust deep beneath the surface of her heart. "It was six moons ago today."

"You think I don't know that!" she cried.

"I know you do. Alana, Landon's death was not an accident. He made a decision. He knew that saving you, saving Reade, was more important than anything else he could have done."

The tears were bitter on her cheeks. "I thought he didn't understand when I gave him Maida. I ordered him to watch over her, but I thought he was too weak, that he would fail me. Fail us. Keep us from escaping Smithcourt."

"He must have thought the same."

Before Alana could reply, could argue against Maddock's implacable logic, the breeze carried a high-pitched laugh to her. "You can't catch me!"

Even as Alana dashed tears from her face, Reade came tearing up the path, looking behind him as he ran, and whooping as if all the Guardians were on his heels.

"Wait for me, you little monster!" Jobina's head appeared over the rise first, but her body was soon in view. She rested her hands on her widened hips, curving her shoulders forward as she struggled to catch her breath. Her belly bulged beneath her tawny shift, seeming to move with a life of its own as the healer gasped for air.

"I should have known you'd be here." Jobina placed the words between the adults like an offering.

"Where else would we be?" Maddock snapped, glaring at the healer.

Alana, though, managed a smile. "There won't be many more days when it's comfortable to make the trek. Sit down, Jobina. You must be exhausted."

The other woman shook her head. "If I sit down now, I'll never get to my feet again."

"And that would be such a loss?" Maddock glared, and Jobina started to respond in kind, but was cut short by Alana.

"Maddock." His name was a warning, but the warrior refused to listen.

"She has no shame, Alana. She's come up here as if she has a right! She's so full with Coren's child that she can hardly make the walk, and then she has the nerve—"

"Jobina! Jobina, look at me!" Reade interrupted Maddock's tirade, and all of the adults turned toward the cliff. "Look, Jobina! I can fly!" Reade spread out his arms, letting the breeze catch his shirt and breeches.

As he leaned forward, the healer called out, "Not so close to the edge, Reade. Step back!"

"You can't make me!" the little boy taunted, but Jobina only eyed him steadily. After a moment, he took a small step toward the adults.

"One more," Jobina called, and Reade reluctantly complied. The healer turned back to Alana and Maddock.

The woodsinger swallowed a smile. "He seems in good spirits."

"Teresa says that he slept through the night. He and Maida both."

"Where is his mother now?" Maddock made the question a challenge.

"She's coming up with Maida and Goody Glenna. They should be here in a moment."

As if in response, there was a flurry of activity at the top of the path, and a half-grown dog came bounding past the adults. "Greatheart!" Reade squealed as the hound dug his forepaws into the earth between the little boy and the cliff.

Alana watched Maddock clutch for his absent sword, reflexively defending the women from the canine threat. Even Jobina blanched a little, settling her hands over her belly. "Reade," she called, and her voice quavered.

The boy looked up with rebellion in his eyes, but then he sighed and turned to the gangly dog. "Sit, Greatheart." The hound complied reluctantly.

"Thank you," the healer said, just as Maida, Teresa, and Glenna came into view.

"Can we go down to the water, Jobina?" Reade's face lit with eagerness. The healer looked doubtful. "You can see us all the way down!"

"Ask your mother."

"Mum, can we?" Reade called. "Can we go to the beach?"

Alana saw how the young mother wanted to say no, how she wanted to keep her son by her side. Reluctantly, though, Teresa nodded her head. "Just don't go in the water. And take that beast with you." Reade tore for the cliff. "Wait for your sister," Teresa called out, and Reade slowly turned about for Maida. The little girl looked as if she'd rather stay with the adults, but Teresa smiled firmly. "Go ahead, Maida. We'll watch you from here."

"But—"

"Go on. We can watch you all the way down the path."

Maida's lower lip trembled, but she moved toward

Reade. Greatheart edged his head under her hand as she approached, and a smile brightened her face as she scrambled to the steep cliff path.

Goody Glenna nodded approvingly as the children began their descent. "They seem to be doing well, Teresa."

"Jobina has been a tremendous help. Sometimes they'll spend all day at her cottage, just playing."

"They've been good for me, too, Teresa." Jobina's tone was respectful.

Glenna nodded approval, but then she turned to Alana with a glower. "I still don't understand why the three of you let them come back with that . . . that beast."

Glenna launched into her never-ending tirade about the hound, but Alana cut her off. "I've told you. We had no choice. Reade wanted him. He needed something, something good, to come out of all that happened in Smithcourt."

"A child needs what he's told to need," the old woman grumbled, but the argument had lost its edge over the summer.

At Goody Glenna's words, Jobina's hands moved protectively over her belly. She looked up at her companions shyly. "My child needs his father," the healer said softly. "I dreamed again last night."

"The only way that brat will meet its father is by digging deep with a spade," Maddock said, sneering.

"You lie! My son will meet his father. Duke Coren will ride out here before our boy is Reade's age."

"Coren is dead, woman!"

"You can't know that!"

"Jobina, you were there. You're a healer! Even if you think you loved the man, you can't deny what you saw!"

"I saw a man bitten by a snake. I saw wounds infected with poison. But I saw no man die."

"Has your child made you deaf? You were sitting

in Goody Glenna's cottage the night we came back to our People. You heard me tell about the Avenger!"

"I heard your story. I heard that the rabbit was corrupted even as you watched. But you forget the entire reason that you were brought before the snake." The healer's voice shook with scarce-pent emotion, and she dashed tears from her cheeks. "I know about the poison that Coren consumed. I know how he tempered his body, how he prepared for the Mothersnake. Besides, *I* am the one who bears his child. *I* am the one he'll ride to find. You don't know anything about this!"

Before anyone could speak, Jobina strode toward the cliff path, disappearing down the incline to follow Reade and Maida. Alana settled her hand over the Tree's scorched bark as she watched the woman disappear.

"Well." Goody Glenna clicked her tongue. "I'd better go after her."

"No, Goody," Maddock sighed. "The path is steep. I'll go."

"You have better things to do. And I can't imagine you'd bring that poor girl much comfort. Teresa will help these old bones get to the beach, and back." Glenna was still shaking her head as she disappeared down the trail with the twins' mother.

"Well," Maddock said after a long, uncomfortable pause. "Goody Glenna was right about one thing."

"What's that?" Alana asked, her attention already recaptured by the wood beneath her fingertips. She could feel the turning leaves on the Tree's healthy side, the tantalizing hint of life beyond the dead patch.

"I have more important things to do." Maddock retrieved his satchel. Suddenly, he was awkward, unable to look Alana in the eye as he spoke, and he gave all of his attention to the leather pouch, fumbling at the ties. "I left the village at dawn this morning, and I had to go miles into the forest before I found these." He drew out a bundle of cloth, finest wool dyed the green of a summer field. "There aren't many left, but I didn't want to wait for mistletoe."

The black currants nestled against their leaves, glowing with juice. Maddock let his satchel fall as he passed the cluster to Alana. "Woodsinger, I offer you these berries as a token of my intention. Will you accept a humble fisherman's hand in marriage?"

The proposal caught Alana entirely by surprise. She knew that she should have expected Maddock's words. She should have been prepared with a response. Instead, though, she could think of only one thing: "We buried Landon six moons ago."

"Aye." Maddock reached out his free hand and brushed her hair back from her face. "He's gone, Alana. He gave his life for us, and now he's gone."

"He gave his life for *me*!" she cried, and she stepped back from the cluster of currants cupped in Maddock's fingers, as if they accused her of some crime. "He gave his life to save me. And now I'm back here, and the Tree is burned, and half our history is lost, and nothing will ever be the same!"

"Nothing *will* ever be the same," Maddock agreed, and he closed the distance between them. "Alana, we've seen things that none of the People should ever see. We'll never forget Smithcourt, or the body that we carried out of that city. We survived, though. The Tree is burned, Alana, but it still lives."

She could not meet his eyes, could not face the raw emotion behind his words. Instead, she forced herself to watch the fruit trembling in his hand. "I am the woodsinger, Maddock. I owe my life to the Tree. It called me before I was wed, and it will not tolerate my taking a man, binding myself to another."

"The Tree gave you the strength for a joining more intimate than any words spoken before the Spirit Council."

Alana felt the blood rush hot in her cheeks, and

she turned away from Maddock. For just an instant, she remembered the strength of the Tree in her own body, the force of that white-hot power as she drove her thoughts into Maddock's, as she felt his body meld with hers. In her heart, she knew that he was right. Still, she hesitated. "Maddock, I won't be good for you. I remember too much. Choose one of the other girls, one who can be happy and make you laugh."

"Alana, you know me better than anyone here in the village. By all the Guardians, do you think that I can settle now for some giggling girl? Do you think I can be happy with some woman who's never seen the world beyond the Headland?"

Alana caught her lip between her teeth. Afraid to answer the warrior, she closed her eyes and reached inside her thoughts for her sisters. "Do you hear him?" she asked.

"Of course, we hear him."

"The boy speaks reason for the first time in all the years *we've* heard him."

"He's a good man, sister woodsinger."

Alana forced herself to ask her question. "But is he a *better* man? I was not willing to go with Landon. How can I take Maddock, instead?"

A handful of the woodsingers laughed, and the sound was like raindrops falling on the Tree's leaves. "Love is not a contest, woodsinger."

"Your feelings for Maddock grew, in part, because of Landon. That does not make them wrong. It does not make them evil."

"The Tree knows your heart, Alana Woodsinger. The Tree will tell."

Alana steeled herself, knowing what she must do. She reached past her sisters to touch the calm, cool rings of the Tree. She felt the solid wood beneath her mind, deep, smooth, unblemished. She remembered the tremendous force that had drawn her into the Tree's core, that had sucked her down to its roots.

She did not need that sort of depth today, though. She did not need to summon that sort of energy.

For Alana felt her mind enveloped by the Tree, gathered in amid the comforting rings of growth and age and long life. She sensed the Tree's amusement, like a parent watching an eager child. She sensed the Tree's acceptance, like a sister welcoming a sibling to the hearth, like a brother offering to share a net of fish. She sensed the Tree's love.

When she pulled away from the oak's embrace, she realized that she'd felt nothing of all that the Tree had suffered. The wise old oak had cordoned off its burned parts; it had stowed away the memory of all it had lost. The Tree had made yet another sacrifice for her. It wanted her to be happy. It wanted her to be with Maddock.

She raised her eyes to the waiting fisherman, scarcely aware of the tears that silvered her cheeks. "I'll always be bound to the Tree, Maddock."

"I'd expect nothing less."

She forced herself to meet his gaze, and she was startled by the fierce devotion that glinted there. She swallowed hard and reached out for the cluster of black currants. Her fingers brushed against his as she took the fruit, but she did not flinch from the touch. "All right, then. Maddock, I'll have you, if you'll have me."

His grin was washed in the early autumn light. "You won't be sorry, Alana Woodsinger."

Before she could respond, a shriek floated up from the beach below. Alana and Maddock moved as one to the cliff's edge, and she reached out for his strong hand as she gazed down on the beach.

Teresa looked out to sea, staring at the distant horizon, where the fishing fleet could just be seen. Goody Glenna and Jobina were sitting on a sea-carved rock, the healer's head cradled in the old woman's lap. Even from this distance, Alana could make out Glenna's hand, stroking Jobina's hair, and she imagined she could hear soft crooning words of comfort. The healer did not even look up as another shriek rose up the cliff side.

Alana turned her gaze to the children. Reade had picked up a piece of driftwood, and he brandished it over his head, making large sweeping gestures. Greatheart leaped for the stick, the dog's entire body shaking with pent excitement.

"Hevva!" Reade cried, as if he were huing in all the People's fishing boats. *"Hevva!"* Maida's laughter rose in another shriek as she splashed about in the surf, looking for her own driftwood branch.

Don't miss the brilliant new novel from the
winner of the Maiden Voyage Award

THE GLASSWRIGHTS' JOURNEYMAN

Mindy L. Klasky

Coming from Roc Books
in June 2002

ROC

THE FUTURE IS CLOSER THAN YOU THINK...
ARCHANGEL PROTOCOL

by Lyda Morehouse

**"An instant classic of SF...
One of the best novels in memory."** —*The SF Site*

First the LINK—an interactive, implanted computer—
transformed society. Then came the angels—
cybernetic manifestations that claimed to be working
God's will...
But former cop Deidre McMannus has had her LINK
implant removed—for a crime she didn't commit.
And she has never believed in angels.
But that will change when a man named Michael
appears at her door...

❑ 0-451-45827-3/$6.99

Prices slightly higher in Canada

Payable by Visa, MC or AMEX only ($10.00 min.), No cash, checks or COD. Shipping & handling:
US/Can. $2.75 for one book, $1.00 for each add'l book; Int'l $5.00 for one book, $1.00 for each
add'l. Call (800) 788-6262 or (201) 933-9292, fax (201) 896-8569 or mail your orders to:

Penguin Putnam Inc.
P.O. Box 12289, Dept. B
Newark, NJ 07101-5289
Please allow 4-6 weeks for delivery.
Foreign and Canadian delivery 6-8 weeks

Bill my: ❑ Visa ❑ MasterCard ❑ Amex _____ (expires)
Card# _____
Signature _____

Bill to:
Name _____
Address _____ City _____
State/ZIP _____ Daytime Phone # _____
Ship to:
Name _____ Book Total $ _____
Address _____ Applicable Sales Tax $ _____
City _____ Postage & Handling $ _____
State/ZIP _____ Total Amount Due $ _____

This offer subject to change without notice.   Ad # N214 (2/01)